"PAY ATT[ENTION TO] YOUR W[ORK,] THE REEFS ARE DANGEROUS BUSINESS!"

"Yes, sir," the Techtenant said earnestly. "But I swear I saw a great beast like a nightmare, shaped like a scorpion, huge as a horse—"

"No, you fool! Talk like this is dangerous to the Plan of Man."

The Techtenant reddened. "I'm sorry, sir. I certainly did not intend to seem Unplanned. But those savage nomads of the Reef are worth considering, even if they do believe the Starchild to be more than human."

The light of the controls flickered madly. Their viewscreen showed a clear picture of the distant Earth's sun, looking somehow dimmer, then darker and darker, until finally . . .

The Techtenant gasped with horror, "The Starchild—whoever or whatever it is—has the power to black out our sun!"

THE STARCHILD TRILOGY

The Reefs of Space
Starchild
Rogue Star

by
FREDERIK POHL
and
JACK WILLIAMSON

A KANGAROO BOOK
PUBLISHED BY POCKET BOOKS NEW YORK

**POCKET BOOKS, a Simon & Schuster division of
GULF & WESTERN CORPORATION
1230 Avenue of the Americas, New York, N.Y. 10020**

ISBN: 0-671-82284-5

First Pocket Books printing December, 1977

3rd printing

Trademarks registered in the United States and other countries.

Printed in the U.S.A.

ACKNOWLEDGMENTS

The Reefs of Space was first published in *World of IF Science Fiction.*
A much shorter version of *Starchild* appeared in serial form in *Galaxy*
Magazine. Copyright, ©, 1964, by Galaxy Publishing Corporation.
A shorter version of *Rogue Star* appeared in serial form in *IF* Magazine.
Copyright, ©, 1968, by Galaxy Publishing Corporation.
The three novels that make up *The Starchild Trilogy* were previously
published in paperback as three separate volumes by Ballantine Books, Inc.

Contents

THE REEFS OF SPACE

1

The major snapped: "Check in, you Risks! What's the matter with you?" His radar horns made him look like Satan—a sleepy young Satan with an underslung jaw, but dangerous.

"Yes, sir," said Steve Ryeland, peering around. This was Reykjavik—a new world to Ryeland, who had just come from a maximum-security labor camp inside the rim of the Arctic Circle. Ryeland blinked at the buildings, a thousand feet high, and at the jets and rockets scattered across the air field. The little man next to Ryeland sneezed and nudged him. "All right," Ryeland said, and went into the bare little Security lounge. On the teletype that stood in the corner of the room—in the corner of *every* room— he tapped out:

> Information. Steven Ryeland, Risk, AWC-38440, and O. B. Oporto, Risk, XYZ-99942, arrived at—

He took the code letters from the identification plate on the machine.

—Station 3-Radius 4-261, Reykjavik, Iceland. Query. What are personal orders?

In a moment the answer came from the Planning Machine, a single typed letter "R." The Machine had received and understood the message and adjusted its records. The orders would follow.

A Togetherness-girl glanced into the lounge, saw the collars on Ryeland and the little man. Her lips had started to curve in the smile of her trade, but they clamped into a thin line. Risks. She nodded to the major and turned away.

The teletype bell rang, and the Machine tapped out:

Action. Proceed to Train 667, Track 6, Compartment 93.

Ryeland acknowledged the message. The major, leaning over his shoulder, grinned. "A one-way ticket to the Body Bank if you want my guess."

"Yes, sir." Ryeland was not going to get into a discussion. He couldn't win. No Risk could win an argument with a man who wore the major's radar horns.

"Well, get going," the major grumbled. "Oh, and Ryeland—"

"Yes, sir?"

The major winked. "Thanks for the chess games. I'll be seeing you, I guess. Parts of you!" He laughed raucously as he strode away. "No side trips, remember," he warned.

"I'll remember," said Steve Ryeland softly, touching the collar he wore.

Oporto sneezed again. "Come on," he grumbled.

"All right. What was that number?"

The little dark man grinned. "Train 667, Track 6, Compartment 93. That's an easy one—ah*choo!* Dabbit," he complained, "I'm catching cold. Let's get out of this draft."

Ryeland led off. They walked unescorted across the pavement to a cab rank and got in. All around them, travelers, air field workers and others glanced at them, saw the iron collars—and at once, on each face a curtain descended. No one spoke to them. Ryeland punched the code number for their destination, and the car raced through broad boulevards to a huge marble structure on the other side of the city.

Over its wide entrance were the carved letters:

They made their way through a wide concourse, noisy and crowded; but everyone gave them plenty of room. Ryeland grinned sourly to himself. No side trips! Of course not—and for the same reason. It wasn't healthy for a man who wore the collar to step out of line. And it wasn't healthy for anyone else to be in his immediate neighborhood if he did.

"Track Six, was it?"

"Train 667, Compartment 93. Can't you remember anything?" Oporto demanded.

"There's Track Six." Ryeland led the way. Track Six was a freight platform. They went down a flight of motionless moving stairs and emerged beside the cradle track of the subtrains.

Since the subtrains spanned the world, there was no clue as to where they were going. From Iceland they could be going to Canada, to Brazil, even to South Africa; the monstrous atomic drills of the Plan had burrowed perfectly straight shafts from everywhere to everywhere. The subtrains rocketed through air-exhausted tunnels, swung between hoops of electrostatic force. Without friction, their speed compared with the velocity of interplanetary travel.

"Where is it?" Oporto grumbled, looking around. A harsh light flooded the grimy platforms, glittering on the huge aluminum balloons that lay in their cradles outside the vacuum locks. Men with trucks and cranes were loading a long row of freightspheres in the platform next to theirs; a little cluster of passengers began to appear down the moving stairs of a platform a hundred yards away. Oporto said abruptly: "I'll give you six to five the next train in is ours."

"No bet." Ryeland knew better than to take him up. But he hoped the little man was right. It was cold on the platform. Chill air roared around them from the ventilators; Oporto, already chilled, sneezed and began to sniffle. Ryeland himself was shivering in his thin maximum-security denims.

At the camp, when their travel orders came through, regulations demanded a thorough medical examination before they left. That was the rule under the Plan, and

3

the examination included a steaming shower. "They want nice clean meat at the Body Bank," the guard guffawed; but Ryeland paid no attention. He couldn't afford to.

A man who wore the iron collar around his neck could only afford a limited look into the future. He could think about the day when the collar came off, and nothing else.

A warning horn shrieked into the pit. Ryeland jumped; Oporto turned more slowly, as though he had been expecting it. Which he had.

Red signals flickered from the enormous gates of the vacuum lock on Track Six. Air valves gasped. The gates swung slowly open and a tractor emerged towing a cradle with the special car they were waiting for. "You would have lost," Oporto commented and Ryeland nodded; of course he would have.

The car stopped. Equalizer valves snorted again, and then its tall door flopped out from the top, forming a ramp to the platform. Escalators began to crawl along it.

Oporto said anxiously: "Steve, I don't like the looks of this!" Out of the opening door of the car two men in uniform came running. They ran up the escalators, raced onto the platform and up the stairs. They didn't look at Ryeland or Oporto; they were in a hurry. They were bearing thick leather dispatch cases the same color as their uniforms.

Bright blue uniforms!

Why, that was the uniform of the special guard of—

Ryeland lifted his eyes to look, unbelieving. At the roof of the shed, amid the ugly web of ducts and pipes and cables, a brilliant light burst forth, shining down on the sphere. And across its top, forty feet above the platform, there was a gleaming blue star and under it, etched in crystalline white, the legend:

THE PLAN OF MAN
OFFICE OF THE PLANNER

The special car they had been waiting for was the private car of the Planner himself!

The first thought that crossed Steve Ryeland's mind was: Now I can present my case to the Planner! But the second thought canceled it. The Planner, like every other human on Earth or the planets, was only an instrument of the Planning Machine. If clearance ever came to Ryeland— if the collar came off his neck—it would be because the

Machine had considered all the evidence and reached a proper decision. Human argument would not affect it.

With an effort, Ryeland put the thought out of his mind; but all the same, he couldn't help feeling a touch better, a degree stronger. At least it was *almost* certain that their destination would not be the Body Bank!

"What was that compartment number?"

Oporto sighed. "93. Can't you remember *anything?* Train 667—the product of the two primes, 23 and 29. Track 6, their difference. Compartment 93, their last digits in reverse order. That's an *easy* one—" But Ryeland was hardly listening. The intimate acquaintance that Oporto seemed to have with all numbers was no longer news to him, and he had more urgent things on his mind. He led the way up the ramp and into the Planner's subtrain car. A woman in the blue uniform of the guard passed them, glanced at their collars and frowned. Before Ryeland could speak to her she had brushed past them busily and was gone. It said a lot for the efficiency of the collars, he thought wryly, that she didn't bother to find out what two Risks were doing wandering freely around the Planner's private car. There was no cause for worry; if they took a wrong turning, the collars would make it their last.

But by the same token, it was highly dangerous for them to wander around. Ryeland stopped short and waited until someone else came by. "Sir!" he called. "Excuse me!"

It was a straight, gray-haired man in the blue of the Planner's guard, wearing the silver mushrooms of a Technicorps colonel ."What is it?" he demanded impatiently.

"We're ordered to compartment 93," Ryeland explained.

The colonel looked at him thoughtfully, "Name," he snapped.

"Ryeland, Steven. And Oporto."

"Umm." Presently the colonel sighed. "All right," he said grouchily. "Can't have you messing up the Planner's car with your blood. Better get secured. This way." He led them to a tiny room, ushered them in. "Look," he said, flexing the knob of the door. "No lock. But I should warn you that most of the corridors are radar-trapped. Do you understand?" They understood. "All right."

He hesitated. "By the way. My name's Lescure, Colonel Pascal Lescure. We'll meet again." And he closed the door behind him.

Ryeland looked quickly around the room, but it wasn't the splendor of its furnishings or the comfort of its appointments that interested him. It was the teletype. Quickly he reported in for himself and Oporto.

The answer came:

R. Action. Await further orders.

Oporto was beginning to look flushed and to tremble. "Always it's lige this," he said thickly. "I ged a cold and if I don't tage care I'm sick for weegs. I'm feeling lighd-headed already!" He stood up, tottering.

Ryeland shook his head. "No, you're not lightheaded. We're moving." The hand at the controls of the subtrain knew whose private car he was driving down the electro-static tubes. The giant sphere was being given a feather-bed ride. They had felt no jar at all on starting, but now they began to feel curiously light.

That was intrinsic to the way of travel. The subtrain was arrowing along a chord from point to point; on long hauls the tunnels dipped nearly a thousand miles below the earth's surface at the halfway mark. Once the initial acceleration was over, the first half of a trip by subtrain was like drop-ping in a super-speed express elevator.

Absently Ryeland reached out an arm to brace Oporto as the little man weaved and shuddered. He frowned. The helical fields which walled the tunnels of the subtrains owed part of their stability to himself. On that Friday night, three years before, when the Plan Police burst in upon him, he had just finished dictating the specifications for a new helical unit that halved hysteresis losses, had a service life at least double the old ones.

And yet he could only remember that much and no more.

Had something been done to his mind? For the thou-sandth time Ryeland asked himself that question. He could remember the equations of his helical field theory that transformed the crude "magnetic bottles" that had first walled out the fluid rock, as early nucleonicists had walled in the plasma of fusing hydrogen. Yet he could not re-member the work that had led him to its design. He could remember his design for ion accelerators to wall the atomic rockets of spaceships, and yet the author of that design—himself—was a stranger. What sort of man had he been? What had he done?

"Sdeve," Oporto moaned. "You wouldn't have a drink on you?"

Ryeland turned, brought back to reality. A drink! Oporto was feverish. "I'd better call the machine," he said.

Oporto nodded weakly. "Yes, call in. I'm sick, Sdeve."

Ryeland hesitated. The little man did look sick. While he was standing there, Oporto blundered past him. "I'll do id myself," he grumbled. "Get out of my way."

He reached with fumbling fingers for the keyboard, his face turned angrily toward Ryeland. That was a mistake; he should have been watching. In the unsteady footing he lurched, reached for the keyboard, missed, stumbled and fell heavily against the teletype.

It toppled with a crash. There was a quick white flash from inside it and a sudden pungent smell of burning.

Oporto got slowly to his feet.

Ryeland opened his mouth and then closed it without saying anything. What was the use? Obviously the teletype was out of commission; obviously Oporto hadn't done it on purpose.

Oporto groaned: "Oh, dabbit. Steve, where'd thad colonel go? Maybe he could ged me something . . ."

"Take it easy," Ryeland said absently. The little man's condition was clearly not good but, in truth, it was not Oporto that was on Ryeland's mind just then. It was the teletype.

Always, since the first days after school, there had been no move Steve Ryeland made, no action he performed, without checking in with the Machine. Even at the maximum-security camp there had been a teletype on direct linkage with the Machine, standing in one desolate corner of the bare barracks.

He felt curiously naked, and somehow forlorn.

"Steve," said Oporto faintly, "could you ged me a glass of water?"

That at least was possible; there was a silver carafe and crystal tumblers, fired with gold designs. Ryeland poured the little man a glass and handed it to him. Oporto took it and sank back against a huge, richly upholstered chair, his eyes closed.

Ryeland roamed around the little cubicle. There wasn't much else for him to do. The colonel had warned them against radar-traps in the corridors; it was not to be thought of that they would go out and take the chance of being destroyed by a single wrong move.

For they were Risks; and the iron collars they wore contained eighty grams of a high explosive. A step into an area proscribed for Risks (and such areas were common all over the world) meant that a triggering radar beam would touch off the explosive. Ryeland had seen that happen once. He didn't want it to happen to him.

Brig or no brig, this room was part of the Planner's private car and it was furnished in a way that Ryeland had not seen in three years. He fingered the drapes around a mock-window and reached out to touch the polished mirror of a hardwood table top.

Three years ago Ryeland had lived in a room something like this. No, he admitted, not quite as lavish. But a room that belonged to him, with furniture that no one else used and a place for his clothes, his books, the things he kept around him. But in that life he had been a cleared man, with a place in the Plan of Man and a quota to be met. That life had ended three years ago, on that fatal Friday afternoon.

Even now, after endless sessions of what was called reconstructive therapy, Ryeland couldn't understand what had happened to him. The vaguely worded charge was "unplanned thinking," but all his merciless therapists had failed to help him recall any thoughts disloyal to the machine. The only material evidence of unplanned activities was his collection of space literature—the yellowed old copies of books by Ley and Gamow and Hoyle and Einstein that he had saved from his father's library.

Of course he knew that the books were not on the list approved by the Plan, but he had intended no disloyalty with his hobby. In fact, as he had many times told the therapists, the special equations of the helical field were related to the mathematics of the whole universe. Without knowing the equations for the expansion of the universe and the continuous creation of matter in the space between the galaxies. he could not have improved the helical units for the subtrain tunnels.

But the therapists had always refused to specify exact charges. Men under the Plan no longer had rights, but merely functions. The purpose of the therapists was not to supply him with information, but to extract information from him. The sessions had failed, because he couldn't remember whatever it was that the therapists had been attempting to extract.

There was so much that he could not remember . . .

Oporto said weakly: "Sdeve, ged me a doctor."

8

"I can't!" Ryeland said bitterly: "If the Plan wants you sick you'll have to be sick."

Oporto's face turned a shade paler. "Shut up! Somebody may be listening."

"I'm not criticizing the Plan. But we have to stay here, you know that."

"Ryeland," Oporto begged, and went into a coughing fit.

Ryeland looked down at the little man. He seemed to be in serious trouble now. Evidently his system was of an ultra-allergic type. Swept clean of disease organisms in the sterile air that blew down on the isolation camp from the Pole, he had been ripe for infection. He was breathing heavily and raggedly, and heat wafted off his forehead as Ryeland brought his hand near it.

"Hold on, Oporto," he said. "It'll only be a little while. Maybe a couple of hours." At a thousand miles an hour, there was no place on Earth much farther away than that.

"I can be dead in a couble of hours," said Oporto. "Can't you ged me a doctor?"

Ryeland hesitated. There was truth to what the little man said. The Plan provided constant immunization for those who lived in areas exposed to disease; but the hypo-allergic, like Oporto, might well lose that immunity in a few months. And Oporto had been breathing sterile air for three years.

"All right," said Ryeland wearily, "I'll do what I can. You come with me, Oporto." Booby-trapped the halls might be, dangerous the trip certainly was; but it was life and death to Oporto.

The door opened easily.

Ryeland, half supporting Oporto, looked out into the corridor. No one was in sight. He sighed; he had hoped that they might find a passerby. Oporto babbled: "Steve, what are you doing? Led me alone. We can't go oud here —the colonel warned us!"

"We have to get you to a doctor, remember?" Ryeland scanned the corridor. At the intersections were curious canopied devices like the sun-shelter over a mogul's howdah. Perhaps they were the radar traps; at least, Ryeland couldn't imagine what else they might be. But there was one back the way they had come, and surely there had been no trap there. . . .

No. Ryeland thought it out carefully. The fact that they had been allowed to get to Compartment 93 didn't prove anything at all; quite possibly the traps had been turned off to allow them to pass. In fact, thinking it over, it seemed certain that the one route that *would* be prohibited would be the corridor going back to the entrance port.

"Oporto," he said, "do you see those doors? I think we can go into one of them."

"You do, Steve? What mages you think so?" the little man asked sardonically.

"Because there's nothing better to try," Ryeland snapped, and dragged the little man with him.

Around his neck the iron collar weighed heavier than ever. If only he were a superman, like that Donderevo whose name stuck half-forgotten in his mind . . . whose fate, somehow, was linked with Ryeland's own.

Who was Donderevo, exactly? The therapists had questioned him so persistently about the man that there had to be some strong reason. Did Ryeland know him? When had he last seen him? When had he received a message from him? What was the message about?

Donderevo was the son of an explorer and trader who had gathered a fortune from the asteroids and the moons of the outer planets, and had built a commercial empire outside the Plan of Man. Ron Donderevo had come to Earth as a student of space medicine at the great technological institute where Ryeland's father was a mathematics professor. While he was there, the Plan had annexed the last reluctant asteroids and moons which had remained outside. Donderevo's father had been defeated in a space fight, resisting the annexation. Donderevo himself had been placed in an iron collar, as a result of a student demonstration. Then one day he had disappeared. The legends said that he had somehow removed the collar, and escaped into space beyond the power of the Plan.

Ryeland remembered meeting him only once, in his own father's study. Ryeland was an eight-year-old Technicub. Donderevo was a grown man, a graduate student, romantic and mysterious with his knowledge of far planets and unknown space. But was that enough to account for the questions?

Ryeland had denied receiving any message from him, but the therapists were unconvinced.

In any event, whatever Donderevo might have been, Ryeland wasn't; *his* collar was on for good, or until the Machine relented.

Ryeland wondered crazily if he would hear the tiny click

of the relay before the decapitation charge went off. Would there be any warning? Would he know?

Or would it all be over, literally, before he knew what was happening?

The only way to find out was to open a door and walk through it.

He pushed a door open, selecting it at random from the half-dozen in the corridor. Oporto broke away from him and, surprisingly spry, ran a few paces down the corridor, whirled and watched him with a face of tense anticipation.

Ryeland didn't stop to think it over, he walked in the door; and nothing happened.

Grinning, embarrassed, Oporto trailed after. "That one was all right, huh, Steve?"

Ryeland nodded; but there was no point in recrimination, although there were a lot of things he had in mind to say to the man who had urged him to take a chance—and then ducked out of the way of the possible consequences. But of more immediate interest was the room they were in.

It was about the size of Compartment 93 and empty. It was quietly furnished: A narrow bed, a table with a few flowers, a large mirror, an array of cabinets. A girl's room, Ryeland guessed, but from the relative modesty of its furnishings, not the room of a girl who was part of the higher brass on this de luxe subtrain. Possibly a secretary's room; perhaps a maid's. Whoever she was, she wasn't in.

But there was another door, leading to a flight of steps. This time Ryeland didn't wait for Oporto. He caught his breath and held it, and when he had passed through and established once again that that particular door was not radar-trapped, he tasted salt and acid on his lip. He had bitten hard enough to draw blood.

But he was through.

The stairs were steep, but it was easy enough to help Oporto up them, with the plunging of the car taking pounds off their weight. They came out into another room, also empty and small.

But this one was sumptuously furnished. It seemed to be a woman's dressing room. It was white and gold, with ivory-backed brushes and combs on a little vanity table, before a gold-rimmed oval mirror. The stairs, Ryeland guessed, were for the use of the personal maid to whoever used this room.

11

And he heard someone singing.

Ryeland took a deep breath and called out: "Hello there! Do you hear me? I'm looking for a doctor!"

There wasn't any answer. The singing went on, a girl's voice, clear and attractive; she was singing for her own amusement. Every once in a while she would go back and repeat a phrase, pause, then start again aimlessly. And under the singing was a sort of musical cooing accompaniment.

Ryeland looked at Oporto, shrugged and pushed the door open.

They looked into a room that was green and silver. Its walls swam with fading, shifting green light. In the center was a round silver tub, six feet across, partly recessed into the floor. From the mouths of carved crystal dolphins tiny jets of perfumed warm water leaped and splashed, in a foam of bubbles, into the tub.

And above the thick blanket of foam protruded one knee, the head and the arms of the most beautiful girl Ryeland had ever seen.

"I—I beg your pardon," he said, awkward and disturbed.

She turned her head and looked at him calmly. On her wet, white shoulders were perched a pair of—birds? No. They were shaped like birds, like doves, but they were made of metal; their feathers were fine silver scales; their eyes were red-lit jewels. The metal things moved restlessly, as the little eyes poked hotly at Ryeland and Oporto. They cooed soft threats, and the rustle of their wings was like thin whispering bells.

Oporto opened his eyes, stared and emitted a strangling sound. "She—She—" He swallowed and clutched at Ryeland. "Steve, it's the Planner's daughter!" he gasped, and flung himself to the floor. "Please!" he begged, writhing toward her. "Please, we didn't mean to bother you!"

But the approach must have alarmed her. Not very much; for she didn't raise her voice; but she stopped singing in the middle of a note and said, quite softly: "Guards."

There must have been a microphone to pick up her words, for there was a sudden commotion outside. But more than that, she had defenders nearer still. The doves on her shoulders leaped into the air and flung themselves at the prostrate little man. Sharp beaks tore, wingtips like knives beat at him. The door opened and four tall women in the blue of the Planner's guard raced in.

2

Death had not been far from Steve Ryeland for these three years. It had worn the neat white smock of Dr. Thrale, the fat, bald, oily man who had been his chief therapist. It had whispered in the soft, asthmatic voice of Dr. Thrale, warning him a thousand times that he stood in danger of the Body Bank, unless he could recall a message from Ron Donderevo, unless he could find the right answers to nonsense questions about a string of words and names that meant nothing to him—*spaceling, reefs of space, Donderevo, jetless drive.*

Death had taken other forms. The concealed trigger of a radar trap, the menacing horns of a radar-headset, the more subtle and more worrisome peril of orders to the Body Bank; these were the deaths he had known and learned to live with. These women, though, carried projectile weapons, not radar. Queer, thought Ryeland, even in that moment, for if carried through the thought indicated that there were some dangers to the person of the Planner's daughter that did not come from classified Risks like himself. Could ordinary citizens—*cleared* citizens—be dangerous to the Plan?

But there was no answer to that question just then. Oporto was screaming under the attack of the silvery doves, the woman guards were bearing down on them.

The girl stopped them all with a single word. "Wait." She swept a mound of bubbles away from her face to see better, exposing a throat of alabaster. Her eyes were green-gray and serene. She looked very lovely and very young.

She caught Ryeland completely undefended.

In the isolation camp there had been no women—not even a pin-up picture; and here he was in the presence of a most beautiful woman, in what should have been the privacy of her bath. Apart from everything else, she could hardly have been unaware of the shattering effect she had on him. But she seemed completely at ease. She said, in a voice more polite than curious: "What do you want?"

Ryeland coughed. "This man needs a doctor," he said hoarsely, looking away.

13

The first of the female guards laughed sharply. She was tall, brunette; a heroic figure of what might have been a lovely girl, if reduced ten per cent in all dimensions. She said in a voice that just missed being baritone: "Come on, Risk! We'll take care of you and your friend too!"

But the girl in the tub shifted position lazily. She waved an arm through the foam, watched the bubbles billow in slow concentric waves and said: "Never mind, Sergeant. Take the sick man to a doctor, if that's what he wants. Leave the other one here."

"But, Madam! The Planner—"

"Sergeant," said the gentle voice, not raised at all; the sergeant turned almost white. She gestured at the others; they half carried Oporto out. The door closed behind them, cutting in twain a look of pure hatred and contempt that passed from the sergeant to Ryeland.

The doves, which had been describing precise circles in the air, shook themselves and returned to the girl's shoulders. Their hot small eyes never left Ryeland, but after a moment they began to coo again.

"You're an iron-collar man, aren't you?" the girl asked suddenly.

Ryeland nodded. "A risk. Yes."

"I've never spoken to an iron-collar man," she said thoughtfully. "Do you mind if we talk? I'm Donna Creery. My father is the Planner."

"I know." Suddenly Ryeland was aware of his rumpled denims, of the fact that he was an intruder on this girl's bath. He coughed. "Don't you think your father—I mean, I don't mind if we talk, but—"

"Good," said the girl, nodding gravely. She shifted position to get a better look at him. The bubbles rippled wildly. "I was afraid you might be sensitive about it," she told him. "I'm glad you're not. What's your name?"

Ryeland raised his chin and spread the collar of his denim shirt to display the iron band.

"Steven Ryeland," she read, squinting to make out the glowing scarlet letters with his name and number. "Why, I think I know that name. A doctor? No. A rocket pilot?"

"I am a mathematician, Miss Creery."

She cried: "Oh, of course! Your folder is on my father's desk. I saw it this morning, when we were leaving Copenhagen."

An anxious eagerness took his breath. For three years he had been trying to learn the charges against him. The

14

therapists had refused to give him information. Their questions had been carefully phrased to tell him nothing—they had asked him a thousand times what the word *spaceling* meant, and punished him more then once for guessing that it meant an inhabitant of space.

"Did the folder tell—" He gulped. "Did it specify any charges against me?"

Her greenish eyes surveyed him, unalarmed.

"You displayed unplanned interests."

"Huh? What does that mean?"

"You possessed a secret collection of books and manuscripts, which had not been approved by the machine."

"No, I didn't." A cold breath touched the back of his neck. "There has been some terrible mistake—"

"The Planning Machine permits no mistakes," she reminded him gravely. "The titles of the forbidden books were listed in the folder. The authors were scientists of the wicked times before the Plan. Einstein. Gamow. Hoyle—"

"Oh!" He gasped. "Then those were just my father's books—a few that I saved. You see, when I was a kid I used to dream of going to space. I've met Ron Donderevo. I wanted to pilot a spaceship, and discover new planets. The Machine killed that dream."

He sighed.

"It transferred me out of the Technicorps and reclassified me as a research mathematician. It assigned me to an installation somewhere underground—I don't know where it was; we were not allowed even to guess whether we were under dry land or the ocean floor or the polar ice. I don't remember, even, if I ever guessed. My memory has . . . holes in it. I had two helpers—a teletype girl and a little man named Oporto, who is a sort of human computing machine. The Machine sent us problems, like the problem of hysterisis loss in the subtrain tunnels. They were problems the Machine couldn't answer, I suppose—even it doesn't know quite everything. Anyhow, we solved the problems.

"Of course I wasn't supposed to see reference books, because I could ask the Machine for any fact I wanted. But for the sake of efficiency it had let me keep a few handbooks, and I had brought those books of my father's among them."

He smiled at her hopefully.

"You see, for a man who had set his heart on space, life in a tunnel isn't very exciting. For a sort of hobby, I read

15

those books about space. They were full of old theories about the nature of the universe. Using modern mathematics, I worked out a new set of equations to describe the expanding universe and the continuous creation of matter in the space bewteen the galaxies—"

Her frown checked him. This was not quite the sort of talk for a young girl in her bath!

"But that was not unplanned," he finished desperately. "It was just a harmless hobby. In fact, it was useful to the Plan. The equations that I used in improving the helical field units were derived from the equations that describe the continuous creation of matter and space."

"And that's what made you a risk?" She looked at him thoughtfully and frowned. "You don't *look* dangerous."

He could find no answer to that. He waited while she waved a hand absent-mindedly. One of the doves left her shoulder to fly, tinkling, to the crystal dolphin. It pecked precisely at a fin-shaped lever on the dolphin's back, and obediently the spray of perfumed water dwindled away. Ryeland watched, more than half lulled by the scent of lilac and the strangeness of his surroundings. The room was warm but not steamy; invisible ducts must be sucking the moisture out. "*Are* you dangerous?" the girl asked suddenly.

Ryeland said: "No, Miss Creery." He hesitated, wondering how to explain it to this child. "The collar isn't a punishment. It's a precaution."

"Precaution?"

He said steadily: "The Machine has reason to believe that under certain circumstances I might work against the Plan of Man. I have never done anything, you must understand that. But the Machine can't take chances, and so—the collar."

She said wonderingly: "But you sound as though you approve of it!"

"I'm loyal to the Plan!"

She thought that over. Then: "Well, aren't we all? But the rest of us don't wear iron collars."

He shook his head. "I never did anything that was against Security."

"But perhaps you did something that wasn't—quite?"

Ryeland grinned. She was amazingly easy to get along with, he thought; the grin became a smile—a real one, and the first one he had worn in some time. "Yes," he admitted, "I did something that wasn't. There was a girl."

16

"Steven, Steven!" Donna Creery shook her head mock-ruefully. "Always a girl. I thought that was only in stories."

"In real life too, Miss Creery." He was almost relaxed ... Then, abruptly, her mood changed.

"Your folder contains another specification," she rapped out. "You are charged with concealing information about a device which is dangerous to the security of the Plan of Man."

"But I'm not!" he protested desperately. "Somebody has made a mistake—in spite of the Machine. For three years the therapists in the maximum-security camp have been working me over, trying to extract information that I don't have."

Her eyes widened, with a calm concern.

"What kind of information?"

"I'm not sure." He winced, with remembered pain. "They were careful not to give me hints, and they punished me for guessing.

"They questioned me about a list of words," he said. "They strapped me down, with electrodes clamped all over me, recording every reaction. They repeated the words a million times. *Spaceling. Reefs of space. Fusorian. Pyropod. Jetless drive.* And two names—Ron Donderevo and Daniel Horrock.

"Putting all those words and names and other clues together, I guessed that the therapists thought that Horrock had brought me a message from Donderevo. A message from space, about things called reefs and spacelings and fusorians. Particularly, about something called a jetless drive. That was what they were trying to dig out of me—how to build a jetless drive."

She frowned.

"What is a jetless drive?"

"There isn't any," he said. "Because a jetless drive would be a system of reactionless propulsion. Crackpots for three hundred years have been trying to invent such a system, but everybody knows it would be a violation of the Third Law of Motion. It's as impossible as pushing a rowboat forward without pushing the water back."

"I see." She was nodding gravely. "Impossible as creating new atoms and new space between the galaxies."

He looked at her sharply. "But I *couldn't* have had a message from Horrock—or anybody else," he insisted desperately. "Not when they seem to think I did. On the Friday it happened, Oddball Oporto and the teletype girl

17

had been with me all day. We were working late, finishing the specifications for the new helical unit. I let Oddball go about eighteen hundred hours, because he was getting a headache. The teletype girl went out with him, to bring coffee and sandwiches for us. They hadn't been gone half an hour, when somebody knocked on the door. I thought it was the girl—but it was the Plan Police."

"That wasn't on Friday." Donna Creery's eyes were veiled, strange. "According to the records in your folder, you were taken into precautionary custody at eighteen hundred hours on a Monday afternoon. That leaves at least three days missing from your story."

Ryeland gulped.

"That couldn't be!" He shook his head. "Oddball and the teletype girl had just gone out—"

"I studied your folder with considerable care." She failed to say why. "I am certain that you were picked up on a Monday."

Ryeland felt a tingle of excitement. This was more than he had ever been able to learn about the case against him.

"I suppose it's possible," he muttered. "At first I was in a place miscalled a recreation center, somewhere under-ground. We weren't allowed to inquire where. The therapy sessions went on around the clock. I had no way of know-ing the time or the date.

"But I still don't know how to build a reactionless pro-pulsion system. And I still believe that the Machine has permitted itself to make a mistake."

Donna Creery shook her head reprovingly.

Ryeland stopped, the collar tight around his neck. This was crazy! Staying here like this with the Planner's daughter! He said abruptly, harshly: "Miss Creery, I'm interrupting your bath. I must go!"

She laughed, like a shimmer of pale music. "I don't want you to," she coaxed.

"But—your bath—"

"I always stay in the tub in these subtrain rides, Ste-ven. It's comfortable, when the up-grav drag begins to work. And don't worry about my father. He rules the world—under the Plan, of course! But he doesn't rule me." She was smiling. She could hardly be twenty, Rye-land thought ruefully, but there was no more doubt in his mind that she knew she was a woman. She said com-fortably: "Sit down, Steven. There. On the bench."

One slim arm, wearing wristlets of foam, gestured at

an emerald bench next to the tub. The doves moved nervously as he approached. Donna Creery said: "Don't be afraid of my Peace Doves." He looked quizzically at the silver-steel beaks. "Oh, I'm sorry they hurt your friend," she apologized, "but they thought he was going to hurt me. You see, even without the guard I am protected."

She waved a hand, and faint music seeped into the room from concealed speakers. "What was the girl like?" she demanded.

"She was beautiful," he said shortly.

"And dangerous?"

He nodded, but under the heavy weight of the collar the stiff hairs at the back of his neck were trying to rise. Dangerous? This girl was far more dangerous to him. He had no right to be here. The Machine would not be blind to this. But Donna Creery said soothingly: "Tell me about her. Was she really lovely?"

"I believed she was. She had long yellow hair and green eyes. Eyes like yours. And she was in the secret police, but I didn't know that until the day of the raid."

Laughter pealed from the girl's lips, and the Peace Doves fluttered their wings fretfully for balance. "And she betrayed you. Are you afraid I might? But I won't, Steven, I promise."

He shrugged. "I've told you. I suppose I was lucky, at that. I was sent to a maximum-security camp. It could have been the Body Bank."

She tilted her head to ponder that, and he watched the red glints flow through the dark waves of her hair. At last she sighed and said, "And for that you became a Risk. But you should have been more careful, Steven. You should not have defied the Plan. And now you have to wear that collar. Can't you get it off?"

He laughed sharply.

She said seriously: "No, I suppose not. But if I were you, I think I might. You said you were a mathematician. If I were a mathematician, and wore the collar, it would be only one more problem for me. I would find a way to solve it."

He said with a touch of anger: "The collar was invented by Colonel Zamfirescu, the best engineer in the Technicorps—before he was salvaged himself. He thought of everything."

"It's only a metal band, Steven."

19

"The toughest armor plate in the world! And inside it there's a decapitation charge, fused with a hydrogen power cell—it won't last forever, no, but it will keep full power for a century! And that's longer than I can wait. And the collar's booby-trapped. If I try to cut it open—if I even try to unlock it, and use the wrong key, or turn it the wrong way—it will kill me on the spot. Have you ever seen a decapitation charge go off, Miss Creery? I have."

She shuddered, but she said: "If I were you, I would run away."

"Not very far! Radar runs faster. And even if you could get away—out to the Cold Planets, say, or to one of the orbiting stations around Mercury—there's a timing device in the collar. It has to be reset periodically, with a key. If not—boom. And you never know when; just that it will be less than a year."

"Oh." She shook her head sadly. "Then you must take it off," she said wisely.

He laughed out loud; he couldn't help it. The idea was preposterous!

"Don't laugh, Steven. Ron Donderevo did," she told him.

"Donderevo! What do you know about Donderevo?"

She said, "Oh, a little. I knew him, you see, when I was very small. I remember seeing him with the collar—and I saw him again, without."

He stopped, staring. He began: "You *saw* Donderevo—"

But there was a sudden, harsh knocking at the door. "Miss Creery!" a worried male voice clamored. "The Planner has sent for that Risk!"

Ryeland sat bolt upright. For a moment he had forgotten; the voice had brought him back to the realities of his life.

The girl said, "You'll have to go, Steven." She whispered, and one of the Peace Doves restlessly rose from her shoulders and circled the room, its hot red eyes fixed on Ryeland. It touched the door, and without sound the door opened. "Be careful," the girl said gently. "And don't think too much about Angela."

"All right," Ryeland said, numb, walking like a mechanical man to where the radar-horned officer of the Planner's guard waited for him, with an expression like malevolent granite. It wasn't until the door had slid si-

20

lently closed behind him that he remembered he had never mentioned the name of the girl who betrayed him, his teletype girl, Angela Zwick.

For all of Ryeland's life the Planner had been watching him. That fearless, genial, giant face had looked down on him from stereo posters in the home of his parents, the barracks of the Technicubs, the classrooms of his school—in every public square, and all the laboratories and buildings where he had worked. Ryeland knew that face as well as his own father's—better—and so did every other human alive.

The Planner sat behind a great hardwood desk in a chair that was all air cushions and cunning springs. He was looking absorbedly through a folder of papers on his desk. Uncomfortably Ryeland stood waiting.

There was no resemblance between the Planner and his daughter. She was brunette and lovely, with the face of a child saint; he was square and silver, a lion's face. His hair was short, gray-white; it sat firmly on his head like a collision mat. And over his head, on the back of the great chair, a steel-gray raven sat frozen; but it was not an ornament, for slowly metal-sheathed eyes opened and tiny bright red eyes peered out at Ryeland.

At last the Planner looked up and smiled. He said in a velvet bass voice: "Son, don't you check in?"

Ryeland jumped. "Oh. Sorry, sir." He hurried over to the gold-plated teletype and tapped out his name. The station plate on the machine said simply: "ONE".

The old man chuckled. "You're Steven Ryeland. I saw you once before, but you wouldn't remember that."

Ryeland started. "Sir?"

"It was a long time ago, boy," the Planner said contemplatively. "I visited your home; you were a baby. Don't look shocked. You see, I knew your father."

Ryeland staggered. He was half floating as the hurtling sphere reached maximum velocity, hundreds of miles under the open air; but it was not that which made him dizzy, nor even the fact that he had not eaten for nearly a full day; it was this man on the other side of the desk. He said incredulously: "Sir, my parents never said anything about knowing the Planner. Surely they would have been proud. . . ."

The Planner laughed, a glorious huge laugh. "My boy," he cried, "it's a wise child, eh? And you are not that wise. You don't know much about your parents. They were

21

not proud of knowing me at all; they were ashamed because, you see, your father hated me very much." He nodded, the smile drying on his face. His voice became like the rasp of a file. "Your father was an enemy of the Plan!" he barked.

"Sir," Ryeland protested, "I don't know anything about my father. He disappeared when I was young. And my mother never told me that."

"She wouldn't," the Planner said savagely. "She was a dangerous woman, but not a stupid one. Neither of your parents were stupid, Ryeland; so how is it that you are?"

Ryeland said baffled: "Sir?"

"You're a Risk!" rasped the Planner. "You should not have dared defy the Plan. That was an act of stupidity!"

Ryeland took a deep breath. Perhaps this was his chance to get his case on the record. He began: "Sir, let me explain. I had no intention of defying the Plan. There was a girl who reported me, and the Machine reclassified me as a Risk. I think this was an error, but—"

"You question the Machine?"

"No, sir. Not the Machine, but the information that—"

"Never mind!" snapped the Planner. "I don't want you to incriminate yourself further. You are your father's son, and you must remember that everything you do is suspect for that reason."

It took Ryeland's breath away. For a moment he couldn't speak. He stood there, weaving slightly in the unsteady footing as the sphere rolled restlessly about in the beginning of its up-drive back to the surface.

Then he burst out: "Sir, do I understand you? You're saying that the Machine considers me a Risk because of what my father may have done before I was born! That's not fair. That's—"

"Fair!" bellowed the Planner, while the raven opened its tiny eyes and whirred restlessly over his head. "What sort of word is that, Ryeland? 'Fairness.' 'Freedom.' 'Democracy.' All those words your father used to use, they run in the blood. And they mean *nothing*. What does 'fairness' have to do with seventeen hundred and fifty calories a day?

"Fairness," he sneered, "is used up, gone, spent! Do you know what your blessed ancestors did, boy? They mined 'fairness' and 'democracy' from the untapped resources of the world. They didn't invent them, they *mined* them—just as the old farmers mined minerals from their

22

cornfields, twenty crops of corn and a foot of soil! Well, the topsoil's gone now. And so is fairness and freedom. The world is a closed system now boy, and there isn't enough to go around!"

The ferocity of the outburst left Ryeland stunned. "But—but sir," he said, "surely the far planets offer *new* frontiers, new resources—"

"Be still!" barked the Planner, the square silver head thrust forward like a hammer. Above him the steel-grey falcon whirred threateningly.

The Planner glowered up at Ryeland, shifting his position in the compensating chair as the subtrain began its up-grav thrust. Weight came back to normal, then more than normal. Planner Creery said: "Ryeland, you're like your father. He never learned that the frontier was gone, but you must. The Plan of Man is based upon a systematic reduction of the pernicious personal liberties that almost destroyed our world. War! Dust bowls! Floods! Forest fires!" Each word was a foul epithet; he spat them at Ryeland. "We have to pay the bill for the waste that has gone before—waste that your father, and those like him, would have spread. Never forget it, boy!"

Ryeland stood silent. There was no reasoning with this man; there was a power and assurance that a gun might shatter, but no human power ever could. After a moment Ryeland said: "I haven't forgotten." Nor ever would, he thought. Not while the collar weighed around his neck.

"The collar bothers you," said the Planner surprisingly, and grinned. It was as though he had read Ryeland's thoughts—easy enough, Ryeland realized. "But we all wear them, boy. Each one of us, from the Planner down to the castoffs waiting for salvage in the Body Bank, must account to the Machine for every hour of every day; and each of us wears the Machine's shackle. On some of us they're intangible," he explained gravely "and I admit that that does make a difference."

Unwillingly Ryeland smiled. Not only power, he realized; the man had personality, charm—even to use on a Risk.

"But if you like," the Planner added, off-handedly "you can get that particular collar off your own particular neck."

For a moment Ryeland couldn't believe what he had heard. "Get the collar off, sir?"

The Planner nodded majestically. He shifted his position again, touching a button. The massive, cushioned chair inclined slightly backward. The raven flapped with a tinkling metallic sound into the air, hovering, as a neck-rest rose out of the chair's back and enveloped the Planner's silver head. The subtrain sphere was well into its upward thrust now. A faint squeal filtered through the soundproofing of the room—testimony of the pressure that forced the car against the invisible, unfeelable wall of electrostatic force. It wasn't friction that made the squeal, but a heterodyne of vibrations from the generators that drove the car. Ryeland staggered as his weight grew.

The Planner said suddenly: "We are all bound to the Plan in one way or another. I must try to find unbreakable links that can replace your iron collar—or you must find them yourself; then the collar can come off."

Ryeland said desperately: "Surely my work proves that I am loyal."

"Surely it does not!" the Planner mocked. He shook his head like a great father bear with a naughty cub. "It is not what you have done already," he reproved, "but what you can do now that will matter. You have worked freely, Ryeland; perhaps brilliantly, but you must work within the Plan. Always. Every moment. The Planning Machine will assign you a task. If you complete it—"

He shrugged, with an effort.

Ryeland was gasping now, the sag of his flesh a trap as the subtrain sphere forced its way up from Earth's molten center. He wanted to talk—question the Planner —perhaps learn the secret of those missing days. But his body refused. All around them was white-hot rock under pressure; only the electrostatic hoops kept it out; they were down many miles, but now rising. It was like an elevator again, but going up. The vertical component of the sphere's speed was rapidly reaching a hundred and fifty miles an hour; and even the Planner's voice, cushioned and protected as he was, began to grow hoarse and slow.

"You'd better go now, Ryeland," he grumbled. "But would you like to know what your task will be?"

Ryeland didn't answer—he couldn't; but his eyes answered for him. The Planner chuckled slowly. "Yes, of course. The Machine thinks you can handle it. It sounds —Well," said the Planner thoughtfully, "we each have our part to play, and mine is not necessarily to understand everything the Machine requires. Your task is to develop a jetless drive."

Ryeland rocked, and clutched frantically at the edge of the Planner's huge desk. "A—a jetless drive?"

The Planner looked somberly amused. "I see," he said. "Perhaps your task does not include understanding it either? But that is what the Machine asks of you."

"You mean—" Ryeland tried to recover his breath. "You mean, a reactionless propulsion system?"

"Precisely."

"Do you know that your torture experts—your reconstruction therapists—have been trying for three years to make me tell them how to build a jetless drive? They seem to think I know how."

"I know." The big man shrugged. "I know their efforts failed. The Machine had received information that you had designed such a mechanism. Apparently that information was mistaken. But the past three years have made such a device more than ever essential to the security of the Plan—more than ever dangerous to the Plan, if it should fall into unfriendly hands.

"The Machine requires a jetless drive. Its records of your abilities and achievements indicate that you are qualified to develop such a device. I have decided to disregard the evidence of your unplanned behavior, the problem of whether your amnesia is real or assumed, voluntary or not. If you want to come out of your collar in one piece, you will design a working method of reactionless propulsion. Now," he said in an exhausted voice, "you must go."

Through a haze Ryeland saw him make a faint motion with the huge gnarled hand that lay on the arm of his chair. The raven shifted position ever so little and beat the air frantically with its steel wings. Across the room a door opened.

One of the Planner's guard officers came in. He was a giant of a man, but he stepped very carefully under the thrust of the sphere's climb.

"Ryeland," whispered the great old man behind the desk.

Ryeland turned, half leaning on the officer in guard blue.

"About my daughter," said the Planner softly. The squeal had become a roar, almost drowning him out. "Donna has a soft heart, which she inherited from her mother; but her brain she inherited from me. Do not attach importance to the fact that she allowed you to talk with her in her bath." And the old man's eyes closed, as the Planner allowed his head to slump back at last.

3

Machine Major Chatterji said comfortingly: "You'll like us here, Ryeland. We're a brisk outfit, brisk."

"Yes, sir." Ryeland looked around him. He was in a steel-walled cubicle with a Security designation. He had no idea where on, or under, Earth he might be.

"You don't have to worry about nonsense," the major chattered. "Get the work done, that's all we care about."

Ryeland nodded. The little major moved with the youthful grace of a kitten. He wore the radar-horned helmet of a risk-pusher debonairely, as though it were part of a fancy-dress costume. He caught Ryeland's glance.

"Oh, that," he said, embarrassed. "Confounded nuisance, of course. But you *are* a Risk and the Machine's orders—"

"I'm used to it."

"Not that you're the only Risk here," Major Chatterji added quickly. "Heavens, no! Some of our best men, and all that."

Ryeland interrupted, "Excuse me, Major." He bent to the teletype and rapidly typed out his identification number and the fact that he had arrived. Without delay the teletype rapped out:

R. Information. Machine Major Chatterji is authorized to reconsider your status. Action. Requisition necessary equipment for expansion of equations re unified force field and steady-state hypothesis.

Ryeland frowned. Major Chatterji, peeking over his shoulder at the gray teletype, cried: "At once, Steve! Oh, we move fast here. I'll have a six-deck calculator and a room to put it in before you can change your clothes, I'll bet you a lakh of dollars!"

Ryeland said: "I don't understand. 'Unified force field and steady-state hypothesis'—what's that about?" But the major was cheerfully ignorant. Administration was his job; Ryeland would find out everything else in due course, wouldn't he? Ryeland shrugged. "All right. But I won't need the calculator—not if Oporto is still around."

"The other Risk?" Machine Major Chatterji winked. "Always stick together," he nodded. "I'll have him detailed to you."

Ryeland looked again at the teletype. The truly important part of the message also needed some thought. *Machine Major Chatterji is authorized to reconsider your status.* Then this man here, with the liquid black eyes and the lean, hooked nose, this was the man who could turn the key that would unlock the iron collar?

Or was that the wrong assumption to make? The Machine was always exact. But sometimes the mere human who read its message failed to understand the meaning. For instance, did that message mean that Machine Major Chatterji could clear Ryeland—or did it mean that he could downgrade him . . . say from Risk to raw material for the Body Bank?

It was a sobering thought.

The faded unreality of everything in his past except his knowledge of science left Ryeland with a nagging sense of bewilderment and loss.

"Why does the Machine need a jetless drive?" Uneasily, he put the question to Major Chatterji. "The ion jet ships are good enough to reach the planets—and anyhow the Plan of Man seems to be retreating from space and burrowing into the Earth."

"Stop it!" Chatterji warned him sharply. "Such speculation is no part of our function."

Ryeland insisted, "The Machine seems to be afraid that a jetless drive in the wrong hands would be dangerous to the Plan. Whose hands could that be? The Plan has conquered all the planets, taken in the whole human race. Except for a few fugitives like Ron Donderevo—"

"Don't talk about him!" Chatterji looked shocked. "Our own function here is enough to keep us busy without any such unplanned talk."

Ryeland shrugged and gave it up, and Chatterji at once reverted to his cheerful bustle.

"We've got to get you settled," he beamed, his gold-rimmed glasses flashing. "Faith! Come in here, girl."

The door opened. A tall blonde strutted in. She wore

27

tight scarlet pants and a brief scarlet jacket. Two centuries before she would have been a drum majorette; under the Plan she had a more important role to play. "This is Faith, Steve. She's one of our Togetherness girls. She'll help you get adjusted here, I promise!"

The Togetherness girl smiled a lacquered smile. She piped: " 'Perform your own function perfectly—and your own function only.' That's our motto here, Mr. Ryeland." It was like a doll talking.

"And a splendid motto it is!" Major Chatterji endorsed, beaming. "Get him started, Faith. And don't forget the Togetherness meeting at nineteen hundred hours."

Ryeland's mind was teeming with jetless drives and the steady-state hypothesis and three missing days and *Major Chatterji is authorized to reconsider* and the fact that the Planner had known about his interview with Donna in her bath. But this was important too; he swept the other things out of his mind and tried to pay attenion to what the Togetherness girl was saying.

"You'll like it here, Steve," she whispered, solemnly squeezing his arm. She smiled up at him, and steered him down a gray-walled concrete tunnel. There were no windows. "This is Point Circle Black. Sounds confusing, doesn't it? But you'll learn. I'll teach you!" Point Circle Black was the headquarters office, where Major Chatterji, the administrative officer, fussed endlessly over his problems of supply and personnel. "Point Triangle Gray." Faith sang, waving at an intersection ahead. "That's the medical section. Tests and diseases, injuries and—" she giggled naughtily—"supply depot for the Body Bank."

Ryeland grunted.

"Oh, that's nothing for *you* to worry about, Steve," she said reassuringly. "Trust Major Chatterji. You do your part and he'll do his; that's Teamwork."

Ryeland mumbled, "I understand. It's just that—well, I've had to face the chance of the Body Bank for three years now. I admit I don't like the idea of being butchered."

She stopped, scandalized, her perfect eyebrows arched, her clear eyes wide. "Butchered? Steve, what an unplanned word!"

"I only meant—"

"The *Planned* term," she said firmly, "is 'salvaged'. And you can't deny the logic of the Machine, can you?" She didn't wait for an answer. She was well into her set

28

speech. "The Body Bank," she parroted, "provides the attack team with the necessary stimulus to insure maximum effort. If the effort is successful, the team has nothing to fear. If the effort fails——"

She shrugged winsomely. "The welfare of the Plan of Man," she said, "requires that they must make their contribution in another way. That is, their physical organs must contribute to the repair of more useful citizens. That's Teamwork!"

"Thanks," said Ryeland grumpily. The isolation camp on the rim of the Arctic Circle, he thought wistfully—it had been hard and dull and uncomfortable; but at least he hadn't been exposed to lectures from teen-aged girls!

Point Triangle Gray was a Security designation; all the names were. The whole area was called Team Center. It might have been under Lake Erie or the Indian Ocean; Ryeland never learned.

At Point Triangle Gray he was given his tests. He caught a glimpse of Oporto, looking healthy enough but somehow crestfallen; they waved, but there was no chance to speak as Oporto came out of one laboratory room while Ryeland was going into another. At least, Ryeland thought, the little man hadn't been salvaged.

Then he forgot about Oporto for five rigorous hours. Point Triangle Gray measured his functional indices and his loyalty quotients with every test that he had ever undergone before and one or two that were brand new to him. The lab men stripped him and clamped him in their metering devices, while the interrogators demanded every detail of his life, back to the toys his mother had given him for his third birthday.

In these tests he tasted the after-bitterness of those sessions in the therapy room at the "recreation center"—those long, endless ages when he was punished and punished again because he could not make sense of the crazy questions the therapists flung at him. He dreaded, each moment now, that in the next moment it would start again. Someone would fling him a question about pyropods or Ron Donderevo. Someone would ask him about the missing three days in his life, or demand that he draw them the plans for a device he'd never heard of.

But it didn't happen; the questions were all routine.

In fact, every one of the questions had been asked him before—some of them a hundred times. Every answer had long since been recorded for the memory drums

29

of the Planning Machine. But the interrogation went on. His reactions were studied in blinding actinic light, and photographed by infra-red in what to him was utter dark. His body fluids were sampled again and again. Whole salvos of injections stimulated and calmed him, and for a short time put him to sleep—while heaven knew what pokings by scalpel and probe investigated the muscle tensions of his innermost system.

But at last it was over.

He was dressed in new crisp scarlet slacks and tunic and propelled into the gray concrete corridors where Faith was waiting, the lacquered smile on her face and her eyes glad.

"You've passed!" she sang. "But I knew you would. And now you're a full member of the Team."

She led him caroling: "Next I'll show you your quarters. They're nice, Steve! And then, oh, there's so much here! You'll like the Togetherness Canteen. You'll have *wonderful* work facilities. Everything is fine—and, of course, that's only fair, isn't it? Because so much is expected of you people on the Attack Team. You're entitled to a great deal in return; that's Teamwork!"

She led him about for an hour, and she did not stop chattering once. She took him to a sort of mess hall to be fed—alone; he was late for dinner, due to the tests at Point Triangle Gray, and the others were all through. The food was General Workers A-Ration—about the same as at the maximum-security camp, though somewhat less of it in terms of calories. But it was pleasant to be allowed to sit and smoke after the meal. And she showed him his quarters.

They were comfortable. A rather surprisingly soft bed, a bookcase (already Machine Major Chatterji had stocked it with conversion tables and reference books), a more than adequate chest for the personal belongings he had long since ceased to own. "Isn't it *nice?*" the Togetherness girl enthused. "But we'll have to hurry, Steve. It's almost nineteen hundred hours!"

The Togetherness Canteen was high over the maze of tunnels that comprised Team Center. Its gray concrete was liberally splashed with bright colors.

It was full of light and sound and people. There were nearly twenty Togetherness girls as pretty as Faith; they danced with laughing officers of the Technicorps, sat with them at tables, sang with them around a piano. There

30

were hurrying waitresses as pretty as the Togetherness girls, or almost, bringing drinks and light refreshment. And there were the officers—Ryeland's new colleagues.

They all wore the crisp scarlet uniform; and his heart bounded, for three of them at least, he saw, wore the same iron collar as himself. But they were *laughing*. One danced with a red-headed girl as tall as he, two were in a card game.

The iron collar did not seem to weigh heavily on these Risks.

Ryeland took a deep, wondering breath. Maybe this place was the place he had hoped for all those three years. . . .

One side of the room was an enormous window, twenty feet tall, made of armor-glass. Outside weathered cliffs were splashed with orange sun, nearly set. The tops of pines swayed in an unheard wind, and a far mountain slope was splotched with evergreens and golden autumn aspen.

Faith touched his arm. "What's wrong, Steve? Afraid of high places?"

He had hardly noticed the scenery; his thoughts had been on his collar. But he blinked and came awake. "I —I didn't know where this place was, until I saw the outside."

"You still don't know," she laughed. "Come along. You'll want to meet the Team leader."

General Fleemer had big bulging eyes and a tight uniform; it made him look like a very important frog. "So you're Steve Ryeland?" The general pumped his hand, the bulging eyes glowing with friendly Togetherness. "Glad to have you, Steve!" He grinned and flicked the iron collar with a fingernail. It rang faintly. "We'll have that off you in no time. Give us results, we'll give you your clearance! What could be fairer?"

He caught Steve by the other elbow, the one Faith wasn't using, and carried him off. Faith trailed along. "Want you to meet some of the others," he boomed. "Here. Pascal! Come over here. Steve, I want you to meet—"

"But I already know Colonel Lescure," said Ryeland. It was the grayhaired Technicorps officer who had conducted them to Compartment 93 on the Planner's subtrain.

The colonel nodded, and took him aside for a moment

31

while General Fleemer rounded up more of the Team. "I didn't want to say anything before—but I knew you were coming here. And I'm glad. Your—ah—interview was a success, eh?" And he nudged Ryeland's ribs.

It occurred to Ryeland that the colonel might not have been nearly as jolly with him if the interview hadn't been a success, but he let it pass. "Yes," he said, "the Planner was quite—"

"Planner?" Colonel Lescure winked. "I mean the *other* interview, son! She's quite a girl!" It seemed, thought Steve Ryeland, that there was hardly a human under the Plan of Man who wasn't aware that he had spent three-quarters of an hour with Donna Creery in her bath.

"Over here!" cried the general, beckoning. "You too, Otto!" As Ryeland reached the general Colonel Otto Gottling stumped over, his face like a rock. He was a jet combustion expert, as it turned out; his chamber had powered the last twelve rockets built for the out-planet run.

Everyone was a specialist and Ryeland found it uncommonly difficult to figure out where the specialties fit together. Colonel Lescure, he discovered, was Director of the Plan of Space Biology, for example. A major named Max Lunggren was an astrophysicist. There were two other mathematicians—one an expert in number theory, the other whose name was vaguely familiar to Ryeland as the author of a paper on normed rings. (Coincidentally—or was it coincidence?—both of them wore the collars of Risks.) The third Risk was a food chemist, a fat, jolly man who owned a fund of limericks.

But some hours later Ryeland received a clue, at least; the evening was not entirely devoted to Togetherness.

When everyone was satisfactorily mellow General Fleemer climbed atop a table and hammered it with his heel for attention.

"A toast!" he bawled. "I give you Teamwork—and the Plan!"

There was a rousing roar. Fleemer drained his glass with them and then turned serious. "Some of you," he cried, "wonder what our Team Attack is aimed at. Well, you'll find out! But for the benefit of the new people, first let me review the overall philosophy of the Team Attack itself. It is the essential tool of our scientific progress, and too important to be taken for granted!"

"Hurray for Team Attack!" bawled one of the iron-collar mathematicians, amid a giggle of the Togetherness girls around him.

General Fleemer smiled, quelling him. He said: "Once upon a time—so our Team historians tell me—science was done by individual men. Some of you may think it is still done that way." He gave a frosty grin to Ryeland and the other Risks. "But that is all over. The turning point came with the Einstein Team, which met at a town called Hiroshima to attack the primary problem of atomic fission.

"Unfortunately," the general said sadly, holding out his glass for a refill, "these pioneers were destroyed by the unexpected success of their first experiment with uranium fission. But the principle of team attack survived!

"Since then the Plan of Man has refined the principles and polished the techniques of Team Attack. When the Plan of Man requires a new scientific discovery, a team is created to make it. Such a team is needed now—and you are my Team, all of you!"

There was prolonged cheering.

Then Fleemer paused. He smiled, and it was a scorpion's smile, vastly out of character in that wattled marshmallow face.

He said: "I'm sure you all understand why you can be counted on to do your best." He nodded merrily to Ryeland and the other iron-collar men. "When you succeed, you will learn that Teamwork operates both ways. *When* you succeed. But if you fail—*if* you fail—why, then. . . ."

He trailed off, and looked somberly at the men for a second.

Then he grinned and drew one pudgy finger across his non-existent neck. "Zzzzt! The Body Bank! *But we won't fail!*"

There was a burst of laughter. Machine Major Chatterji leaped to a table, his glasses gleaming. "Three cheers for General Fleemer and the Plan of Man! Hip, hip—"

"Hooray!" The cheer was loud but ragged.

"Hip, hip—"

"Hooray!" Louder now. The whole room was together.

"Hip, hip——"

"Hooray!" Ryeland found himself thundering along with the rest. He couldn't help it. He had been born under the Plan of Man. He could not doubt it. It would have deprived his life of meaning, as the iron collar that was the

Plan's gift to him had, for a time, nearly deprived it of hope.

There was a loud applause. And General Fleemer, still smiling, raised his hand. "What the Machine needs," he said, "is a new physical principle." He shrugged winsomely—as best he could with those blubber shoulders. "I'm not a scientist, and I don't know just how tough this job is going to be. Probably some of you think it's going to be *very* tough. Well," he said, chuckling, "the rest of you are just going to have to convince them otherwise!" And he touched his finger jestingly to his throat.

Ryeland tried, but got little information from the others. It wasn't so much that they refused to tell; it was more that he couldn't understand. The Machine would give him a detailed directive, they assured him, and wouldn't he have another drink?

And an hour later Faith offered to show him a short-cut home to his quarters. They linked arms and wandered off through the gray-walled corridors. "Here's an area you've never seen," she caroled. "See that? Point Nexus. That's the Message Center."

"Lovely Message Center," said Ryeland comfortably. Funny. Even the iron collar didn't seem as hard or as cold. She was a sweet kind of girl, he thought dreamily. Of course, the Togetherness girls were coached, reared—all but bred for that. But she reminded him of the Fair Lost One, Angela—about whom the Planner's daughter had known more than she should. But of course it could have come from his personnel folder, and—

"Point Crescent Green," sang the girl, pointing to another stenciled emblem on the wall.

"Lovely," said Ryeland automatically, and then took a closer look. "But what's going on?"

The girl hesitated.

She stopped in the middle of a word and frowned at Ryeland. "I tell you," she said after a moment, suddenly gay, "maybe this short-cut isn't such a good idea. Back the other way there's—"

"No, but look," Ryeland insisted planting his feet as she tugged at him. It was quite late now, but there were a couple of guards in Team scarlet, and one of them was turning a key to slide back a massive, lead-shielded door. Beyond was the floor of an enormous pit, lit by a bright single light, high up.

Ryeland recognized it for what it was: A rocket land-

34

ing pit. There were the great spreading girder arms of the gantry, the enormous ducts for the jet-baffles yawned black in the floor. A piece of his mind catalogued the information that rocket landings commonly took place here; dim in the gloom behind the brilliant light were the enormous doors that would open to the sky.

But there was no rocket in the pit.

There was something else, something in a heavy metal cage.

"What *is* that thing?" Ryeland demanded. It looked a little like the seals that Ryeland had seen sunning themselves on the rocks off the maximum-security camp; but it was golden—metallic gold, the gold of the setting sun on bright metal, as it lay bathed in the wash of harsh light from above.

The thing was alive. It was, however, no animal that Ryeland had ever seen.

It lay on the floor of the great metal cage as though exhausted by efforts to escape. The golden fur was bloodied and torn about its head. Some of the bars were bent and bloodstained.

Whatever it was, it had fought to get free!

The Togetherness girl said worriedly: "Come away, Steve. Please! Major Chatterji doesn't want anyone to see the spaceling until—" She gasped, confused. She begged: "Forget I said that! I shouldn't have taken you this way at all, but—Oh, please, Steve, come away."

Reluctantly he let her lead him away. The guard had hurried inside and the enormous metal doors were closed; there was nothing more to see in any case.

But what was it that he had seen?

4

At 0700 hours the next morning the teletype rang him out of a deep sleep. Hardly stopping to open his eyes he leaped to answer. It clattered:

Query. Is Steven Ryeland, Risk, AWC-38440, present?

Ryeland blanched and instantly tapped out his acknowledgement. All human instincts ordered him to add an apology, but the Machine was not interested in apologies, only

35

in compliance with its rules. It rapped back at him without pause:

Information. Steady-state hypothesis rests on theory of Fred Hoyle English astronomer physicist 20th century stating that clouds hydrogen gas are continually formed between stars thus replenishing matter converted into energy in stellar power processes. Action. Produce necessary mathematical statements showing when under what conditions process can occur. Action. Make statement as to feasibility additional mathematical statement providing basis for neutralizing or reversing hydrogen formation process.

Ryeland stared. There was a brief tap at the door and the Togetherness girl danced in, carrying a tray with tea and toast and a glass of pinkish fruit juice. "Good morning, Steven! Rise and shine. I—oh!" He impatiently motioned her to be silent; the teletype, as though that were not enough for him to worry about in a single transmission, emitted the whir of marking impulses for a moment and then clattered out a new message:

Information. Experimental evidence available indicating existence of drive mechanism not subject to Newton Third Law Motion. Information. Said mechanism referred to as Jetless Drive. Action. Produce necessary mathematical statements providing basis for reproducing Jetless Drive in Plan space vehicles. Action. Review work of Colonel Gottling unified force field as necessary first step.

Ryeland pulled the tape out of the machine as soon as it was finished and sat staring at it. Somebody, he reflected, had been transferring information from his forbidden books into the Machine!

Gently Faith removed it from his fingers. "Breakfast," she scolded. "A bath. You'll think better when you're more awake!" Groggily Steve allowed himself to be propelled toward the bath, his mind a whirl of hydrogen clouds and non-Newtonian force fields.

The steaming shower woke him. By the time he was dressed and sitting down to breakfast with the Togetherness girl he was alert. "Jetless drive!" he said. "But there can't be such a thing. Newton's law!"

"Drink your tea, Steven," she said soothingly. "Would the Machine ask you to do it if it were impossible?"

"But I can't—well, *what* experimental evidence? I haven't seen any."

The Togetherness Girl looked inconspicuously at the watch on her wrist. "Colonel Lescure will be waiting, Steve. Drink your tea."

The colonel was very crisp in his uniform and white smock. He said: "You're jittery, Ryeland. Relax."

Steve touched his iron collar significantly. The colonel smiled. "Oh, sure," he said, "but you want to get it off, don't you? And the best way is to relax, because your first job is to listen. I have to tell you about the reefs of space."

The reefs of space! Ryeland gulped and tried to relax. A numbing fog of bewilderment and pain swirled up around him, across the lost years at the maximum-security camp. He was lying stretched on the couch in the therapy room, with the cold electrodes clamped to his wrists, and the blinding light blazing into his face. Dr. Thrale was standing over him, fat and gentle and apologetic, wheezing out the words *spaceling* and *pyropod* and *jetless drive* and *reefs of space*, and methodically charting his reactions.

"Relax, Ryeland." The colonel's voice buzzed out of a great gulf of distance. "We must take this problem one step at a time. The first step is the information which I am to give you now."

"Sure," Ryeland gasped. "I understand."

He was trying desperately to relax. Perhaps this information would answer the riddle of those three lost days.

"Let's have a drink," the Colonel was suggesting. "Talking's thirsty work."

Ryeland hesitated. Alcohol had always been forbidden, at the academy and at the isolation camp.

"Come on," said the colonel, twinkling. "A transfusion won't hurt the story."

He opened a cabinet and took out glasses and a little box. While he poured drinks, Ryeland urged: "Reefs of space? Meteor clouds, perhaps?"

Pascal Lescure laughed. "More like coral reefs. Here." He touched glasses. "That's better," he said comfortably, tasting his drink, and he opened the little box.

A collection of fantastic little animals modeled in plastic spilled out. Ryeland glanced at them only abstractedly;

his mind was on what Lescure had said. "But coral is built by living organisms."

The colonel nodded. "The reefs of space are built by living organisms, too—working over vastly longer stretches of time."

Ryeland set down his untouched glass violently, slopping it over. "What organisms live in space?"

"Why," the colonel said seriously, poking at his plastic toys with a finger, "creatures very much like these. They were modeled from life. And before that—the creators of the reefs themselves, simple little one-celled organisms, originating—everywhere!"

Ryeland forced himself to speak slowly, methodically: "The Machine's orders came this morning. I'm to investigate the steady-state hypothesis. And ever since then I've been thinking—about Hoyle's steady-state theory, and about another speculation he made. That life was born before the planets were, created by the chemical action of ultraviolet light in the cooling clouds of gas and dust around the sun. But how could it survive? The clouds disappear as the planets form."

"Life adapts," the colonel said heavily, and poked at his dragons.

He took a fresh drink. "Leaving out the intangibles," he lectured, "life is a phenomenon of matter and energy. The Hoyle Effect provides the matter, in the clouds of new hydrogen that are always being born between the stars. And life makes its own energy."

"How?"

"By fusing the hydrogen into heavier elements," the colonel said solemnly.

He flicked a switch. A screen slid down out of the ceiling. An image appeared on it, the image of little darting bodies, flashing with light, crossing the field of vision. The picture might have been one of pond life under a microscope, except for the difference in shapes . . . and for the fact that these creatures gave off a light of their own. "The fusorians," said the colonel somberly. "Hardy little things. They fuse hydrogen atoms and generate energy, and they live in space."

Fusorians! Ryeland felt his body tense as though an electric shock had passed through it. He was conscious of the colonel's gaze on him, and tried to relax, but the colonel studied him thoughtfully for a moment.

He said only: "No wonder you're excited." He blinked

at Ryeland mildly. "This thing is big. It means that the planets are not lonely oases in a dead desert of emptiness. It means that they are islands in an infinite ocean of life —strange life, which we had never suspected."

"But why haven't any of them ever appeared on Earth?" Ryeland demanded. Infuriating how slowly Lescure spoke! It was life and death to Ryeland—perhaps it was the answer to all his questions—but the colonel treated it only as another lecture, and a rather dull one.

The colonel shrugged. "Perhaps they drown in air. I suppose the heavier elements are their own waste products, and therefore poisonous to them." He took another pull at his drink. "Perhaps these creatures built the Earth," he said meditatively. "It accounts for the proportions of heavy elements better than the theories of the cosmologists. But of course it doesn't really matter—not to the Plan, I mean."

Ryeland frowned. There had been something almost disloyal about the colonel's tone. He changed the subject. "These things—" touching the plastic models—"they aren't fusorians?"

"No. They're pyropods. They live in the reefs." Irritably the colonel waved a hand. The screen glowed with another picture.

Ryeland leaned forward staring. "Fairyland!" he breathed.

The colonel laughed harshly. The view on the screen was of a delicate tracery of glowing vines and plants, where birdlike things moved effortlessly among the branches.

"Call it that," said the colonel. "I called it other things when I was there. You see, there *is* a constant new flow of matter into the universe. There *is* a steady rebirth of hydrogen between the stars. I know—I've seen it!"

Nervously he took another drink. "It was a few years ago. The pyropods had been seen, but none had been captured. The Planner ordered me out on a hunting trip to catch one."

Ryeland frowned. "Hunting? But the Plan of Man has no energy to waste on that sort of thing! Every calorie must go to some productive use!"

"You're an apt pupil," the colonel said wryly, "but it was the Machine's decision, not mine. Or so the Planner said. At any rate, we took off for the planet beyond Pluto. Was there one? It was necessary to assume one, to provide a home for the pyropods—or so we thought. We knew they had no home from Pluto sunwards. . . .

"It was a long trip. You know why interstellar flight has never been possible. There's power enough for us to reach the stars, but the difficulty is in finding the reaction mass to hurl away. Once you pass Orbit Pluto you begin to face those problems in practice. We were in the old *Cristobal Colon*, with hydrion jets. Our reaction mass was water. All we could carry was barely enough to land us on the hypothetical planet. We were to reload there for the flight home, if we found it." The colonel chuckled dryly. "We didn't find it," he said.

"Then—how did you get back?" Ryeland demanded, startled.

"We blundered into something. What we called the Rim. Don't confuse it with the Reefs of Space—it wasn't them, not for billions of miles yet. It belongs to the solar system, a scattered swarm of little asteroids, strung in a wide orbit all around the sun. A ring of snowballs, actually. *Cold* snow—mostly methane and ammonia; but we found enough water to refill our tanks. And then we went on. The Machine's orders had been definite."

The colonel shivered and finished his drink. "We went out and out," he said, mixing a fresh one, "beyond the Rim, until the sun was just a bright star behind—then not even particularly bright. We were braking, on the point of turning back—

"And then we saw the first Reef."

Colonel Lescure waved at the strange scene on the screen. He began to look alive again. "It didn't look like much at first. A mottled, lopsided mass, not much bigger than the snowballs. But it was luminous!"

Ryeland found himself gulping his drink. Silently he held out the empty glass and the colonel refilled it without pausing.

"An unearthly place. We came down in a brittle forest of things like coral branches. Thickets of shining crystal thorns snagged at our spacesuits when we went out exploring. We blundered through metal jungles that tripped and snared us with living wires and stabbed us with sharp blades. And there were stranger things still!

"There were enormous lovely flowers that shone with uncanny colors—and gave off deadly gamma rays. There was a kind of golden vine that struck back with a high-
40

voltage kick when you touched it. There were innocent little pods that squirted jets of radioactive isotopes.

"It was a nightmare! But while we were reviving and decontaminating our casualties we worked out the natural history of the Reef. It was a cluster of living fusorian colonies!

"We counted almost a hundred species. They must have grown from a few spores, drifting in the interstellar hydrogen. The rate of growth must be terribly slow—a few inches, perhaps, in a million years. But the fusorians have time.

"We looked at each other. We knew we had found something more than we had been sent for.

"We had found a new frontier."

Ryeland was on his feet, a sudden uncontrollable surge of emotion driving him there. "Frontier? Could—could people survive out there?"

"Why not? They're rich with everything we need. There's hydrogen for power, metal for machines, raw materials for food. We brought treasures back with us! We loaded our ship with every sort of specimen we could carry. Fantastic diamond spikes, and masses of malleable iron in perfectly pure crystals. Living prisms that shone with their own cold glow of fusion. Spongy metal mushrooms, in hundred-pound chunks, that tested more than ninety per cent uranium-235. Much more than critical mass! And yet they didn't explode, while they lived. But one chunk did let go after we had jettisoned it in space, and after that we were careful to divide the masses."

"So *that's* why the Machine needs a jetless drive?" Ryeland saw a ray of understanding, stabbing through the gray fog of confusion which had followed him from his suite in the maximum-security camp. "To reach the reefs of space—because they're beyond the range of our ion drives!"

"I suppose so." Lescure nodded. "Though such thinking goes a little beyond our function."

"But why would the Machine want to explore them?" Ryeland frowned at him. "Is there something in the reefs which could threaten the security of the Plan?"

"Better not exceed our function," Lescure warned him. "I imagine the planets are pretty well protected from the life of space, by their atmospheres and their Van Allen belts. But of course there was the pyropod that rammed us—"

41

"Pyropod?"

For a second Ryeland was lying on his couch in the therapy room again, with the cold electrodes clamped on his body and Thrale's apologetic voice lisping out the words that had been senseless to him then, *jetless drive ... fusorian ... pyropod.*

Lescure's eyes had narrowed.

"Ryeland, you appear unduly agitated. I don't quite understand your reactions—unless you have heard this story before."

"I have not." That, at least, was true. The therapists had always been careful to tell him nothing at all about pyropods or fusorians or the reefs of space.

For another uncomfortable moment, Lescure stared.

"Relax, then." At last he smiled. "Forgive my question. I asked it because there was an unfortunate breach of security. One member of my crew jumped ship after our return. He had managed to steal unauthorized specimens and descriptions of the life of space. Of course he went to the Body Bank."

His eyes brushed Ryeland again, casually.

"I forget the fellow's name. Herrick? Horlick? Horrocks?"

Ryeland sat still, feeling numb.

Colonel Lescure waved carelessly, and the screen retracted, shutting itself off. "Drink?" he demanded. Ryeland shook his head, waiting.

Lescure sighed and poked through his plastic toys. "Here," he said suddenly.

Ryeland took the tiny thing from him, a two-inch figurine in black and silver with a wicked, knife-edged snout. Lescure's glazed eyes remained on it in fascination. "That's the one that attacked us," he said.

"This little thing?"

The colonel laughed. "It was ninety feet long," he said. He took it back from Steve and patted it. "Vicious little creature," he said, half fondly. "Evolution has made them vicious, Ryeland. They are living war rockets. They've been hammered into a horrible perfection, by eternities of evolution."

He swept the whole menagerie back into its box. "But they are only rockets," he said thoughtfully. "They need mass, too. We've cut up a dozen of them, and the squid is as much a rocket as they. . . . Perhaps that accounts for their voracity. They'll attack anything, with a hungry

42

fury you can't imagine. Mass is not plentiful in space, and they need what they can find.

"At any rate, this one rammed us, and—well, we had another dozen casualties." The colonel shrugged. "It was touch and go, because the thing was faster than we. But ultimately the survivors manned a torpedo station, and then the contest was over.

"Even the pyropods have not achieved a jetless drive."

"If there *is* such a thing," said Ryeland.

Colonel Lescure chuckled. He looked thoughtfully at Ryeland, as though choosing which of several to make. Finally he said: "You don't think the Team Attack will succeed?"

Ryeland said stiffly: "I will do my best, Colonel. But Newton's Third Law—"

Colonel Lescure laughed aloud. "Ah, well," he said, "who knows? Perhaps it won't succeed. Perhaps there is no jetless drive." Hilariously amused, though Ryeland could not tell why, he tossed the box of plastic figurines back in a cupboard.

"Ugly little things, good night," he said affectionately.

Ryeland commented: "You sound as though you like them."

"Why not? They don't bother us. If they haven't attacked the earth in the past billion years or so, they aren't likely to start very soon. They aren't adapted for atmosphere, or for direct, strong sunlight. Only a few of the strongest ventured in beyond Orbit Pluto to be sighted, before our expedition. None was ever seen in closer than Orbit Saturn—and that one, I think, was dying."

Ryeland was puzzled. "But—you spoke of danger."

"The danger that lurks in the Reefs of Space, yes!"

"But, if it isn't the pyropods, then what *is* it?"

"Freedom!" snapped Colonel Lescure, and clamped his lips shut.

5

Faith carried Ryeland off to his next interview. "You liked Colonel Lescure, didn't you?" she chattered. "He's such a *nice* man. If it were up to him, the reefrat wouldn't be suffering—" She stopped, the very picture of embarrassed confusion.

Ryeland looked at her thoughtfully. "What's a reefrat?"

"Here's Major Chatterji's office," said Faith nervously, and almost pushed him through the door.

Machine Major Chatterji got up, smiling blankly through his gleaming glasses, waving a copy of Ryeland's orders from the Machine. "Ready, Ryeland," he called. "We're all set for you now."

Ryeland advanced into the room, thinking. "I'll need my computer," he said. "And someone to look up all the work that's been done on the Hoyle Effect, boil it down, give me the essential information."

"Right! You can have three assistants from Colonel Lescure's section. And I've already requisitioned a binary computer."

"No," said Ryeland impatiently, "not a binary computer. *My* computer. Oddball Oporto."

Major Chatterji's gold-rimmed glasses twinkled with alarm. "The Risk? But Ryeland, really!"

"I need him," said Ryeland obstinately. The Machine's orders had been perfectly clear.

Chatterji surrendered. "We'll have to get General Fleemer's okay," he said. "Come along." He led Ryeland out through a short corridor to an elevator; Faith tagged after inconspicuously. The three of them went up, out, down another hall. Chatterji tapped on a door.

"All right," grumbled a voice from a speaker over the door, and it swung open. They walked into a silver room, with silver walls and furnishings plated in silver. General Fleemer, in a silver robe that he was knotting about him, stumped in from a bedroom. "Well?"

Machine Major Chatterji cleared his throat. "Sir, Ryeland wants the other Risk, Oporto, assigned to him."

"For calculation purposes, General," Ryeland cut in.

"He's a natural calculator. What they used to call an *idiot-savant*, or the next thing to it."

The general looked at him through his deepset eyes. "Will that help you solve the jetless drive?"

"Why," Ryeland began, "I haven't started on that yet. This is the Hoyle Effect. The Machine ordered—"

"I know what the Machine ordered," the general grumbled. He scratched his nose reflectively. "All right, give him his man. But Ryeland. The important part of your work is the jetless drive."

Ryeland was startled. "General, the Machine's orders didn't give priority to either section."

"*I* give priority," said the general sharply. "Get along with it, man! And get out."

In the corridor, Chatterji vanished toward his office and the Togetherness Girl took over again. "A very fine man, the general, don't you agree?" she chatted, leading him back to the elevator.

Ryeland took a deep breath. "Faith," he said, "there's something funny here. General Fleemer lives awfully well! And he seems to take it upon himself to, at least, interpret the Machine's orders. Is that customary, in Team Attack?"

The Togetherness Girl hesitated. She glanced at Ryeland, then led him down the corridor without speaking for a moment. She stopped before another door. "General Fleemer," she said, "is a fine man. I knew you'd like him. And you'll like Colonel Gottling too, don't think you won't!" And without any more of an answer than that, she opened the door to Gottling's office for him and left him there.

But Colonel Gottling proved himself very hard to like.

He was a huge man with a face like a skull, the horned helmet over it. He stood fingering the controls of his radar-horns angrily as Ryeland reported in on the teletype. "Hurry up, man," he muttered, and clumped out of his office, motioning Ryeland ahead of him. "You're next," he snapped. "Lescure had his whacks at the creature and he failed. They wouldn't let *me* handle it the way I wanted! And now it's up to you."

Ryeland said, "I don't understand. What creature?"

"The spaceling! The reefrat! The creature with the jetless drive."

Ryeland said humbly, "Colonel, I don't know what you're talking about."

Gottling spread his bony hands and stared at the ceil-

45

ing in exasperation. "What under the Plan is this? What kind of idiots do they salvage for top-priority Teams these days? Do you mean you never heard of the reefrats?"

"Only the word," Ryeland admitted. "But didn't you just say 'spaceling'?"

"Same thing!" Gottling stopped in an anteroom, jerking a thumb at a file cabinet. He barked: "Here! Here's everything you want to know about them. Everything from resting weight to the chemistry of what passes for blood. The only thing I can't tell you is what makes them go, and I could tell you that if they'd let me alone with the thing!"

"But—"

"You fool, stop saying 'but'!" howled Colonel Gottling. "Look here!"

He opened a door. Beyond was a big room, once a repair shop attached to one of the rocket pits, now hastily improvised into a laboratory. There were unpainted partitions, unconcealed electric wiring. Chemical lab benches held glassware and flasks of reagents, reeking acidly. There were transformers; an X-ray generator; various bulky devices that might have been centrifuges, biological research equipment—heaven knew what.

And the lab was busy.

There were at least two dozen men and women in scarlet Technicorps smocks working at the benches and instruments. They glanced up only briefly as Colonel Gottling and Ryeland entered and checked in, then quickly went back to their work without speaking.

Evidently the cheery good will among the brass didn't extend to the lower echelons.

Colonel Gottling, in a good humor again, lighted a long, green-tinted cigarette and waved at the room. "It's all yours now," he grunted. "Temporarily."

Ryeland looked at him.

"Or permanently," grinned the colonel, "provided you can tell us what makes the spaceling fly. Me, I think you can't. You look soft, Ryeland. The collar has not hardened you enough. Still—Do you want me to tell you something about the spaceling?"

"I certainly do," Ryeland said fervently.

"All right, why not? It's fairly intelligent. Lower primate level, at least. It is a warm-blooded oxygen-breathing mammal which—why do you look that way, man?"

46

Ryeland closed his mouth. "It's just that I thought it lived in space."

Colonel Gottling guffawed. "And it does! An oxygen-breather, living in open space! Amusing, is it not? But it possesses some remarkable adaptations."

"Such as what?"

Colonel Gottling looked bored. "You should have asked Lescure these questions. I am a rocket man. But first, of course, there is the jetless drive. Then there is something else—a field of force, perhaps, which enables it to hold a little cloud of air around it, even out in interstellar vacuum."

Ryeland said thoughtfully: "Could the two effects be linked?"

"Could they? Of course they could, idiot! But are they? I do not know." But Gottling was mellowing; treating Ryeland like an idiot had put him in a good humor. He said condescendingly: "It is possible, of course. I have thought that myself. If the reefrat can accelerate its own body without reaction, perhaps it can also accelerate gas molecules centripetally, also without reaction. How can one know? But—"

"But let us look at the spaceling," he said abruptly. "Then we can talk better."

He led the way through the laboratory and out the other side.

They went through a steel door into a sort of airlock. Racks in the walls held bulky protective suits and red-painted emergency gear. A warning sign glowed on the inner door of the airlock:

DANGER!
LANDING PIT—WAIT
FOR DECONTAMINATION

"It is safe," Gottling assured him. "The pit was de-conned months ago, before the spaceling was brought in."

He pulled a lever. Motors groaned; the inner door, an enormous lead-lined mass of steel and fire-brick, inched slowly aside.

Like a Viking in his radar horns, the colonel stalked into the landing pit, Ryeland following.

The pit was an enormous circular cavern. Floodlights blazed on the blackened concrete floor. Even the decon

47

crews, with all their foamants and air-blasting, had failed to remove the black breath of the jets.

Ryeland recognized it at once. It was the pit of which he had caught a glimpse the night before, with the Togetherness Girl. He lifted his eyes, looking for the sky and a settling rocket instinctively; but the dark armored walls lifted up into shadowy mystery. The cranes and the stages above were dark shapes in the dimness. No light passed the enormous doors, hundreds of feet up, that closed off the sky.

Gottling touched his arm and pointed.

Out in the black concrete stood a room-sized cage. Inside the cage was a pale cloud of greenish light; and in the center of the cloud lying motionless on the bare steel floor—

"The spaceling," said Gottling proudly.

It had struggled.

At close range, Ryeland could see how frantically fierce that struggle had been. The steel bars of the cage were thicker than his wrist, but some of them were bent. Red blood smeared them, and matted the spaceling's golden fur. It lay gasping on the stainless steel floor.

"She's skulking now, but we'll put her through her paces," Gottling bragged.

Ryeland said: "Wait, Colonel! The thing's injured. In the name of heaven, you can't—"

"Can't?" blazed the colonel. "Can't?" His finger reached up and touched the buttons of his radar-field suggestively. Under the triggering radar horns, his skull-like face glowered. "Don't tell me what I can't do, fool! Do you want me to expand my field radius? One touch of this and there won't be enough of you left to salvage!"

Ryeland swallowed. Involuntarily his hand reached toward the collar, with its eighty grams of high explosive.

"That's better," grunted Gottling. He clapped his hands and called: "Sergeant, get busy! Goose her!"

A Technicorps sergeant in red came trotting out of the shadows. He carried a long pole tipped with a sharpened blade. Black wires led from it to a battery box on his shoulder.

The spaceling rolled its battered head.

Its eyes opened—large, dark, limpid eyes—a seal's eyes; and they were terrible, it seemed to Ryeland, with suffering and fear. A shudder rippled along the creature's smooth featureless flanks.

48

"Goose her in the belly!" Gottling shouted. "Mr. Ryeland wants to see her do her tricks!"

The spaceling screamed.

Its cry was thinly edged with terror, like the voice of a hysterical woman. "Stop it," Ryeland gasped, shaken.

Colonel Gottling blared with laughter. Tears rolled out of his piglike eyes, down the bony cheeks. Finally he got control of himself. "Why, certainly," he gasped. "You're next, as I said, eh? And if you believe you can tell us how the creature flies without even seeing her do it—" he shrugged.

Writhing on the floor of the cage as though it had already felt the prod, the spaceling screamed in fright again.

Ryeland said hoarsely: "Just make him take that prod away."

"As you wish," the colonel nodded urbanely. "Sergeant! Return to duty. And you, Ryeland, I will leave you alone with your friend. Perhaps if I am not here to eavesdrop, she will whisper her secret in your ear!" Bellowing with laughter, Colonel Gottling shambled out of the pit.

After an hour, Ryeland began to appreciate the difficulties of the problem.

Back in the file room, he found a summary of the existing knowledge of the spaceling; he took it to the landing pit and read through it, watching the spaceling, trying to allow it to become accustomed to his presence. The creature hardly moved, except to follow Ryeland with its eyes.

The notes on the spaceling showed a fruitless and painful history. The spaceling had been captured by an exploring Plan rocket retracing the steps of Lescure's *Cristobal Colon*. A section of notes, showing how the capture had been effected, was missing; the account took up the story with the creature being brought into the hastily converted rocket pit. It had been chained at first, so that the first investigators approached it with impunity. Then the chains had been taken off—and, in quick order, half a dozen investigators had been bashed rather severely against the bars. The spaceling did not seem to have attacked them; they simply were in the way of the thing's terrified attempts at escape. However, after that the observations had been conducted primarily from outside the cage. And mostly—at least in the last two weeks, since

49

Colonel Gottling had taken over charge of the specimen —with the help of the goad. Or worse.

There were reports of blood tests and tissue samples. Ryeland glanced at them, frowned and put them aside; they meant nothing to him. There were X-ray studies, and reams of learned radiologists reports. Also of no value to Ryeland, whatever they might have meant to Colonel Pascal Lescure.

Then there were physical tests. Dynamometers had measured the pull against the chains. Telemetering devices had registered the change in the recorded curves of its vital processes under various conditions—at rest, as it "flew," and "under extraordinary stimulus," as the report primly put it. Meaning, Ryeland supposed, under torture.

No radiation of any sort had been detected. And someone had thought to surround the creature with plumb-bobs to test for an incident side thrust; there was none; the plumbs were undisturbed.

No thrust!

Then this nonsense that everyone had been spouting so glibly was not nonsense after all!

For if there was no measurable thrust against its environment to balance its measured dynamometer pull— then the spaceling had, indeed, a true jetless drive.

Ryeland looked up from the notes to stare at the spaceling, slumped in the bottom of its cage, its great eyes fixed on him. Jetless drive!

He suddenly felt very small and, for all the Togetherness and the Teamwork, for all the joint effort embodied in the Plan of Man, very alone. Jetless drive—here in this creature lay the seeds of a fact which would destroy Newton's Third Law, change the shape of the Solar System. For unquestionably, with such a drive, the scope of the Plan of Man would widen beyond recognition. Out past the useless, frozen methane giants, the Plan would drive to the stars!

Ryeland shook his head, confused.

For suddenly he didn't want the Plan of Man expanded to the stars. That word that Pascal Lescure had used— "Freedom!"

It did not seem to live under the Plan.

Abruptly his reveries were ended; there was a rumble like thunder in the pit.

Ryeland leaped to his feet, astonished, while the spaceling mewed worriedly in its cage. A blade of light split the dark above. He looked up, and a slit of blue sky widened.

There was a confused clattering behind him and someone came running into the pit. The Technicorps sergeant, shouting: "Mr. Ryeland, Mr. Ryeland! Get out of the way. Some crazy fool is coming in for a landing!"

The sergeant raced over to the cage and began frantically trying to unbolt its heavy fastenings, to push it on its tiny wheel to the side of the pit. There was a wild cataract of flame thrusting into the opening gates of the pit overhead, radio-triggered; and a tiny rocket came weaving in, settling on a cushion of bright white fire.

Ryeland thought grimly: "Thank God it's only a little one!" A big one would have been the end of the spaceling —and of himself and the Technicorps sergeant as well. But this little speedster had plenty of room to land without incinerating them all. It was a one-man craft, built for looks and play; it dropped to the black concrete on the far side of the pit, a hundred yards away, and though heat washed over them like a benediction, it did them no harm. A sudden gale roared through the floor ducts, sweeping the rocket fumes away.

A ramp fell.

A slim figure in white coveralls ran lightly down the ramp and across the concrete, confusingly half-familiar birds fluttering about its head.

Ryeland was galvanized into action. "Stop it!" he shouted. "Keep away from that cage!"

The intruder ignored him. Swearing, Ryeland raced to intercept the stranger. He took a dozen angry strides, caught a slim arm, swung the intruder around—and gasped. Silvery doves tore fiercely at his face and head.

"Get your hands off me, Risk!" It was a girl—*that* girl! He could see now that her white coveralls did not disguise her sex. Her eyes were a greenish blue, and very familiar eyes; her voice, though charged with indignation, was a familiar voice.

She gestured, and the Peace Doves fluttered muttering away. "What do you mean?" she demanded, shaking his fingers off her arm.

Ryeland gulped. It was the Planner's daughter, Donna

51

Creery. "I—" he began. "I—I didn't know it was you! But what do you want here?"

"Want?" The ocean-water eyes flashed. "I want to know what you people are doing—what you think you're doing by torturing my spaceling!"

6

The girl stood staring at Ryeland. She was an entirely different creature from the lovely girl in the bubble bath, almost unrecognizable. The Donna of the Planner's private subtrain car was a teen-ager in the process of becoming woman, with the sad shyness of youth and its innocence. But this girl was something else. This was the Planner's daughter, imperious. And not a child.

Ryeland took a deep breath. Planner's daughter or no, this girl was in his way. The only way he had of getting the collar off his neck lay through the creature in the cage. He said sharply: "Get out of here, Miss Creery. The spaceling is dying. It mustn't be disturbed."

"*What?*" The Peace Dove, settling on her shoulders, whirred and muttered.

"You aren't allowed here," he said stubbornly. "Please leave!"

She stared at him incredulously; then, without a word, turned to the cage. "Here, sweet," she whispered to the great seal-like animal. "Don't worry, Donna's here." The spaceling lifted its head and stared at her with great, limpid eyes.

Ryeland said harshly: "Miss Creery, I asked you to leave."

She didn't bother to look at him. "There's a good girl," she cooed, like a child with a puppy. "Where's the damned door?"

Ryeland was angry now. "You can't go in there!" He caught at her arm. It was like catching a tiger by the tail; there was a quick movement, too fast to follow, and she caught him a stinging blow across the face with her open hand. Sheer astonishment drove him back; and by the time he recovered his balance the Planner's daughter had found the catch and was inside the door of the cage.

The spaceling came heaving seal-like toward her, whimpering.

It was a bad spot for Ryeland. If anything happened to the girl, there was no doubt in the world that he would be held responsible. Gottling would see to that. And then good-bye dreams of freedom.

In fact, more likely it would be good-bye head!

Ryeland swore angrily. The Peace Doves squawked and rose into the air, circling around him. He paused, searched around, found a length of heavy chain just outside the cage door. Heaven knew what it had been used for—though the stains on it suggested one possibiility. He caught it up and dove into the cage after the girl.

"Stop," she said calmly. "I don't want to turn the Doves loose on you."

"Then get out of here!" he demanded. The floor of the cage was slippery with a kind of odorous slime. Part of it was the spaceling's blood, undoubtedly, but there was more —decaying small things that Ryeland couldn't recognize; perhaps they were animals that had come with the spaceling. The stench was powerful and sickening, but Ryeland didn't let it stop him. If that girl could stand it, that dainty creature who lived in an atmosphere of lilac blossoms and ease, certainly he could!

She was bending over the creature, reaching down to caress its golden fur. "Drop that chain," she ordered over her shoulder. "It's afraid of you."

It flinched from her touch at first. Then it relaxed. It licked at her face with a long black tongue. A sudden rumble filled the cage, like the purr of a giant cat.

There was an eruption of noise from outside. Colonel Gottling, radar-horned, deep eyes blazing fury out of the face like a skull, came racing in with a dozen men in Technicorps scarlet. "Get her out of there, you fool!" he roared, waving the electric prod at Ryeland.

The spaceling saw him and the enormous purr stopped. The creature began to whimper and tremble. "Hold it!" cried Ryeland. "You're frightening the spaceling. It may attack Miss Creery!"

But Donna Creery needed no help from him just then. On her knees in the bloody slime, she looked up from the torn, blood-crusted fur of the creature and her eyes were a hawk's eyes. "Colonel Gottling," she said in a thin voice that cut like knives. "I've been wanting to talk to you!"

The skull-faced colonel swallowed but stood his ground.

"You must get out of there, Miss Creery! The animal is dangerous. It has already wounded half a dozen men!"

"And what were the men doing to the spaceling?" The girl bent to pat the golden battered head. Two or three fat green flies were buzzing through the thinning cloud of light around the wounds on the spaceling's flanks. "Filthy," she said with scorn. "I want this cleaned up!"

She stood up and gestured Ryeland ahead of her out of the cage. "I want a meeting of the whole Team," she said coldly, closing the cage door behind her, "and I want it now! Meanwhile, Gottling, have your men clean that cage out. And if I catch any of them using that prod again, I'll see how they like it used on themselves!"

Gottling turned purple. In a voice stiff with self-control he said: "It is no longer my project, Miss Creery. Mr. Ryeland has taken it over."

"I give it back," said the girl. "I have another use for Mr. Ryeland."

Ryeland said, shocked: "But the Machine ordered—"

"I'll take care of the Machine," she said calmly. "Get started on this cage, you men! The spaceling needs her symbiotic partners and they're dying fast." She turned to the door. "Now let's have that meeting," she said grimly. "I want to get a few things straight!"

They were back at Point Crescent Green. The Team was buzzing like flies around the spaceling's wounds.

Donna Creery dominated the meeting. Major Chatterji tittered shyly and General Fleemer made half a dozen speeches on Teamwork; Colonel Gottling was in an icy rage and Colonel Lescure fluttered objections. But not one of them could stand up against the girl.

She blazed: "If that animal dies, she's going to take the lot of you with her! I've got news for you. There's a shortage of salvage material at the Body Bank." She stared around the room appraisingly. "Some of you would make pretty good spare parts. Do I make myself clear?"

"Quite clear," General Fleemer said humbly. "But, Miss Creery, our Team objective—"

"Shut up," she said mildly. "Yes? What is it?"

Machine Major Chatterji said with great respect: "There's a message for you on the teletype."

"It can wait." There was an audible gasp but the girl paid no attention. "From this date forward, Mr. Ryeland is in charge of the Team."

General Fleemer choked and sputtered: "Miss Creery, a *Risk* can't be put—"

"Yes, a Risk can," Donna Creery contradicted. "Oh, all right. Here, I'll get orders for you." She walked through them to the teletype, calmly pressed the "Interrupt" switch —another gasp swept through the Team—and began to type. In a moment the Machine's answer rattled back:

Action. Fleemer Team will comply with directive of Donna Creery

"Anything else bothering you?" she demanded.

"Nothing," croaked General Fleemer. His toad eyes bulged more than ever.

"All right. Now the rest of you clear out. Ryeland, I want to talk to you."

Whispering among themselves, but not audibly, the Team filed out of the conference room. Donna Creery stretched and yawned, the Peace Doves fluttering and cooing. "That's better," she said drowsily. "What are you doing?"

Ryeland coughed. "There seems to be a message coming in for you, Miss Creery," he said.

"There always is," she sighed. She stood behind him, one arm casually on his shoulder, reading:

Information. Planner Creery en route from Mombasa to Capetown. Information. Donna Creery personal rocket refueled and serviced. Information. London Philharmonic acknowledges receipt of opening season program instructions. Action. Request choice of soloist Beethoven piano concerto. Information. Moon colony Alpha-Six requests presence Donna Creery 25th anniversary celebration. Information.

"The usual run of thing," the girl said absently. "It can wait." She looked around. "This place depresses me. Haven't you got a room of your own? Let's go there." She didn't wait for an answer; she got up and beckoned Ryeland to follow.

He was not surprised to find that she knew the way. There seemed to be very little this girl didn't know!

But the situation was getting out of hand.

This girl was giving orders to an entire Research Team. It wasn't her place to do that. Everybody knew that! Under the Plan of Man it was the Machine that gave orders. Human beings—even Planner's daughters—were supposed to do their own job (perfectly) and nobody else's. That was plain logic, the logic of the Plan.

He stood stiffly holding the door to his room, meditating what to say to her. She walked in, looking curiously about; he followed, leaving the door ajar.

"Oh, close it," she said impatiently. "Don't you think my Peace Doves are chaperones enough?" She laughed at the expression on his face, threw herself at full length on his bed and lit a cigarette. The dislodged Peace Doves cooed complainingly and found roosts for themselves on the iron headboard.

Grudgingly Ryeland closed the door. He nodded to the teletype. "Don't you want to check in?"

"The Machine'll find me," Donna Creery said cheerfully. "You watch." And, sure enough, the words were hardly out of her mouth when the keys began to rattle away:

Information. Marseilles Planning Council asks Donna Creery give annual Plan Awards. Information. Life Magazine requests permission use photograph Donna Creery on Woman of the Year cover. Information—

"Someone's always available to tell the Machine where I've gone," the girl told Ryeland seriously. "And if not—well, the Machine can usually make a pretty good guess where I'll be. It knows me pretty well by now."

She spoke, Ryeland noticed wonderingly, as though the Machine were an old friend. But she didn't give him much chance to speculate on that; she said abruptly: "You're not much, Steve, but you're better than those others. Can you keep my spaceling alive?"

"*Your* spaceling?"

She laughed. "It's mine because I like it. Everything I like belongs to me—that's the way I want it." She added seriously: "But I don't know yet whether or not I like you."

He said, the back of his neck bristling, "I have my duty, Miss Creery. I'm going to do it! I hope it won't mean any further discomfort to the spaceling, but, if it does—Do you see this?" He tugged angrily at his collar. "I want that off! If I have to kill a million spacelings to get it off, I'll do it!"

She stubbed out her cigarette lazily. "That isn't what you told Gottling," she observed.

"How do you know what I told Gottling?"

"Oh, I know very many things. Why shouldn't I? The Machine goes everywhere, and my father is practically part of the Machine. And, oh, yes, I like the Machine, and everything I like—" She shrugged winsomely.

Ryeland stared. She was mocking him. She had to be. It was a joke in terribly bad taste, but surely that was all it was. He said stiffly: "Miss Creery, I don't appreciate that sort of remark about the Machine. I believe in the Plan of Man."

"That's terribly good of you," she said admiringly.

"Blast you," he yelled, pushed a step too far, "don't make fun of me! The Plan of Man *needs* the jetless drive, you silly little skirt! If the spaceling has to die so the Plan can discover its secret, what possible difference does that make?"

She swung her feet to the ground and got up, walking over close to him. Her face was relaxed and sympathetic. She looked at him for a second.

Then she said suddenly: "Do you still love that girl?"

It caught him off balance. "What—what girl?"

"Angela Zwick," she said patiently. "The daughter of Stefan Zwick. The blond, twenty years old, five feet four and a quarter, with green eyes, who became your teletype operator late one afternoon and made you kiss her that very night. The one who turned you in. Do you still love her?"

Ryeland's eyes popped. "I—I know you've got special sources of information," he managed, "but, really, I had no idea—"

"Answer the question," she said impatiently.

He took a deep breath and considered.

"Why, I don't know," he said at last. "Perhaps I do."

Donna Creery nodded. "I thought so," she said. "All right, Steve. I thought for a moment—But, no, it wouldn't work out, would it? But I admire your spirit."

Ryeland took a deep breath again. This girl, she had a talent for confusing him. It wasn't possible for him to keep up with her, he decided, it was only possible for him to cling to the basic facts of his existence. He said stiffly: "It doesn't take spirit to defend the Plan of Man. If the Plan needs to learn the secret of the jetless drive, that's my plain duty."

57

She nodded and sat again on his bed, the Peace Doves settling gently on her shoulders. "Tell me, Steve, do you know *why* the Plan of Man requires this information?"

"Why—no, not exactly. I suppose—"

"Don't suppose. It's to explore the reefs of space. Do you know what the Plan wants in the reefs?"

"No, I can't say that—"

"It wants Ron Donderevo, Steve."

"Ron?" He frowned.

"The man who got out of his iron collar, Steve," the girl said, nodding. A man you might like to know again. That booby-trapped, tamper-proof collar, that nobody can possibly get off until the Machine authorizes it—the Machine wants to talk to Donderevo about it, very badly. Because he took *his* collar off, all by himself."

Ryeland stared at her.

She nodded. "And Donderevo is out in the reefs now," she said, "and the Machine wants to do something about it. It might simply destroy the reefs. I understand you are working on some such project. But if it can't do that, it wants to send someone out there to find him.

"Someone with a radar gun, Steve! To kill him! And that's why the Machine wants the secret of the jetless drive!"

7

Ryeland's new authority as leader of the Attack Team did nothing to endear him to his colleagues.

He didn't care. He had work enough to keep him busy. Oddball Oporto made himself useful. The little man's talent for lightning computing saved Ryeland a good deal of time. Not that Oporto was faster than a computer. He wasn't; but Oporto had a distinct advantage over the binary digital types in that problems didn't have to be encoded and taped, then decoded.

Still, in the final analysis there were not too many problems to compute. In fact, that was the *big* problem: Ryeland could find no handle by which to grasp the question of the jetless drive.

But Oporto made himself useful in other ways as well.

He had a prying nose for news, for example, which kept Ryeland informed of what was going on in the Team Project. "Fleemer's got the sulks," he reported one day. "Holed up in his room, doesn't come out."

"All right," said Ryeland absently. "Say, where's my *Physical Constants of Steady-State Equations?*"

"It's indexed under 603.811," Oporto said patiently. "The word is that Fleemer is having an argument with the Machine. Messages are going back and forth, back and forth, all the time."

"What?" Ryeland looked up, momentarily diverted from the task of scribbling out a library requisition for the book he needed. "Nobody can argue with the Machine!"

Oporto shrugged. "I don't know what you'd call it, then."

"General Fleemer is filing reports," Ryeland said firmly. He beckoned to Faith, brooding in a corner. The Togetherness girl came eagerly forward, saw the slip, looked glum, shrugged and went off to get the book.

"Sure," said Oporto. "Say, have you heard anything from Donna Creery?"

Ryeland shook his head.

"I hear she's in Port Canaveral."

Ryeland snapped: "That's her problem. No doubt the Planner's daughter has plenty of occasions for off-Earth trips."

"No doubt," agreed Oporto, "but—"

"But you could mind your business," said Ryeland, closing the discussion.

Faith came back with the book. Ryeland verified a couple of figures and turned a sheet of calculations over to Oporto. "Here, solve these for me. It'll give you something to do," he said. He stood up, looking absently around the room. This was his A Section, devoted to the Hoyle Effect. He had a whole sub-Team of workers going here. Still, he thought, it was a waste of time.

"No sweat," said Oporto cheerfully, handing back the completed equations.

"Thanks." Ryeland glanced at them, then dumped them on the desk of one of the other workers. There wasn't much to be done but routine; he could leave it to the others now. That was why it was a waste of time. All the prior art was in hand and digested, it was only a matter of checking out the math now. Then he could answer the Machine's questions—but in fact, he knew, he could pretty well answer them now. Under what conditions could hydrogen growth occur? That was easy. Basic theory gave most of the answer; an analysis of the data from Lescure's expedition in the *Cristobal Colon* gave a clue to the rest. And what was the possibility of halting or reversing the formation? That was easy too. Humans could have little control over the processes that could build stars. With finite equipment, in finite time, the probability was zero.

But it was a measure of the Machine's—desperation? Was that a word you could apply to the Machine—a measure of the Machine's, well, urgency that it could even ask such questions as these.

Ryeland said uncomfortably: "Come on, Oporto. Let's go take a look at the spaceling."

And that was B Section, and it was going badly indeed.

Jetless drive! It was impossible, that was all. If Ryeland hadn't had the maddening spectacle of the spaceling right there before him, he would have sworn that the laws were right.

For every action, Newton had stated centuries before, there is an equal and opposite reaction. That law of motion accounted for every movement of every creature on Earth. The cilia of the first swimming paramecium propelled the creature forward by propelling an equal mass of water backward. It was the same with the thrust of a propeller, in water or in air. Rockets thrust forward by reaction, as the mass of the ejected jet's hot molecules went one way, the vessel the rockets drove went another. Action and reaction!

It was an equation that was easy to write—Mass times Acceleration equals Mass-prime times Acceleration-prime —and it was an equation that was hard to doubt.

But it did not happen to be true. The evidence of the dazed little creature from space made a liar out of Newton. The spaceling's trick of floating without visible reaction confounded the greatest genius the world has ever known.

The spaceling showed no reaction mass at all.

Whatever it was that permitted the spaceling to hover, it (call it "X") did not:

Disturb the currents of the air; affect plumb-bobs hung all about; register on photographic film; discharge a gold-leaf electroscope; disturb a compass; produce a measurable electric, magnetic or electronic field; add to the weight of the cage when the entire structure was supported on a scale; make any audible sound; affect the basal metabolism of the spaceling itself; or produce a discoverable track in a cloud chamber.

"X" did, on the other hand, do a few things.

It affected the "brain waves" of the spaceling; there was a distinctive trace on the EEG.

It seemed to have a worrisome effect on certain other mammals. This was noticed by chance when a cat happened to wander into the rocket pit; when the spaceling lifted itself the cat was "spooked", leaping about stifflegged, fur bristling, eyes aglare.

And finally, it worked. Whatever "X" was, it lifted the spaceling with great ease.

They even wrapped the spaceling in chains once, more than six hundred pounds of them. And as if amused the spaceling floated with all six hundred pounds for an hour, purring to itself.

It was maddening.

Still, thought Ryeland, though the comfort was small— at least the thing seemed healthier. The wounds were healing. The small symbiotic animals that were left seemed to survive. The spaceling showed life and energy.

Donna Creery would be pleased.

Nobody else seemed very pleased with Ryeland, though. General Fleemer stayed in his room, venturing forth only occasionally to make sardonic comments and get in the way. The other high brass of the Team didn't have Fleemer's ready escape, since they had specific tasks; but they made sure to be as unpleasant to Ryeland as they could manage.

Only Major Chatterji was affable at all, and that was second nature to him. He came by every hour on the hour for a report. He was very little trouble. If Ryeland was busy, the major waited inconspicuously in the background. If Ryeland was free, the major asked a minimum of questions and then departed. Ryeland was pretty sure that all the information went, first, to the Machine and, second, almost as promptly to General Fleemer; but he could see no reason why he should attempt to interfere with the process. And he could also see no reason to believe he would be successful if he tried.

He kept busy.

Oporto said one afternoon: "Say, it's definite about your girl friend."

Ryeland blinked up from his papers. "Who?" He was

genuinely confused for a moment; then he remembered Oporto's previous remarks. "You mean Miss Creery?"

"Miss Creery, yeah." The little man grinned. "She's off to the Moon. Her daddy, too."

"That's nice," said Ryeland. Carefully he kept his voice noncommittal, though he wondered who he was fooling. No matter how well he disguised his interest from Oporto, he couldn't disguise it from himself: Something inside him reacted to the thought of Donna Creery.

Oporto sprawled lazily over Ryeland's desk. "Well, I don't know if it is so nice, Steve," he said seriously. "Maybe they ought to stay home and attend to business. Did you hear about the Paris tube collapse?"

"What?" Ryeland wearily put down the sheaf of reports and blinked at his friend. His eyes smarted. He rubbed them, wondering if he needed sleep. But that didn't seem reasonable, he figured; he'd had at least eight hours sleep in the previous forty-eight. In any case, he didn't have the time; so he put the thought out of his mind and said: "What the devil are you talking about, Oporto?"

The little man said: "Just what I said. The Paris subtrain to Finland. The tube collapse. More than a hundred people missing—and that means dead, of course. When a tube gives out a hundred miles down you aren't 'missing.' "

Ryeland said, startled: "But that isn't possible! I mean, I know the math for those tubes. They can collapse, all right, but not without plenty of warning. They can't break down without three hours of field degeneration—plenty of time to halt transits."

Oporto shrugged. "A hundred dead people would be glad to know that, Steve," he said.

Ryeland thought for a second. "Well," he said wearily, "maybe you're right, maybe the Planner ought to be around to keep an eye on things like that . . . Oh, hello, Major."

Chatterji came smiling in, peering amiably through his gold glasses. "I wondered if there was anything to report, Mr. Ryeland."

While Ryeland searched through the papers on his desk, Oporto said: "We were just talking about the Paris trouble, Major."

Chatterji's brown eyes went opaque. There was a marked silence.

Ryeland took it in, and realized that Machine Major Chatterji was concerned about the tube failure between

Paris and the Finland center. Odd, he thought, why should Chatterji care? But he was too weary to pursue the subject further. He found the requisition he was looking for and silently passed it across to Chatterji.

The major glanced at it casually, then intently. His crew-cut black hair seemed to stand on end. "But, dear Ryeland!" he protested, blinking through his gold-rimmed glasses. "This equipment—"

"I've checked it with the Machine," Ryeland said obstinately. "Here." He showed the teletape to Major Chatterji.

Action. Request approved. Action. Concert with Major Chatterji. Information. Power sources at Point Circle Black not adequate to demands.

"But, my dear *Ryeland!*" The major's expression was tortured. "It isn't only a matter of power sources. Think of the other considerations!"

"What the Plan requires, the Plan shall have," Ryeland quoted, beginning to enjoy himself.

"Of course, of course. But—" The major studied the list, "You have enough electronic equipment here to run a university lab," he wailed. "And some of it is dangerous. After the, uh, accident Mr. Oporto was talking about, surely you understand that we can't take chances."

Ryeland stared. "What does that have to do with the Team project?"

The major said angrily, "The Plan can't stand accidents, Mr. Ryeland! This equipment creates radiation hazards, if nothing else, and there are eighty thousand people in Points Circle Black, Triangle Gray, Crescent Green and Square Silver alone. They can't be exposed to this sort of thing!"

Ryeland tapped the teletape meaningfully.

"Oh," sighed the major, "if the Machine approves . . ." He thought for a moment, then brightened. "I have it! An orbiting rocket!"

Ryeland was taken aback. "What?"

"An orbiting rocket filled with all the equipment you want." Chatterji said eagerly. "Why not? Everything run by remote control. I can requisition one for you at once, Mr. Ryeland! And you can fill it with all the dangerous equipment you like—what do we care what happens to any wandering spacelings, eh?" He winked and giggled.

63

"Well," said Ryeland doubtfully, "we could do it that way."

"Of course we could! We'll arrange a TV repeater circuit with remote-controlled apparatus. You work in your lab, the equipment is out in space. Perform any experiments you like. And that way," he beamed, "if you blow the lab up you destroy only one ship, not all of *us*." He bustled off.

It was astonishing what the Plan of Man could accomplish. The rocket was loaded, launched and orbited in forty-eight hours.

Ryeland never saw it. He monitored the installation of the equipment he wanted via TV circuits, tested the instruments, gave the okay—and watched the fire-tailed bird leap off its launching pad through a cathode screen. At once he put it to work. The only thing they had learned about the force the spaceling generated, what the Planner had called the "jetless drive", was that it was indetectable. But that in itself was a great piece of knowledge. Ryeland's researchers had turned up another fact—a high-energy nuclear reaction which turned out less energy than went into it—and it was just possible, it was more than possible, it was perhaps a fact, that that missing energy was not missing at all, but merely not detectable.

Like the energy of the spaceling . . . Ryeland determined to recreate the nuclear reactions which were involved.

Until the morning that the Togetherness girl woke him with news: "Rise and shine, Steve," she sang, bringing him his breakfast. "Guess what! General Fleemer's going to be at the Teamwork conference today."

Steve got groggily to his feet. "That's his privilege," he said thickly, and looked at her, young, pretty, fresh—though she had been with him, tirelessly running errands, through half the night. "Don't you ever get tired?" he asked sourly.

"Oh, no, Steve!" Eat your breakfast." She perched on his chair, watching him, and said earnestly: "We're not here to get tired, Steve. We have our job! We Togetherness girls are the connecting wires that hold the Plan of Man's circuit together."

He gaped at her, but she was serious. "That's right," she nodded. "The Plan of Man depends as much on us as on the transistors and condensers and capacitors—that's you and the other brass. Everyone is important! Don't

64

forget, Steve: 'To each his own job—and his own job only.'"

"I won't forget," he said, and wearily drank his citrus juice. But the girl had something on her mind, he saw. She was waiting for an opportunity to speak to him. "Well? What is it?"

She seemed embarrassed. "Oh, Uh—it's just that—well, there's talk, Steve. The girls were wondering about something."

"For heaven's sake, say it!"

"We wondered," she said primly, "if our Team really had anything to do with these accidents."

Ryeland blinked and rubbed his eyes. But rubbing his eyes didn't change anything; the girl still sat there with the mildly embarrased, mildly apologetic expression. "Accidents? Faith, what are you talking about?"

"The Paris-Finland tube," she recited. "The Bombay power plant explosion. The cargo-jet crash in Nevada. *You* know."

"No, I didn't know. Half those things I never heard of. Oporto's been falling down on the job."

"There are others, Steve. And what the girls are saying—" She paused. "I only wondered if it was true. They say our Team project has caused them. They even say that you, Steve—"

"That I what?"

"Oh, I suppose it's ridiculous. General Fleemer said it wasn't really true, anyway, that you had something to do with it. But they say you were involved in planning the subtrains..."

He grumbled, "They say some weird things. Excuse me while I dress, will you?"

He couldn't put it out of his mind. It was foolish, he thought testily. How did rumors like that start?

At the day's Teamwork conference, sure enough, General Fleemer had done them the unusual honor of attending. Ryeland scowled at him thoughtfully, then remembered the silly rumor. "Before we get started," he demanded, "has anybody heard anything about our work causing accidents?"

A dozen blank expressions met his stare. Then the head of the computer section coughed and said hesitantly, "Well, there was some talk, Mr. Ryeland."

"What kind of talk?"

The computerman shrugged. "Just talk. One of the

65

data-encoders had heard from a cousin who heard from
somebody else. You know how it goes. The story is that
our work here has upset the radio-control circuits, heaven
knows how."

"That's preposterous!" Steve exploded. "What the devil
do they mean by that?" He stopped himself. It wasn't the
computerman's fault, after all. "Well," he said grimly,
"if anybody hears anything else like that, I want it reported to me!"

Heads nodded; every head but General Fleemer's. He
barked testily: "Ryeland! Are we going to gossip about
accidents, or is the Team going to chart its course for the
day?"

Ryeland swallowed his temper. In spite of the fact that
Donna Creery had put him in charge of the Team, General
Fleemer's seniority made him a bad man to tangle with.

"All right," said Ryeland, "let's get on with it." Then
he brightened. "I saw your report, Lescure. Want to elaborate on it?"

Colonel Lescure cleared his throat. "After a suggestion
by Mr. Ryeland," he said, nodding, "we instituted a new
series of X-ray examinations of the spaceling. By shadow-
graphing its interior and using remote-chromotography
analytic techniques I have discovered a sort of crystalline
mass at the conflux of its major nervous canals. This is in
accordance with the prediction made by Mr. Ryeland."

Fleemer demanded harshly: "What does it mean?"

Ryeland said eagerly: "It means we're making head-
way! There had to be some sort of such arrangement for
controlling and directing the jetless drive. After yesterday's
computer run, and some further calculations Oporto did
for me, I asked Colonel Lescure to make the tests. He did
—on overtime, as you see."

"What this means," he said, beginning to lecture, "is
that we have found *where* the spaceling's force is generated and directed. And there's one other thing we
learned from yesterday's calculations. Phase-rule analysis
indicates zero possibility of any electromagnetic or gravitic
force. I have the report here, ready for transmission to the
Machine."

General Fleemer nodded slowly, looking at Ryeland.
After a moment he said, "Does it account for what happened to the mining colonies in Antarctica?"

Ryeland was puzzled. "I don't understand . . ."

"No? I refer to the explosion of the power reactor last

night, which destroyed them, at a very great loss to the Plan of Man. Not the only loss, Ryeland. A spaceship has been lost through a failure of its helical field accelerator. The same helical field which was involved in the reactor explosion—and in other accidents, Ryeland. The same field which you helped to design."

"The design is not to blame," Ryeland protested desperately. "If there have been accidents, they must be due to mechanical failure or human error or deliberate sabotage—"

"Exactly!"

"How could I be to blame for accidents in Antarctica and a hundred miles down and out beyond the Moon?"

"That's exactly what the Machine will want to know."

"Perhaps it is only chance," he suggested wildly. "Coincidence. Accidents have happened in series before—"

"When?"

"I don't remember. I—I can't recall."

He stammered and gulped, and walked away. The veil of gray fog across his past was thicker. Everything except his science was a swirl of unreality and contradiction.

Alone in his room, he tried again to come to grips with that old riddle of the three days missing from his life. What had the therapists suspected that he had done in that lost interval? Why had they expected him to know anything about a call from Dan Horrock, or about fusorians and pyropods and spacelings or about how to design a reactionless drive?

Lescure's story had given him clues, but they were too fragmentary to make much sense. Horrock had left the *Cristobal Colon* with unauthorized specimens and descriptions of the life of space. Did the Machine suspect that he had been in contact with Ryeland, before he was recaptured and consigned to the Body Bank?

Ryeland turned the puzzle over, and saw no light.

According to Donna Creery, there had really been three days between the knocking on his door and the arrival of the Plan Police. Had the knocking he remembered really been Horrock?

If so, what had erased his memory?

He stared at the wall and probed through the fog in his mind. He tried to remember Horrock, still perhaps in his uniform, soiled from his flight, perhaps bleeding from some wound, panting with terror and exhaustion, lugging

67

the black canvas space bag that held his stolen notes and specimens—

The images had become queerly real. Were they all imagination?

Had Horrock brought him some information vital to the invention of a jetless drive? He couldn't recall. He fell at last into a restless sleep, into a nightmare in which he and Horrock were in flight from the Plan Police.

The next morning Ryeland went directly from his room to the spaceling's cage in the rocket pit—and stopped, appalled.

The spaceling lay crushed and bleeding in its cage.

Ryeland ran to the cage and let himself in. The creature had grown to know him. It lay wrapped in a fading glow of misty green, eyes dulled; but as he entered its eyes brightened angrily. It lifted off the floor. Suddenly apprehensive, Ryeland dodged outside and slammed the cage door—just in time. The spaceling darted toward him with flashing speed. The cage rocked as she struck the closing door. Anchor chains clanked. Fresh blood ran down the bars, and a flap of golden fur was torn loose. She collapsed again, mewing piteously.

Ryeland felt the first real rage he had known in years.

He spun on his heel. "Gottling!" he bawled. "What the devil have you been up to?"

The colonel appeared, looking sardonically self-satisfied. "Mr Ryeland," he nodded.

Ryeland took a firm grip on himself. Gottling looked more like a skull than ever, the radar horns giving a Satanic expression to a face that was cold and cruel enough to begin with.

But those radar horns were not merely ornament. Team leader or not, Ryeland was a risk. The cold, complacent smile that twisted the corners of Gottling's thin lips was enough of a reminder of their relative status. One touch of the radar button on Gottling's harness and it was the end of Ryeland.

But this was too much. Ryeland blazed: "You've been torturing the thing again!"

"I suppose so," Gottling agreed mildly.

"Damn you! My orders were—"

"*Shut up, Risk.*" There was no smile at all now. Gottling thrust a teletape at Ryeland. "Before you go too far, read this!"

Ryeland hesitated, then took the tape. It read:

68

Information. Agreed present line of investigation unnecessarily slow. Information. Danger of additional accidents possibly related Ryeland method of research must be investigated. Information. Possibility Ryeland engaged in direct sabotage subtrains, reactors, ion drives. Action. Direction of Team project returned to General Fleemer. Action. Supplementary lines to be initiated at discretion Colonel Gottling.

Ryeland stared at it, dazed. The Machine had reversed itself again!

But in truth it wasn't his own position, difficult though it had suddenly become, that concerned him. It was the spaceling. "Supplementary lines!" he thundered. "Man, you'll kill her!"

Gottling shrugged, contemplating the spaceling. It lay gasping on the steel floor, looking up at them.

"Perhaps I will not wait for her to die," the colonel said meditatively. "Pascal does not wish to perform a vivisection, but he would hardly dare refuse the orders of the Machine. Even he." He smiled frostily and commented: "You are all alike, Pascal Lescure and the Planner's daughter and you, Risk. Blood frightens you. But pain is not contagious. You need not fear to observe it in others, it will not infect you. Indeed," he beamed, "there is much to learn in the pain of others."

Ryeland said tightly: "I'm going to report this to Donna Creery."

The colonel widened his eyes. "Oh? You need the Planner's daughter to fight your battles?" He allowed a silence to hang over them for a moment. Then, forgivingly: "But it does not matter, for you will not find that possible, Ryeland. Miss Creery is on the Moon. So you see, Risk, what happens to the spaceling from now on is entirely up to me."

8

Ryeland flung open the door of his room and headed for the teletype in the corner. Oporto and the Togetherness girl were there. He paused, distracted for a moment; he seemed to have interrupted something, but what? It didn't matter. He barked: "Oporto! What's Donna Creery's call number?"

Oporto coughed. "Gee, Steve. I don't know. Three? Fifteen?"

"Cut it out, Oporto," Ryeland warned dangerously.

"Three." Ryeland thumped the teletype keyboard:

Query. Permission for direct hookup communication Donna Creery station 3.

The teletype hardly hesitated:

Information. Refused.

"Well," Oporto said reasonably, "what did you expect? The machine can't have its circuits tied up with—"

"Shut up." Ryeland was typing again, demanding a connection with the Planner himself.

Information. Refused.

"You see, Steve? You aren't getting anywhere. What's got you so steamed up?"

Ryeland told him in half a dozen sentences what was getting him so steamed up. "Oh, that's too bad," murmured the Togetherness girl. "The poor thing."

Oporto seconded: "Tough. Well, what are you going to do? We're only Risks. We can't buck Gottling and all those." He sneezed, and complained: "See, Steve, you're gedding me all upset. I bet I'm catching a code."

Ryeland looked at him blankly; he had not heard what Oporto had said, and hardly knew the other two were in the room with him. What could he do? Cut off from the Planner or his daughter, he had no chance to keep Gottling from murdering the spaceling. That was the end of the project. If what the Planner had told him was true, it actually endangered the Plan itself; for the jetless drive, the spaceling's queer method of propulsion, was important to the safety of all the Plan. Yet the Planning Machine would not allow him to—

He blinked and the room came into focus. "The Planning Machine!" he said aloud.

"What? Steve," moaned Oporto, "now what are you going to do?" But Ryeland didn't answer. He sat at the keyboard of the machine and with a steady hand tapped out an account of what had happened. Colonel Gottling had deliberately controverted the orders of Donna Creery and the Machine itself. The spaceling was in danger. The Plan itself was threatened. He finished, and waited.

And waited.

And waited for long minutes, while Oporto and the girl whispered behind him. It was incredible that the Machine should take so long to answer! Ryeland asked himself feverishly: Was it turned on, was the wire cut, could it be possible that the Machine's circuits were so overloaded that the message was not received? He was actually bending over, hardly aware of what he was doing, to be sure that the machine was properly plugged in when abruptly it whirred and rattled.

Ryeland was up like a shot.

But the message was unbelievably short. It said only:

R.

"Received and understood," Oporto said sympathetically from behind him. "Gee, Steve. That's all? Well, that's the Machine for you. It isn't up to us to question—Steve. Hey. Steve! Where are you going?" But Ryeland was already gone.

Ryeland hurried down the corridors to General Fleemer's quarters. He had wasted time and it was now late; he would be waking the general up, but he didn't care about that, not now. He tapped on the door and then, without pausing, banged hard.

"A minute, a minute," mumbled a grumpy voice. A wait. Then the door was flung open.

General Fleemer was in lounging pajamas, bright purple tunic, striped purple and scarlet pants. The collar and cuffs were picked out in silver braid, and the room behind him was silver. Silver walls, silver-mounted furniture on a silvery rug. It was a startling effect. Fleemer growled irritably: "Ryeland? What the devil do you want?"

"I have to talk to you, General." He didn't wait for an invitation, but slipped past him into the room. Then something stopped him and he paused, stared, distracted even from the important mission he was on.

There was a statue by the fireplace, a bright silver statue of a girl. But it moved! It opened silver eyelids and looked

71

at him. With pink-tinged lips, like metallic copper in a silver face, it said: "Who is this one?"

"Go in the other room!" the general barked. The silver statue shrugged and stood up. It was no statue but a girl; the motion revealed it as she stared at Ryeland and left.

Ryeland blinked. Dusted with silver to look like living metal, even her hair silver—the general had a remarkable private life. But it was no business of Ryeland's at this moment. He said briskly: "Sir, Colonel Gottling is about to destroy the spaceling. I'm afraid he is deliberately trying to sabotage the project."

Suddenly the general was no longer a cross, sleepy little fuss-budget. His cat's eyes slitted down, his face abruptly became stone. "Go on," he said after a second.

"Why—that's all there is, sir. Isn't it enough? If Colonel Gottling goes ahead with vivisection it will kill the creature, I'm certain. Miss Creery left specific orders—"

"Wait," said the general, but did not invite him to sit down. He turned his back to Ryeland and strode over to his desk. He pressed a button on his desk phone and leaned over to yell into it. "Gottling? Get down to my quarters. Ryeland's here."

Mumble-mumble from the desk phone. It was directional; Ryeland couldn't understand the words and wasn't meant to. "On the double!" the general barked, cutting off discussion, and broke the connection. Without looking at Ryeland he slumped in a chair, shading his eyes with his hands, and remained there until there was a crisp knock at the door.

Colonel Gottling walked in. He did not seem disturbed, not in the least. And he was not alone. Machine Major Chatterji came smiling and bowing behind him. "What a *lovely* room, General! Oh, really lovely. It takes exquisite taste to transform our dreary barracks into—"

"Shut up." General Fleemer stood. Ryeland waited, poised for whatever excuse Gottling might offer, ready to confront him with the facts as soon as the general began his accusation.

But the general did not begin. The general did not speak to Gottling at all. He said: "All right, Chatterji, have you got the orders?"

"Yes, General. Certainly! Here you are. I knew you'd be wanting them, so—" The general moved slightly and Chatterji was still. Fleemer took a sheet of teletype communication paper from the major's hand and passed it to

Ryeland without comment. Ryeland glanced puzzledly at it.

Then he felt a sudden quick burning sensation, as though a knife had reached him unsuspected. The message said:

Information. Ryeland, Steven, Risk, change of status approved. Action. Subject will therefore be transported to stockpile HJK without delay.

"Stockpile HJK?" Ryeland repeated aloud. He shook his head, dazed. "But—there's got to be some mistake here, because, look, stockpile HJK is Heaven. I mean—"

"You mean the Body Bank, as it is otherwise known." General Fleemer nodded wisely. "That's correct, and that is where you're going. You were perfectly right about Gottling sabotaging the Project, you see. Your only mistake was in thinking that he was alone."

9

Heaven was on the island of Cuba.

The subtrain took nearly an hour to get there. Ryeland hardly noticed. They rode in a gray steel ball, far less luxurious than the Planner's private car. When they stopped, Ryeland, still dazed, still shocked, got out and blinked at a massive concrete archway over a steel gate.

The letter in the concrete read:

Resurrection under the Plan

The station was gray concrete. Air ducts blew a clammy breath at them. A guard in white, a red heart stitched on the breast of his tunic, came forward to take charge.

The major who had convoyed Ryeland's detail, twenty-two new cadavers for the Body Bank, turned them over gratefully and went back into the subtrain without a look. He didn't like this escort detail. No one did. It was a reminder of mortality; even a machine major could be made to realize that one bad blunder, or one bad break, could put him in Heaven too. "Come on!" bawled the guard, and apathetically the twenty-two walking collections of spare parts followed him through the gate.

A narrow corridor. A long rectangular room, with wooden benches. Ryeland sat and waited and, one by one, they were admitted to a smaller room. When it was his turn Ryeland walked through the door and a girl grasped his arm, thrusting it under the black-light. Her hair was red, the same bright red as the heart that was stitched on her uniform. Under the light his tattoo glowed faintly. She read off his name and number in a rapid drone. "Steven Ryeland," she said in the same continuous drone, "when you entered this gate you leave life behind as an individual you have failed to justify your place in the Plan the tissues of—"

She yawned sharply. She shook her head and grinned. "Excuse me. Where was I? The tissues of your body however may still serve the Plan before you enter have you anything to say?"

Ryeland thought. What was there to say? He shook his head.

"Go ahead, then. Through that door," said the girl.

Behind Ryeland the door clanged with a steel finality.

First there were tests.

Ryeland was stripped, scrubbed, weighed, measured, X-rayed, blood-tested, tissue-tested, ascaulted, palped and all but sniffed and tasted. A bit of his flesh was snipped and whisked to a complex bench where a team of girls put it through a process of staining and microscopy. From their studies a genetic map was made of his chromosomes, every allele and allomorph in place, and coded into binary symbols which were stamped on his collar.

It was interesting. Transplants of body organs did not survive, not even with suppressants, if the donor and subject were too different in their genetic makeup. Antibodies formed. The new tissue was attacked by the environment it found itself in. It died. So, usually, did the patient. The more delicate the tissue involved, the closer the genetic resemblance had to be. It was an old story. Any cornea can be imbedded in any other eye; the tissues are crude and simple, mostly water. Millions of humans can transfer blood from one to another—blood is a tissue little more complex than the cornea.

But more highly specialized members are transferable, without suppressants, only between identical twins.

Suppressants—something like the allergy-controlling phar-maceuticals which once helped hold down hay fever—can make the range of tolerance broader; but, even so, genetic patterns must be matched as closely as possible. It was good that it was interesting. Ryeland was able to keep his mind on it. He did not find himself dwelling on the fact that he was now in the position of the spaceling under Gottling. He did not have to contemplate the prospect of what was essentially (however gentle, however carefully anesthetized for him) the Death of a Thousand Cuts.

And then they turned him loose, without warning.

He had expected a cell. He was given a millionaire's playground. He tripped over a tuft of grass and, blinking in warm Caribbean afternoon sun, found himself in a broad park, with trees and comfortable-looking cabins. He started forward, then happened to think of something and returned to the guard. "What do I do now? Who do I report to?"

"Nobody," said the guard, gently closing the door. Nobody at all, any more."

Ryeland walked down a broad green lane toward the glint of water, it was as good a direction to go as any. He had never in all his life before had the experience of being without orders. It was almost more disturbing than the sure prospect of dismemberment that lay before him. He was so absorbed in the feeling that he hardly heard someone calling to him until the man raised his voice. "You! Hey, you new fellow! Come back here!"

Ryeland turned.

The man who was calling him was about fifty years old —the prime of life. He should have been a husky, bronzed creature with all his hair. Statistically he should hardly have needed even glasses. Forty good years should still be ahead of him at least.

But the man who limp-stumped up to Ryeland had none of these things. He was totally bald. (In a moment, as the sunlight caught it, Ryeland saw that what had seemed to be the man's scalp was a plastic covering.) He walked with a shoulder-cane—almost a crutch. And what he walked on were not flesh-and-blood feet but prosthetic appliances. One eye was only a patch; the other was drawn into a squint by another area of pink plastic that covered the place where once he had had an ear.

"You! Did you just come in?" he cried. His voice was deep and vibrant; that, at least, he had kept.

Ryeland said, keeping his expression polite with some difficulty, "Yes, that's right. My name is Steve Ryeland."

"Never mind *that*. Do you play bridge?"

The difficult expression collapsed for a second, but Ryeland got it back. "I'm afraid not."

"Damn." When the man scowled it pointed up another peculiarity of his face. He had no eyebrows. "How about chess?"

"Yes, a little."

"Speak up!" the man barked, turning his good ear irritably to Ryeland.

"I said yes!"

"Well, that's worth something," the man said, grudging the words. "Um. Maybe you could learn bridge, hey? We're a good house. No rough stuff, no stealing. And no basket cases." He said proudly: "I'm the senior inmate in the house. Take a look at me. See? I've got plenty left."

Ryeland said slowly, "You mean I can pick out the house I live in? I don't know the rules here yet."

"There aren't any rules. Oh," the man shrugged, "no fights resulting in bodily injury, no hazardous sports—they salvage you *total* for that sort of thing. You know. What you've got, it doesn't belong to you any more. It's the Plan's and you're supposed to take care of it." He hitched himself forward on his shoulder-cane. "Well, what about it? You look all right to me. Take my advice and come in with us. Never mind what the other houses say —those Jupiters will be talking about their pingpong table, and what good is that when tomorrow morning you maybe won't have what to play pingpong with!" He grinned confidentially, revealing a set of casually placed artificial teeth.

Ryeland went with the one-eyed man, whose name turned out to be Whitehurst. The man was a good salesman, but he had not exaggerated the value of choosing the right hut. Ryeland could see that for himself; some cottages had a rundown, disreputable air, the inmates lounging around, surly and bored. Whitehurst's house was busy if nothing else.

It was amazing, but Ryeland found Heaven rather pleasant. There was food—*good* food. Whitehurst told him proudly, no synthetics or retreads! (The tissues had to be kept up.) There was plenty of leisure. (The patient had to be always in shape for major surgery.) There was . . . well . . . freedom, said Whitehurst, almost embarrassed as he said it and unwilling to explain. But Ryeland found out that it was so. If Heaven was a jail, at least the walls were out of sight. There was no fear of making a mistake and falling to ruin; there was no farther to fall.

The physical plant was ideal. Small cottages dotted a green landscape. Palms stood on green hills. There was a grove of oaks and cedars by a lake, and the lake contained actual fish. The tropic sky was a permanent milky blue, with high-piled cumulus to give it life.

Whitehurst's cottage called themselves the Dixie Presidents. No one remembered what doomed antiquarian, generations before, had selected the name, but it was the custom to name each house and successive inmates kept the names; it was a tradition. The Dixie Presidents were an all-male cottage, by choice. It was up to the inmates. Not all the houses were so monastic. There were as many women as men in Heaven, and the co-ed cottages were given to wild sounds late at night. But that was up to the inmates too.

Listening to the evening conversation of his fellow inmates, Ryeland found a few things which struck him as odd. The cottage across the way was occupied by a family group. Strange! Their name was Minton—Mr. Minton, Mrs. Minton and their five grown children. What mass crime had the Minton family committed to be scrapped en masse? It was queer.

The principle that lay behind the Body Bank he knew well. It had been explained to him in detail on his travel orders, even if he had been the one man alive under the Plan who didn't know all about it from infancy. Each human under the Plan of Man was required to make a contribution toward the good of all. If inefficiency, malevolence or carelessness kept him from doing what he was asked, he would then be permitted to contribute in another way. He would be scrapped. His limbs and organs would be put to the use of more valuable citizens, replacing parts damaged through accident or disease.

It was a project more attractive to the recipient than to the donor, of course. Yet it did have a sort of rough justice, and Ryeland thought he could bring himself to tolerate whatever might happen—the world's good was more important than his own!

And yet . . .

One thing *did* bother him. In his life he had known or

77

heard of a fair number of persons who had been scrapped for the salvage of their parts in the Body Bank.

And yet he could not remember ever, not even once, having encountered a man who had benefited from these organs . . .

Now at last, when it was too late to matter, Ryeland had time to return to the riddle of his three missing days. He was tormented with the possibility that he had once known a precious secret which could somehow transform the Plan of Man—if he could just recall it.

That night after he had watched the bridge game for a few minutes he lay trying to remember. Had there been a knocking twice on his door, on Friday and again on Monday? If Horrock had really come to him, what message could he have brought? Even if a jetless drive could be invented, how could it threaten the Plan? Who besides Donderevo was free from the Machine?

He found no answers. The fog was thicker in his memory. Even the fat, apologetic face of Dr. Thrale was growing dim. He no longer flinched when he remembered the cold electrodes clamped on his body. He fell asleep and dreamed that he had discovered a jetless drive.

It was a broomstick. He rode it through a jungle of five-pointed tinsel stars, with General Fleemer astride a spaceling close behind him. Fleemer was goading and spurring the spaceling, and it was screaming horribly.

"Reveille! Reveille! Everybody up!"

Ryeland woke up with a start; he had been dreaming that he was in the Body Bank, in an unusually soft bed, and woke to find it true. He sat blinking at the bunk across from him. It looked more like a surgical supply house than a human being's bed. The cords of a bone conduction hearing aid dangled from the stainless-steel shafts of a prosthetic arm. A self-powered wheelchair bore ten pounds of assorted steel, copper, rubber and plastic. As in the ancient joke about the wedding night, there was more of Ryeland's roommate on the bureau than in the bed.

The roommate was a plump man of rosy complexion, what there was left of it, and ill temper. His name was Alden. "Come on, Ryeland," he screeched faintly in the high-pitched whisper of the newly deaf. "You know the rules of the house. Give me a hand."

"All right." There was plenty of time before morning shape-up and breakfast, so Ryeland had been told; there

had to be, for the senior members of the community needed
plenty of time to get their miscellaneous artificial parts in
place. As a newcomer, still complete in his organs, Ryeland had obligations. The juniors took care of the seniors.
Seniority ruled—not age, but length of time in Heaven. It was a fair system, it was explained to Ryeland,
and it was enlightened self-interest besides. "You'll find
out," Whitehurst had said grimly. "Wait till you're missing
a few little chunks."

In the morning the conversation was less placid, less
polite than at night. It was odd too, thought Ryeland,
listening carefully. In the morning the one universal topic
was Escape. Perhaps it was only the wake-up irritability
of the normal human, but even the advanced basket cases
from the huts next door laid their plans and carefully
measured the daily patrol of the guard helicopters. Alden
muttered for twenty minutes about the chance of swimming to a miraculously borrowed fishing submarine that
some incredibly loyal friend from Life might arrange to
have out beyond the breakers. It was foolish, it was pathetic. There was hardly enough left of him to bother escaping
with. And his tone the night before had been bland resigna-
tion: "You'll learn, my boy," he told Ryeland, "we're here
for a *reason*. It's *right*." It was puzzling.

In the night Ryeland had been bothered by something
sticking him in the ribs.

Once Alden was wheeled away he searched, and there,
thrust under the seams of the mattress, was a flat aluminum case. He opened and spilled out lump sugar, maps,
terribly amateurish faked travel orders from the Machine.
And a journal.

The journal was the work of some previous occupant
who signed himself only by initials—D.W.H.—and it
covered a period of almost three years. The first entry
was sober self-appraisal:

June 16. I arrived in Heaven this morning. I can't
get out. If I did get out, there would be no place to
go. But if I let myself give up the hope of *somehow*
getting out I might as well be dead. Therefore I will
try to escape. And I will not brood.

The last entry, in a palsied hand, was less sober, less
analytic:

79

May the—what? 9th, maybe. Just a min. bfr shape-up. I think I've got it! Nbdy ever looks at the scrap-heap carcasses! I've seen some that look better than I do now and, whoosh, they're down the chute & out on the barge when they clean up. So tonight's the night. All I have to do is pass one more shape-up. I've plenty left. Aprnces don't matter. If I can just—There's the bell. More ltr.

The remaining pages were blank.

Breakfast came before the morning shape-up and Rye-land, stuffing the journal back in the mattress, went thoughtfully out to eat.

The food was all Whitehurst had promised! There was no rationing here, none at all. Sugar. Coffee. Real, thick cream. Ham with red gravy; cereal with more of the thick cream; fruits and hot biscuits.

Ryeland ate until his stomach bulged. He began to feel better. The world seemed calmer, brighter; his housemates left off grumbling and plotting and began to laugh and shout along the long tables.

Ryeland sat next to Whitehurst and brought up the subject of the previous occupant of his bunk.

"Oh, him," said the one-eyed man. "Old Danny. He was here for *ever*, considering. I mean, he must have been a very popular type, they took so much of him. I thought they'd never salvage him total, though all he had keeping him going at the end was a whirl-pump heart and twice a day filtrations on the kidney machine. Funny thing about Danny, his bidding was good enough but when he played a hand—"

"What happened to him?"

Whitehurst scowled. "Took both lungs at one time. Pity, too. He still had two arms, clear down to the fingers."

The bell summoned them out to the morning shape-up.

There were three of them a day, Whitehurst whispered, and you *had* to be present. Otherwise total salvage, right away. The white guards with red hearts appliqued on their tunics moved up and down the ragged lines, checking the tattooed identification against lists. "Gutnick, Fairt-weather, Breen, Morchant," the one at the house of the Dixie Presidents chanted. "Nothing for you boys. You can fall out. Alden, Hensley—Hensley? Say, how did that name get on the list? Wasn't he scrapped last week?" Half a dozen voices agreed he had been; the guard scratched the name off his list. "Lousy administrative work. Say. Who are you?" He took Ryeland's arm. "Oh, Steve Ryeland. Welcome to our little community. Nothing for you today, though. Whitehurst. Oh, yes. Come on, Whitehurst, you're in business."

Ryeland got away as soon as he could. The others were laughing and relaxed, but seeing Whitehurst led away had chilled the soft warmth that had spread over Ryeland at breakfast. At any moment it might be his name that was on the list; if there was anything at all he could do about it, the time to do it was now.

He retrieved the journal from his bed, escaped the back way and found a sunny spot on a hill. He sat down against a stone retaining wall and studied the diary of the late D.W.H.

There was nothing about the man's life-in-Life in his journal. But whatever he had been he was a man of method and intelligence. He had begun by systematically investigating his surroundings. From the first month's entries Ryeland learned a number of possibly useful statistics. There had then been 327 inmates in Heaven, counting twelve children under the age of eighteen (and what had *they* done to be here?) This was not the only Heaven; there probably were a number of others; twice shipments of inmates had gone out through the gate, to replenish another Heaven temporarily low in stock. There were never any guards inside the walls except at the shape-ups. Usually about a dozen came in then, and D.W.H. had once been able to count the outside guards at fifteen more. Heaven roamed over nearly a hundred acres, and there was a map, heavily erased and redrawn, tucked into the journal. A note on the map told Ryeland that the walls were electrified and impenetrable, even down to a depth of fifty yards under the surface. Apparently someone had actually dug that far!

The beach was not fenced, but there was a heavy steel net and, beyond that, a persuasive tradition of sharks. The only other break in the wall was the building through which he had entered, and its satellite structures—the clinic, the administration building, the powerhouse. And the sanitation building. It was there that the "scrap-heap" had attracted D.W.H.'s attention. It was near the beach, and a chute led to a barge which, towed to sea, disposed of the left-over parts of the inmates as well as the more ordinary wastes of a community of several hundred.

Ryeland mused thoughtfully over the map. Only the scrap disposal chute looked promising. Yet the writer had not thought of it until after some months and, judging by the increasingly panicked and incoherent quality of his notes, his judgment must by then have begun to deteriorate. Still, it was worth a thought. He said a man could escape that way. Perhaps a man could . . .

If he had a place to escape to.

Ryeland put that thought out of his mind and read industriously in the journal until movements outside the cottages revealed that it was time for the mid-day shape-up.

10

No Dixie President was called at noon. Only when they were dismissed did Ryeland realize he had been holding his breath almost continuously. Gutnick, the man next to him in line, winked and said: "It gets you that way at first. It keeps on getting you that way too."

Ryeland said only: "What's that?"

Gutnick turned and looked. Down the gravel path two guards were solemnly pushing a wheelchair and a hand-truck of appliances. All were connected to the occupant of the wheelchair. There was little left of the man, if it was a man. All of his head was swathed in bandages—if that was his head. Only a little gap showed where the mouth was. The auxiliary handtruck carried a considerable array of pumps and tubing, stainless-steel cylinders and electric equipment.

Gutnick said, "Oh, him." Gutnick could not wave, as both his arms had been needed elsewhere, but he inclined his torso and called: "Hi, Alec. What did you lose this time?"

The bandaged head moved faintly. Nothing else moved on the man. The nearly invisible lips parted to gasp, in words like puffs of smoke. "That you, Gutnick? Just the other kidney, I think."

"You've got plenty left," lied Gutnick cheerfully, and they went in to lunch. Ryeland could not get the basket case out of his mind.

"I didn't think they bothered to keep us alive, with that much gone."

"I guess Alec's something special. He's senior in all Heaven. He's been here—" Gutnick's voice was respectful—"almost six years."

Ryeland didn't have much appetite; but after he'd taken a few bites he had to stop in order to feed Gutnick anyway; and then he himself began to perk up. It was astonishing, he marveled after lunch, trudging aimlessly around the walks of Heaven, how the food here made life so bearable. It showed that a good diet made a happy man. It showed—why, he thought with a sudden miserable flash of insight, it showed nothing at all except that even a doomed creature like himself could submerge the forebrain in a wallow of physical pleasures. He determined to go right back to the house and get the diary, study it, plan—

Someone was calling his name.

He turned, and Oddball Oporto was rushing toward him. "Gee! Ryeland! It's you!"

Oporto stopped. So did Ryeland; and then he realized that what they were doing was appraising each other, looking for missing parts. So soon it had become a habit in this place.

"You don't seem to be missing anything," said Ryeland.

"I've only been here two days. Got here right ahead of you—I saw you come in. I guess you stopped to turn in your gear? They didn't bother with that, with me . . . I should've stayed in Iceland, hey? Not that I hold it against *you*," he finished glumly.

"Sorry."

"Yeah. Well, where you living?" Ryeland told him about the Dixie Presidents, and Oporto was incredulous. "Gee! Those moldy old creeps? Say, why not come over to our place? There's two vacancies right now, and some of the boys are real sharp. You know, you lose a few parts and there isn't much left but the brain; so what you want is a few little problems to work on. Well, fellow next to me, he has a whole bunch of stuff from the *Lilavata*— old Hindu math problems, mostly diophantine equations when you come down to it, but—"

Ryeland said gently: "I'm working on a different problem right now."

Oporto waited.

"I want to get out of here."

"Oh, no. Wait a minute! Steve, don't be crazy. A fellow like you, you've got *years* here. Plenty to look forward to. You don't want to—"

"But I do want to," said Ryeland, "I want to get away. It isn't just my life, though I admit that's got a lot to do with it."

"What else? Oh. You don't have to tell me. That girl."

"Not the girl. Or not exactly. But she's part of it. Something bad's happening with the spaceling and Colonel Gottling. It ought to be stopped."

Oporto said dismally. "Gee. Steve. You don't want to talk like that. Anyway—" He stopped.

Ryeland knew Oporto well enough to wait him out. He prompted: "Anyway what?"

"Anyway," said Oporto with some hesitation, "I don't know why you want not to bother with *her*. I thought that other girl was more important to you. You know, 837552 —I forget her name."

Ryeland took it like a blow between the eyes. That number—he didn't have Oporto's queer memory for any arithmetical function, but surely it was the number of . . .

"Angela Zwick," he whispered, remembering blonde hair, blue eyes and a mouth that testified against him at his hearing.

"That's the one. Well, now! So you didn't forget her?" Oporto was enjoying his bombshell. "Why not go see her? She's been here quite a while—over in a cottage by the lake."

"She's really *here?* But she was with the Plan Police." Ryeland was dazed. Had the Plan come to this, that it scrapped its own undercover agents?

"Well," said Oporto judiciously, "I guess you'd say she's here. Anyway, there's a quorum present. Why not go see for yourself?"

The first sensation was shock, and a terrible embarrassment. Ryeland scraped one foot against another, staring at the girl in the wheelchair. He said her name gruffly, and then he met her eyes and could say nothing else. Angela? This thing in the chair, was it the girl he had known? She had no arms and, from the flatness of the lap robe that draped her, no legs either. But her face was intact, blue-green eyes, golden hair; her husky, warm voice was the voice he had known.

"Steve! It's *good* to see you!" She was not embarrassed at all, only amused. She laughed. "Don't gawk. But I know how you feel. You've only just arrived, and I've been here twenty-one months."

Ryeland sat awkwardly on the grass before her. Her cottage lay in a little clump of woods, and there were neatly tended beds of flowers around it. Flowers! Ryeland could not remember ever having seen flowers around a dwelling before, only in parks. Though this was a kind of a park, at that.

Angela said softly: "I wondered if I would ever see you again, after what happened." She cocked her chin, and a tiny motor droned; the velvet-covered chin rest that supported her head seemed to have switches in it, so that she could move the wheels of her chair. Facing him, she said seriously: "You don't blame me, do you?"

Ryeland muttered: "You did your job under the Plan."

"So *wise* of you to say that, Steve. Ah, Steve! I'm glad to see you again." She lifted her lovely chin. "We've got so much to talk about. Take me down by the lake," she commanded . . .

For nearly three years Ryeland had rehearsed the speeches he would make to Angela Zwick if ever they chanced to come together, but in this place they were all wrong, he forgot the words. He had raged silently in his bed, he had pleaded with the stony fields of the isolation camp; now, facing the girl, he found himself engaged in a little conversation. They chatted. They laughed. It was pleasant. *Pleasant!* And she had put the collar around his neck.

"There is always peace in serving the Plan," she told him wisely, reading his mind.

They stopped by the lake and he sat down. "I don't even mind the collar any more," he murmured, suppressing a yawn.

"Of course not, Steve."

He scratched his shoulderblades against the bole of a palm. "I never thought I'd stop minding that. Why, I remember talking to a fellow about it in the isolation camp. He said I'd get over it. I said—"

He stopped, and frowned faintly.

"What did you say to him, Steve?"

"Why," he said slowly, "I told him that I'd never stop hating the collar unless I was dead, or drugged."

She smiled at him with mandarin calm.

Back at the cottage of the Dixie Presidents, Ryeland thumbed through the journal that had once belonged to his predecessor in the bunk. There was an entry that he wanted to read again.

He found it:

> This place is insidious. The atmosphere is so tran-
> quil—God knows how!—that it is very tempting to
> relax and let what happens happen. Today Cullen came
> back from the clinic giggling because a nurse had told
> him a joke. He had lost both eyes!

And two days later:

> Yesterday I lost my other leg. It is painful, but
> they gave me shots for that. I wonder why it doesn't
> bother me. I keep thinking of Cullen.

Frowning, Ryeland closed the book and went out to stand in the afternoon shape-up. The other Dixie Presidents were already there, and their greetings were chill. Ryeland paid very little attention, although he knew they were annoyed because he had spent so little time conforming with the customs of the cottage. He hardly even noticed the guards, with their scarlet hearts blazoned on their white tunics, as they came droning down the line with their rolls.

There was something more important on his mind.

Ryeland was reasonably sure that his mind was functioning as well as it ever had. But he was finding it hard to think this matter through. *He didn't mind the collar.* That was the first term in the syllogism. Something in the diary supplied the second term. What was the conclusion?

"Come on, I said!" said a guard's voice, annoyed, and Ryeland woke up to the fact that his name had been called.

He gawked. "Me? Are you calling me?"

"You. That's what I said, man! You're on orders today. Come on to the tissue bank!"

11

The group of scrapped men waited for the elevator.

The man next to Ryeland was whispering feverishly under his breath, his eyes fixed on the elevator door as though it were the gate to hell. He caught Ryeland looking at him and threw him a wild smile. "First time for you? Me, too, But I figure it won't be much, you know."

"All right, all right." The guards began to herd them into the opening elevator door. "Move along, now!"

The elevator dropped swiftly and let them out in an underground hall. Blue asepsis lamps winked on the walls, a hum from the air ducts told of purifiers at work. The guards ordered them to sit down. There were a dozen long, wooden benches. The waiting room was not at all crowded, though there were twenty or more walking cadavers in it. Ryeland looked around at them. Some seemed to have all their faculties and parts; if there was anything missing, it was not such as would appear on the surface. Many showed signs of being nibbled away—a leg missing, an ear, a finger or two. And some were so much prosthesis, so little flesh and blood, that it was a wonder that the surgeons could find anything left to take from them.

The nervous man switched seats to join Ryeland and hissed in his ear: "See, the way I see it, they're not going to take much the first time. Why should they? For instance, your body might not transplant right. They can't tell. They'll have to do a couple little jobs first and see how they take, before they try anything big. I'm *positive* of that, friend . . ." He stopped as the door opened, his eyes like a tortured kitten's. But it was only a nurse walking through, and she paid no attention to them.

Ryeland took time from his own worries to comfort the man. "That's right," he said. "That figures." It didn't, of course; the Plan knew all it had to know about them already. But the nervous man seized at the reassurance.

He babbled: "Now, all we have to worry about is something *little*. Maybe some clumsy oaf lost a couple of fingers somewhere. Well, they'll take a finger. Or a couple of fingers . . ." He glanced wonderingly at his hand. "A couple of fingers. They'll take—But what's that? You can spare them. Or a foot, maybe. But they aren't going to take anything big the first time, because—"

The door opened.

A young, slim guard walked in. He was bored, and the look he gave the waiting cadavers was not intended for anything human. "Eckroth?" he called, reading from a list. The man next to Ryeland jumped. "Come on!"

The nervous man stared frantically at Ryeland, swallowed, stood up and left, into a door that closed, silent and final, behind him.

Ryeland sat and waited.

One by one the cadavers were summoned to their operating rooms to give to the Plan what the Plan demanded of them. Ryeland watched them, because it was better to think of them than to think about himself: the oldster with the fire-blue eyes, weeping into the maze of tubes that had replaced his breathing apparatus; the young girl with the curiously flat dressings along one side of her body; the men and women of all sizes and descriptions. Ryeland was almost the last of them all to be called.

But at last it was his turn. A nurse beckoned to him. He stood up, feeling strangely empty. A queer premonitory, tingling raced all over his peripheral nervous system, like a pain looking for its proper place to settle down and begin aching.

What would it be? A foot, an arm, a set of teeth, some internal organs?

"Oh, come *on*," said the nurse, looking ruffled. She was a pretty girl with red hair. She even wore a ring on her finger. Ryeland marveled. This girl was engaged! Somewhere there was a Plan-fearing man who looked at her with affection and warmth. And, here, she was the embodiment of something that was going to deprive Steve Ryeland of a part of his body.

He walked stiffly after her. There was a roar in his ears: the drumming of his blood. It was very loud; he felt his heart thumping, very strong. Colors were bright, an antiseptic odor in the room was very sharp. His senses missed nothing. He felt the stiffness of his worn red uniform. The blue glare of the sterilamps was painfully bright.

He was in a small room, dominated by a neat, high operating table, stainlessly white.

Ryeland looked at the table and licked his lips.

Unexpectedly the nurse giggled. "Oh, I swear. You cadavers take everything so hard. Don't you know why you're here?"

Ryeland nodded stiffly. He knew very well. Still, it was odd that he didn't see the bright metal gleam of instruments.

She said, humorously exasperated: "I don't think you do. Your blood, friend. That's all I'm going to take from you today. Maybe next time it will be different, of course. But right now we only need half a liter of your good red blood."

Flat on his back, with his arm strapped to the table and a crisp, cool sheet covering his legs, Ryeland lay. He was watching his blood slowly fill a liter beaker up to a measured mark. His blood was wine-purple colored, and it seemed to flow very slowly.

There was nothing at all painful about the process. Of course, it wasn't exactly pure pleasure. There was a queer jumpy sensation in his skin, a sort of warning of something that *might* hurt—as though the nerve-ends, evolved to cope with grosser wounds and warn of instanter dangers, did not know quite what to tell the brain, and could only express a sort of worry. The tube made a faint vulgar sound from time to time, like a siphon sucking air, but there was no other noise. The nurse had left him. It was amazing how still the world was. . .

And it was amazing how clearly Ryeland could think.

He was tranquil.

More than that, he *knew* he was tranquil.

More still, he was beginning to realize that he had been tranquil—stupidly, crazily tranquil—ever since he had arrived in the Body Bank! And so was everyone else! It accounted for the cheerful amputees and his heedless roommates at the Dixie Presidents. Tranquil! But it was not natural, and so it was due to drugs.

Ryeland lay lazily watching the thick froth at the top of the beaker of his blood and marveled that he had not seen it before. Even the man who wrote the diary had never seen it, though he had come so close. Drugs!

The Plan of Man understood that there were circuits in the human brain not subject to reason. Self-preservation was one of them. The Machine would not risk a sudden flare-up of that instinct. The Machine must have known that, whatever the mood of the Body Bank's raw materials as they went in, however carefully conditioned to their duties under the Plan of Man, the threat of dismemberment and death could upset all conditioning.

Therefore the Machine had taken steps. The obvious step—how was it that no one had seen it?—was to flood the cadavers with tranquilizing drugs.

The nurse came in. She tapped the beaker lightly with a finger, fussed with the tubes, and in a moment deftly removed the needle from Ryeland's arm. She was humming to herself. She pressed an alcohol pad over the little puncture in his arm and ordered: "Hold it that way to keep the pad in place."

Ryeland was hardly listening. Tranquilizing drugs, he thought, like an echo; it explained everything. It explained why D.W.H.'s careful plans had come to nothing; before they could mature, the drive that would make them reality had been sapped. It explained why Ryeland himself had loafed for irretrievable days. The only astonishing thing was that he had found out.

The nurse straightened his arm, plucked off the pad and pointed. "Out that way."

Ryeland started obediently out the door, then stopped, shocked to alertness at last.

An orderly was guiding an electric stretcher down the hall. On it, his eyes closed, lay the nervous man from Ryeland's group of donors. He looked to be asleep. Surely he had lost something—but what? Arms were there, legs showed under the sheet, there was no mark on the motionless face.

Ryeland said to the nurse: "Excuse me. That fellow. What happened with him?"

The nurse peered past him. "Oh, that one." A shade came down over her eyes. "That was a big one. Did you know him?"

"Yes."

"I see." After a second she said briskly: "We needed a whole spine. There wasn't much point in trying to salvage any of the rest of him."

Ryeland stumbled out into the corridor, following the corpse of the nervous man, who never again would have to be nervous. He glanced over his shoulder at the nurse and said: "Good-by."

She said: "I'll be seeing you."

Outside Heaven, thirteen billion human beings worked, studied, loved, quarreled and in general fulfilled their tiny assigned missions under the Plan of Man. In Saskatchewan an engineer turned a switch and the side of a mountain lifted itself, grumbled and slid into a lake, revealing an open vein of low-grade uranium ore, one of the last deposits left to tap. In the hillside town of Fiesole, in Italy, a Technicorps colonel made a field inspection of the new reservoir. The water level had risen a gratifying nineteen inches since his last report. He observed, from his flat-bottomed boat, how a certain jumbled pile of masonry he remembered seeing was now almost entirely submerged; it was the Pitti Palace, but he had never heard the name. (The Ponte Vecchio was already twenty feet under the bottom of his boat.) Under Honduras, a subtrain shaft collapsed and eighteen hundred migratory agricultural workers were simultaneously cremated and dissolved in molten rock. The Planner, returned from the Moon, signed an order which would ultimately lower the level of the Mediterranean sea ninety feet, creating thousands of miles of new land around its dwindled shores and providing an enormous hydroelectric station at the Straits of Gibraltar. . .

But on of the isle of Cuba, no echo of these rumblings penetrated. Everything was calm. Everything was pleasant. And Steve Ryeland fought against it as hard as he could. He quarreled vigorously with his Dixie Presidents. The senior cadaver was hurt, shocked and mortified; as a consequence, half an hour later he lost count of trumps and suffered an eight-hundred point penalty in the afternoon's bridge game. Ryeland was well pleased. Quarreling stimulated his adrenals. He went out to find someone to quarrel with.

His logical candidate was Angela, and he found her where he had left her, sunning herself in front of her cottage. "Steve, dear," she whispered, but he did not want to be charmed.

He said brutally: "I just made my first donation. Guess what it was?" He gave her a chance to scan him and look perturbed, then said: "Nothing much, only blood. Lucky, eh?"

It was terribly bad manners. She said, "Yes, Steve, that's lucky. Must we talk about it? Oh, I know! Let's go down to the lake again. It's warm today, and there's bound to be a breeze at the fountains—"

"That's all you care about, isn't it?"

"Steve!"

"Food and comfort. Are those the only things that matter to you?"

Angela said petulantly, "Steve, you're in an unpleasant mood this afternoon. If you don't want to come with me I'll go alone."

"Do you care?"

She opened her mouth, closed it, looked at him and shook her head. She was angry; but she was also untouched by it. As Ryeland was an irritation, she removed herself from it.

He stood there thoughtfully. Even after Angela had flounced away, as best a woman with neither arms nor legs can flounce, he stood there, thinking. Knowing that there were tranquilizers flooding his bloodstream was one thing, knowing what to do about it was something else. He could keep his adrenal glands combating the drug by quarreling, even by exercising, but it was wearing. It would be better to keep the drug from his system in the first place...

It was very simple.

It needed only one thing, Ryeland saw. He would merely have to stop eating and drinking entirely.

By lunchtime the next day he began to see the flaws in that scheme.

He had worked it out very carefully. He had to eat something, otherwise he would die, and that would be no improvement at all. He settled on eating sugar. That day after the noon formation he entered the mess-hall, carried his tray to a corner—and abandoned it there, untouched. He filled his pockets with sugar, as inconspicuously as he could. It was a calculated risk. All foods were suspect, sugar included. But even the thorough Machine would not be likely to bother with sugar.

Of course, water was out of the question. Already Ryeland was beginning to feel parched. He thought of making a still, somehow, and purifying the water from the lake. It would attract attention . . . but he was getting very thirsty.

He went to see Angela and tried to take his mind off his thirst. They roamed about, the girl in her remarkably agile wheeled chair. She found him hard to endure that day. They sat by the lake and Steve Ryeland stared at it longingly. Water, lovely and clear. Beautiful water. Sweet water! But it was the source for all the drinking water in Heaven, and undoubtedly it was already treated. He talked about swimming and clinking ice in a glass and the spray from the prow of a boat until Angela, faintly exasperated, said: "Go swimming, then. No, don't worry about me." Gentle smile. "I'd rather not, for reasons which are apparent, but you go ahead. It's what you want, isn't it?"

And it was; but Ryeland refused vigorously until he thought of something and then went to get a pair of trunks. Why not go swimming? It was a trick torpedoed sailors had learned centuries before. If one merely lay in the water and relaxed, it would help control thirst. It wouldn't help much. But it would help a little—perhaps it would keep him alive until his brain was clear and he could think surely enough to find a way out. But, oh, that water was tempting!

He lay in the shallows and played a sort of game. It was for high stakes, his whole life riding on the turn of the wheel. He let the water come up to his chin. He let it touch his lip. He even let a few drops of it into his mouth; then he filled his mouth and held the water there.

It would be so easy to swallow! So simple to ease his thirst! And surely, he said reasonably to himself, his eyes closed against the thirst, swishing the water back and forth with his cheeks and enjoying the sensation, surely *one* little drink would be of no real importance. . .

Sputtering and coughing, he floundered out of the lake.

That had been a close one. But he had learned something; the thirst was a counter-irritant; already he was fully aware of things that had been tempered and dull even an hour before. The puncture inside his elbow hurt. The nurse had been clumsy with the needle. The denims had chafed his thighs raw—a poor fit, miserably poor—and what a joy, he exulted, to be able to realize it.

Angela was looking at him suspiciously. "What's the matter with you?" she demanded.

"Nothing."

"You act—oh, I don't know. As if the Machine canceled your orders here. As though you were going to get rid of your collar."

And even that was not impossible, thought Ryeland. If only he could hold out until somehow, some way there was a chance. He toweled himself dry and said. "Why not? Donderevo did it."

"Steve," she scolded, "that's unplanned thinking! I'm disappointed in you. Nobody else can escape the way Donderevo did, and even if you could, your duty to the Plan—"

"Wait a minute." He stopped toweling and turned to

look at her. "What did you say? What do you know about Donderevo?"

"I know how he escaped. After all, this is where he escaped from."

Ryeland heard a ripping sound, and glanced down to see that his hands, without command from his brain, had clenched so tightly on the towel that it had parted. He dropped it to the ground and whispered: *"How?"*

Angela writhed carelessly, angling her head to start the motors that turned her chair away from the sun. She frowned thoughtfully, then said, "Well, I don't suppose it would do any harm. You can't possibly duplicate his escape. No one can."

"Angela! How did he do it?"

"Not by any method you can follow, Steve." Her smile teased him. "He found a group on the staff here who could be tempted into unplanned thinking—and he tempted them, with talk of space outside the Plan. He managed to corrupt them, with promises of freedom and wealth in the reefs of space. He bribed them to remove his collar—surgically."

"Huh?"

"The thing was expertly planned," she said. "The disloyal surgeons forged the requisitions, and issued false documents. Donderevo was called out of the lineup one morning, exactly in the ordinary way. In one operating theater, he was disassembled, down to the head and the spine. All the parts were rushed into the adjoining theater —and put back together, without the iron collar."

"But don't go getting any ideas," she warned him. "Because the plot was eventually discovered. The surgeons who had participated were promptly junked. Unfortunately, by that time Donderevo had escaped."

"How did he get away?"

"That was the most important part," she said. "You see, the surgeons made a rather ingenious effort to cover their tracks. They used junk parts to assemble a complete patchwork man inside the collar. This junk man took Donderevo's place, until it was too late to trace him."

Ryeland shivered in the warm sunshine. That method of escape semed gruesomely drastic, even if it had been open to him, which it was not.

"Let's do something more amusing," Angela urged him.

"There's one more thing I want to know." He looked

at her, caught with an unpleasant fascination. "How did you happen to know all this?"

She stretched her torso lazily in the sunshine, with a slow, graceful, serpentine movement.

"I suppose I can tell *you*, Steve." She smiled at him confidentially. "After all, it's no secret between us that I once worked for the Plan Police. The fact is that I first came here on the Donderevo case. It was not broken until I had managed to persuade one of the guilty surgeons to use the same method to help me escape."

She yawned, smiling with a feline satisfaction.

"If you came here as a spy, why are you—"

He stopped, feeling a horrified embarrassment.

"Why am I still here? Don't be ashamed to ask that, Steve. I'm here because by the time I finished my task I was—well—as you see me. Naturally the Plan could not divert resources for my sake . . . so . . . I was declared surplus. Oh, I won't deny it disturbed me a little, at first. But I came to accept it. And you will too, Steve. You see, you have no other choice."

12

Accept the fate he would not, though he was powerfully tempted. A rain shower in the middle of the night woke him and he ran out, careless that he woke his cabin mates and left them staring, to find a standpipe under the eaves and drink, drink, drink. It gave him the strength he needed. The next morning he could see a difference. He held out his hand before him and it shook. It shook! He was nervous.

He was also very hungry.

Water was not, for the moment, a problem. He had found a jug that would do and carefully filled it from the drain of a dozen roofs. It tasted of zinc and tar. But he was off the drug. . .

And hungry.

He did not dare to eat in the commissary.

Oporto came to see him at breakfast and that little dark face missed nothing. "Not hungry, Steve?"

Ryeland pushed aside his untouched plate—ham hash!

lovely, irresistible coffee!—and said, "No. I'm not hungry." Later, in the hut of the Dixie Presidents, Oporto still tagging along, the little man pointed at the jug of rain water. "What's that?"

"It's water. In case I get thirsty," said Ryeland, allowing himself a small drink.

Oporto's face remained thoughtful.

Ryeland found a sense of doom pressing in on him, a fear that dried his mouth and bothered his digestion—damaged already by the curious nature of the few substances he dared eat. He enjoyed it. He welcomed the fluttering of terror between his shoulderblades. He looked around him at the other cadavers of Heaven, and they were zombies, dead-alive, the victims of asphodel. They laughed and smiled and walked about (when they had what was needful to walk with), but they were dead men. Not Ryeland. He was alive, and in a panic. And very hungry.

He managed to shake Oporto just before the second shape-up, and seized time to study some of the entries in the journal:

Oct. 16. The only examination given to the discarded parts in the trash pile is visual. They are under the observation of a guard stationed on the watch balcony of the North Clinic. Sometimes he isn't there, but I do not know why.

Nov. 5. Today I was in the North Clinic on the fifth floor, where the guard is stationed. I found out why he is sometimes absent, I think. Twice he was called in to help move patients; apparently this is part of his job. Since I was strapped to the table with a spinal tap I couldn't watch closely, but it seems evident that each time he is called inside he will remain there for at least half a minute, and that the periods at which he is most likely to be called are those when the operation schedule is heavy. Probably the three hours or so following each shape-up would be the best time. The morning and lunch shape-ups are no good. First, I would not be able to conceal my absence for more than a couple of hours; second, they don't usually dump the scraps until night anyway. That leaves only the night. Unfortunately not much

96

operating is done then . . . Today it was the left leg, including the femur.

Dec. 3. Unusually heavy call-outs at the shape-up this morning. The rumor is that there was a nuclear explosion in Baja California and a great many spare parts will be needed. I wonder. Tonight?

Ryeland turned the page, but he already knew what he would find.

The next entry was the last. It had been close for D.W.H., but not quite close enough.

Hunger was beginning to prey on him seriously. His system began to refuse the sugar.

Oporto was openly suspicious now. He walked with Ryeland all over Heaven. Down by the palm-fringed lake he sat with his back against a boulder and watched Ryeland grimly hurling rocks at the hanging coconuts. Ryeland did not succeed in knocking one down, but he did, after visiting a few clumps of palms, find one that had fallen. "I guess you like coconut milk a lot," Oporto said sulkily, seeing how greedily Ryeland hammered off the outer husk and bashed in the shell.

"I love it." Actually the nut was overripe, and the milk had a foul taste.

"Tastes good with garlic, huh?" Oporto was referring to some wild roots Ryeland had found, dark green spears thrusting out of the grass with a cluster of muddy little strong-flavored knobs underground; Oporto had found him nibbing them experimentally.

Ryeland said: "Leave me alone, will you? I—ah—don't feel very well."

Oporto sighed. "I'm not surprised." But he wandered away after a while.

Ryeland dismissed him from his mind. He felt weak and starved. It was only psychological, he told himself; why, shipwrecked mariners had lasted for months and years on little more than what he had so easily come by!

But they had not, it was true, been subjected to the thrice-daily temptation of a loaded table from which they dared not eat.

And there was another consideration. He looked longingly at the little fish in the lake, for example. He could easily catch one. What was to stop him from broiling it over a fire?

But he had already attracted enough attention, he dared no more. Surely the guardians of Heaven would know what to do with a cadaver who had stumbled on the necessity of avoiding their drugs. Once they found one such it would be only a name on the shape-up list, a needle in the arm, and all the drug his system could absorb thrust into him at one moment. Will power would not help him then.

Yet he could not avoid suspicion entirely, not as long as he continued to reject the all but irresistable food of Heaven. Already he was concerned over his mates in the Dixie Presidents, not to mention Angela Zwick and, above all, Oporto, whose behavior was no longer suspicious but sure. There was no doubt; Oporto knew.

The next morning he got away from the others and scouted the periphery of Heaven. Reluctantly he decided that what everyone said was true; the fence was impassable. It would have to be the garbage heap.

The leftover bits from the cadavers in Heaven were deposited in a stainless steel sump next to the North Clinic. The pit was empty at this hour; it had been sluiced clean, its tons of abandoned humanity chuted into a barge and towed away. The hot sun had baked it gleaming. It was surrounded by a wire fence, and that in turn screened by red-flowered bougainvillea bushes. Ryeland wondered if the fence was electrified. Probably not. . .

It would, he thought, be wise to make his bid for freedom soon. The quicker he tried, the more likely that he would retain all his parts. Even now, he saw, there was some sort of activity going on; guards were on the roof of the North Clinic, working around what looked like searchlight projectors. Ryeland scowled. If they flooded the garbage heap with light, that would make things more difficult. Still the projectors were peculiar; they had reflectors but no lenses, and they seemed to be rather small for the task involved. Ryeland crossed his fingers. Perhaps they would be for some other use entirely. He could only hope.

"Sdeve! Sdeve Ryeland!" a familiar voice called loudly. It was Oporto—shouting, waving, smiling.

Ryeland waited, suddenly wary. How had the little man known he would be here? And what was this sudden excitement in his manner? Oporto was sniffling, almost quivering. "Whad a mess, hey, Steve You hear about id?"

"About what?"

"Another tube collabze! Eighdeen hundred people this time. You know whad I think? Sabotage. Thad's whad I think."

Ryeland shook his head. He was not feeling over-friendly to the little man; he was still wary. Still, there was the chance that Oporto knew something, even here, cut off from the world as they all were. "Sabotage by whom?"

"Anti-Plan elemends," Oporto explained cheerfully. "They've been happening all over the world, you know. Thousands dead! Commudication wrecked!" He glanced over his shoulder, smiled, and said quite loudly: "Or don'd you think so, Steven Ryeland?"

Ryeland's nostrils flared; he smelled danger. He looked where Oporto had glanced, and saw what Oporto had seen. Three big men in the white uniforms, coming toward them with purpose. He understood why Oporto had spoken his name so loudly; and the little man nodded, quite unabashed. "Yes, Steve, Judas Isgariot, thad's my other name."

The guards looked as though they were spoiling for a touch of resistance from him. He didn't offer it. He let them take him to the clinic, and when the needle was presented to his arm he stared at it without emotion. The shot was painless enough, even though he knew what it was. It was asphodel again, but this time he was ready for it. "Don't give us any more trouble, Zero-Dome," growled the guard, and released him at the gate of the clinic.

Ryeland's body responded at once to the shot. He accepted it; it was warmly comforting; it would not matter now. He almost laughed out loud. He could not feel betrayed by Oporto, even; Oporto could no longer commit betrayal; he was no longer trusted. And meanwhile . . . Ryeland could eat!

There was a guard brooding over the tables assigned to the Dixie Presidents at lunch. Ryeland conscientiously gorged himself on roast pork and sweet potatoes, with three cups of coffee. It tasted very good. Why not? It didn't matter any more. Meprobamate is not a narcotic; it doesn't keep you from thinking. It only eases jitters—that sovereign incentive to action!—and for Ryeland the worrying fear had already served its purpose. He had his plan. He would carry it out that night, if he could; the next night certainly. He recognized quite calmly that, now that Oporto had told the guards he was avoiding food, he would no longer serve any purpose by not eating; they

99

would pick him up and inject him. All right. It didn't matter, nothing mattered, he was on his way out.

He could hardly wait for sundown and escape.

It was time, too. There were heavy callouts that day. Ryeland's bunkmate had gone at breakfast and had not returned by lunch—wouldn't ever return, now, said the wise old heads; if you didn't come back by the next shape-up, you weren't coming back at all. Five names were called at noon. At dinner, seven more—why, thought Ryeland through his comfortable haze of meprobamate, that left only three in the entire cottage who had not been called for some donation that day, and Ryeland was one of them. Clearly he was pushing his luck.

After the evening shape-up he looked one last time around Heaven and strolled away. Just in time.

For as he was almost out of earshot in the gathering dark, a white-clad guard came down the shell path. Ryeland paused, listening. "Ryeland," the guard was saying, and something with the word "clinic."

Rumble-rumble; the bass voice of one of the few survivors of the Dixie Presidents, answering.

"Oh." The guard again, not very interested. "Well, when he turns up, tell him to report. She can wait."

Ryeland hid himself in the night. What they wanted with him he could not know; but he was very sure that his time was even shorter than he had thought. But who was the "she" who could wait? Angela?

He could hardly think so, but—well, why not go to see her? If it turned out to be Angela, who had somehow inveigled a guard into being messenger-boy for her, there was no reason he should not find out why. If it turned out not to be her . . . he was surely all the better off for being as far as possible from the cabin of the Dixie Presidents.

It wasn't Angela. She was completely ignorant of why the guard had been looking for him, and completely disinterested.

Uneasily, keeping an alert eye open for any possible guard who might come their way, he sat down beside her in the warm tropical evening. More to see what she would say than to relieve his feelings, he told her about Oporto's reporting him to the guards and his consequent new dose of tranquilizer. "Very right of him, Steve. You shouldn't go against the Plan!"

He shook his head ruefully. "I can't understand you," he admitted. "To work for the Plan—yes. That's duty.

But to betray a friend—" He stopped, and looked quickly at her, but she only laughed.

"I know, Steven. But you're wrong. Do you remember what I was doing when we first met?"

"Running a computer."

"That's right! And we would set up problems—oh, enormous problems. I loved that job, Steven! And the computer would solve them, one-two, click-click, ting-a-ling! It could do it without fail; well, it was part of the Plan, you see. Only one unit in the master Plan of Man that the Machine itself runs. Do you know why it was never wrong?"

"You tell me," he growled. She was so calm!

"Because we tested it!" she cried. "There was a special test-circuit switch. After a big problem we'd send a charge —oh, five times normal voltage!—through every last tube and transistor and relay. If anything was going to fail, it would fail then—and we'd know—and we could replace it. And . . . well, Steven," she said, quite serious, "that's what I am, you see. I'm a test charge."

She leaned forward against the high restraining chair-arms that kept her limbless body from toppling. "You can't be allowed to fail the Plan!" she cried. "You must be found if you are weak . . . and replaced. Oporto and I, we have one purpose under the Plan of Man: to find and report the bad tubes. Did I trick you? I don't know; is the excess voltage flushing out a computer a 'trick?' You were a bad tube. Admit it, Steven; you could fail. You *did* fail! And the Machine is better without you!"

Ryeland paced about. The girl watched him solemnly, her eyes large and compassionate. He said at last, unwillingly: "And you are willing to serve the Machine, even after it lops your arms and legs off?"

"I'm willing."

"Then you're crazier than Oporto!" he roared. "The Machine is a monster! The Plan of Man is a hoax!"

She refused to be shocked. "It keeps thirteen billion of us alive," she reminded him.

"It keeps thirteen billion of us enslaved!"

"Do you have another way!"

He scowled. "I don't know. Maybe—out in the Reefs of Space—"

"The Reefs of Space are no longer of any importance to you, my dear. Just like Ron Donderevo. Oh, he was a real man——and maybe there are Reefs, I don't know. But there's nothing there for us." She moved her head, and the obedient wheels brought her closer to him. "And is it so bad, Steven? Being slaves? I know you have ideals—I respect you for them, truly I do! But this is a matter of life and death for Mankind. And isn't it true that, for almost all of us, under the Plan of Man there is happiness?"

He laughed shortly. "It comes in the drinking water!"

"All of it?" She leaned back lazily, looking at him with candid huge eyes. "What about me, Steven. Don't you want me?"

It caught him off-guard. He flushed. "I—I don't know what—"

"Because I'm here, Steven," she went on softly. "If you wanted me, I'm here. And I'm helpless; I can't resist you."

He swallowed. "You—You could scream for help. The guards would—*Damn you!*" He leaped away from her. "I'll never forgive you that, Angela! You've dragged me down to your level, haven't you? But you can't do the same trick again!"

She said, calm, real regret in her voice, "I don't know what you mean, dear." And after a moment Ryeland realized that there was truth in what she said. She meant it; she was his to take, if he chose, and she would not have blamed him. He said brutally:

"You're a high-voltage test circuit, Angela, yes, indeed! But you've already burned me once. I don't intend for it to happen again!"

There was no longer any doubt of what he had to do in his mind. He was inside a wall; well, a wall had two sides. He would reach that other side! Perhaps he would be alive; more likely he would be a cadaver, stripped of useful parts. But he would reach it.

Because . . . because, he thought, on the other side of that wall were many things. There was freedom—maybe —in the Reefs of Space. There was, perhaps, the man who knew how to remove collars.

And there was Donna Creery.

Abruptly he turned to Angela again, surprised at his own thought of the Planner's daughter, unwilling to think farther in that most dangerous of directions. He said, "I —I didn't mean—"

"Don't apologize, Steve. You of all people—"

He became conscious that she had stopped in the middle of a thought. "What were you going to say?"

"Oh . . . nothing. Nothing much. Just that . . ."

102

"Angela!" he said angrily. "You've always kept secrets from me! Please don't keep on with it—not here! Now, what were you going to say? Something about me 'of all people'? Am I any different from other people?"

Her wide, lovely eyes studied him serenely. Then she said: "Don't you know that you are?"

Her cool regard made him uncomfortable. He had to gulp before he could ask what she meant.

"Haven't you been aware of anything strange about yourself?"

He was about to shake his head, when something froze him. He recalled the riddle of the three days he had lost. Suddenly he remembered a time when he thought he had heard her voice, from the dark outside the circle of pitiless light that blazed down on the therapy couch, before she had sacrificed her limbs to the Plan.

"You must have noticed that you are different, Steve," her soft voice taunted him. "Have you ever wondered why?"

For a moment he wanted to strike her. The iron collar was suddenly tighter around his neck, so tight that he could scarcely breathe, so tight that he felt the veins throbbing at his throat. He sat numb and silent, staring at her.

"Did you think you were human?" Her voice was contemptuous, merciless. "I thought you might guess, when I was telling you how Donderevo got away. You are the junk man."

"Junk—what?"

The hair stood up at the nape of his neck. He shuddered in the sun. The collar was heavier then lead, colder than ice.

"I told you that a thing was patched together out of waste parts. A decoy for the guards to watch while Donderevo got away. Well, Steve, that's what you are."

He sat still, breathing carefully through the cruel constriction of the collar.

"If you're good-looking, Steve, that's because the surgeons were trying to put together a reasonable likeness of Ron Donderevo, who was a handsome man. If you dislike the Plan, it is because your brain and your glands were patched together from what was left of several of its most distinguished enemies. If you have an unusual mastery of helical field theory, it is because one lobe of your brain belonged to the man who invented it. If the rest of your memory is somewhat blurred or contradictory, it is because the rest of your brain was stuck together from odds and ends of tissue."

"No!" he whispered hoarsely. "That can't be true—"

But the collar choked off his voice. He felt weak and numb with a hideous feeling that it could be true. "If I was ever here before," he argued desperately, "I can't remember anything about it."

"That goes to prove it." Angela's slow smile was innocently sweet. "The men who assembled you were research scientists, as well as enemies of the Plan. They had been using bits of waste brain tissue in effort to improve upon nature. When they were putting your brain together, they seized the opportunity to create a mental mechanism dangerous to the plan."

Dazed, he could only shake his head.

"There's proof enough, if you don't believe me," she said. "Look at all your feats of sabotage. The subtrain tubes and fusion reactions and ion-drive accelerators that you have demolished with your *improved designs*—"

Agony wrenched him.

"I don't remember—"

"That's the final perfection of your mental mechanism," she said calmly. "The disloyal surgeons equipped your new brain with a self-erasing circuit, to protect you from any temptation to reveal your secrets under torture. Aren't you aware of the blank in your past?"

"I—I am." Shuddering, he nodded.

"That's all you are." A lazy malice glinted in her smile. "All the special attention that you have been receiving for the past three years is proof that you functioned remarkably well as a sabotage device, but your function has been performed. I suppose you are setting some sort of precedent, now that all your organs are about to be salvaged for the second time. But in spite of that, Steve, I can't help feeling that you are trying to carry your head a little too high. Actually, you're nothing more than a hundred and sixty pounds of bait that those traitors filched from the sharks."

13

Shark meat! If that was all he was, then this was the place for him!

Ryeland lurked in a clump of the bougainvilleas near the garbage pit, watching the guards on the roof, while the sun went down and the sky purpled and the stars began to find pockets in the cloud cover through which they could appear.

The searchlights—or whatever—were not turned on.

Numbed, Ryeland watched and tried not to think. That was one less worry. Still, there were guards on the roof; he would have to wait until it was darker. The guards were idly looking out over Heaven to the sea. It was a warm night, a fine tropic night.

But what was before him was an ugly spectacle.

It was odd, Ryeland thought dreamily, that the Plan of Man permitted itself this touch of natural human horror. The world was so cuddled in cotton batting, so insulated against shock, that it would seem this sight should have been hidden away. Before him lay some tons of meat and bone—amputated, exsanguinated, raped of corneal tissue and bone grafts, of healthy arterial sections and snips of nervous tissue.

What had been taken from the pale cold cadavers behind the fence was that mere nothing, life. What remained was good organic matter. And that was another queer thing, thought Ryeland. It would have been a superb animal feed! Or, if on this one point the Plan of Man had reason to be tender, why, how many thousands of acres of mined-out farmland could be rejuvenated with the protein and phosphate in those corpses?

The Plan did not choose to use them in that way. Each night the accumulated parts were chuted to a barge—the barge towed out to sea—the contents given the deep six. Fish, crabs, drifting jellies and moored bivalves would ingest their flesh. Why? Men would eat the fish; why not shorten the chain?

Ryeland shifted uneasily, and turned his thoughts away

—for, if Angela told the truth, from this sort of rubble his own body had been built. . . Anyway, it was almost time.

There was a murmur of public-address speakers from the cottage areas. He couldn't hear the words, but it was unusual for them to be used at all so late at night. Then another cluster of speakers spoke up—nearer, this time. It sounded as though a name were being called.

Ryeland swore under his breath. The sentry nearest him stood rigid as the Machine itself, gazing out over Heaven. Couldn't he at least take a break, stretch, yawn, gaze at the stars—couldn't he do *anything* but remain alert and watchful at his post?

The loudspeakers again. It was the circuit around the lake, Ryeland guessed. And the tone was becoming irritable, as though the guard in his microphone room atop the Clinic was being annoyed by higher authority . . . and was passing his annoyance on to the cadavers of Heaven.

Then closer still; and Ryeland heard the name this time. His own name. "Ryeland!" Only it came bouncing off half a dozen speakers at once, each delayed a tiny fraction of a second by distance and echo: "RYELAND*Ryeland*ryeland," ricocheting away.

He was not surprised; he had been more than half expecting it. He listened to the measured words, cadenced to let the echo of each fade before the next word was spoken: "You . . . are . . . ordered . . . to . . . report . . . to . . . the . . . South . . . Clinic . . . at . . . once!" And off toward the lake Ryeland could see lights moving.

Ryeland took a deep breath. He would have to chance it, even if the guard did not look away—

He caught himself, poised. The guard moved. He turned his head and nodded, to someone out of sight; and then, so quickly that Ryeland might scarcely have noticed he was gone if his eyes had not been glued to the man, the guard stepped inside.

Ryeland ran, climbed, swung himself over the fence, ripped off his clothes, balled and hid them under a body and flung himself, naked and acrawl with revulsion, onto the heap of pale, cold corpses.

There was classic terror. It was like the buried-alive man of humanity's oldest, most frightening story: the awakening in the narrow box, the dark, the smell of damp earth, the hollow muffled sound of the hammered coffin lid with six feet of graveyard dirt above. It was like the war wounded given up for dead, awakening in one of

Grant's wagons after Shiloh, or the mass graves of Hitler's Sixth Army outside Stalingrad—the dead all around, the man himself as good as dead.

Ryeland thanked God for meprobamate. He lay face down and limbs under him, as much as he could. No reason to make a guard wonder why a relatively intact corpse should be on the heap. He did not move. He smelled an acrid, sour reek that nearly made him vomit and he was, in a moment, bitter cold. He swore silently. It had not occurred to him that the metal walls of the trashbin would be refrigerated.

He waited. And waited.

He dared not look up, dared hardly breathe. It would be, he calculated, at least a matter of hours before the bin would tip and chute its contents into the barge. His flesh crawled and tried desperately to shiver, but he would not allow it.

A bright light flared.

Ryeland froze. He heard a murmur of voices. But that was all right; it probably was time for changing the shift of guards, and that was good, because it meant time was passing even faster than he had dared hope. The light would be only a routine inspection, of course. . . Another light flared, and another.

The area of corpses was flooded with light, he was drowning in light; over him he could hear the wash of copter vanes adding their light to the scene. He dared not move. He dared not even blink, though the lights were cruel; but it was in vain; everything was in vain. There was a sudden string of orders and a commotion at the steel ladder that admitted workmen to the sump. Four guards ran in. They did not hesitate; they picked their way rapidly across the stainless-steel floor, stepping on torsos, pushing limbs aside. Straight to Ryeland.

"Good try," one of them grinned. Then, without humor, "But don't do it again."

They hurried him to the ladder and up it. They had not allowed him to retrieve his clothes. Now that it was too late his body was racked with shivering. He stammered, "How—how did you know?"

The guard caught his elbow and lifted him to the roof of the North Clinic. He was not unkind. He gestured to the row of searchlight-like things that Ryeland had feared might be floodlights. "Infrared scanners, Ryeland. Sniffed out your body heat. Oh, you can fool them—but not while

107

you're alive, not without clothes on to hide your heat. And clothes would have given you away anyhow," he added compassionately, "so don't feel bad. You just didn't have a chance." He opened a door and shoved Ryeland, reeling, into a hall of the Clinic. "Now get a move on. Somebody wants you. Somebody important."

14

They rushed him through the corridors, into a room, left him there for a moment; they threw a pair of coveralls at him, gave him barely time to squirm into them and paid no attention to the fact that they were four sizes too small. "It doesn't matter where you're going," rumbled the guard with the white tunic and the red heart. "Come on!" And they led him to another room and once again left him.

Through an open door Ryeland saw an operating theater.

Thank heaven for meprobomate, he thought without emotion, for this was undoubtedly the end of the trail. The asepsis lights were burning over the twin tables; a full O. R. crew was in view behind the transparent contamination-bar. On one table was a man of Ryeland's approximate build, with a great sighing bellows box pumping air through a complicated nest of piping. A lung machine? Yes. And the man, Ryeland knew, was about to get new lungs. And the lungs would have to come, of course, from Ryeland . . .

Or would they? Ryeland was baffled. For both tables were occupied, the one with a cadaver from Heaven as well as the one with a useful citizen come to collect a new part.

It was very queer.

But it only meant, probably, he assured himself, that he would be the donor for the next useful part. It was not kind of them to make him witness the operation, of course. But the Plan of Man was only impersonally kind. He glanced at the scene, looked away, then watched with helpless fascination. Faintly he could hear the brisk, businesslike orders of the surgeon, slitting skin, slicing through muscle, sculpting bone . . .

The operation was nearly over when he heard a sound behind him.

He turned.

Donna Creery walked in the door.

Donna Creery! She looked at him as though he were furniture. "Took you long enough to get him," she said grumpily to the man behind her—chief surgeon of the Clinic, by his bearing and his frown. "All right. I've got this—" she waved a radar gun—"so he won't give me any trouble. Will you, Ryeland?"

The surgeon said doubtfully, "It's most irregular."

"You've seen the Machine's order," purred Donna Creery, and waved a strip of factape.

"Oh," said the surgeon hastily, "of course, Miss Creery. You know I wouldn't—But it's most irregular, all the same."

Donna nodded coldly and beckoned to Ryeland. "The Machine does not have to be regular," she said. "Now show us how to get to my rocket."

They were out of the clinic beyond the wall, out to a landing pit. And there was Donna Creery's rocket speedster, squatting on its fins. The girl whispered: "Chiquita!"

Ryeland said strongly, "Wait a minute, Miss Creery. Where are you taking me?"

She looked at him thoughtfully. "I have orders from the Machine," she said after a moment. "They direct me to take you to another Heaven, where you are needed for a rush repair job on an important member of the Planning Staff."

"That sounds peculiar," he protested.

"Oh, very. Chiquita!" The girl stamped her foot and glared into the ship.

There was a golden movement inside, then a faint blue luminous haze.

The spaceling floated out.

Its tawny eyes were fixed worshipfully on Donna Creery. It wriggled felinely in the air, curled, spun—in pure joy, it seemed—and halted, poised in the air, before her.

Ryeland started to speak. "Shut up," whispered the girl. "There isn't time to argue. You've got to get out of here before they come to take you back."

"Back? But why should they do that? The travel orders from the Machine—"

"—are forged." She met his gaze calmly. "Yes. I forged them myself, so I should know. So the surgeon will be looking for you, as soon as he gets around to filing a routine report of compliance with the Machine. And that will be—what would you say? Five minutes?"

"But I don't understand!"

"You don't have to understand!" the girl blazed. "There isn't time! I'm trying to save your life. Also—" she hesitated. "Truthfully there's another reason. My father needs you."

"The Planner? But—but—why would *he* have to forge orders from the Machine?"

"I can't tell you now." She stared around. No one was in sight. She said grimly, "Heaven help you if anything goes wrong. I can't take you in my rocket; there isn't room. Anyway, that's the first place they'll look. I don't think they'll bother *me*. But if you're there—" She shrugged.

"Then what am I supposed to do?"

"Do?" she cried. "Why get on Chiquita's back! What do you think I brought her for? Just get on—she knows where to take you!"

Ryeland rode the spaceling; it was like mounting a running stream.

A slim golden shape, more slender than a seal, floating in the air; gold, pure gold that blended into black at the tail, it was the strangest mount a man ever bestrode. Donna said a quick word of command. The spaceling purred faintly, rippled its lazy muscles and *whoom*. It was like a muffled slap of metal. Suddenly they had leaped a hundred feet into the air.

There was no shock, no crushing blow of acceleration. There was just a quick vibrant lift, and they were high in the air.

Through the thin coveralls that were his only garment Ryeland felt the purring vibration of the spaceling's body. Down below he saw the Planner's daughter already entering her rocket. She did not intend to wait for trouble. The jets flared. Ryeland heard the sound—but it was receding, receding although the rocket had already begun to climb; they were climbing too, and *fast*. Ryeland was breathless. He clung to the spaceling. There was no pressure; only his arms held him to that bare, warm, smooth back. His stomach fluttered. His breathing caught. Down below he saw men moving, insects on the lawn and the walks. But they were not looking up, probably couldn't see him if they did; it was still night, and the hovering helicopters, with their floodlights were between him and the ground.

They were nearly a thousand feet in the air now. Donna's rocket, a black dot in the center of its own petaleo flame, seemed plastered against the concrete of the pit below. Only the fact that its size stayed constant showed that it was following them; then even it began to dwindle.

Off to the northeast was a storm, the warning cirrus veil across the sky, the dark towering cumulonimbus, the rain squalls already marching across the dark mountains of Cuba. The spaceling turned toward the storm. "Wait!" cried Ryeland. "Don't go into *that!*" But the spaceling didn't understand, or wouldn't. It purred warmly, like a fat kitten, and arrowed toward the menacing cloud with its violent gusts.

And still Ryeland felt no motion.

All his body was accelerated uniformly by the spaceling's field, whatever it was. The air came with them, the pocket which the spaceling wore like a halo, its blue shroud of faintly glowing light. Their flight was not quite noiseless, though nearly; the only sound was a faint distant tearing, though they were barreling through the sky at surely sonic speed. Incredible! Ryeland's mathematician's mind fitted pieces together; the spaceling, he thought, must form a capsule which instantly shapes itself to meet the resistance—forming the perfect streamline shape for its needs, blunt teardrop at a hundred miles an hour, needle as it approached sound's speed, probably wasp-waisted area-rule profile at higher speeds.

And still there was no sense of motion, though Heaven had dropped away behind them and was gone.

Now they were over water. All around them was cloud. They were hurtling into the furious wall of towering thunderstorms that was the forefront of a hurricane.

Cold rain drenched him in an instant. That was curious, thought the objective, never-stilled part of his mind; rain penetrated the capsule where the rush of air did not! But there was no time to think of it. The rain was pelting icewater, uncomfortable, chilling. It disturbed the spaceling, too. Its satisfied purr changed to a complaining mew; it shook and shuddered. But it plunged on.

Ryeland was hopelessly lost.

The storm was the same in all directions, a dim void of fog and icy water, flickering with distant lightning. But the spaceling knew where it was going . . . he hoped.

They drilled through the top of the clouds and came out above them into clear air. Underneath them the shape of the storm revealed itself in a great spiral, the hurricane

111

wheeling around its open eye. A bright light burst on him. It was the sun, rising again on the western horizon—they were *that* high! It was a blaze of incandescence in the dark; and still they climbed.

A great elation possessed Ryeland.

He had done the impossible! He had escaped, with all his limbs and faculties, from the hell they called Heaven!

He was no longer a numbered carcass; he was a man again. And Donna Creery had done it, where he had failed; he owed her something. He wondered briefly what it was she had failed to tell him about her father; then dismissed it. That wonder was lost in the greater soaring wonder of free flight. The sky was black around them— surely the air was thin now. And still they climbed, while the vast hazy floor of sea and cloud became visibly convex.

And still they climbed; and the air *was* thin now.

That was all wrong! Ryeland knew that much; the spaceling's field should hold the air. But the creature itself was gasping now, panting. Its purring and mewing had turned into the choking cough of a tiger. They still climbed, but Ryeland could feel the creature falter.

They were at a dangerous altitude. Suddenly he was breathless. His drenched body was chilled through, even in the white, bright glare of the naked sun.

It was the spaceling's wounds that were endangering them now, Ryeland realized. Gottling's torture chamber had left its marks. The creature's symbiotes had been destroyed, or some of them had. Its fusorians that gave it power, its parasitic Reef animalcules that made it possible for a warm-blooded air-breather to live in space in the first place, their numbers had been greatly diminished. They were not all gone, for there was still some air. It filled his grasping lungs, kept his body fluids from boiling out, screened him at least a little from the cold and the even more deadly UV of the sun. There was some air . . . but was there enough?

Ryeland laughed grimly, with almost the last of his breath. "That's what I'll find out," he panted, hoarsely . . . and passed out. He was not conscious of the moment when he blacked out; he only knew that he was going.

When he awoke, it was with sheer wonder that he was alive.

Donna Creery's perfect face bent over him, making the wonder all the greater. "I made it," he whispered incredulously.

The girl said seriously, "Yes, so far. But don't crowd your luck, Ryeland. We're still in trouble."

He stirred to get up—and floated free, until the girl's restraining hand pushed him back against the metal acceleration couch. They were in a spaceship, apparently in free-fall. He looked around. Automatically he said, "I've got to find a—" He stopped. He had been about to ask where the teletype was, so that he could check in with the Machine. But that was no longer necessary, of course.

Donna Creery gestured at the cabin of the spaceship. "You like it, Steven? It's yours."

He was startled. "Mine?"

"Oh, yes. Do you remember the ship that General Fleemer equipped for you, with remote controls from Point Triangle Gray? This is it—with some changes. I've removed the remote controls. But it was a perfectly good interplanetary rocket, right in orbit where Chiquita could bring you to it. Only—" she looked worried. "Only I'm surprised that Father isn't here."

Ryeland shook his head.

"I'm sorry," he said. "I don't understand. Why does the Planner want me here?"

She said, "He ought to tell you himself, but perhaps I can. Did you know, Steven, that in the past two months there have been over a hundred major seismic shocks? And they always seem to strike centers of population. My father thinks—well, it doesn't sound right when I say it. He thinks the Machine is doing it."

"The Machine!"

"I know, Steven. But Father is worried. He has discovered that General Fleemer and others have been tampering with the Machine! Father is a good man, Steven, and he says he does not understand this. But I do. Fleemer wants to control the Machine—because he wants to control the Plan of Man—and destroying the project for discovery of a jetless drive is only one step in his plan. All those seismic shocks and accidents with subtrain tubes and fusion reactors and the new ion drives—they're all part of it, too. Deliberate sabotage!

"And, oh, Steven! How well it has worked! The Machine is only transistors and relays, you know; it knows nothing but what is fed into it. Fleemer has managed to corrupt its input circuits, and now the Machine is almost openly hostile to Father, and the whole crux of the matter right now is the jetless drive. The Machine has come to

113

think that such a drive will destroy the Plan of Man. It has overruled Father's orders on it—oh, a thousand times —so that Father has to resort to subterfuge and tricks. He let me rescue you, as one of his moves. But I'm afraid it's too late."

She moved away, peering worriedly at the viewports on the spaceship's panel. "They don't seem to be following. Not yet, anyhow."

Ryeland noticed he was shivering. It was not cold in the ship, but he had only the ill-fitting coveralls to wear and they were soaked through. "Who?" he demanded.

"The Plan Police," she said, surprised. "General Fleemer will be after Chiquita, even if they don't suspect you are with me. Though we can't count on that, of course; it wouldn't be unreasonable for the Machine to inform them that I had rescued you from Heaven. He was going to kill Chiquita, you see, so I stole her." She frowned as Ryeland shook his head.

"Why shouldn't I steal her?" the girl flared. "She was mine! And the only safe place for Chiquita is out in space—out on the Reefs, if I can get her there. And, of course, that's the only safe place for you."

Ryeland said angrily, "You're asking me to run away from the Machine! You want me to be an outlaw!"

"Oh, Steven, what do you think you are? Have you forgotten Heaven already? I saved your life . . . You're lucky you got here," she said seriously, stroking the spaceling. "I wasn't at all sure Chiquita could make the jump from atmosphere."

"Neither was I."

She smiled, and for a moment she was the impish, confident girl who had interviewed him in her bath. But quickly her face clouded again. "I wish Father would come," she said. "Chiquita can't live forever without getting back to the Reefs to replenish her fusorians. And I— well, I sent my own rocket back to Earth and crashed it where they'll find it. Perhaps they'll think we were both killed. But," she said calmly, "they would have to be stupid to be deceived very long, and the Machine is never stupid. It's—I don't know—unbalanced, now. But it is thorough. Father and I discussed it thoroughly; he knows the Machine well. He thinks we have about twelve hours."

"Then what?"

"Why, then the Machine will trigger your collar."

Involuntarily Ryeland's fingers came up to touch the dull metal that encircled his neck.

The girl was right; that was what the Machine would do. Twelve hours? He didn't know; but probably the Planner did. All right. Then in twelve hours they had to be out of range.

"Can we get away from the Machine's radar beam in twelve hours?" he demanded.

"I don't know, Steven. I think so. The Machine may not realize that you are in space."

The girl restlessly prowled toward the viewports. "But Father isn't here. I don't know how long we can afford to wait. Once we get out to the Reefs, of course, there's nothing to worry about. You won't have your collar any more."

He looked startled. She smiled. "Don't you remember, Steven? Ron Donderevo. The man who got his iron collar off; he's out there. I'm sure he can do the same with yours."

Restlessly Ryeland touched his collar. "Please," he begged. "Tell me what you know about Donderevo" . . . about, he thought silently, the man this junk body of mine was built to replace.

"You know everything there is to tell. Or almost," she said. "He was once a friend of my father—in spite of all their differences over the future of the Plan of Man. It was Donderevo who first told my father something about the spacelings and the reefs, and convinced him that the Machine should try to develop a jetless drive.

"Unfortunately, when the Plan took over his people, Donderevo engaged in disloyal activities. For that reason he was classified as a Risk and finally sent to the stockpile. The fact that Father communicated with him while he was in the stockpile, and finally connived at his escape, is one of the charges that Fleemer is using now in his effort to discredit Father with the Machine.

"I think Donderevo might be able to help Father now, in this fight with Fleemer for control of the Machine and the future of the Plan. At least he could tell the Machine more about the reefs than it got from Lescure's reports— after Fleemer had finished doctoring them. And that's where we must go, Steve—to find Donderevo, out to the Reefs of Space!"

Ryeland was suddenly afraid to tell Donna how desperately he wanted to see Ron Donderevo. Donderevo

115

might help him remove the iron collar. Donderevo might help him clear up the fog of oblivion and contradiction in his past. But it was also possible that Donderevo would tell him that the collar could not be removed—not without the elaborate surgical facilities available only at the stock-pile. It was even possible that Donderevo would affirm what Angela had told him—that he was a junk man, a meat machine patched together from a few bits of waste tissue, not worth saving from the collar.

If that were true, he thought, he couldn't stand for Donna Creery ever to find it out. The Planner's daughter—and a few pounds of salvaged human garbage. The gulf between them would be too wide for any warm emotion to cross.

Donna Creery looked again at the viewports and sighed. "I don't know why Father isn't here," she said, "but we dare not wait any longer. I'll send him a message and we'll go. Even the Machine's normal radar beam might reach out this far; we're got to get out of range." She smiled. "It isn't only for your sake, you know. If that collar were triggered in this little ship . . ."

She pursed her lips gravely and shook her head.

15

Ryeland was deep in a dream of an armless, legless blonde with Oporto's grinning face coming at him with a sonic hacksaw. When the earth began to shake, his body vibrated like a harpstring . . . and he awoke. Donna Creery was leaning over him.

Uncomfortably he stretched and rubbed his tingling hands and ankles. It took him several seconds to wake up. Not unusual; the sleep that spans interplanetary distances is not lightly thrown off. They had put themselves under for what was to have been a voyage of a hundred and fifty days. Were they at the end of it already?

But Donna's face was worried, and there was a loud excited mewing from the ship's cargo lock. Ryeland groaned and tried to shake the aches out of his bones. Thank heaven they were in space, he thought. The mild thrust of Hohmann-minima orbits kept the endless contact of body-to-bed from producing the bed sores and bruises that would have been inevitable on Earth. "Steven!" the girl cried frantically.

"Sorry," he mumbled, shook himself and woke up at last. "What's the matter?"

"Chiquita's gone crazy!" He grunted and climbed up, peering into the cargo hold. The spaceling was flashing about the lock like a tom on the trail of a skulking mouse. She was mewing frantically.

"Are we here?"

"No, Steven! But Chiquita got so excited that she triggered the alarms and woke me up. We should be traveling for days yet!"

"All right. Let's see what's bothering her."

"But there's nothing to see. We're in deep space now, Steven. Far out beyond Pluto—and yet surely not as far as the Reefs. There couldn't possibly be anything here that could bother her . . ."

She stopped, listening.

Both of them heard it at the same moment. It was an irritated hammering sound.

They stared at each other.

It came again, a muffled banging on their ship's hull. "Let's take a look," Ryeland said grimly. The viewports showed nothing, but on the outer door of the airlock was a small window, shielded against chance radiation. Ryeland slipped the catch and slid open the shields.

A man stared in, with an expression of impatient annoyance.

A man!

Ryeland and the girl looked at each other and then at the face that peered in on them. It was quite impossible. But it was undeniably true.

The man did not even wear a spacesuit. He wore a ragged blanket, hammering on the valve of the airlock with the handle of a long knife. He was a lean little red-bearded man, not young.

Donna cried out suddenly. "Steven! I know him. His name is Quiveras. Why, he brought Chiquita to Earth—to rescue Donderevo from the stockpile." She hesitated, then said abruptly: "Open the lock, Steven."

"What?"

"Open the lock, man!"

"But the air—"

"Oh, there's no worry about that," she said impatiently.

"Look!" She pointed behind the man's head where a smooth-lined shape rippled. Another spaceling! No wonder Chiquita had been so upset; undoubtedly she had sensed its presence, a creature like herself though larger and darker. "He's got his own air. The spaceling carried it. How do you suppose he lives? Open the lock!"

Ryeland hesitated. Reason told him the girl was right; there could be no other explanation. Reason was certain; but his emotional conditioning against opening a door to the great exploding suck of space was too powerful to give in to mere reason without combat; it took a great deal of self-discipline for Ryeland to turn the valve key. But he did it. A metallic whine; a hiss of equalizing pressure. And the lock was open, and they were still breathing air—queerly scented air, with a faint, hot, chemical bouquet, but not unpleasant.

The little man hurried inside.

He whistled sharply and his spaceling followed. It was a red-nosed, stub-winged seal, its nose pulsing with red light. Its huge eyes peered around the chamber; it was whining shrilly with pleasure and excitement.

"Wait!" cried the little man. The spaceling was frantic, but obedient; it paused in the lock while the man spun the closing valve. Then Quiveras said, "All right, Adam. Go meet your friend."

The two spacelings flew at each other.

Around and around the narrow cargo compartment they spun, mewing and purring in soprano-baritone counterpoint. Quiveras grinned. "Ah, the children! How happy to see each other they are!" He bowed and took off his rag of a hat. "And I, sir and madam. I am Quintano Quiveras, your humble servant."

He looked again at Donna Creery and smiled with real pleasure. "Ah, the Planner's daughter! It is good to see you! And you, sir; it is good to see you as well, though I do not as yet know your name."

"Steve Ryeland." He put out his hand, and gravely they shook.

Donna managed to say: "We're pleased to see you too, Mr. Quiveras. But—"

"But what is Quiveras doing here?" The man smiled and bowed again. "Ah, perhaps I may help. My Adam felt the presence of Chiquita here." He reached out and stroked the golden she-spaceling; the two of them hung poised, their flanks touching, just behind him. "So he

118

wished to join you; and then, there is another reason."
The smile left his face. "My Adam and I, we have been
watching you for some time. Adam has excellent vision,
apart from the way that spacelings have of knowing another spaceling is near even when vision is of no use. And
Adam saw something. With his help, I saw it too."

"What's that?"

"Why," said Quiveras seriously, "perhaps you do not
know it, but you are being followed by a heavy war
rocket of the Plan of Man."

Involuntarily Ryeland's fingers stole up to touch his
collar. Donna Creery's face turned chalk-white. Their
signal to the Planner must have been intercepted; Fleemer
knew where they were.

The equations of military affairs in open space admit
of only one solution: The faster vessel could always force
battle on the slower. The logic of the radar-pulse that
would trigger the collar on Ryeland's neck made it certain
that the battle could be decided only one way. If they
fled, the Plan cruiser would overtake them. If they stopped
their jets, it would calculate course and position from the
last recorded points with no chance whatsoever of error.
The jets made a magnificent target, their light and heat
a beacon for a million miles. Every effort at escape would
plot another blip on the Plan cruiser's thermal screens.

And then the radar pulse would detonate the collar.

Ryeland said harshly: "Can we fight? Are there any
arms on the ship?"

Quiveras's gnarled face took on an expression of surprise. "Fight against the Plan? Oh, no, my young friend.
We do not fight them; that is their way. We follow our
way. We merely run away." He nodded. "We are some
millions of miles from the Reefs, yes; it is a considerable
journey. But at the end of the journey is freedom. Perhaps even—" he followed Ryeland's stroking fingers on
the collar with his eyes—"freedom from that thing about
your neck."

"We have no lifeboat!"

Quiveras pursed his lips. He pointed to the two spacelings, frolicking about.

Ryeland said with quick comprehension: "The jetless
drive! Of course. They can get us away from our rocket,
and as they do not use thermal propulsion, the Plan ship
won't be able to spot them. But—the female is injured,
Quiveras. She almost killed me before, in just a few

minutes in space. Look." He indicated the ridged scars Colonel Gottling had left on her golden fur.

"But she's had time to heal, Steven!" cried Donna Creery. "Don't forget we've been aspace for over four months!"

Quiveras looked suddenly worried. Ignoring the girl, he dropped to one knee and crooned to the spaceling. Chiquita frolicked over and hung before him, purring faintly as he stroked the scars. At last Quiveras looked up, his gnarled face concerned. "These were bad wounds, Miss Creery. I did not think you would treat her like that."

"It wasn't I!"

Quiveras shook his head. Obstinately, he said, "They are bad. I do not know if she will ever altogether heal."

Ryeland said stonily, "Are you telling us that we can't get away by spaceling, then?"

"Oh, no!" The little man was upset. "I did not mean to frighten you. My Adam can hold enough air for us all, I promise. We must go quickly."

"No," said Ryeland.

The girl and Quiveras paused, staring at him.

"Not like that," he said. "This rocket was equipped for me, to work out some of the problems of the jetless drive. I need that equipment—for, if it is as important as you say, we must have it. The spacelings will have to tow it— No," he said, not letting Quiveras object, "I know it will be difficult. But I must have it. And one other thing."

Quiveras looked at him coldly, then at last smiled. "Very well. If you are willing to go slowly, Adam and Chiquita can pull along whatever it is you want. What is the other thing?"

Ryeland said: "I want to set a fuse on this ship's fuel compartment. I don't want them poking around in it after we go; I want to blow it up."

In ten minutes they had locked out some tons of computers, electronic instruments, a power source and a handfull of other gear; Ryeland took another five to wire contacts to a time-lock and set them to explode the ship's fuel, and then they were ready to leave the spaceship.

It was like making up one's mind to leap off a building. They stood in the open airlock, and there outside was the universe of stars. Ryeland felt more helpless and small than ever before in his life; how could human flesh survive that great cold barrage of light?

But Quiveras assured them that the spaceling's bubble of gas had remained about the ship, held there by the

120

spaceling even through the ship's hull. And in fact, they could see strange shapes and colors, hardly visible, with their eyes still used to the bright ship's interior and dazzled by the distant display of multitudinous suns.

Ryeland and the girl joined hands and leaped, and they floated into the world of the spaceling.

They felt nothing, but they began to move away. The two spacelings swam among them, apparently unheeding, but the jetless drive their bodies produced was moving them all at a tangent to the rocket's line of flight, diverging from it slowly. As they drew off from the ship, the captive air the spaceling carried with it detached itself from its resting places along the hull of the ship. The bubble condensed. The air became denser. Scraps of solid material drifted into place.

Behind them, in a long string pointing toward the rocket ship they had left, an occasional glint of starshine showed the trail of instruments Ryeland had demanded they take with them. But they saw them only briefly, and then the spaceling's world was coalescing about them, and it was a fairyland.

It was incredible! Donna and Ryeland stared about, unbelieving. As the bits and pieces sorted themselves into their accustomed relationships they became a cool green cloud, so bright that Ryeland could hardly see the stars outside. Strangeleafed vines twined through the cloud, laden with clusters of unfamiliar fruit. Small creatures that were half fish and half bird flitted through the vines.

They were at the center, and as the air reached earth-normal density the invisible small creatures that gave it light and life were thickly packed about them. They could move. Ryeland roamed restlessly around the mad little bubble of life they inhabited, with naked space only yards away, staring, thinking, asking quick questions of Quiveras. The little man had apologetically few answers for him, but the facts spoke for themselves. "Incredible!" he muttered. "Fantastic!" He caught himself on a tendril of vine eighteen inches from the faint veil that marked the end of the bubble and stared out at the stars. He could recognize no constellations; great Orion and the mighty Southern Cross alike were out there, but buried in a swarm of thousands of lesser lights, invisible on earth but here a snow-sprinkling of radiance. One great blue-white needle lanced him, and he knew that he had found one star at least. That

121

could only be Sirius, many magnitudes brighter than from Earth's surface, painful to look at directly.

Behind him Donna said hesitantly, "Steven, what is all this?"

Ryeland turned at last to confront her. "It's remarkable! I think I understand it, though . . . The drive field holds this little cloud of air. Moving through space, it picks up dust and hydrogen gas. These vines have fusorian cells, that fuse the hydrogen into oxygen, carbon and all the other elements—and also release light and heat enough for the spaceling's metabolism, or for ours. I'd guess," he said thoughtfully, "that there's a fair proportion of heavy elements in those plants. Conservation of energy. Fusion liberates nuclear energy at the light end of the scale; if the fusorians made only light elements there would be too much release of energy, we'd all be dead in a moment, one way or another. But up past silver fusion *takes* energy. . . ." He shook his head. "Sorry. But I can't help running on about it. This is a complete little world, with its own complete economy."

Donna asked simply, "What about food?"

Quiveras interrupted. "Ah, *food!*" he cried. He launched himself through the air like a swimmer in water, the vines like a strange seaweed. He gathered his hands full of the bright fruits and came soaring back. He begged: "Try them! They are good. Platinum? Gold? I do not know about heavy elements, Mr. Ryeland. But I know about flavor!"

At that moment a great soundless flower of fire unfolded behind them. They all whirled to look.

Ryeland said soberly: "There goes our rocket. I hope we're going to like this place, Donna. It's all we've got now."

They gathered close to the film at the very rim of the bubble, peering out. "Not too close," warned Quiveras. "You must not stick even your little finger through it. You will be blown out, you see."

Ryeland looked startled, then, after a moment, nodded. "Of course. Anything much larger than a molecule is not reflected, eh? And once the field was penetrated, it would be forced out by the pressure differential." Very cautiously they settled themselves to peer out at the ship they had left behind. The flame was gone, but even in its microseconds it had heated metal to red incandescence and they could see a ruddy skeleton that was all that was left of

122

the craft's main supporting beams. The hull and fitting were scattered by the blast; but near the dark red glow they could make out faint points of light. The war rocket, Quiveras declared positively. The lights they saw were the flare of its auxiliary rockets as it matched position with the abandoned hulk.

The spacelings hung looking out through the tangle of glowing vines, searching the dark outward sky. They made soft murmuring and whimpering sounds. Quiveras listened to them, stroking their sleek fur, crooning to them gently.

"They are watching the Plan rocket," he told the others. "The ship radiates its own infrared. They can see it well, now that it is coming closer."

"Closer?" Ryeland was startled.

"Of course, Mr. Ryeland. The Plan is not stupid."

"But—they must think we are dead! And even if not, they have no way of tracing the spacelings' jetless drive—"

"Nor have they," Quiveras told him solemnly. "The Plan is merely thorough. I can understand what they are saying in that cruiser. 'Did they have an escape vessel? If so, where would they be going?' To the Reefs. And the Plan knows where the Reefs must be."

The spacelings were growing uneasy. "And our friends here are tiring." Quiveras said soberly. "They need rest. Carrying all of us, and all of your equipment. Mr. Ryeland—even for two of them it is a great load. They cannot go faster, and so they are going to try to hide. There."

He pointed out through the glowing vines.

Ryeland looked. The brillance of their little atmosphere was in his way. He kicked himself—very warily!—to the other end of their bubble and hung, clutching a vine and staring; but if there was something to see his untrained eyes could not make it out.

Quiveras followed. "It is a cluster of Reefs," he explained. "There, near those three blue-white stars."

Ryeland's Earth-adapted eyes were not equal to the task. But Chiquita and Adam slipped close to him and hung among the bright leaves, their sad eyes staring into the star-sprinkled space ahead. Ryeland shook his head. "I don't see anything at all."

"Nor did I," Quiveras agreed, "until the spacelings showed me. We are not equipped to find a pebble in the dark, countless miles away; but they are."

Ryeland said doubtfully, "Even if there are the Reefs

123

there, and we get to them—can't the Plan rocket follow us?"

Quiveras shrugged. "Of course. But the Reefs are in a thicker cloud than this little bubble of Adam's, Mr. Ryeland. There are swarms of the little fireflies that you call fusorians; they'll fog his search screens. There are hunks of bigger stuff that will slow him down—perhaps even wreck him, Mr. Ryeland, if he should be careless! Still, he may get through and find us. Yes. It is a chance, but we have no choice but to take it."

They drove on for hours, there was no way of measuring just how long. As destination and pursuer were alike invisible to Ryeland, there were only the shrouded stars as reference points, and their great distance was not affected by the tiny crawl of the spacelings. Adam and Chiquita seemed hardly to be working, as they slipped supplely about through the vines, yet Quiveras assured Ryeland they were moving nearly as fast as the Plan cruiser, in spite of the trail of machines that followed them.

Then Quiveras said. "We are almost there!"

Ryeland sought among the stars for "there." What made it hardest was that there was neither bow nor stern to their tiny captive world, no sure way of knowing which way they were going. He could find nothing. The stars shone splendid and unobscured, as he hung at nearly the edge of their air capsule—red stars, blue-white giants, clouds of nebular matter . . .

Then he saw the Reef ahead.

16

It appeared first as a pale point of light that suddenly grew into a bulging, uneven sphere of splendor. It was a jeweled ball, floating in space, and the jewels were forests of crystal.

They came closer, like a comet, then slower. Ryeland saw spiked trees of crystal carbon—diamond!—glittering with their own inner light. There was strange bulging brain-shaped masses of blue and violet, patches of ghostly white sand, a frozen forest with bright metal leaves.

It was an incredible fairyland to Ryeland and the girl,

but Quiveras surveyed it with a shrewd professional eye and shook his head.

"Not a good place to hide," he said, peering at the glowing ball. "Still, that solid part might be useful. The Reefs are mostly hollow—because they're dead inside."

Ryeland nodded. "I suppose the surface organisms are the ones that pick up the free hydrogen and grow. The ones inside die of starvation."

Quiveras was not listening. He cried gleefully: "Yes! There is a cave!—If it is not already occupied."

Ryeland stared at him. Quiveras shrugged. "These Reefs do not have much gravitation; something must be holding the air there, as the spacelings do. It could be another spaceling. It could be small cells in the Reef itself—each Reef is its own world; I do not pretend that I know what to expect on this one. But it could be something quite bad." He raised a hand. "Wait. Let us see."

The jeweled ball swam closer. "Watch," ordered Quiveras. "See how Chiquita enters the air of this Reef. Adam is pulling us now; Chiquita is controlling our atmosphere. Do you see?"

The female spaceling was darting about, while Adam hung motionless. "I did wonder about that," admitted Ryeland. "When the two spheres meet, air pressure will be forcing them apart."

Quiveras shook his head. "See, she airlocks the Reef in." Ryeland stared. They came closer to the Reef and closer. From the frightened movements of the little fishbirds, he saw that the shell was being contracted; yet there was no increase of pressure— "I see!" he cried suddenly. "She is setting up another shell, big enough for both us and the Reef! Then she'll collapse our inner shell, letting the air leak out as it contracts to keep the pressure steady!"

Quiveras nodded. There was a sudden vibration, as though the shock-front of a distant explosion had raced past them, and a clicking in their ears. The inner shell was finally gone.

Ryeland stared about his new world. The steady rain of starlight, even through their light-fogged atmosphere, gave him a view of a wonderland. The sun itself, hardly brighter than Sirius, made yellowish sparkles in the crystal branches of the—could he call it "vegetation"? But Quiveras gave him little time to admire the world.

"Now we must do our part, Mr. Ryeland," he grinned.

Ryeland saw that the two spacelings were hanging at a

distance from the dark cave mouth, regarding it with huge wet eyes. Their red noses flickered swiftly. They whimpered, and a shudder ran along Chiquita's scarred flank. "What is our part?"

Quiveras said calmly: "The spacelings have natural enemies—clumsy, armored killers. Very slow—too slow to catch the spacelings out in space. But extremely deadly. They wait for them in places like these." He said politely, "So we must ferret into this burrow, Mr. Ryeland, if you will do me the honor to join me."

Quiveras propelled himself to the mouth of the cave, peered inside, looked at the others and shrugged. "We will see," was all he said. Calmly he unwrapped a bundle of rags and took out an old Plan Police handweapon. He was not very skillful with it; he worried at it until he had opened the clip, checked the number of charges it contained—Ryeland saw that it only held four; undoubtedly Quiveras had found it difficult to obtain them—snapped it closed and balanced it in his hand. Then with the heel of his worn boot he kicked at a stalagmite of greenish crystal until it broke free. It was eighteen inches long or more and quite sharp. It made a queer but serviceable sword, Ryeland thought, and then realized that it made an even better torch. The interior of the cave was dark. The crystal sword glowed with its trapped fusorian cells.

Quiveras scrambled into the cave and Ryeland followed, unable to look at the girl.

It was a strange dark lair of winding passages. The entrance was worn smooth—alarmingly—as though large bodies had been scraping in and out. Ryeland thought swiftly of the probable age of the Reef, and felt somewhat reassured. Time moved along different scales out here. Change could be lightning fast, or ponderously slow; those ledges might have been worn smooth a hundred million years ago. The dark passages, smooth-worn rock walls made of the bodies of once-living fusorians had perhaps been dead when the Earth was still a boiling incandescent blob. There simply was no way to tell. Nor had Ryeland any idea of how long or deep the passages might be. They were as labyrinthine as the maze inside a head of sea-coral, where tiny crustaceans wait for tinier fish to blunder in.

Quiveras paused where the passage branched—and, within sight, both divisions inside a dozen yards branched again. He was staring at the wall. As Ryeland joined him, he saw what Quiveras had seen.

The worn sides of some of the passages bore curving parallel scars, as though they had been rasped by the claws of some incredible monster.

Quiveras said cheerfully, "That one looks the most used, Mr. Ryeland. If we only knew when, eh? Well, I'll try it—asking you, if you please, to remain here on guard." He turned away, hesitated and said solemnly: "You see, it is you who must take the post of danger. For if a pyropod should come from one of the other passages while I am gone . . ." He made a grave face, spread his hands politely and left.

Ryeland clung to a projection of rock and waited.

Pyropod . . .

He heard the word again, in the soft, apologetic, wheezy voice of Dr. Thrale. He was lying again on the therapy couch in the recreation center, clamped into the cold electrodes, helplessly enduring the merciless probing into his blank memory. He shuddered again, flinching from the pitiless pressure to make him reveal the secret he had never known—

Or had he really ever known how to build a jetless drive? That haunting fog of black oblivion and insane contradiction flowed into his brain. Through it, he heard the lazy malice of Angela's voice, mocking him with her explanation of the riddle. He was a junk man, a meat machine designed to sabotage the Plan, without a memory because he lacked a past.

A queer companion for the Planner's daughter. He resolved again not to tell her what he was. Now when they were alone, when he and Quiveras were the only human beings in her world—could she stand the shock of learning that even he was no real human being?

He shook himself impatiently, as if mere motion might dispel that paralyzing fog and reveal his true identity. That old riddle would have to wait—perhaps until the timing mechanism detonated the collar, and answered it forever. The problems of the present were more urgent now.

It was warm in the cavern, far from the surface of the little deformed globe, where the fusorian cells poured endless heat and light into the atmosphere. But he found himself shivering. Pyropod? Yes. He had heard the term. He did not want to recall just what he had heard about it.

Quiveras disappeared, the needle-sharp crystal blade giving a strange light. It disappeared around a bend in the passage, and then for a time there was no light at all.

Time passed.

It was dark . . . silent . . . empty. Ryeland felt as though the dead walls around him were closing in. He wiped slippery sweat from his palms, listening, reaching out, because he could not help himself, to touch the walls to make sure that they were not about to squeeze him . . . Then involuntarily he felt himself grinning. Claustrophobia —here! Billions of miles from the Earth, a floating dust mote in the middle of absolute emptiness! The incongruity reassured him; and he was calm and cheerful when, at last, he saw the glow of light appear again in the passage Quiveras had taken.

The crystal sword came into sight and Quiveras hailed him cheerfully. "A dead end, and nothing there. Very well." He drew even with Ryeland and gazed at the other passages. "I think," he said, with some doubt, "that we will leave these others for now. They do not seem occupied, and it would take us weeks to explore them all. Consider yourself fortunate, my friend. You have not yet been introduced to a pyropod."

At Quiveras's hail the spacelings came swimming gracefully down the tunnel, their red noses blinking as they probed its depths with infrared. Donna Creery followed more slowly, exploring the caves with a child's wonder and awe. "Is it safe?" she asked.

Quiveras said calmly, "We will never be safe while Ryeland's collar is with us. If you mean are we safe from pyropods, I do not know. From a full-grown one, yes. I do not guarantee there is not a cub lurking somewhere, but if there is we will find it out and meanwhile shall we not try to make this place into a home?"

They worked for three hard days, while the spacelings fluttered and mewed restlessly—because, Quiveras said without emotion, the Plan cruiser was still somewhere about. As there was nothing they could do about it, they did nothing. To their little world they did a great deal.

They carried aerial fusorian vines into the caverns, choosing cubicles for sleeping, for eating, for rest, curtaining and cushioning them with the vines, bringing shining crystals of ruby and topaz for heat and illumination. Donna cried out at its beauty. Indeed it was beautiful; and they were not finished. With Quiveras for a teacher, Ryeland learned how to weave nets and ropes out of the fiber from the vines. The surface of the reef provided crystal and great branching arms of metal, pure copper, pure aluminum, pure silver. They hammered the metal into crude tools. And finally they made a sort of curtain, woven from the vines and crusted with broken pieces of crystal, which they stretched across the mouth of the cave to conceal it.

Quiveras stood back and regarded it.

"Well," he said doubtfully, "it could be thicker and it could look more natural and those gadgets of yours could be hidden in better places. But if the Plan cruiser sniffs around here it might miss you, at that."

"Miss us? What about you?"

"I, Miss Creery, will go out to the main Reefs." Quiveras's gnarled face looked eager. "I'll get help, more spacelings. And I'll bring back Ron Donderevo!"

Ryeland and the girl were sorry to see him go, but their sorrow was nothing compared to the unhappiness of the two spacelings at being separated. Adam would carry Quiveras; Chiquita would have to stay with them, to maintain their atmosphere and to be ready to carry them away in desperate flight if the Plan cruiser should grow too inquisitive.

They watched him leave, all three of them, Ryeland, Donna Creery and the spaceling. He was gone out of sight in a moment. Ryeland thought he caught a single reddish wink from Adam's nose—perhaps the male spaceling turning restlessly as it drove away, to bid a last farewell to Chiquita. Then there was nothing. They stared till their eyes watered, but it was useless. The Plan cruiser could be lurking a mere hundred miles away—a thousand men on spacelings could be within ten miles. Without radar gear they were blind. Out there were only the stars.

Ryeland's mind drifted out among those stars wonderingly. He tried to imagine the clouds of new hydrogen, constantly being born of the Hoyle effect, and the myriad drifting fusorians that built the hydrogen into heavier elements that might someday be planets. There were other Reefs out there, the first concentrations of matter like the one they occupied, the larger ones that provided a home for the exiles of the Plan—great ones, even, that might in some remote millenium become the cores for first condensations of titanic new suns. They were all invisible.

Donna Creery touched his arm. "It's lonely," she whispered. "Let's go back inside."

"Inside our cave!" he said harshly. "Back to the stone age! Is this the sort of life that's fit for a princess of the Plan?"

She shrank away from him, and in a moment went with the spaceling silently inside the sheltering drift of vines. Ryeland roamed about, trying to work off the sudden storm of anger and helplessness that was beseiging him. He tried to calm himself.

But calm was impossible to him. Calm, he knew, was a sensation he would not be likely to feel, until he had managed to rid himself of the choking, threatening thing about his neck—and until he had managed to bridge that gap in his past, until he had escaped that dreadful, creeping cloud of forgetfulness and contradiction—

Or until the collar's explosion brought him the permanent calm of the grave.

Time passed. They both found plenty to do. Alone now, except the spaceling, they were queerly constrained in each other's company. Ryeland hardly recognized the bright, sure brat of the bath, with the angry Peace Dove and the fighting guard within instant call. Donna was quieter and younger now. They spoke of her father, and for the first time Ryeland was able to think of that semilegendary Olympian figure as a human being. Donna was terribly worried about her father. "But we *couldn't* wait for him, Steven. Only—I wish we had."

He asked her again why the Planner had had to hide from the Machine, and got the same answer he had been given before. It was no answer. "I don't know, Steven, but he was worried. And it's your equations that are the key to it." And that, of course, drove Ryeland out to stare at the banked machines he had brought with him from the rocket, but all he could do was stare. They needed space and order, and on this little reefling there was neither.

They lived like primitive islanders, catching the tiny flying things with nets made of vines, feasting on the shining fruits. Ryeland's mind was queasy at the thought of the radiation they were absorbing with every luscious bite, but his stomach was delighted. And, he thought, they were not the first to eat them and live. Perhaps the radiation was purely photonic; perhaps a sort of bioluminescence, like the green glow of a firefly.

Ryeland asked the girl again how Fleemer and his allies had got the better of her father, and got the same answer he had been given before. It was no answer. "I don't know, Steve. Except that it is all about the jetless drive. Father told me that he approved the search for an interstellar drive as part of the original Plan, built into the Machine. When he first learned about the spacelings, from Donderevo, he knew that a reactionless drive was possible. He began to organize an effort to learn how to build it. Immediately, he ran into fanatical opposition from men like Fleemer. I don't know the reason for their opposition. It must have been something more than just the desire to grab Father's place. Somehow, they were able to manipulate the Machine. They have got it under their own control. But I still believe that we could rescue the Machine and Father and the Plan of Man—if we knew the secret of the spacelings."

That, of course, drove Ryeland to begin assembling and testing the computers he had brought from the rocket. But the crawling fog was thicker in his mind. He sat staring at the banked computers, but he could think of no approach more promising than those he had tried when he was still on Fleemer's team. He couldn't be sure that the failure of the team attack was altogether due to Fleemer's sabotage.

Anyhow, he reflected, there wasn't much that he could do in his cave on this reeflet. Even if he had been given the blueprints for a perfected reactionless drive, he had no shop equipment.

Hopelessly, he gave up the effort.

Days passed. Weeks passed. The spaceling roamed sadly around their little world, still worried. They could not read its ways as Quiveras had, but its worry was plain. Was it the Plan cruiser, still skulking about? Or a nearer menace? They simply could not tell. Donna grew sulky and unhappy, until they had a brief, brittle quarrel of words one day and it exploded into weeping. She clung to him. "I'm sorry. It's just that I always had so much. Servants, clean clothes, cooked food. Power, too. And now—"

She smiled up at him. Queerly, Ryeland thrust her away then. He was churned up inside with feelings he could neither analyze nor handle. It was his turn to be sulky and irritable, because, though he did not know it, his inner self was becoming a battle ground—the site of a struggle between his common sense, on one hand, and on

131

the other a growing, potent love for the Planner's daughter . . .

Even his dreams were haunted.

He slept restlessly, and felt that he was choking . . . He was in his office, miles under the surface of the Earth in the hidden complex of air-conditioned tunnels that held the Machine and its attendants. He heard the knocking on the locked door, and got up to open it for Angela.

But it wasn't Angela.

It was Donna Creery, white-smocked like the nurses at the stock-pile. She had brought the coffee and sandwiches on a plastic tray, but she screamed and threw them on the floor when she saw his face.

"It's Donderevo!" she was screaming. "It was Ron Donderevo—"

He wanted to tell her who he was, but suddenly he was strapped to the therapy couch in the recreation center, with shocks of paralyzing agony stabbing from the electrodes on his body. She was coming toward him again, in the white smock with a stitched red heart on her perfect breast, reaching for him with a long hooked scalpel.

"You might as well tell us now." She was wheezing at him with Dr. Thrale's apologetic, asthmatic voice. "Tell us how to build a jetless drive."

He wanted to tell her. The specifications were clear in his mind, amazingly simple; he couldn't understand why there had to be so much fuss about such a simple thing. But his voice was paralyzed with the shocks that made waves of dazing pain from the collar around his neck. And Donna wouldn't let him talk.

Now she wore a horned radar helmet. She was taunting him, with Fleemer's ugly voice. *One touch, Ryeland. Only one little touch on the detonation button, and your precious secret will die with you!*

Now she had Angela's face.

But she still had hands, like Donna. He saw her touch the deadly little button. The collar about his neck blossomed and swelled—

He awoke strangling.

"I was dreaming!" He tugged frantically at the collar. No! It was no dream. The collar was there, and surely it was about to explode. His exacerbated imagination felt it pulsing against his rasped throat. He thought he heard a sound from it, a tick, a whine, a purring of faint unstoppable engines. "No!" he shouted and leaped up out of the little nest of leaves where he slept. It was exploding! Not in a year, not in a minute—*now*. He flung himself wildly about in the no-gravity, shouting.

Donna Creery came swiftly to him, and the terror in her face woke him, drowning his imaginary terrors.

"What's the matter?" he demanded harshly.

"Steven! It's Chiquita. She—she was wandering about the lower passages, where we've never been, and—" She stopped, unable to speak on. Behind her the spaceling came, slowly, painfully, mewing tragically.

Chiquita's flank was a horror, raw flesh and golden ichor, with the mark of a great sharp claw.

17

There were four cartridges in the clip. Ryeland checked them, blessed Quiveras for having left the gun and started down the passages. He didn't say anything to Donna Creery; he didn't know what to say.

Then there was a pyropod on their Reef . . .

Ryeland's throat was raw and dry. Pyropods. "Flamefeet." Outer-space animals which, Ryeland thought, sounded vaguely like Earthly squids. Ryeland tried to picture one, and failed; but Quiveras had said there was a possibility that the caverns in their Reef might house one. And Chiquita's terrible wounds had converted that possibility into something far stronger.

Ryeland paused at the end of the passages they had explored, and picked up the discarded crystal sword Quiveras had left there. It was still bright; it was all the light he had. Then he dove into the first of the great convoluted burrows.

In five minutes he was at an end; the tunnel narrowed sharply, so that he could hardly move, and poised bits of rubble showed that nothing of any size had passed that way in finite time.

He went back again. Another tunnel, a much longer one this time, but again a dead end. It was difficult to maneuver; in no-gravity, he could not walk, and the shape and constriction of the tunnel made it hard to leap.

He came to another branch and stopped.

There were two tunnels, both enormous, both dark and soundless. The air was the air the spaceling had brought, but it had a sharp strange odor, like burning gunpowder.

And one of the tunnels was scarred with the enormous claws that had left their sign near the surface.

Ryeland plunged in without giving himself time to think.

He came almost at once to a chamber. He paused and hung in its entrance, peering about in the faint light his crystal sword gave. It was roughly spherical, so vast that its farther walls were dim; and in a niche at one side of it was a clutter of tangled objects.

Warily he approached.

It seemed to be a sort of midden, and the blood began to pulse in his ears. It contained odd-shaped objects that might have resembled the bones and fangs and carapaces of animals like no animals that had ever lived on earth. He stood staring at it, every sense poised. Then, with infinite pain, he approached. There was no sound. There was no motion. Gently he poked the crystalline light into a gap in the tangle. But nothing moved and there was nothing revealed.

Ryeland moved back and considered.

Space had its own scale of time. The discarded bones and the claw-marks in the rock might look just as fresh after another hundred million years. Undoubtedly the cave had been abandoned.

He turned.

Something screamed behind him. He had only time to halt his turn, to start to move his head back.

And the heap of bones exploded.

What kept Ryeland from dying at once was the tiny scope of the cavern, compared to the scale of interplanetary distances. The pyropod, rocket driven, enormously strong, hadn't the room to maneuver or even to build up speed. But it blasted up at him with frightening speed. It was huge—as Earth animals go—larger than a horse, and armored with mirror-bright scales. It had a solitary eye, a wide mirror on a stalked central organ. It had a single, enormous claw at the end of a writhing, flexible trunk. It roared like a rocket at takeoff—which it was—and the great heavy-metal claw snapped violently.

But the trash in its way screened Ryeland for a moment; he was thrust back and out of the way, and the pyropod flew past to gouge great chips out of the wall of the cavern.

Ryeland took quick aim and fired.

Even in the roar of the pyropod's drive, he could hear his bullet scream away, and knew that it had hit that armor and ricocheted off. The pyropod did not turn to strike toward him again; it turned away, in fact, and its thin bright tail whipped toward him. White fire jetted out furiously. The tail! The tail was a more fearsome weapon than the claw—the mighty drive that could hurl it through space could char him in a second. But Ryeland was already moving, and the blast missed him entirely, though a backwash of flame from the wall caught his leg and (he discovered later) raised great angry blisters on his skin. Ryeland crashed into the wall, spun like a racing swimmer in a pool, raised the gun again and fired—rapidly—one, two, three!

And then his cartridges were gone . . .

But one of those bullets had struck a target. The stalk that held its eye was hit. The bulb exploded; the creature was blinded. It blundered about the chamber like a rocket gone mad, colliding with the walls, recoiling, plunging wildly again. The blazing jet licked perilously close—

And then the jet was screaming away, bouncing and roaring through the tunnel, out and out and away . . .

Ryeland was hurt badly, burned, bleeding, aching in every muscle; and he had no breath left at all after that quick violent encounter. But he did not pause. He leaped to follow the pyropod. Donna was up there!

He sailed through dark space, his crystal torch long since lost, tried to see through the utter dark, tried to shield his head from striking against the wall. It was good, now, that the tunnel was so narrow; there was really only one way to go.

And after interminable moments there was light.

He drove toward it, rounded a bend, and saw Donna Creery hurrying toward him—alive! She bore a coiled branch of the vine with its moons of luminous fusorians.

"Steven! Thank God!"

She tossed a loop of the vine to him: he caught it, and they drew themselves together. Ryeland caught her roughly. "The pyropod! What became of it?"

"Gone," said Donna Creery. "It went right by, out into space. Not having a nucleonic harpoon, I let it go. I think we've seen the last of it."

"It was hiding in a pile of bones," said Ryeland, suddenly drained. "I—I think I hit its eye."

135

"Yes. At least, it acted blind. And—oh, Steven!"

He looked at her, not comprehending. Reaction? He tried to reassure her. "It won't be back, Donna. You said yourself—"

"No, no. It's Chiquita, Steven. I think she's dying."

He nodded, hardly hearing. "Poor thing. Well, we've avenged her, I guess."

"And what about avenging ourselves? Have you forgotten, Steve—if Chiquita dies, there's nothing to hold our air!"

The spaceling lay motionless in a little cave lined with vines.

Now and then she struggled restlessly—not to move, but to bring fresh air about her. She seemed both bloated and gaunt. And the great wounds along her side were now crusted with dirty ocher scabs.

"Poor Chiquita," the girl whispered, stroking the soft fur. Donna crooned at the creature, and its great dull eyes fastened on her.

Ryeland looked the spaceling over. Her belly was swollen angrily, but the flesh had shrunk from the rest of her body. Her fur was lusterless and unkempt. The flame-red brilliance was gone from her nose; it was cold, black, dry. He touched her: hot. Did she have a fever? Ryeland could not know, but surely she was hotter than when he had clung to her neck, fleeing the Body Bank. The spaceling seemed to know that he was trying to help. She licked her black tongue out at him feebly; it was all the effort she could make.

Ryeland said reluctantly, "I—don't think there's anything we can do for her."

"The light seems to bother her."

"All right. That much we can do." But it wasn't easy, in this little world of luminous crystal and vine. They found some growths that glowed only faintly and tugged them into place, thicker and thicker, until the little nook where Chiquita lay became a dim green hiding-hole. Chiquita looked faintly grateful, but mostly she looked sick.

They left her and went out to the surface to look at the stars. It was maddening, it was utterly maddening, to be so helpless! Ryeland clung to the edge of the tunnel, staring out toward emptiness. Somewhere out there, invisible but sure, lay the other Reefs. The great outer Reefs where fugitive humans managed lives that were free of the

Plan—where, above all, lived Ron Donderevo, the native spaceman who had been a student of the science of the Plan, a guest and a prisoner of the Planner. He had worn the iron collar of a Risk—the selfsame collar that choked Ryeland now, if Angela had told the truth. He had talked to the Planner about a jetless drive, had been consigned to the stockpile, had ridden Chiquita back to the Reefs.

But—was he superhuman?

Could he remove Ryeland's collar—here in the reefs, without all the elaborate surgical facilities that had been available at the stockpile? Could he fill the gap in Ryeland's tormented memory—or was there really any gap to fill, except the time before the dissected scraps of a hundred salvaged enemies of the Plan had been assembled to make a thinking thing without a past?

By now Quiveras might have reached him. By now they might be on their way! Perhaps in a few days Quiveras and the stranger would come to the little Reef and look for Ryeland and the girl.

And what would they find?

Ryeland knew that the most probable answer was . . . death.

Time passed, and the spaceling stayed alive. But she was weaker and worse every day.

The Reef became a dream to Ryeland. He lost all sense of time. He had no watch and there were no celestial objects to mark days or years very conveniently. He thought of a calendar, and tried to construct one. The sun was bright enough to be visible, but the trouble was that their little Reef had no perceptible rotation. No force from another object had ever set it spinning, perhaps; the same stars hung always over the tunnel mouth. It could tell them nothing of time. Painfully Ryeland located winking Algol and began a star-watch; its period would be his clock.

Donna said gently: "It won't help. You don't know when the collar will go off."

And he realized that she had seen farther into his mind than he himself. It was the ticking year that he was trying to measure, the year which was in any event his maximum hope of life as long as that collar sat sullenly about his neck. Chiquita might not die, the Plan cruiser might not return, but his assassin was with him at every moment. At one of those moments it would strike. That was the ultimate deadly promise of the iron collar. You could flee the radar guns of the Plan Police and even outrun their

137

cruisers. You could in the Reefs of Space perhaps even avoid the wash of pulsed radar which the Machine would flood through the system. But the timing element would not be stopped and would not be merciful. In less than a year it would go off . . .

And Ryeland's guess, based on Algol's cycle and a careful recollection of how they had slept and eaten, was that no less than six months had already passed.

Chiquita was now terribly sick.

The great claw-gashes had begun to heal, but her fever was high. She seemed thirsty, but she would not drink; she seemed in pain, but she hardly moved. Only a low whimpering mew came from the little bower they had made for her.

Ryeland made a decision and went out onto the shell of their Reef to put it into practice. It was only a matter of moments before Donna followed. "What are you doing?" she demanded sharply. He stopped, caught working over the equipment the spacelings had transported from the ship for him—the equipment that he had not used and now was proposing to put to a use completely unconnected with his original intention.

He said, "How's Chiquita?" But she would not be diverted.

"What are you doing?"

Ryeland said, "Rigging up a radio. I've got all the parts. I—I thought I might be able to reach Quiveras and ask him to hurry—"

"Or maybe you thought you might reach that Plan cruiser?"

Ryeland said strongly: "All right. Why not? Maybe we pushed our luck too far! Things weren't so bad back in the B—back on Earth, I mean. The Plan of Man is reasonable. They'll take us back if I surrender, and even at worst, it can't be worse than waiting here to die."

"Steven!" She reached up to stare into his eyes. "I won't have you going back!"

"Who the devil," he yelled in a cold counterfeit of rage, "do you think you're ordering—" But she stopped his lips.

"Don't say it," she whispered. "I won't let you. And anyway, I'm afraid it's too late."

It took him a second to react. "Chiquita!"

He raced far ahead of her down to the dying spaceling. Chiquita had sunk into a sort of coma, motionless, barely breathing. Her belly was more and more misshapen, as with terminal malnutrition—or whatever might correspond to it in the structure of a creature from space—and the rest of her body as wasted as the gaunt, starved babies of Oriental famines of old times.

Ryeland reached out a hand to her—

And drew it back.

It was too late; it was all over. The spaceling had stopped breathing entirely.

Absently Ryeland brushed the dull fur on her cooling neck. Dead, yes. No matter what secrets her alien metabolism held, there was no doubt that life had gone.

And now . . . how long would the field that contained their air persist?

Ryeland had no idea. In a firefly, he remembered, the bioluminescence lingered for hours after death. Was this a related effect? Probably not. The strange force that drove the spaceling was something far removed from a mere greenish glow. It might last for a few minutes. It might—at any split second it might—disappear, and kill them instantly in a soundless explosion of released air.

Donna said softly, "Steven. Let's go outside where we can see the stars."

The Reef was a small hollowed planet, wheeling slowly now, perhaps because of some dying convulsion from Chiquita. From the mouth of the cave the whole stardusted splendor of the heavens was revealed. The sun itself, yellow and distant, came up through tangled vines to look at them, like the headlight of a far-off locomotive.

"The sun," whispered Ryeland. "Still the brightest star. We haven't come so far."

They looked out at the mighty constellations, strange in their powdery mask of lesser stars but still identifiable —mighty Orion, the misty cluster of the Pleiades, the vast silvery sweep of the galaxy. There it was, thought Ryeland soberly, the terrible, wonderful new empire that they had hoped to help claim for Man. And they had failed.

It was very strange and wonderful, but he felt almost at peace. They were still alive. It was a fact that brought with it a sense of unbounded wealth. As everything had been lost with the death of the spaceling, now each tiny moment that they were somehow spared was a treasure. Each second was a joy.

Ryeland anchored himself to a ledge of space coral, all silver and ruby, with Donna very light in his arms. They talked, not consecutively. There were things each had to say.

The one central fact—the fact that they were clinging to life by only the feeblest of grips—they did not mention.

Donna said:

"Father's probably still on Earth. He can't have got my message. He'd have followed if he did. He's a busy, a driving man, Steven, and I used to hate him, but—Oh, Steven! Now I am only sorry for him."

Ryeland said:

"You wouldn't remember. You were bathing, and I blundered in. I was embarrassed. I guess you were, too. No, you probably weren't. And you had the Peace Dove. It nearly killed—what was his name? Oporto." Cloudily it struck him as odd: he had almost forgotten the man who had been the nearest thing he had to a friend.

Donna said:

"That was Father's idea, the Peace Dove. If you hate black . . . call it white, and love it. So he took that murdering thing and called it 'Peace'. He always boasted. 'The Planner is the first ruler in all Earth's history who has never needed a bodyguard.' But what would you call those things? My Peace Doves. His Hawks."

Ryeland said, with a sudden rush of amazement:

"Donna! We're still alive!"

18

They looked at each other in wonderment, for sure enough, it was true. They had not died of air-strangulation. Around them their little world was still intact.

"But surely the spaceling was dead!" Donna cried.

"No doubt of that. I don't understand this."

They looked around anxiously. The stars blazed down on them, and that was all there was to be seen beyond the confines of the tiny air bubble that made their world.

"Look!" cried Ryeland. "Something's happening." At the edge of the reeflet, suddenly, like a vanishing ghost . . . . *puff!* There was a soundless explosion of faint, misty fog. And a colony of flying fish, a lacy pattern of vines, a clump of blossoms with liquid gold in their cups—they fluttered, shook, flung madly away; and then that corner, too, was still; but it was dead.

The shape of the bubble had changed. One corner of their little world had lost its air—*poof!*—like the winking of an eye. For one eternal moment Ryeland thought that this was what they had been waiting for. The spaceling, Chiquita, had died at last; the strange forces that allowed her to hold air about her, and them, had loosened their grasp, and they were face to face with death. Donna, who felt the abrupt clutch of fear, clung to him tightly.

But Ryeland whispered thoughtfully. "It isn't right, Donna. Something's happening, but not what we expected at all. If the field went, it should go all at once."

"But what could it be, then, Steven?"

"Let's go see!" Like biped spacelings themselves, they turned and dove into the cavern. Quickly, quickly. Crazed, confused thoughts floated through Ryeland's mind: Their dying little world . . . all worlds, dying . . . all the planets of the sun, doomed to death, doomed because Ryeland had failed to give them inertialess travel in time . . . doomed to die without giving seed to space.

They stopped, clutching at palely glowing vines.

In the very green darkness Chiquita lay. She was surely dead. There was no possibility of a mistake.

But beside her—

Beside her something moved! Beside that shrunken, lifeless skin, something quivered, curled and lifted. It came frolicking toward them, flying—something small, smaller even than Donna, a mere doll beside the dead Chiquita, racked and shrunken though she was.

It was a spaceling!

A baby spaceling! Its red nose winked swiftly; it looked at them with bright, friendly eyes. "Oh, you darling!" cried Donna, holding out her arms to it, and it licked at her face with a slim, quick, black tongue.

"Look there!" croaked Ryeland, astonished beyond words, pointing. There was another tiny, seal-like creature . . . and a third, and a fourth, and—there seemed to be a dozen of them, frolicking and darting with their tiny noses blinking comically, pink light and orange, red and almost purple.

Ryeland said softly: "Chiquita may be dead, but her children are not."

There were eight of them in all, as well as they could count their quicksilver, gamboling shapes. Eight baby spacelings, frolicking like pups. Had they been born after the death of the mother, in some reproductive mystery of the spacelings? Had they been born before, and wandered off? Ryeland could not know. He only knew that they were here.

"Thank heaven," whispered Donna, as Ryeland carried one out into the light to see it.

"Thank Something," murmured Ryeland. "Look, Donna. They're just like adult spacelings, but tiny. Born fully formed—obviously, they are able to maintain a field, able to use the jetless drive! Fortunately for us. Though," he said remembering the lost corner of their paradise, "I think they could stand a little more practice."

He stopped, looking up, jaw hanging.

Out there somewhere past the air curtain, something moved and winked.

"The Plan rocket!" cried Donna in terror.

"No! No," shouted Ryeland, leaping up. "Don't you see? It's too small too close. It's a spaceling! Quiveras has come back, and—look! There's someone else. He has brought Donderevo back with him!"

Donderevo! Six feet eight inches tall, a dark-faced man with blue eyes that blazed. His spaceling brought him daintly into the air bubble of their little haven, and Ron Donderevo sprang free. "Donna!" he cried, and caught her hand.

Joyously Donna threw her arms about him, pressing her face against his bronzed cheek. When she drew free, she said: "Ron, this is Steve Ryeland."

"I remember," Ryeland whispered breathlessly. "When I was a Technicub, about eight years old. And you were a medical student from space, wearing a collar because your people hadn't accepted the Plan—"

Chuckling, the huge man gripped his hand. Ron Donderevo's fringed leather jacket was open at the throat. His neck was a brown muscular column. A thin scar circled it, but he wore no collar.

"And I remember you," Donderevo rumbled. "I admired your father. A philosopher and a historian, as well as a mathematician. He's the scholar who helped me understand the real meaning of the space frontier."

"Your collar?" Ryeland interrupted him. "You really got out of it?"

"Out of the collar, and out of the place they call

Heaven." Donderevo nodded solemnly. "I was luckier than your father."

"I was never told what became of him."

Ryeland caught his breath to ask another question, but the sudden iron constriction of his own collar stopped him. He wanted to know how Donderevo had got away, but he was afraid to know the answer. He was afraid that Donderevo would confirm the strange story of Angela Zwick—that Ryeland was the imitation man that the anti-Plan surgeons had assembled in Donderevo's collar, to cover his escape.

"Ron?" Donna's voice was quick and quivering with concern. "Can you get Steve out of his collar?"

"Not quite the way I was taken out of mine." Ron Donderevo shook his shagged, craggy head. "Mine was removed in the surgical center at the stockpile where I had been sent for salvage. Half a dozen surgeons helped, using the best equipment—"

"What was done with your collar?" Ryeland interrupted.

"I promised not to tell," Donderevo said.

"Was a patch—?" Ryeland had to gulp and start again. "Was a patchwork man assembled in it? A kind of living dummy to take your place until the spaceling could carry you away?"

"Right." The big man nodded casually. "I don't suppose it matters to anybody now."

It mattered very much to Ryeland. His flesh turned numb and cold . . . as it must have been before it was sutured and cemented back into the likeness of a man. His knees felt weak.

"What's wrong, Steve?" Donna asked. "You look so pale!"

He couldn't tell her that he was that decoy, that patchwork of junk meat.

"I was hoping you could take my collar off," he told Donderevo. That was a matter desperate enough to account for his agitation. "If you learned medicine on Earth, can't you—can't you possibly do the operation?"

Donderevo started to shake his head, and suddenly looked hard at Ryeland's face. He glanced at Donna, and peered again at Ryeland. His own face twitched and stiffened, gray beneath the bronze.

"I suppose I could try," he admitted reluctantly. "Of course you understand that I lack the experience and the fine equipment those surgeons had. Operating here, with only a portable surgery, without trained assistants, I can promise you one chance in four that you'll survive the operation—one chance in five that you'll walk again, even if you do survive."

Ryeland fell dizzily back against a great crystal branch. Twittering iridescent bird-fish, jarred loose, swam tinkling away.

"And yet," rumbled Donderevo compassionately, "you are right, Steve, for you have no chance otherwise. The Plan can kill you in ten seconds, as easy as that. The rocket is less than three million miles away. Push a button—*poof!*—your code impulse is transmitted—you're dead. And so am I," he said earnestly, "and poor Quiveras here, and Donna. So you are right, for you see, Steven, we must save you somehow or you may kill us all."

"Describe it to me," said Ryeland emptily. "Tell me what it entails. Exactly."

Donderevo hesitated, and then began.

Ron Donderevo, that huge man, his hands soft as a maiden's, his voice deep as a tiger's growl; Ron Donderevo had performed many an operation for the Plan.

But on Earth, in the Body Bank, he said with meticulous care, there were things that could not be duplicated here. There were nurses and surgeons beyond counting. (Here was only young Donna and old Quiveras, neither of them trained.) There was equipment by the warehouseful. Here was only what had been packed in on the back of spacelings. Enough, yes—if nothing went wrong. But there were no extras. If a blood pump should fail, there was no other. There in the Body Bank was the unmatched reservoir of human parts that constituted a reserve against spoilage. And here were only the four of them, and no more parts than they needed to go around.

The first step, he said, would be to create an atmosphere of asepsis around the anesthetized Ryeland. Easy enough, particularly in the negligible gravity of the spaceling's bubble, and particularly where the only ambient germs were those the four of them had brought in. A soft hissing from a yellowish metal tube Donderevo had brought—he demonstrated it—accounted for a polyantibiotic spray.

Then—scalpels, retractors, sutures, clamps. Sterile and inherently inhospitable to microscopic life, they came out of the gleaming containers at Donderevo's orders. Donna was whitefaced but steady as she listened and looked at the instruments. She shrank away as he described how

144

the first scalpel would trace a thin red line around Ryeland's neck, just under the collar; but then she was all
right.

The epidermis and dermis would have to be slit and
pulled back, like a stocking from a leg. Red flesh and
white muscle would swiftly be cut and retracted. The great
trapezius muscles would have to be cut, caught and held—
it was important that muscles be kept under tension. The
small blood vessels of the neck needed to be tied off; the
large ones—the carotids, the jugular, the vertebral blood
supply—were to be cut and quickly clamped to the plastic
tubes of a double-chambered mechanical heart—not because Ryeland's own heart was out of circuit, yet, but
because there was blood loss, constantly, from every vessel
and uncountable capillary, from the disturbed cells themselves. Extra reserves of blood were needed and held in
the mechanical heart's chambers, for a man's own heart
was not equal to the task.

Then the nerves, carefully dissected out and clamped
to the wondrous organic silver leads that alone had made
major replacement of parts possible. Nervous tissue does
not readily regenerate in the higher vertebrates—not without help. Organic silver is the solder that holds the parts
together; organic silver in the form of braided wire strands
is the "connection" that permits the extension of a nerve,
so that performance is not lost during surgery. As the
cervical ganglia were cut, great sections of Ryeland's body
would convulse quiveringly.

Then the bones. Sonic saws to slice into the third cervical vertebra. The spinal cord—opened, sealed, tied. The
fluid dammed inside its chamber—

"That's enough," interrupted Ryeland, his face frozen
into a mask. "I get the picture. I don't need any more."
His eyes sought Donna's, and he tried to speak to her . . .
but could not. "Go ahead," he said. "Operate!"

He stepped forward, swung himself onto the operating
cradle and lay patiently while Donderevo and Quiveras
strapped him in. Then Donderevo nodded and Donna
moved forward, her face trembling on the verge of repressed tears, in her hand the soft flexible mask that sealed
his lips and plugged his nostrils. He moved his head aside
quickly. "Good-by, my dearest," he whispered. "For a
while." Then he allowed her to fit the mask.

Crashing, crashing, the crystal trees swam down on him.

The little reeflet folded into a bud, with himself in the heart of it like the pure liquid gold in the cup of one of its strange flowers . . .

And he was unconscious.

19

He was unconscious. But his mind was racing on.

He was dreaming. He was remembering. The haunting fog came swirling up out of the past. It had followed him all the way from Earth. It was all around him now, cold and silent and clinging. It covered Donna and Ron Donderevo, and distorted them. Everything changed, twisted into hopeless contradiction.

He was no longer in the portable surgery. Now the straps that held him were those of the therapy couch in the recreation center. The people over him were Dr. Thrale and General Fleemer.

"Tell us, Ryeland," Thrale's soft insistent voice was wheezing. "We know about the knocking on the door, after the teletype girl left your office to bring sandwiches and coffee. We know you left the papers on your desk and went to open the door. Tell us who came in."

Suddenly, he knew.

Somehow, the anesthetic had cleared away that clinging fog. It wasn't Angela Zwick! It wasn't even the Plan Police —they really hadn't come until the following Monday. It was a thin man in a blood-spotted fatigue uniform, bent under the bulging weight of a soiled space bag.

"Horrocks—"

"Shhh!"

Ryeland let him into the room and locked the door again. Horrocks dropped the space bag and stood leaning on the desk. He was panting heavily. Droplets of red foam sprayed out of his mouth and spattered over the sheafs of yellow teletape on the desk.

"You're hurt," Ryeland said. "Let me get a doctor."

"That can wait," Dan Horrocks gasped. "I've got a message for you—that's got more priority. From an old— friend of yours."

Ryeland helped him into a chair and listened to the mes-

146

sage. It came in gasped words that were sometimes incoherent. The old friend was Ron Donderevo. Horrocks had met him at a tiny colony on an uncharted asteroid twenty billion miles outside the Plan, when Colonel Lescure's ship had stopped there to pick up reaction mass.

The message itself took a long time for the stricken man to deliver, and longer still for Ryeland to grasp. It began with the existence of the Reefs of Space and the fusorian life that had built them. The point of it was the way the spacelings flew.

"Donderevo wants you to know space isn't dead," Horrocks panted hoarsely. "A living frontier—alive and infinite. Rockets can't—can't reach it usefully. We've got to have—propulsion—with no reaction mass."

In the dream he tried to tell the wounded man that any sort of jetless drive was forbidden by the Third Law of Motion.

"Wrong—" the wounded man interrupted him. "Spacelings—fly! Donderevo said—tell you that. All you need to know. Except the fact—your father taught him. The historic effect—effect of the free front—"

Horrocks coughed, spraying Ryeland with flecks of red.

"Sorry!" he gasped. "Mean frontier. Closed frontier—closed society. That's the Plan." He paused to cough again, turning painfully away from Ryeland. "Open frontier—that's the reefs. Freedom. Forever!"

Ryeland needed time to understand that agonized summary of a fundamental fact, but later, when he began to grasp it, he thought he knew what had happened to his father. The Plan existed to regiment the closed society that had spread to the last frontier that rockets could reach. His father had seen the infinite promise of the new frontier of interstellar space—but even a dream of that open frontier was treason to the closed world of the Plan.

"Donderevo knows Planner—Creery," Horrocks finished faintly. "Thinks we can trust—trust him to understand—that man is more—important than the Plan. If we can show him a working drive. But he says—he says trust—nobody—nobody else."

Even after his message was delivered, Horrocks didn't want a doctor. He let Ryeland give him a eubiotic emergency shot from the survival kit that he had stolen from the *Cristobal Colon,* and hid in the rest room across the corridor before Angela Zwick came back with the sand-

147

wiches and coffee. By the time Ryeland had got rid of her, Horrocks was gone.

The message was unbelievable—but Horrocks had left the red-spattered space bag. Ryeland dumped it on his desk, and shivered with wonder. There was a great, glowing octahedral crystal of carbon coral. There were dazzling stereos of reefs and pyropods and spacelings. There was a notebook of Ron Donderevo's observations, proving that the spacelings really flew without reaction.

Forced to believe, Ryeland's mind reacted. As Donderevo had told Horrocks to tell him, all he needed to know was the fact that the spacelings flew. With that simple datum actually accepted, the rest was obvious.

As a mathematician, he knew that equations had to balance. As a physicist, however, he had learned that the balancing quantity might be physically elusive. The neutrino, required to balance the equations of a nuclear reaction, was one such example. In his own equations of mass-creation and space-expansion, which described the Hoyle effect, the new mass equalled x — an unknown quantity, more elusive than even the neutrino, which he had failed to identify in nature.

But now he saw it. Printed in the simple fact of the spaceling's flight, it was plain as the fact that two plus two is four. The unknown quantity which equalled the new mass in his equations was at last identified.

It was momentum! The momentum of the expanding universe, which ultimately pushed the receding galaxies beyond the velocity of light!

With a professional satisfaction, he noted that the Third Law of Motion had not been violated. It had simply been transformed. The kinetic energy of the flying spaceling was balanced by a precisely equivalent energy of new mass. The reaction was governed by the classical equation of energy and mass, $E = mc^2$. The enormous last factor, the squared velocity of light, meant that a tiny mass was the equivalent of enormous kinetic energy. That was what had made his x so hard to identify. On its longest jetless flight, a spaceling would add only an imperceptible breath of new hydrogen to the cloud of atoms that its own motion had created.

Locked alone in his office, Ryeland went to work. A surging elation had swept away all his fatigue, and even the fear that Horrocks had brought. That single substitution of momentum for the unknown quanity in his own cosmological equations had given him the theory. A simple transformation described the field conditions required for the creation of new mass and the equivalent momentum. The problems of material and design were more troublesome, but by Sunday noon he had set up the complete specifications for a reactionless propulsion system with an effective thrust of half a million tons.

Suddenly hungry and groggy, he stumbled across the hushed dimness of the tunnel to wash his face in the laboratory that had not been scrubbed since Horrocks had sprayed the basin with blood. He ate the last dry beef algae sandwich, and the last bitter drops of cold yeast coffee and went to sleep in his chair, wondering dully how to go about reaching Planner Creery without trusting anybody else.

He woke early Monday morning with a stiff neck and the fading recollection of a nightmare in which he had been running with Horrocks from the Plan Police. He hid the space bag behind a filing cabinet, stuffed the blood-sprayed teletapes into the incinerator, and packed his specifications and the stereos in his briefcase.

Two hours before the time for Angela and Oporto to come, he hurried away, into the maze of gray-walled tunnels that housed all the linked computers of the Planning Machine and the working quarters of the Planner's staff.

Trust nobody . . .

The tunnels were dim and empty. Cool air roared here and there from the ducts. The Monday morning white-collar rush hadn't begun, but now and then he met a maintenance man in gray overalls. It was strange to think of the solid miles of Earth above, when he had the key to the stars in his hands.

Through he had never been to the Planner's office, he knew the way. Outside the automatic elevator, a guard looked at him sharply and waved him on past the warning sign: RESTRICTED! RISKS REQUIRE ESCORT BEYOND THIS POINT.

He was not a Risk. He wore no security collar.

Outside the Planner's suite, another guard studied his badge and tapped the number into a teletype. Waiting for the Machine to answer, Ryeland held his breath. But the guard looked up from the clattering machine, with a reluctant respect easing his official frown.

"Go in, sir."

A teletype girl in the waiting room wanted to know his

business. He informed her that he had a confidential report for Planner Creery. She wanted to know the nature of it. When he insisted that it was too confidential for any ears except the Planner's, she made an appointment for him to see an executive associate.

The executive associate was a huge, blue-faced frog of a man. A polished wood slab on his desk was impressively lettered: *General Rudolph Fleemer*. His bulging eyes were sharp, with a quick curiosity about Ryeland's confidential report.

Unfortunately, Planner Creery had not returned from a weekend cruise with his family. He would doubtless be in his office later in the week, but even then pressure of accumulated work would be extreme. Although Planner Creery was well aware that Ryeland's distinguished achievements in helical field engineering had been useful to the Plan, the extent of his duties forced him to delegate most responsibilities to subordinates. General Fleemer implied that people who refused to trust the Planner's associates were seldom able to see the Planner himself.

Reluctantly, when he saw that he could do no better, Ryeland left a message stating that his business involved Ron Donderevo and a new space propulsion system. General Fleemer promised sullenly to signal him later in the week, if Planner Creery chose to see him.

Noon had passed before Ryeland got back to his office. If Oporto and the teletype girl had come to work, he saw no sign of them. The blood-spattered space bag was still in place behind the filing cabinet, and a long yellow strip of teletape from the untended machine was piling up on the floor. He locked the office door and looked around for a place to hide his specifications for the jetless drive.

There was no space behind his reference books. The gap between the filing cabinet and the wall was already dangerously conspicuous. His desk had no drawers. In fact, he reflected, there was no room in the Plan for personal secrets or private documents. He found no hiding place—none better than his memory.

He was dropping the specifications into the incinerator slot, when he heard the loud impatient knocking on his door . . .

Again in the dream he was an unwilling guest in the deeply buried recreation center. The suites on both sides of him were occupied by disloyal surgeons who had been trapped in some plot against the Plan. The therapy room

150

down the tunnel held the unplanned thing that they had assembled from scraps of waste tissue, which raved insanely in its straps and bandages while it was alive.

Then the surgeons were gone. There was only Horrocks, in the next suite, and Oporto in the one across the corridor. He was seldom aware even of them, because the stewards kept him most of the time in the therapy room where the junk man had died.

He was strapped to the couch, with the iron collar on his neck and electrodes clamped to his shivering flesh. Merciless light blazed down on his face. The white-smocked fat therapist stood over him, wheezing questions in a soft apologetic voice.

What was the message that Horrocks had brought him from Ron Donderevo? Where were fusorians and pyropods and spacelings? What was the way to build a jetless drive?

At first he could have answered, but a burning shock from the collar paralyzed his voice whenever he tried to speak. Even when he was utterly broken, abjectly willing to trust anybody with what he knew, they wouldn't let him say a word. They gave him no chance to understand, left him no will even to dream of escape.

Donderevo? Reefs of space? Jetless drive?

The soft insistent voice and the agony went on, until all his past was lost in a fog of pain and insane contradiction. Even when the collar didn't shock him, he didn't try to speak. He didn't even try to think of the answer. His mind had been erased.

20

Ryeland awoke, blinking against a glare of light and found a man in white bending over him.

It took him a long time to understand that it was not Dr. Thrale, but Donderevo; longer still to realize that the crystal glint and glowing color of the cave was right and natural, so sure he had been that he would find himself in the aseptic white of the therapy room. He was in the operating cradle. The straps on his body had been loosened. Things began to click into place. There was Donderevo, yes, and the girl with her back to him undoubtedly was Donna Creery, and the other figure—

He sat up involuntarily, eyes wide. For the third figure in the room was not Quiveras. It was a Technicorps officer, watching him with the calculation of a poised cobra.

With a sudden spasm of desperate hope and fear Ryeland's hands came up to his neck.

They touched the familiar hard curve of the collar. He still wore it. He was still a Risk, his life hanging on the whim of every guard with a radar pistol or on the flipover of a relay in the distant synapses of the Machine.

"What—" For a moment his voice was paralyzed, still half in the dream, remembering the violence of the shocks that had conditioned him not to speak the truths he knew. But he fought to get words out: "What went wrong?"

Donderevo said compassionately, "We were too late. Before we had more than started the spacelings let us know the Plan cruiser was nearby. It breached the bubble around this reeflet. We sewed you up, and now we are all back in the Plan of Man." Unconsciously his hand touched the scar on his own throat. "I'm sorry about your collar, Ryeland," he said, "but if I'm not mistaken it will be no long time before I'm once more wearing one of my own."

The nurse turned, and Ryeland had his third shock. For it was not Donna. "Where is she?" he demanded.

"Safe," rumbled Donderevo. "Or as safe as any one under the Plan. Her father was in the cruiser. She's with him now."

"May I—" Ryeland had to stop and gulp, because a memory of agony had paralyzed his throat. "May I see them?"

"I'll tell them you're awake," Donderevo said. He moved toward the doorway, and turned back with a hesitant expression. "I had better warn you that you can't expect much help from Creery. You see, he's not the Planner any longer. In fact, he's wearing a collar of his own."

Ryeland was sitting on the edge of the portable cradle with a sheet wrapped around him, when Donna brought her father into that crystal-lighted cave of space. Though the former Planner was smiling tenderly at his daughter, his face looked pinched and gray. He wore the thin denim of a Risk. The chrome-steel collar shimmered with reflected crystal glints.

Two officious men followed Creery. One was a stocky

Technicorps colonel, who looked bleakly Satanic with his radar horns. The other was a communications sergeant, with a gray-cased portable teleset slung to his body.

Donna nervously repeated what Donderevo had already told Ryeland about her father's arrival.

"I was hoping," she finished wistfully, "that Father could unlock your collar."

"Not even my own." Creery's stiff smile faded. "You can see that things have changed. Our old friend General Fleemer is acting Planner now. I have been reclassified, and assigned to this hazardous special mission." He glanced uncomfortably back at the colonel.

Donna's face twitched. She whispered, "What's your special mission, Father?"

"It is concerned with the Plan of Man," he said. "You see, since the Machine has been reliably informed of the limitless extent of the Reefs of Space, it has been projecting a new phase of the Plan. In this second phase, the abundant resources of the space frontier will end any need for the strict regimentation of the original Plan. Unfortunately, this second phase cannot begin until the new frontier is actually open to the masses of mankind. Obviously, that requires a reactionless space drive."

The former Planner paused. His haggard eyes looked sharply at Donderevo, regretfully at Ryeland, blankly at the Technicorps colonel.

"General Fleemer managed to convince the Machine that I was no longer competent," he said. "I suppose you know about the numerous failures of the helical field equipment that you had designed." His dull stare came back to Ryeland. "Fleemer laid all those disasters at my feet. As a result of such apparent executive errors, I was replaced.

"I insisted on one last chance to find a reactionless drive. I had enough power left so that Fleemer was unable to block the assignment. That's my mission now. I saw the spacelings that came out to meet the cruiser. I must learn how they fly!"

His voice was hopeless.

"If Ryeland couldn't find the answer," Donderevo said, "I doubt that it exists."

"But—I found it!"

The collar was very tight. For a moment Ryeland's throat was paralyzed again. The old fog of agony and con-

153

tradiction thickened in his mind. He looked at the man and at Donna. Her smile was sunshine, clearing the fog.

He remembered. He could speak.

He explained his theory of the equivalence of momentum and new mass, which related the flight of the spacelings to the expansion of the universe. He recited the specifications that he had memorized before the Plan Police burst into his office on that lost Monday.

The colonel watched, a skeptical Satan, while they discussed the design and dictated the specifications to the sergeant at the portable teleset. They waited, while the message was digested by the special section of the Planning Machine aboard the cruiser.

Time passed—while slow radio pulsed the message to Earth.

Ryeland looked at Donna Creery's anxious face—and remembered the bandaged patchwork man who had raved and died in the therapy room down the tunnel from his suite in the recreation center.

Then he himself was not the junk man!

That part of Angela's story had been a malicious lie!

The teleset clattered.

Ryeland crowded with the former Planner and Donderevo and the girl to read the tape. Officiously, the colonel waved them back. He peered at the tape, and reached to finger the buttons of his radar gear.

But his expression changed.

"I knew it, Mr. Planner." His voice was suddenly smoothly affable. "I knew that Fleemer was nothing better than a conniving traitor, who will certainly get his comeuppance now! Any man with a spark of wit knew that jetless flight had to come."

Grinning, he offered his hand to Creery.

"I want to be the first to congratulate you, Mr. Planner. And you, too, Mr. Ryeland. The special section of the Planning Machine in the cruiser has completed its preliminary evaluation of your invention.

"It has relayed a message to the master complex of the Machine on Earth, alerting it to prepare the Plan of Man for transition to the second phase, in which the freedom of the space frontier will render our present strict security controls both impossible and unnecessary.

"As a first step toward the effectuation of that second phase, it is propagating a radar pulse—"

Ryeland heard a click at this throat.

154

His collar snapped open.

As if moved by the same pulse, the girl stepped forward and into his arms. Together they moved out of the cave into the faerie shimmer of the reeflet. To one side hung the great gray mass of the Plan cruiser, no longer an enemy. Beyond lay the stars.

The stars. The limitless frontier for mankind—the space between suns, where hydrogen is constantly born to make new worlds, as freedom is constantly born in the hearts of men.

"A billion billion new worlds," whispered Ryeland.

And the girl said firmly: "Our children will see them all."

STARCHILD

1

It was the day, the hour, and the moment of Earth's vernal equinox . . . and the near stars blinked.

A dozen of them flickered at once. Blazing Sirius and its dense dwarf sister. The bright yellow twins of Alpha Centauri. Faint red Proxima . . . the distant sparks of Eta Eridani and 70 Ophiuchi A . . . the bright Sun itself.

The vast cosmic engines declared a vacation in their processes: the fusion of smaller atoms into large, the flow of surplus mass into energy, the filtration of that energy through layered seas of restless gas, the radiation of their atomic power into space.

By the shores of Earth's oceans, within the crater walls of Luna, on the sands of Mars and the ringed satellites of Saturn, out past the Spacewall to the Reefs, the great billion-headed human race stirred and shook and knew fear. The whisper spread out into the galaxy, propagated at the speed of light: *"The Starchild!"*

That was the way it began.

The flickering of the neighbor stars lasted only a moment, and it was seen first on the Reefs nearest each star.

157

Then slow Pluto caught the twinkle of 70 Ophiuchi A while Neptune, lumbering in its dark orbit on the far side of Sol, was the first to catch the dimming of white-hot Sirius. On Earth, where the fat old Planner sat chuckling on his golden chair, every momentary pulse of darkness arrived at once. His chuckles stopped. His pouchy face darkened. As his astronomers reported in, he exploded in wrath.

His first reports came from a hardened station in the zone of twilight on the planet Mercury, where sliding concrete doors uncovered a pit beneath a saw-toothed crater rim.

A silvered dome pushed out of the pit, out of the ragged shadow, into the white blaze of the near sun. The barrels of a dozen optical and radio telescopes, pyrometers, telescanners, and cameras thrust out at the great orb, under the blazoned slogan that the dome displayed to the universe in letters of cast bronze:

THE MIGHTIEST REWARDS
THE MOST FAITHFUL

And inside the insulated, refrigerated observatory, three astronomers watched a thousand boards and gauges and dials. They were waiting.

For they had been warned.

The senior officer on duty lifted his eyes from a chronometer dial and growled, "Five minutes!"

The other two men squinted at their instruments in silence. The grizzled Technicaptain peered at them through the pale lighting of the screen that dominated the glitter of instruments. On it swam the visual image of the sun, golden and engorged, reaching out with fat, slow tendrils or superheated gas as it lay above the rock-fanged horizon of the planet Mercury.

"Yeah," he grumbled, half to himself. "We're ready."

The junior member of the team was a lean young Technicadet, an ambitious young man already embittered by the harsh facts of survival and promotion in the Technicorps. He dared a comment: "Ready for nothing, if you ask me. This is idiot business!"

The senior officer rolled a yellowed eye toward him, but said nothing.

"So?" murmured the third man. He was a plump little Techtenant who had found a satisfying philosophy in his recent promotion. "The Machine's business is idiotic, then?"

"Now, look! I didn't mean—"

"No. But you didn't think, either. The Machine discerns the greater plan; we only execute the parts. If the Machine attaches importance to this fanciful creature, the Starchild, then we may not question its motives."

The Technicadet gestured at the huge solar globe angrily and cried, "Look! What could put *that* out?"

The Techtenant shrugged, and the senior officer said only, "Four minutes."

The cadet's military courtesy was worn thin under the abrasion of their long, tense vigil. He scowled at his telemetering pyrometers and grumbled, "Not a flicker! We've been here three miserable weeks, and we haven't seen a thing."

The Technicaptain rumbled, "We'll stay here three years if the Machine orders it. The Machine is above injustice or error. The Machine was built to rule the Plan, and it is guarded against human blunders."

"Oh, yes, sir. But we've seen nothing at all," cried the Technicadet. "No Starchild. No major sunspots—or whatever it is we are supposed to expect."

"Practice patience," advised the fat captain. "Or you may find yourself serving the Plan more personally. There is always a need for spare parts in the Body Bank! Three minutes."

The Technicadet subsided grudgingly apologetic. All three men sat strapped in their observation chairs, watching the great golden image of the sun. Wreathed in its red coronal streamers, pocked in its middle latitudes with a trail of small black spots, it hung over the black horizon like a god's eye. The instruments around them clicked and murmured.

"I remember," the Techtenant said at last, as if to himself, "when that Sun was only another star in the sky. No brighter even than great Vega."

The Technicadet cried eagerly, "You were out in the Reefs?"

"Two minutes," growled the captain, but his eyes were on the young Techtenant.

He nodded. "Looking for my sister's . . . boy friend?

159

Fiance? Looking for Boysie Gann. Because he was looking for the Starchild. And we didn't find either of them."

The cadet said simply, "I've never seen the Reefs."

"A beautiful thing," said the Techtenant. "There are spiked forests of silicon plants, shining with their own light. Like jewels, and sharp enough to shred your space-suit. There's a growth that makes great brain-shaped masses of pure silver. There are thick stalks of platinum and gold, and there are things like flowers that are diamonds."

The cadet's breathing was suddenly loud. The grizzled old captain turned to look at him, all his recent scorn now frozen into longing—and a sort of fear. He snapped: "Pay attention to your work, man! The Reefs are dangerous business!"

"Yes, sir," the Techtenant agreed earnestly. "I saw a great beast like a nightmare, shaped like a scorpion, huge as a horse—"

"No, you fool! Dangerous to the Plan of Man. There is something there that nearly destroyed us once. If the Starchild has his way—"

He stopped himself and said only, "One minute."

The Techtenant reddened. "I'm sorry, sir. I certainly did not intend to seem unplanned. I don't mean to suggest that those savage nomads beyond the Spacewall are worth con-sidering, even if they do believe the Starchild to be more than human."

"Tend your instruments!" The captain set the example, resolutely taking his eyes from the men and the screen, clamping them on the bank of gauges and dials before him. A vagrant thought stirred his mind of the blond Together-ness girl who had first whispered the name of the Starchild to him. What had become of her? The Body Bank?

—But there was no time for that. It was only seconds now.

In spite of all the insulation and the cold air sighing from the vents, the dome was suddenly stifling. The cap-tain felt a trickle of perspiration running down his sides. "Twenty seconds!"

The captain stood with his eyes frozen on the black chronometer needle that raced to meet the red, still one he had set. When they touched it would be the vernal equinox on Earth. And the Starchild's threat would be proved an empty bluff . . . or would not.

Suddenly the whisper of the instruments changed. A camera shutter began clicking gently.

160

"Ten seconds!"

The shielded floor lamps shut themselves off. Only the instrument lights rivaled the phosphor glow from the image of the great yellow sun in the screen.

"Five seconds! . . . Four! . . . Three! . . ."

Twenty reels of tape began to spin shrilly in the darkness; the breathing of the men was like sobs.

"Two! . . . One! . . .

"Zero!"

The captain gulped and rubbed his eyes.

There was a dimming. Then the filters went down, and then there was a burst of flame—then darkness.

The lights were gone. All of them. The Sun's image had winked out. He heard a gasp from one of the other men, then a shout. "The Starchild! He's done it!"

And the other man sobbed, "We're blind!"

That, too, was how it began. But there was more.

Like a ripple from a pebble dropped into a still pond, a wave of darkness spread out from the sun. Three minutes after the instant of the vernal equinox it reached that clucking camera in the dome on Mercury, unseen by those sightless eyes.

In not quite three more minutes, it struck the men watching from the orbital stations above the eternal hot, dank clouds of Venus. A falling shadow of fear, it darkened their screens, whitened their faces, silenced their talk. But their instrument lights remained visible. They had not been blinded by that last great burst of light from the Sun.

Eight minutes from the Sun, the wave of blackness washed over Earth. All across the sunward face of the planet a crushing night came down. Bewildered, men paused and fumbled through the endless seconds before the city lights came on. Terror electrified those who had heard the whisper of the Starchild's threat. On the dark side of Earth and on Luna, astronomers blenched as their near, familiar stars flickered. Some had heard whispers of the Starchild too, and of a Writ of Liberation. Others merely knew that the images in their great spaceborne mirrors, or in the scopes that peered up from Earth's highest mountains, suddenly were missing familiar points of light.

They came back . . .

But the Sun did not. Not then. Not for half an hour and more, and while it was gone there was panic.

To the Planner on his great golden chair the news came and quenched his chuckling good humor. His huge soft face turned pale with fear.

To a man named Boysie Gann, locked in the dungeons of the Machine, no word came—but he knew. For he heard a guard whisper to another, *"The Starchild!"*

To a girl with haunted dark eyes, telling whispering sonic beads before a console of the Machine, the word came in a language that Man had not invented, and few men could understand. Her name was Delta Four, and she did not fear. She did not care at all. . . .

And that was how it began for them, and the wave of darkness raced on into infinite space.

Twelve minutes from the Sun it swept Mars, halting the dedication of an enormous new project to extract oxygen and water from the dead crust of the planet. The Deputy Planner of Mars, a poorly planned individual who had seen the Writ of Liberation with his own eyes, snatched a gun from his honor guard and shot himself.

During the following quarter hour that shadow bathed the asteroids, terrified a few, left others unconcerned. For either they did not know, being buried in the mining shafts that hollowed out the precious cores of the tiny planets, or they were so dazed and uncaring with the eternal hardship of their toil that nothing could frighten them again.

The racing wave of light overtook the scattered outposts of the Plan on the Moons of Jupiter. It darkened Saturn's rings, swallowed the satellites of Uranus and Neptune. It fell upon the Spacewall Command complex on distant Pluto, where only those whose eyes fell upon the Sun by chance noticed it—but they were afraid.

It drowned the Spacewall itself—more web than wall, a net of far-scattered stations whose laser beams and patrol craft kept watch on the little-known infinities beyond, alert to guard the Plan of Man against vagrants from the Reefs, or such enemies as the Starchild.

A wave of unexpected terror, it sent the crews of a thousand slow-wheeling spaceforts shouting to their emergency stations. It awakened sirens and horns on ten thousand lonely patrol ships. It set the laser beams winking with a million signals of confused alarm.

A day or so beyond Pluto it washed the frontiers of the solar system, the snowball protoplanets of solid methane and ammonia that the distant gravitational arms of the Sun had never gathered into actual worlds.

162

And then at last, days beyond that last fearful outpost of the Plan, it began to bathe the Reefs of Space.

Out on the reefs, those living asteroids grown through unending ages by the minute fusorian organisms, feeding on the thin seas of interstellar hydrogen, the wave of shadow no longer meant terror. It was only another event in a life that was filled with danger and surprise.

On one lonely worldlet a prospector stopped to peer in annoyance at where the Sun had been. He fumbled in his pack for a luminous crystal of fusorian diamond, and bent over his drill again.

On another reef a lay preacher in the Church of the Star glanced at his watch, then at the sky. He was not afraid when he saw that Sol was gone from its accustomed position. He had been expecting it.

He left his work to face the blue blaze of Deneb, knelt, whispered a few words of supplication and thanksgiving. Calmly then he bent back to the unfinished space boot on his last, for he was by trade a cobbler.

The shadow washed over a grave, but no one saw it. No one could have, for no one was there. Not even the cadaver; the grave was empty.

The shadow rested lightly on a city of stern, hardfaced refugees from the Plan of Man—on a great cluster of reeflets where a mighty space armada was being fashioned from fusorian steel—on a girl named Quarla Snow, who stood watching it flicker out with tears bright in her eyes.

On another living rock, a herdsman stood guarding a calving member of his herd from a flight of marauding pyropods. Lying behind a sheltering ledge of organic iron, one eye on his parturient spaceling while he searched out the armored killers with frugal flashes from his laser gun, he failed to notice that the Sun had gone out.

That was how it began, for every man, woman and child alive.

And thirty-nine minutes later the Sun began again its mighty outpouring of heat and light, but the wave of brilliance that followed the dark looked down on a changed solar system.

The Sun's atomic engines ran again. Hydrogen fused into helium through the carbon cycle. Filtered energy flowed toward the solar surface. Radiation poured into space.

Three minutes from the Sun, the wave of radiation

crashed against that insulated dome on Mercury. It was recorded by the clucking camera, analyzed by the thousand automatic instruments. Sobbing with joy—or fear! —the blinded astronomers flashed the word to Earth: *The Sun lives again!*

But its light reached Earth before their message.

That first rebirth of light brushed a high mountain on Earth, where the Planner sat on his golden chair, the gray metal falcon that perched on his shoulder darting a red-eyed glare about the room, whirring its steel wings. The Planner was staring at a sheet of creamy parchment that bore the heading:

WRIT OF LIBERATION

It had been delivered to him by the hand of one of his own guards, who had found it at his door. It said:

> The Starchild requires the release of all of his followers who are held in the service of the Plan of Man by security collars.
>
> The Starchild requires that all of his followers who have been consigned to the Body Bank for salvage shall be restored to their original state, and then that they too shall be released.
>
> The Starchild finally requires that the barrier called the Spacewall shall be dismantled, and that free passage between the worlds of the Plan and the Reefs of Space shall be permitted.
>
> The Starchild is aware that the Plan of Man considers itself invulnerable, and thus he has arranged a warning demonstration. At the moment of the vernal equinox on Earth the Sun will be extinguished. Twelve near stars will blink.
>
> If the Planner fails to meet the Starchild's requirements after this demonstration, further measures will be taken. These will result in the destruction of the Plan of Man.

"Unplanned nonsense," groaned the Planner. "Impudence! Treason!"

A tall Technicolonel said uneasily, "Sir. We must take measures—"

"Measures," grumbled the Planner while his steel falcon clashed its pinions. "What does the Machine say?"

164

A girl in a hooded gown said, "No data, sir." Her voice was like distant music, her expression serene.

"No data! Find me some data! Find who this Starchild is! Tell me how he did this thing—and how I can stop him from doing it again!"

The Technicolonel coughed. "Sir, for some years we have had reports of a Church of the Star. A new religion, apparently springing from the Reefs—"

"Always the Reefs! They should have been destroyed twenty years ago!"

"Yes, sir. But they were not. And the pioneers—that is, sir, the tramps and vagabonds on the Reefs—they invented new superstitions. They worship, I believe, the star Deneb. Alpha Cygni—the star at the top of the Northern Cross. They have imagined a paradise on the planets that they imagine to orbit around it. They wish to migrate there, or some of them do—though at maximum drive for conventional spacecraft," he continued earnestly, "they might average some one per cent of the speed of light, in which case Deneb, at four hundred light-years distance, would not be reached for forty thousand—"

"Get to the point!" cried the Planner fretfully. "What about the Starchild?"

"Well, sir we had heard rumors of such a person in our investigations of this cult. Some time ago we decided to send a . . . uh . . . a special investigator to secure intelligence concerning him and it. The investigator's name was Boysie Gann, sir, and—"

"Bring him to me! Is he here on Earth?"

"Yes, sir. But . . . well, sir, he did not return as we expected. In fact"—the Colonel's face was a picture puzzle of confusion—"I *must confess,* sir, that we don't properly know how he *did* return, as—"

"Fool!" shouted the Planner. "Bring him to me! Never mind what you don't know. Bring me Boysie Gann!"

And that too was how it began; but in fact, some parts of it began earlier.

For Boysie Gann it began many months earlier, when he was a spy.

2

For Boysie Gann the beginning was on Polaris Station, that great metal wheel that floats in the icy space past Pluto, one link in the Spacewall between the Plan of Man planets and the Reefs.

Boysie Gann was twenty-six years old and already a Machine Major.

Boysie Gann was six feet tall, brown-haired, blue-eyed. He was broad through the shoulders and slim at the waist. He moved like a cheerful cat. He looked like a fighter, and he was.

He reported aboard the Polaris Station with a grin and a disarming look out of his bright blue eyes. "Boysie Gann reporting, sir," he told the deck officer. "Technicadet Gann, at your service." And that was a cheerful lie. He was no cadet, but at the spy school on Pluto the briefing officers had given him a new rank to make his job easier. A Machine Major was a man of importance. He would be watched. A cadet could go anywhere, see anything.

The deck officer assigned him quarters, procured him help in stowing his gear, shook his hand to welcome him aboard, and ordered him to report to the commandant of the Station, Machine Colonel Mohammed Zafar.

Gann's assignment was to investigate rumors of strange anti-Plan activities on the Polaris Station. Gann was a soldier of the Plan, and he could hardly conceive of anything anti-Plan that was not at the same time corrupt, slovenly, evil, and wrong. He had come to the station expecting to find it rundown and rusty, manned by surly malcontents.

Yet the discipline was good. The men were on their toes. On the way through the plastic passages of the wheel, stepping high in the light gravity of the station's spin, he saw that the metalwork was bright. Confusing, thought Gann, mildly perplexed; but he knew his duty and he knew how to do it.

He knocked on the door of the commandant's office and was ordered inside. He came to full attention and a brisk salute.

"Technicadet Gann reporting as ordered, sir!"

The Machine Colonel returned his salute methodically. Here, too, Gann was faintly surprised, though he allowed none of the surprise to show through his military bearing and engaging grin. Machine Colonel Zafar was a short brown man in meticulously pressed dress whites, who looked as solid and enduring as the Plan itself. "Welcome aboard, cadet," he said. "Give me your orders, please."

"Yes, sir!" Gann's orders were also a lie. They showed him to be a relief laser operator fresh out from Earth. They did not mention his true rank, or his intensive training on Pluto. The commandant read them carefully, then nodded.

"Cadet Gann," he said in his soft, precise voice, "we are glad to have you on Polaris Station. As you know, this station is a major unit in the Spacewall. Our primary job is to detect and intercept any unauthorized traffic between the Plan of Man and the areas beyond Pluto—the wastes that are called the Reefs of Space. Our secondary job is to monitor as much activity in the Reefs as possible. Our radar, laser, and optical systems are the heart of our mission—and so, Cadet Gann, what you do is the most important part of our work here. Don't fail us."

"Sir," said Boysie Gann earnestly, "I won't fail you! I serve the Plan of Man without question or pause!" And he saluted and left.

But before he left he dropped his orders and retrieved them, with a flashing grin of apology to the colonel.

He left with his shoulders high. For in the instant when he was bent out of the commandant's sight, picking up his papers, he had planted a listening bug under the projecting rim of Machine Colonel Zafar's desk.

Within an hour of Gann's arrival on Polaris Station he was fitted with an iron collar.

He had expected it. In so sensitive an installation as the station, every man wore one of the Machine's collars, so that at any instant, wherever he might be, any one of them could be destroyed. There was no other way. A space man gone amok—a traitor loose in the fuel stores—a drunken armorer at the studs of the station's mighty missiles—any individual could do so much harm that it was necessary to have instant control over every man aboard.

Still, it was an uncomfortable feeling. Gann touched the collar lightly, and for once the smile was gone from

167

his cheerful face. It was disturbing to know that someone somewhere—the distant Machine on Earth, or one of its satellites nearby, a security officer on Pluto, or the commandant here on the station—could at the surge of a radar pulse detonate the decapitation charge.

His bunkmate was a tall, lean Nigerian, Technicadet M'Buna. Lounging in the security office waiting for Gann, M'Buna saw his involuntary gesture and laughed. As he held the door and they started off to their duty post M'Buna said, "Makes you nervous, eh? Don't worry. If it goes off, you'll never know it!"

Gann grinned. He liked M'Buna, had at first encounter already realized that here was an intelligent, patient friend. Yet he said at once, "Nobody likes a collar. And—" he acted a pause, glancing around—"I hear there are people somewhere who do something about it. Out on the Reefs. Men who know how to get the collars off . . ."

M'Buna said uncomfortably, "I wouldn't know anything about that. Here's our station."

Gann nodded and let it pass. But he had not failed to notice that M'Buna had overlooked one essential act. What Gann had hinted at treason to the Plan. M'Buna's duty was clear: he should have called Gann on it and established exactly what was meant by the hint. . . . And then reported Gann at once.

Huge as an ocean liner, flimsy as a dragon kite, Polaris Station was a big plastic wheel. Its spin was just fast enough to keep the crew's soup in the plate and the plate on the table. The hub was stationary, with the radar-laser search dome on the north face, the entry locks on the other.

The station had been set up first, more than a quarter century before, as a base for exploring the Reef cluster immediately to the galactic north of the sun. The snowball that had supplied reaction mass for the old nuclear rockets was still in detector range, swinging a hundred miles from the station in their coupled orbits. Now there was no need for reaction mass, but the snow-asteroid still had its uses. It served as a cosmic garbage dump, the unreclaimed wastes and offal of the station hauled out there after every watch and left on its surface so that free-orbiting particles of trash would not return false signals to the search instruments back at the station.

Within forty-eight hours of reporting aboard the station,

Machine Major Boysie Gann had bugged the offices of the commandant, the executive officer, the quartermaster, and the intelligence chief. Each tiny instrument was broadcasting a sealed-wave pickup of every word that was uttered in those sacrosanct chambers. Gann himself spot-monitored the transmissions when time allowed. The rest of the time the great records machine on Pluto received the signals, taped them, and transmitted them to Earth and the buried citadel of the Planning Machine itself.

But all his bugs produced nothing.

Gann's orders had been less than explicit: *Seek out and identify enemies of the Plan.* Beyond that there had been only rumors. A vast smuggling enterprise, shipping valuable strategic materials from the inner Plan Worlds to the Reefs. A strange new cult that threatened to unite the Reefs against the inner planets. A leader preaching a hegira, a security leak . . . But which of these was true, if any, Gann had not been told. It was not security doctrine to tell agents precisely what they should be looking for, on the grounds that their time was most productively employed when they could develop and follow up on many of their own leads.

Yet here there were no leads at all.

No real leads, at least. A few unguarded remarks at mess. Some slipshod accounting of spare parts for the laser banks. These were anti-Plan irregularities, to be sure, and men had gone to the Body Bank for far less. Men would go to the Body Bank for them now, from Polaris Station, for Gann had promptly filed the names and data. But he was certain that what he should be looking for was something bigger and worse than an occasional disgruntled or sloppy officer.

Within one week Gann had proved to his own satisfaction that if there was any major anti-Plan activity going on, it was not on Polaris Station.

He had to look elsewhere.

But where else was there?

It wasn't until he had been there twice that he realized where the "elsewhere" had to be.

Like all the noncommissioned personnel, Gann took his share of KP, garbage detail, cleanup orderly, and so on. It was not usually a burdensome chore. The radar ovens and cybernated housekeepers did all the work; the only thing left for the men in charge was to make sure they were working properly. Even the short hop from the station to the snowball for garbage disposal was a welcome break in the routine.

He shared his garbage tour with M'Buna, and they spent their time chatting desultorily at the controls of the "scow"—actually a reactionless space tractor—while the garbage pods steered, unloaded, and returned themselves. M'Buna had never referred to Gann's leading remark about collars. Nor had Gann ever been able to draw him into any unplanned talk; he had given up trying. They talked about home. They talked about promotion. And they talked about girls.

For Gann there was one girl, and her name was Julie Martinet. "No bigger than a minute, M'Buna," he said earnestly, "and with those beautiful dark eyes. She's waiting for me. When I come back—"

"Sure," said M'Buna. "Now, this girl I knew in Lagos—"

"You're talking about *a* girl," said Gann. "Julie is *the* girl. The only one who matters."

"How come you never get any mail from her?" asked M'Buna.

And Gann froze.

"She doesn't like to write letters," he said after a moment, but inside he was cursing himself. So foolish a slip! There was a reason, and a perfectly good one, why he got no letters from Julie Martinet. They were piling up for him on Pluto; he was sure of that; but they could not be forwarded here. There was too much risk of someone reading one, and learning from some chance comment that Gann was not the simple laser tech he appeared.

As soon as he could, Gann changed the subject. "Say," he said, "what's that on the scope?" It was a tiny blip, settling down feather-light toward the surface of the snowball protoplanet. A clutter of trash, of course. Nothing more. It was by no means unusual for some part of the garbage cargo to rebound from the tenuous clutch of the snowball's gravity and wheel around in space for minutes or hours before finally settling into place.

But M'Buna glanced at the radar display and said casually, "The commandant, I suppose. He comes out here every once in a while to check things over."

Carefully, trying to hide his excitement, Gann said, "Wonder what he does there." M'Buna shrugged, reached forward, and turned a switch. The pod had emptied itself and returned to the ship. "Tell you what," Gann went on. "Let's look."

He didn't wait for an answer. The pod back, the scow ready, there was nothing to stop him. He fed the ion stream to the reactionless drive and cut in the course-correcting side rockets. The scow began to move.

M'Buna said tautly, "No! Cut it out, Gann. The Old Man isn't going to want us skylarking around without permission."

But Gann wasn't listening. He was watching the screens intently.

If Machine Colonel Zafar was paying surreptitious visits to the ice-planetoid, there had to be a reason. He was going to find out what that reason was. He cut in maximum magnification on the screens, and the surface of the little protoplanet of frozen gases leaped up toward him.

The thing was eight or ten miles thick, shaped more like a broken cinder block than a sphere. It was unusually dense, as the distant, orbiting blobs of frozen methane and hydrogen went; if it ever drifted in near the sun, it would make a major comet. In the screen its greenish crust of solid gases looked like a blizzard in slow motion. Disturbed by the impact of the waste they had dumped, the whole snowball was quivering and shaking, its light gas-snow rising in sheets and falling again.

There was absolutely nothing to be seen . . .

But even a tiny planetoid has a great deal of surface, by human standards. Somewhere on that surface Colonel Zafar had gone in his flying suit. Gann reached again for the controls to circle around.

Some noise warned him.

He turned, and saw M'Buna leaning toward him, a strange expression of mingled pity and hate on his face; and in M'Buna's hand was a glittering metal pencil, pointed at him.

In that split second of time that was left to him Gann thought wildly: *If only I could get the report in, I've sure found something anti-Plan going on now* . . .

And that was the last thought he had for a long time. He heard a hiss and just had time to realize that the sting on his cheek was a nerve pellet fired from M'Buna's contraband gun. That was all. Blackness closed over him, and cold.

3

A nerve pellet is an instant anesthetic. It is also something more.

It does not wear off. Not ever. The victim of a nerve pellet does not recover consciousness until he is given an antidote.

When Gann woke up, he had no idea of how long he had been under the influence of the nerve pellet. But what he knew for sure was that he was no longer in the control room of the garbage scow.

Nor was he anywhere else in the universe where he had ever been before.

He lay on an uneven, rocky ledge. Under him was a soft, moist—and warm—blanket of something that seemed to be a lichen, a kind of clinging moss that grew in thick, flaky scales. It was glowing with a soft steady light. On the rocks around him the light was greenish in hue. Farther away, on higher ridges, it shone purple and red.

And above the rocks the sky was velvet black, with a single dazzling star blazing down on him.

Boysie Gann struggled to his feet—and soared into the air.

As he came down he stared about him. When he looked away from the rocks and that bright star his eyes adjusted and he could see other stars. All the familiar constellations . . . And then it hit him.

That bright star was the sun.

He was on one of the Reefs of Space.

Gann never knew how he came there. The man who would surely know was M'Buna, and Gann never saw M'Buna again. But it was clear that while under the influence of the nerve pellet he had been transported and marooned. Alone, without a radio, without instruments, without a ship or spacesuit, he might live out his life on that Reef—but he would die there in the end. For he could never leave.

It was surely a good way to dispose of an unwanted

man—simpler even than murder, since there was no body to get rid of.

He was stiff and cold. His wrists were swollen and his ankles numb. Evidently his captors had not trusted to the nerve pellet to keep him quiet, but had shackled him as well. But the shackles were gone now, with every other evidence of who it was who had brought him here. His head hurt. He was parched and hungry.

He began to look around him more methodically.

His first needs were food and water; but he could not resist a look around at the wonder of the place. Bright metallic fern fronds tinkled like wind gongs from an overgrown vale to one side. A distant whirring sounded like a flock of grouse. Impossible that there should be grouse here, Gann knew; yet there might be some sort of life. The Reefs of Space were created by life, like the coral atolls on Earth's warm seas. Life inhabited them all . . .

But it was not always—not even often!—life of a sort compatible with humankind. For the Reefs were formed from clusters of fusorians, feasting on the hydrogen formed between the stars according to the laws of the Neo-Hoyle Hypothesis, converting it into heavier atoms, then into atoms heavier still. The life in the Reefs was sometimes warm-blooded, carbon-based, oxygen-breathing animal. But more often it was metal or crystal—at best worthless for food; at worst, a deadly danger.

The bright star Sol was near the south celestial pole, Gann discovered. That put him more or less galactic north of the sun—and, therefore, almost straight out from Polaris Station. How far out? He had no way of knowing, except that the major Reef clusters were thought to be some two hundred astronomical units from Sol. At a guess, twenty billion miles.

Gann turned his eyes from the stars and looked about him. He had a world to explore. It might be less than a hundred yards in its longest axis, but it was all he had.

He rubbed his aching wrists and ankles and began to explore. He climbed carefully out of that small, glowing green dell—carefully, because he knew the danger of a reeflet. The fusorian symbiotes held an atmosphere, somehow; but it was like a soap bubble, and if Gann was so incautious as to step too high and soar through it, he would find himself in the hard vacuum of the space between the stars, and death would come in a horrible explosive burst as his blood boiled off and his cells ruptured.

He climbed toward the ridge, paused, and looked around.

Ahead of him was another dell, this one bearing some sort of glittering bush. The plants were shoulder-high, with plumes of narrow gloss, sprinkled with what seemed to be individual fusorian cells that glowed with their own light. Each leaf darkened from green at the base to black at the tip, and each ended in a bright red berry.

Queerly, they grew in rows.

They looked, in fact, like a truck farm in Earth's populous market valleys, and at once Gann's hunger surged forth. They looked like food; He started toward them at a shambling run . . .

And from behind him a voice spoke. "Well, good for you. See you woke up finally. Headed right for the feed-bag too, eh?"

Machine Major Boysie Gann's training had prepared him for any shock. It was trained reflex that stopped him in midflight, turned him, brought him back down to the glowing mossy surface of the reeflet in a half crouch, ready to do battle.

But there was nothing warlike in the figure that was coming toward him. He was a stubby little man with a big belly and a dirty yellow beard. His clothing was woven out of some kind of rough fiber. It was ragged and filthy and half unbuttoned.

And clinging to his bald brown head was a black-fanged, green-scaled, red-eyed creature the size of a capuchin monkey. It looked like a toy dragon. And from under the knife-sharp edges of its scales seeped little wisps of smoke.

Boysie Gann said warily, "Hello."

"Why, hello," the man said in a mild voice. "You was sleeping. Figured I'd best leave you to sleep it off. Nice to have you here. I wasn't expecting company."

"I wasn't exactly expecting to be here."

The man nodded and thrust out a dirty, gnarled hand. "Figured that. Couple fellows dropped you five, six hours ago. Looks like they gave you a rough enough time, so I let you be."

The creature on its head wheeled to face Gann as its owner moved, glaring at him with hot red eyes. Gann shook the man's hand and said, "I need some water. And food."

174

"Why, sure. Come along then." He nodded, the creature scrambling back and forth, and turned to lead the way across the cultivated field toward what seemed to be a tiny black lake. "Omer don't like strangers," he called over his shoulder, "but he won't bother you none. Just don't make any sudden moves is all. Omer's a pyropod —just a baby, of course, but they can be mean."

Silently Gann agreed. The little creature looked mean enough, with its oozing plumes of smoke and fiery eyes. They loped across the glowing rows of the man's little farm and reached the shore of the lake—no more than a pond, really, fifty feet across, its surface disturbed with the slow, tall waves of low-gravity fluids. On its far bank a sharp cliff rose in a glitter of metallic outcroppings, softened by glowing plants and mosses, and in the base of the cliff was a metal lean-to that hid the mouth of the cave.

"That's home," said the man cheerfully. "Welcome to it, such as 'tis. Come in and rest yourself."

"Thanks," said Gann. "By the way, we didn't really introduce ourselves."

"Oh? Guess you're right," said the man. "I'm Harry Hickson. And you"—Gann started to speak, but Hickson didn't pause—"you're what you call it—Machine Major Boysie Gann, out of the spy school on Pluto."

For twenty-four hours, Gann rested in the cave of the hermit Harry Hickson, and his thoughts were dark. How had Hickson known his name? Even more, how had he known that he was not a shanghaied radar-laser tech, but a graduate of the spy school?

There was no answer in Gann's brain, so he shut off his mind to conjectures and applied it to restoring his physical condition and reconnoitering his surroundings.

Evidently he had been unconscious for longer than he had thought on the ship that had dumped him on this reeflet, for he had lost weight and strength and there was a straggly stubble of beard on his chin. But Hickson fed him and cared for him. He gave Gann a bed of sorts to sleep on—only a stack of reeking blankets, but as good as the one he slept on himself—and fed him from the same pot of greasy stew as himself. The diet was crude but filling, supplemented with fruits and roots and shoots of the plants he grew on the rock. The reddish berries, which tasted like a sort of acid citrus fruit, were

175

a good source of all necessary vitamins, Harry told him earnestly, and one of the lichens was a source of protein.

Gann did not question the food. Clearly it had kept Harry Hickson alive for a long time—the cave showed that it had been his home for months or even years—and it would keep Gann alive for at least as long as he intended to stay on the reeflet.

And that would not be long. For he had learned from Hickson that there was a way of communicating that would bring help if he needed it. "Never needed it, o' course," he said, fishing a long string of a rhubarb-like vegetable out of his bowl of stew and licking his fingers. "But it's comforting to know it's there . . . Say, you worried about that collar, Boysie?"

Gann stopped in mid-gesture, suddenly aware that he had been tugging at it. "Not exactly," he said quietly.

"Get it off of you, if you like," Hickson offered mildly. "No trouble. Done it lots o' times."

Gann stared. "What the Plan are you talking about?" he demanded. "Don't you know what this is? These things are built with automatic destruct circuits, as well as the remote triggering equipment. If anybody tries to take them off—" He touched both sides of the collar with fingertips and flipped them up and outward, pantomiming the explosion of a decapitation charge.

"Oh, sure, I know all about *that*," said Hickson. "Hold still. No, not you, Gann. *You*, Omer! Don't wiggle so. Makes me nervous."

He got up from his squatting position at the rude plank table where they ate and came around behind Gann. "Just you sit there, Boysie," he said. "Can move if you want to—it don't matter—but don't look toward me . . . Omer, confound you! Get your claws outa my scalp! Raised him from an egg, that little devil, right here in my own smoke pot, but he gets jumpy when he knows I'm going to . . . Well, here we are."

And something moved around Gann's neck. He couldn't see what Hickson was doing, was sure that the tubby little hermit had not brought any tools or instruments. Yet there was a sudden constriction at his throat.

He heard the lock snap . . .

The collar fell off his neck and clattered to the floor of the cave. Gann leaped to his feet and spun, white-faced, to be ready for the explosion. But no explosion came.

"Now, rest easy, Boysie," complained the hermit. "You're

spooking Omer here. That thing can't blow up any more." Casually he picked up the collar and lifted it to examine it in the light of a mass of luminous diamond that would have been worth millions on earth. "They make them real nice," he said admiringly. "Lot of detail in this thing. Too bad it can't be something more useful." And he tossed it to the rear of the cave. "Well," he said, "you about ready to move on now?"

Gann stood silent for a second, looking at him. "Move on where?" he asked.

"Oh, don't worry, Boysie. I know what you were thinking. Plain as day. You figure I ought to go back and get examined by the Planning Machine, 'cause you don't quite understand what I'm up to, but you think it's unplanned. Well, that's right. Unplanned is what I am. And I don't mind if you do what you're thinking, and take my laser-gun and call help so you can get out of here. But I'm not going with you, Boysie. Make up your mind to that."

"All right," said Gann, surrendering. But in his mind he was not surrendering at all.

Hickson had put it very mildly when he said that Gann wanted to take him back for study. Gann not only wanted to; he intended to. In fact, he had never intended anything as hard in his life—had never been so determined or insistent, not even about his career in the service of the Machine, not even in his great love for Julie Martinet.

This man Harry Hickson was an unplanned disaster in the making.

Whoever he was, however he did what he did, he was a terrible danger to the Plan of Man. Gann could almost hear the instructions of his briefing officer back on Pluto —if he had been able to report Hickson's existence to him, and if the briefing officer could issue an order: *Subject Hickson is a negative factor. His uncatalogued knowledge must be retrived for the Plan. Then each organ of his unautomated body must be obliterated* . . .

But how to get him back into the jurisdiction of the Planning Machine?

There had to be a way. There would be a way. Machine Major Boysie Gann was sure of it. All it required was that he be patient—then, when his chance came, be ready.

Gann said, "If you mean it, then let's take your gun and signal right now. I'm ready to move on."

Harry Hickson led Gann to a point of red-scaled rock,

puffing and wheezing. On his bald scalp the fledgling py-ropod wheeled and slithered, keeping its bright red eyes on Boysie Gann.

"See up there?" called Hickson over his shoulder. "That star there next to Vega . . ."

Boysie Gann followed his pointing finger. "You mean Theta Lyrae?"

The hermit turned and looked at him, mildly surprised. "That's right, Boysie. You fellows learn a lot in that spy school. Too bad you don't . . . Well, never mind that. One I mean, it's just below Theta Lyrae. The faint red one. Forget the name, but that one right there. That way's Freehaven."

Gann felt his blood pound. "Freehaven? I've heard of it. A colony of reef rats."

"Aw, Boysie, don't say it like that. They're free men —that's all. That's the biggest place in the Reefs, Free-haven is. Like a . . . well, what would you call it? A kind of a town only it's one whole cluster of Reefs, maybe a hundred thousand miles across. And maybe half a billion miles from here."

"I see," said Gann, thinking with exultation and pride, *What a prize to bring back to Pluto! A whole city to be planned and returned to the brotherhood of the Machine!* He could almost see the glowing jet trails of the Plan cruisers vectoring in on the cluster . . .

"Don't get your hopes up," Hickson said dryly. "You ain't there yet, Boysie, and maybe even when you get there you won't find it too easy to pick up a phone and call the Machine. Now hush a minute while I send for your ride out there."

He picked up the clumsy old laser gun he had taken out of its greasy rag wrappings back in the cave, checked its power settings, raised it, and aimed carefully at the distant red spark that was the line-of-sight to Freehaven. Three times he snapped the trigger, then lowered the gun and turned to Gann.

"That all there is to it. Take 'em a while to get here. Might as well go back to the cave."

But he paused, glancing at Boysie Gann as if he was mildly embarrassed about something. Then he seemed to come to a decision.

He turned back to the stars, set down the laser pistol, and stretched out his arms. His lips moved, but Gann could hear no sound. On his bald pate the pyropod hissed

178

and slithered. The hermit's whole body seemed stretched, yearning, toward—toward what?

Gann could not tell. Toward Freehaven, perhaps. Toward the faint red star that marked its position—or toward Theta Lyrae nearby—or toward the great bright giants of the Summer Triangle that marked that part of the sky, Vega, Altair, and Deneb . . .

Then Harry Hickson relaxed and the pyropod scuttled down from his scalp onto his shoulder as the hermit raised one arm and made a sinuous, undulating motion. Like the wriggle of a snake, Gann thought. Or the looping movement of a swan's neck.

Swan? Some faint old memory stirred in Boysie Gann's mind. Something about a swan—and a star . . .

But it would not come clear, and he followed Harry Hickson back to the cave.

Harry Hickson's little reeflet was one drifting island in an expanding infinity of matter and space. The doctrine of the Neo-Hoyle Hypothesis was clear: The universe was limitless, in space, in time—and in matter. New mass was forming everywhere in the form of newly created hydrogen atoms as the old complexes of matter—the stars and the planets, the dust clouds and the galaxies—were spinning slowly apart.

Hickson's reeflet was an infant among bodies of organized matter, probably only a few millions of years in age, in size no more than a dust mote. Yet it was like most of the universe in that; for most matter is young. The spiraling growth in rate of creation of new matter makes that sure. Some galaxies, and even some of the reefs between them, are old beyond computation and imagination, because the steady-state universe has neither beginning nor end. And life is the oldest phenomenon of all. Older than the oldest stars—but yet young, though those scattered and forgotten stars are black and dead.

Life in space has lived—literally—forever.

Every possible biology has been evolved, through every conceivable evolutionary test.

Watching Harry Hickson play with his pet pyropod, Boysie Gann reflected that the strangest life form he knew was man. For here was the pudgy, balding hermit—unplanned and deviant, a deadly danger by every standard of the Planning Machine—solemnly attempting to teach his pyropod to fly.

179

He lifted the little horror off his head and set it carefully on a high ledge, then retreated. Spitting and hissing, its red eyes glittering, its scales seeping the smoke of its internal jet fires, it wailed in a thin, raucous screech for him to come back. Then, despairing, it launched itself out into the air, missed Hickson by yards and crashed into the rock wall at the far side of the cave, where it remained, writhing and hissing, until Hickson took pity on it and picked it up. "It's a wonder it doesn't dash its brains out," muttered Gann the fifth time the little beast crashed into the rock.

"Oh, I guess so," Hickson agreed mildly. "Don't suppose it has any, really, though. A pretty clumsy kind of beast it is—right, Omer?" And he patted the little monster with the appearance of real affection for a moment, then sighed and set it down. He carefully inverted a crate and set it down over the pyropod, then put a mass of silvery fusorian coral upon the crate.

The pyropod squalled and hissed, but Hickson ignored it. "Hoped I could teach it to fly before I go," he said regretfully, "but I guess I won't make it. Boysie, your transportation ought to be here in an hour. Care to see what the pilot's gonna look like?" He thumbed an old-fashioned two-dimensional color print out of a button-down pocket in his ragged coat and handed it to Gann. It was a pretty, quite young girl, one hand resting on the head of a seal-like creature, before a background of a glowing purple and silver Reef. "Name's Quarla," said the old man affectionately. "Quarla Snow. Daughter of an old friend of mine. He treated me, couple years ago. Doctor, he is, and a good one. Don't know much about what ails me, though . . ."

The hermit seemed to realize he was rambling and caught himself up short. "Guess that's all," he said, smiling with a touch of embarrassment. "Swan bless you, Boysie. Give Quarla my love." And in a moment, before Gann could realize what he was about to do, the old man had turned, pushed aside the metal door that overhung the entrance to the cave, and stepped out.

Gann shook his head, half in rueful amusement, half in surprise. "Hey!" he called. "Hickson! Where are you going? Wait for me!" And he hurried to the door of the cave and out onto the sward the old hermit had so carefully cropped.

The man was not there.

His footprints were there, still visible in the faint bruises on the lichenous surface of the earth.

But Harry Hickson was gone.

Gann ranged the surface of the entire reef in the next few hours, shouting and searching. But there was no answer to his call, no sight of Hickson anywhere.

The man had simply vanished.

4

In the cave Machine Major Gann found the old man's laser gun—an ancient Technicorps model that must have been smuggled into space before the Spacewall was set up. It gave him a small feeling of confidence to carry it, though there was no visible enemy to shoot it at.

He needed that confidence.

No man can be alone. Each man has his place in the Plan of Man under the benevolent guidance of the Planning Machine. Each man serves the Plan, so that the Plan may serve all men ...

That was doctrine, and Boysie Gann found himself foolishly repeating it as he clambered up the red-scaled rock to the point from which Hickson had signaled to Freehaven. It did not help very much.

No man can be alone . . . but Boysie Gann felt very much alone indeed, on that tiny floating islet of reef, under the blazing stare of a billion stars.

There was no reason for him to be on this point of rock, rather than anywhere else on the surface of the reeflet. He had no reason to believe his rescuer would come to look for him there. Had no reason to be sure there would be a rescuer at all, in fact, for what the half-demented hermit, Harry Hickson, had said could not be accepted as reliable . . .

Yet he stayed there, waiting, for hours. He leaned against a cairn of rock and scanned the skies. Only the distant, unfriendly stars returned his look. He sat, leaning against the rock, and drowsed. No sound or motion disturbed him. Then . . .

There was a faint blur of greenish mist in the low black sky, moving at the threshold of vision.

Gann sprang to his feet, eyes peering into the immense emptiness above him. The greenish blur was so faint that he could not be sure it was real. Yet . . . surely there was something there and, following it, a cluster of even fainter reddish sparks.

Gann raised the laser, checked the settings to make sure he was not firing a blast of destruction into the sky, and thumbed the trigger thrice, as he had seen Hickson do, pointing it toward the greenish blur.

A moment . . . then the green glow veered toward him.

It was his rescuer—he was sure of it. But what were the red sparks? Even as he watched, the tiny, distant coals veered too, following the greenish glow. Rapidly they grew nearer . . .

Then one of the red sparks dashed ahead of the rest, with a long blue trail of incandescence faintly visible behind it. It was like an ominous comet as it dived through the greenish cloud.

Noise smote Gann's ears abruptly: a sudden roaring, like the jet of an old-time rocket.

The things had come at last into the shallow atmosphere of his reeflet. He heard the shriek of their motion through the air—and something else.

Something was screaming.

The red spark thundered overhead, out of the green cloud, toward Gann like some deadly ancient missile homing in on a radar trace—then at the last moment rose up a dozen yards above his head, and as it passed he caught a sudden glimpse of nightmare.

Metal scales like broken mirrors. Enormous talons, dripping something that glowed and was golden, something that splattered to the ground near Gann like a soft, fitful rain. The red spark divided into two red, monstrous, blinking eyes, mirror-rimmed, in a head like a maniac dragon's. And the roaring blue flame was the tail of the thing.

"Pyropod!" breathed Boysie Gann aloud, transfixed.

He had never seen an adult before—had heard of them only as distant rumors, like the sort of ghost stories unplanned parents used to tell their children. The baby pyropod that had been Harry Hickson's pet had not prepared him for the huge, menacing reality that shrieked through the air above him now. He stood, stunned.

A pyropod is a living rocket, flame-footed and deadly. Their chemistry is not that of Earthly air-breathers; their

182

primeval genesis came from the same noncarbon evolutionary strain that shaped the fusorians. On their plasma jets, nuclear in temperature, fired by fusorian symbiotes, they can outrun a Plan cruiser and outfight any Terrestrial beast in search of prey. And to the pyropods, anything that moves is prey. Their jets take enormous quantities of reaction mass. Their appetites are insatiable. Scavengers of space, they will attack anything.

Fortunately for the continuation of life on the inner planets and the Reefs of Space, atmosphere is a slow poison to the pyropods and gravity damages their reflexes. They are beasts of the interstellar void, ship-sized monstrosities at their hugest, big as cave bears even when barely mature. Standing in shock, watching the great beast, Boysie Gann stared at the red eyes pulsing in their telescopic mirrors, wheel and flash back toward him, imagined the black talons ripping metal or rock like bread . . .

And realized, almost too late, that he was the target of those monstrous talons now.

Instinctively he raised the laser gun and fired.

The charge was minimal, only the message setting; yet the great pyropod felt it, screamed, and soared away. Gann hurled himself to the shelter of the rock cairn, staring about. The torn green cloud of luminosity was dissolving in the night sky above him. Streamers of mist scattered and faded. And where the cloud had been, Gann could see what had brought it.

A spaceling. One of the warm-blooded, seal-like creatures that roam the space between the stars, natural prey to the pyropods, friend to man. It had brought the cloud —for it was the spaceling's ability to hold atmosphere about it, in a Ryeland-effect field, that permitted them, as oxygen-breathers, to live in space at all.

The spaceling had been grievously wounded. Even from so far away, Gann could see the hideous slash that ripped along the whole length of its sleek, golden body as it came tumbling down. Something was clinging to its fur —a rider? Gann could not be sure; but what he was certain of was that the end for both the spaceling and its burden was very near.

The pyropod that had attacked him had wheeled again and was diving on the wounded seal-like beast. A louder howling drowned out the spaceling's scream as the pyropod came out of the dark over a purple-scaled ridge, red eyes pulsing and dripping talons reaching again.

Gann reacted without thought. He twisted the crystal of that old laser to maximal intensity, steadied the tube on the rocks of the cairn, and fired into those dreadful flashing eyes. They exploded.

The pyropod bellowed in agony. Its eyes were gone —eyes or eyelike structures; actually, Gann knew, they were more like laser search gear. But whatever they were, they were gone now, burst like the shattered hull of a subtrain when the field of its tunnel fails and the fluid rock crushes it. The pyropod drove blindly up and away, squalling until its sound was cut off like the dropping of a curtain.

It had passed beyond the atmosphere into space. Blind and wounded, it would not, Gann thought, be back. And a blessing that was, since an orange light was blinking on the laser gun, warning him that the fuel cell was fully exhausted.

He knew there were other pyropods still out there, somewhere beyond the veil of air. He could see their faint red sparks circling, and the blue trails of their fiery exhausts. They veered all at once, and drove in toward the retreating comet tail of the pyropod he had wounded. There was a puff of incandescent vapor . . .

Dimly Gann realized that its mates had destroyed the wounded one, torn it open and were now wheeling and diving, fighting for their shares of the kill. But he had no time for them. The spaceling had tumbled to earth halfway across the little reeflet, and Gann stumbled and leaped across the red-scaled rocks to find it.

It was lying at the edge of Harry Hickson's little plantation, spurting glowing yellow blood across the green moss. Beside it was its rider, bent over the terrible wound, trying with both hands to stanch the flow of blood.

The rider was a girl. Hickson had been right. It was the girl in the photograph he had displayed.

The spaceling moaned and shuddered as Gann drew near, its voice a faint, inarticulate sob. The girl was sobbing too.

"Can I help?" said Boysie Gann.

The girl, Quarla Snow, turned quickly, startled. She stared at Gann as if he were himself a pyropod, or some more fearsome monster from legend. There was fright in her eyes—and yet, queerly, thought Gann, almost relief as well, as if she had expected something even worse. It

184

was the expression of a man who finds himself confronted by a wolf, when he expects a tiger.

"Who are you?" she demanded. Her voice was low and controlled. She was tall and strong, but very young.

"Boysie Gann," he said. "And you're Quarla Snow. Harry Hickson told me you'd be here."

Her hand flew to her mouth. Her eyes widened in fear. For a moment she seemed about to run; then she shook her head in a pathetic gesture and turned back to the spaceling.

Its golden blood had ceased to flow, its body to move. The sounds it had uttered were still.

"Sultana's dead," the girl said softly, as if to herself.

"I'm sorry," Boysie Gann said inadequately. He glanced aloft—the pyropods were out of sight entirely now—then back to her. Quarla Snow's face was lightly tanned, almost to match her honey-colored hair. She was nearly the color of her spaceling. Her white coveralls were splashed with that golden ichor, her hands dripping with it. Yet she was beautiful.

For a moment a buried emotion trembled inside Boysie Gann, a memory of Julie Martinet and the taste of the fresh salt surf on her mouth when he kissed her on the beach of the little Mexican resort, Playa Blanca, long ages ago when they had said good-by. This girl did not in the least resemble Julie Martinet. She was blond where Julie had hair like night; she was tall, and Julie tiny. Her face was broad, friendly, and even in her sorrow and fear it showed contentment and joy in life, while Julie Martinet was a girl of sad pleasures and half-expressed sorrows. Yet there was something in both of them that stirred him.

He said hastily, "Those things may be back. We'd better do something about it."

The girl's tears were drying on her cheeks and her expression had become more calm. She looked down at the dead gun in Gann's hands and half smiled. "Not with that, Boysie Gann. It's empty."

"I know. We'd better get back to Hickson's cave. He may have left other charges."

"Left them? But I thought you said he was here!" The shadow fell over her face again, her eyes bright and fearful.

"He was, yes. But he's gone. Disappeared. I don't know where."

The girl nodded absently, as if she were too dazed to

take in what he had said. She dropped to her knees beside the dead spaceling and stroked its golden head. "Poor Sultana. I'll never forgive myself. When I got your signal I . . . well, I was frightened. I didn't know what to do. Dad was gone on an emergency call. He'd taken our ship, and . . . I decided to ride Sultana out here by myself."

Her mouth set white for a moment. "I didn't really think of any danger. There aren't many pyropods in these clusters any more—been hunted out years ago, though they keep straying back. But I'd outrun them on Sultana often enough before. I didn't think about the fact that she's . . . that she was . . . getting old."

She stood up and touched Gann lightly on the arm, a gesture of reassurance. "But you're not to worry. We aren't marooned here; Dad will come for us in the ship as soon as he gets home. I left a message."

Gann nodded. "So he'll wait a while," he said, comprehendingly, "and then, if you haven't returned in—what? a day or so? Then he'll come looking for you."

But Quarla Snow shook her golden head, her expression unreadable. "No. He won't wait. Not even a second. I said in my note that Harry Hickson's old distress signal had come. He'll be here as fast as his ship can bring him, to see who sent Harry's signal."

Gann stared. "Harry did. Harry Hickson. I told you!"

"I know you told me," the girl said, her voice calm but with an undercurrent of wonder and of fear. "But you see, it couldn't have been Harry. I—no, wait. I'll show you."

And she turned and led him away from the cultivated little field, back up to the red-scaled crest of rock, where he had rested his laser gun on the cairn of rocks to fire at the pyropod. "See?" she said, touching the cairn.

He bent closer to look, and there on the lowermost rock, on one half-smoothed face of a boulder, was a faint scratching of carved letters, whittled out a line at a time with a laser gun, almost invisible unless you knew just where to look:

Harry Hickson
Died of a fusorian infection
Deneb light his way

"You see?" said the girl. "Harry could not have sent the message. He died here three years ago."

5

All this was months before the Writ of Liberation. On Earth the old Planner sat in silent, joyous communion with the Planning Machine. In solarian space the great Plan cruisers arrowed from satellite to planet, from asteroid to distant Spacewall post, carrying the weapons and the orders of the Machine to all the far-flung territories of the Plan of Man. On the island of Cuba, in the Body Bank, a Nigerian ex-Technicorps man, broken for inefficiency, gave up the last of his vital organs to serve some more worthy servant of the Plan, and died. (His name had once been M'Buna. He had been captured and court-martialed for desertion.) A girl named Julie Martinet, in a dormitory hall far below the surface of the Peruvian Andes, sat with stylus in hand deciding on which letter to write—one to the man she loved "but had not heard from"; the other an application for special duty in the service of the Machine.

And out on the Reefs, in the sprawling hundred-orbed community called Freehaven, Machine Major Boysie Gann began to understand that his greatest opportunity for service—and his greatest hope of reward!—had been handed to him on a silver platter.

For he was at large in Freehaven, the very heart of the Reefs of Space. And he knew, or thought he knew, a way to get back to the worlds of the Plan.

True, there were some puzzling problems. Some of them, indeed, were almost frightening.

What could Quarla Snow hope to gain by pretending that Harry Hickson was dead? What did she think Gann had seen on the little reeflet? A ghost? It was no ghost that had fed him, healed him, taken the collar from around his neck.

And it was no coincidence, he was coming to believe, that had brought him to Hickson's world in the first place.

There was no proof, of course. But he was sure that M'Buna, perhaps Colonel Zafar as well, was in some way related to Hickson and the treasonable activities that

187

were going on all around him in this unplanned, decadent, dangerous world of the Reefs. He had heard hints. An unguarded word, a look, a remark that was halted before it began. Nothing tangible, but enough to make him sure that there were links between the Reefs and the Plan worlds—links that extended even into the Technicorps, even into the vital defenses of the Spacewell itself.

If he could get back— No! he thought. *When* he got back, with the proof of this spreading rot, with the names of the conspirators and the evidence that would send them to the Body Bank, then no reward in the Machine's power would be too great to give to Machine Major Boysie Gann. And Julie Martinet would be waiting. . . .

Meanwhile there was a lot of work to do.

Gann dared not make notes or attempt to secure tapes or photographs; but he missed no opportunity to scout and examine every part of this queer community of Freehaven. Even the name was strange and somehow disconcerting. Freehaven.

As if "freedom" were important!

Yet Boysie Gann could not help but notice that strangely the decadent, unruly mobs that dwelt in Freehaven seemed somehow sturdier, somehow happier, in some way more alert and even more prosperous than the billions who lived under the all-powerful and protective embrace of the Plan of Man. . . .

It was confusing.

But his duty was clear. Gann set himself to learn all there was to know.

Freehaven consisted of a couple of thousand people, scattered over a hundred fusorian-grown rocks and a hundred thousand miles of space. Many of the rocks had been terraformed, Gann learned, with the lichenous air plant he had first seen on Harry Hickson's little reef. The rest of them were airless, but all of them supplied useful metals and minerals to the bustling economy of Freehaven.

Gann was not sure just what he had expected—tattooed savages, perhaps, dancing to a wild tomtom—but he had surely not been prepared for this modern, busy community. There were farms and herds—of spacelings and even, in one case, a stock farm with sixty head of what seemed to be Guernsey cattle, stolen somehow from the Plan of Man and transported in some improbable manner out to this hydrogen-based worldlet twenty billion miles

188

from the sun. On one airless reef that was mostly pure fusorian iron was a steel mill—one of the small nuclear-powered units developed by Technicorps engineers for use on the asteroids, to save the high cost of lifting terrain steel into space. Gann marveled at it all. He admitted it to Quarla Snow and her father, with whom he was staying as guest—or prisoner, he was never sure which—at a meal when he was served as fine a steak as he had ever tasted, with wines that bore the bouquet of French vineyards.

Dr. Snow boomed, "It isn't only the food that is good here, young man. It is life! It has a flavor here that the Plan worlds will never taste."

Boysie Gann said engagingly, "You may be right. I . . . well, you have to excuse me. You see, I've never known anything but the Plan."

Quarla's father nodded briskly. "Of course. None of us had, before we made our way out here. None but Quarla, at any rate, and a few others like her who were born here. They've lived in freedom all their lives."

Gann said, with just the right inflexion of doubt, "But I don't understand. I mean, how does it work? Who tells you what you're to do?"

"No one, boy! That's the whole point of freedom! We came here because we didn't want to live under the collar of the Machine. We work together, and as you see we work well. Prosperity and happiness! That's what we've built out of nothingness, just as the fusorians build our worlds for us out of thin gas and energy. Why, when Harry Hickson and I came here—" He broke off and tugged at his chin, frowning at Boysie Gann.

"Yes?" said Gann. "You and Hickson . . ."

"It was different then," said Dr. Snow shortly. "Boy, do you still want us to believe that story of yours about Hickson? A man I helped to bury myself, right under the rocks of his home?"

Gann said carefully, knowing that he was on dangerous ground, "Well, sir, of course I don't know anything about Hickson. But what I told you was true. The man who summoned Quarla said he was Harry Hickson, and I had absolutely no reason at all to doubt him at the time."

Snow nodded somberly and said no more; but Gann noticed that he no longer seemed to enjoy his meal.

Gann put the matter from his mind. He was thinking of something bigger. He was thinking of the gratitude of the

189

Machine when he returned, riding one of Quarla Snow's spacelings—as she was even now teaching him to do—bringing word of the community of Freehaven and its precious crop of several thousand splendid candidates for tissue salvage at the Body Bank!

He rose and strolled outside with Quarla. Harry Hickson's pet pyropod, which Quarla had insisted on rescuing from the cave when her father arrived to take them off the reeflet, hissed and slithered around the area outside the door where its staked chain permitted it to move.

He took her hand and held it, as they looked over the green ramble of glowing vines toward the distant beacon that was the central urban area of Freehaven. "You promised to let me ride one of your spacelings," he said, squeezing her hand and grinning. "If I'm going to be a permanent inhabitant here, I'd better start learning my way around."

She looked at him thoughtfully, then smiled. Under her golden hair her eyes were an intense blue. "Why not?" she said. "But not out of the atmosphere, Boysie. Not at first."

"I thought the spacelings brought their air with them."

She nodded but said firmly, "Not out of the atmosphere. For one thing, there might be pyropods."

He scoffed, "So close to Freehaven? Nonsense, Quarla! What's the other thing?"

She hesitated. "Well," she began. She was saved the trouble of answering. A pale blue wash of energy brightened up the sky over their heads.

Both of them turned to look; a spacecraft was coming in for a landing, full jets blazing to slow its racing drive. Whoever it was who was piloting the craft, he was in a hurry. In a matter of seconds the ship was down on the lichenous lawn before Dr. Snow's clinic, its lock open, a man leaping out. He glanced toward Quarla and Boysie Gann, cried, "Emergency!" and turned to receive something that was being handed to him out the lock of the ship.

Quarla cried, "I'll get my father. Boysie, run and help them!" Gann was already in motion, hurtling across the lichenous ground, though the two men in the rocket needed little help. What was coming through the lock of the ship was a man on a stretcher, wrapped in white sheets. In the light gravity of the Reef the two of them were perfectly adequate to handle it. Gann bore a hand anyway.

"Sick," panted one of the men. "Don't know who he is, but he collapsed in my spaceling corral. Thought it might be something dangerous—"

Gann nodded, helped lift the stretcher on which the sick man was thrashing and babbling . . .

And almost dropped it, light gravity or not.

He stood there, jaw hanging, eyes wide. Face streaming with perspiration, eyes vacant, head tossing from side to side in delirium, the face of the man on the stretcher was nevertheless very familiar to Boysie Gann. It was the face of Machine Colonel Mohammed Zafar.

If ever Boysie Gann had needed all the wits and wiles that had been drummed into him in the spy school on Pluto, now was the moment. "Dangerous," the reef rat who had brought Zafar had called him. He was more than dangerous; he spelled a strong probability of disaster for Boysie Gann. Zafar of all people would know him —and if, as Gann was morally certain, Zafar and M'Buna had been joined in some anti-Plan scheme on Polaris Station, Zafar would surely now know that Gann was no simple radar tech.

He dared not risk Zafar's recovering consciousness and identifying him. Yet his every loyalty to the Plan of Man demanded that he take every chance to learn more about Zafar from the colonel's disjointed ravings.

Dr. Snow made it easy for him, without knowing it. "You, boy!" he snapped. "Stay out of here. Quarla too! May be contagious . . . But stay where I can find you if I need you," he added, bending over his patient.

The two of them stood at the door of the emergency room, Quarla's hand, forgotten, in Boysie Gann's. "He's bad, Boysie," she whispered. "Don't know what it is. I haven't seen anything like that since Harry—" Then she stopped, and went on, in a different tone, to the men who had brought him: "You'd better wait until my father's examined him. You might have been exposed."

In the emergency room Dr. Snow was lifting a bimetal thermometer out of Zafar's slack, mumbling mouth. Boysie Gann strained to hear what the man was saying, but all he could catch were words like ". . . trap for minds . . ." ". . . living dust and lying dreams . . ."

Dr. Snow's expression was serious. "High," he muttered, then glanced toward the group at the door. "Quarla!" he called. "You'll have to compound an injection for me. Standard broad-spectrum antibiotics, afebrilium, analgesics. Call his weight—let's see—ninety kilos. And make the dosage maximum."

Quarla nodded and hurried to the pharmacy room, while Snow bent back to the man. Even at this distance, Gann could see that the former Machine Colonel's face was contorted in agony and fear. There was more than sickness in Zafar's wild muttering; there was terror. He pushed himself erect, eyes staring, and shouted: "Graveyard of the galaxy! Starchild! Beware the trap! Beware your heart's desire!" Then Quarla was back with a spray hypodermic. Her father took it from her, pushed her out of the room again, and quickly injected the man.

Zafar slumped back onto the examining couch, eyes closing, still mumbling to himself.

The doctor watched him for a second, then came toward the group at the door. "He'll sleep for a while," he said. "Nothing else to do at this moment. We've got to see how he responds to the drug."

The man who had brought him said, "Doc, what is it? Are we all going to . . ." But Dr. Snow was shaking his head.

"I can't answer your question," he said. "I don't know what it is. But I don't think you're in any danger. I've seen only one other case like this, three years ago. But I was exposed, and so was my daughter, and several others —and no one was infected."

He hesitated, glancing at Gann. Then he said abruptly, "The other case was Harry Hickson, Mr. Gann. It killed him."

Boysie Gann started to speak, then nodded. "I understand."

"Do you?" Dr. Snow's voice was heavy with irony. "I don't! I don't understand at all. Let me show you something—then tell me if you understand!" He stood away from the door, reached out a hand, and switched off the lights in the emergency room. "Look!" he cried. "Do you understand that?"

The four in the doorway gasped as one. "Father!" cried Quarla, and the men swore softly. Inside the emergency room, in the semi-darkness Dr. Snow had brought about, Mohammed Zafar's leather-colored skin was leather-colored no longer. Like the spilled blood of the spaceling Gann had seen murdered, Zafar's skin was bright with a golden glow! His face shone with the radiance of a muted sun. One wasted hand, dangling out of the sheets, was limned in a yellowish, unsteady light like the flicker of a million flashing fusorians.

Quarla choked, "It's . . . it's just like Harry, Father!"

The doctor nodded somberly. "And it will end the same way, too. Unless there's a miracle, that man will be dead in an hour."

He sighed and reached to turn the light on again, but there was an abrupt hissing, swishing sound and something darted past them, over their heads. "What the devil!" cried Dr. Snow, and turned on the lights.

Something was on the dying man's head, something that scuttled about and glared at them with hot red eyes, like incandescent shoebuttons.

"Father! It's Harry's—I mean, it's the pyropod! The one Boysie and I brought back!" cried Quarla Snow.

Gann said tightly, "Look! He broke the chain." Then he laughed shakily. "Harry would be pleased," he said unsteadily. "At last the thing's learned how to fly."

Machine Colonel Zafar lived longer than the hour Dr. Snow had promised, but it was obvious that the extra time would not be very long. He was sinking. For minutes at a time he seemed hardly to breathe, then roused himself long enough to mumble incoherent phrases like "The Starchild! But the Swan won't help him . . ."

Snow was working over his laboratory equipment in the corner of the room, pausing every few minutes to check his patient's breathing, and shake his head. He summoned Quarla and Gann to him and gestured to a microscope.

"I want to show you something," he said, his face somber and wondering. "Look." And he stepped aside.

Quarla looked into the slim chromed barrels of the microscope, then lifted her head to stare questioningly at her father. He nodded. "You see? Mr. Gann, look."

Slowly Boysie Gann took her place. "I'm not a scientist, Doctor," he protested. "I won't know what to look for."

But then he was looking through the eyepieces and his voice stopped. He did not need to be a scientist. The spectacle before him, standing out clear in three dimensions in the stereoscopic field of the microscope, was nothing he had ever seen before.

Straw-colored erythrocytes and pale eosinophiles floated among colonies of benign microorganisms that live in every human's blood. Rodlike and amoeboid, radial or amorphous, all the tiny bacteria were familiar, in a vague, half-remembered way, to Gann.

All but one.

For dominating the field were masses of globular bodies, dark and uninteresting-looking at first, but bursting under his eyes into spurts of golden light. Like the luminous plankton of Earth's warm seas, they flared brilliantly, then subsided, then flared again. It was like tiny warning lights signaling disaster in the sample of the sick man's blood—hundreds of them, perhaps thousands—so many that the field of the microscope was brilliantly illuminated with a flickering golden glow.

"Great Plan!" whispered Boysie Gann. "And this is what made him sick?"

Dr. Snow said slowly, "It is the same thing I saw in Harry Hickson's blood. Just before he died."

He took his place at the twin eyepieces and glanced for a second at the tiny golden spheres. "Fusorians," he said. "It took me a month with paper chromatography and mass spectrograms to verify it in Harry's blood, but that is what they were. Colonies of fusorian symbiotes gone wild. They're killing him."

He stared blankly at the microscope, then roused himself and hurried back to his patient. Machine Colonel Zafar was gasping for breath, his eyes wide and fixed on the ceiling, his fingers working aimlessly, his whole skin suffused with that golden glow.

"Quarla!" rapped Dr. Snow. "Seal the room! We'll give him a positive partial pressure of oxygen! . . . It won't save his life," he added wearily, "but it may prolong it—by minutes, at least."

The girl hurried to close the door tightly against its resilient seals, while her father adjusted valves on his mediconsole. Boysie Gann heard a "white" sound of hissing gas and felt a quick increase of pressure in his ears. He swallowed and heard Quarla's voice, queerly distant, say, "Father! He's—he's trying to get up!"

Machine Colonel Zafar was sitting up. His eyes were less remote, his breathing easier in the hypobaric atmosphere. But the golden glow was even more intense, the perspiration streaming from his brow.

And his eyes were on Boysie Gann. "You!" he cried. "Swan take you! Get back to the Machine, you traitor!" And he made the curious looping gesture with his arm that Gann had seen in Harry Hickson . . .

And then Boysie Gann remembered what the star was that lived in the heart of the Swan.

"Alpha Cygni!" he cried. "Deneb! The star in the constellation of the Swan!"

Zafar fell back on an elbow, glaring at him. "Your dirty mouth profanes the sacred name," he hissed. "The Starchild will punish you. In the heart of the Planner's citadel—in the bowels of Terra, where the Machine plays with its human toys—the Starchild will seek out and destroy its enemies!"

His eyes closed and he gasped for breath. Gann looked at Quarla and her father, but their expressions were as clouded as his own. "Starchild?" whispered the girl. "Father, do you know what—"

The doctor rumbled, "No, Quarla. I know nothing. Only rumors. A myth that there is a Starchild, and that he will bring the faithful of the Church of the Star home to Deneb's planets one day."

"No rumor!" shouted the glowing, golden man, and he paused to cough hackingly. "The Starchild lives! I've seen him in the heart of the Whirlpool! He has touched me with his radiant hand!"

But Dr. Snow was beside him, thrusting him back down on the bed, hushing him. "No!" cried Zafar wildly. "Don't stop the word of the Starchild! See here!"

And with a convulsive effort he drew out of the pouch of the one garment he still wore a stiff, cream-colored sheet of parchment. "The Writ of Liberation!" he shouted. "The Starchild gave it to me to send to Earth. And I send it—now!"

The pyropod that had belonged to Harry Hickson scuttled wildly about, its red eyes bright orange in the high-oxygen air. It hissed and shook its scales; and Zafar's eyes, too, were almost orange, glowing with tiny, dancing golden atoms, even in the pupil. They seemed blind—or fixed on something far more distant than the walls of the doctor's clinic.

Boysie Gann felt a shudder, as if the floor of the room were shaking. It had not moved.

He staggered and thrust out a hand to support himself, yet there was no motion. "To Earth!" cried the sick man, and threw the sheet of paper from him. "Swan, carry it! Starchild, guide it! To Earth . . ." He broke off.

The doctor tried again to calm him, but the dying man thrust him aside. "To Earth!" he cried. "And you—spy, traitor, slave of the Machine! Swan take you . . ."

Gann opened his mouth to say something, anything, but words would not come. The room lurched again, more violently. Sickeningly. The others did not seem to notice, yet the shock came again. He stumbled and almost fell, caught himself and reached out instinctively for the fluttering sheet of paper Zafar had thrown into the air.

It slipped away from him . . . and disappeared. One moment it was there. The next moment it was gone. Where it had been Gann saw a queer flow in the atmosphere, like flawed glass, spinning.

The whirlpool grew. It enlarged and came near him, and the room moved around him once more. Frantically he tried to leap back, to save himself, but he was falling, falling into the whirlpool . . . falling . . . and falling . . .

He fell for what seemed to be a thousand years while the room turned queerly dark and disappeared. Quarla's worried face, the doctor's look of shock, Mohammed Zafar's dying glare of hate—all disappeared, and around him he saw the dim shapes of stars and planets, of galaxies and dust clouds, rippling and glowing . . .

He fell for a long time, through what seemed to be a distance of billions upon billions of empty, airless miles.

And was.

For when the falling stopped and shaken and frantic he staggered to his feet, he fell flat and cut his face, bloodied his nose against a gray, soft-lighted metal floor.

He was in full-earth gravity.

He was on the Reefs no longer. He was on a planet. And around him stretched long empty corridors of metal walls and spinning tapes and glittering lights. Machine Major Boysie Gann was home at last. He was in the catacombs under Earth's surface that housed the mighty electronic masses of the Planning Machine.

6

And that was how it began for Boysie Gann, with a twenty-billion-mile drop that landed him in a place where no one could possibly be, in the heart of the Machine.

A warm wind blew between the narrow walls of the corridor. There was a faint distant hum, overlaid by the whir and hiss of rushing tape, the drone of enormous far-off machines. Gann stood up, gasping with the effort of moving his new weight—nearly a hundred kilos, when for months he had had to carry only a fraction of that, or none. He looked around, dazed.

He was in a long corridor. At the end of it, hundreds of yards off, was a brighter light that seemed to be a room.

He stumbled toward it, stanching the flow from his nose with the back of a hand, coughing and tasting the acrid blood at the back of his mouth.

The gray light turned out to come from a strange round chamber, its roof a high concrete dome. The great floor was broken with little island clusters of consoles and control panels, unattended. The wall, almost circular, was pierced with twenty-four dark tunnels like the one he had come from.

Gann leaned dizzily for a moment against the frame of the door through which he had entered. Then, summoning his strength, he shouted, "Help! Anyone! Is anybody here?"

The only answer was a booming echo from the great concrete dome, and the distant whirring of the tapes.

The control stations were empty, the corridor vacant. Yet as Gann stood there he began to feel that the place was somehow alive. As the echoes died away his ears began to register fainter, more distant sounds—a muffled mechanical murmur, a hum and whir. All the corridors were as empty as the one he had left. He peered into them one by one, saw nothing but the endless banks of computing equipment, the jungle of thick cables that roofed them.

Almost on tiptoes, humbled by the immense hush

around him, Gann went to the circular islands of consoles in the middle of the chamber. One unit, glowing with illuminated dials and buttons, faced each radiating tunnel. He stood entranced, watching the race of indicator lights across the face of each console.

He had never seen this place in his own person before, yet it was all familiar to him, had been repeated a hundred times, from a hundred angles, in the texts and visual-aid lectures at the Technicorps academy. He was in the very heart of the Planning Machine—the most secret, the most elaborately guarded spot on nine planets. The nerve center of the Plan of Man.

And the Planning Machine did not even know he was there!

That was the fact that most shook Boysie Gann, almost terrified him, not only for himself, although surely he was on dangerous ground—men had gone to the Body Bank for far less. His fear was for the Plan of Man itself. How was it possible?

With all its storage of facts on every act of every human being in the Plan—with its great taped mass of data covering every field of knowledge, every scientific discovery, every law—the Planning Machine seemed to have no way of telling that an unauthorized human being was at large in its very heart.

Gann found himself sobbing. Dizzied, he clutched at the edge of the nearest console and frantically tried to make sense of the unfamiliar glitter of dials and scopes and racing lights. There was a linkbox! For a moment he was hopeful—yet the linkboxes to the Machine were meant only for those who had received communion, who wore the flat plate in their skulls that gave the Machine access to their cranial nerve centers. Dared he use the linkbox?

But what else was there? Gann thought swiftly, crazily, of punching a button at random—throwing a switch—turning a dial. Any small change would alert the Machine. Serving robots or human techs would be there in moments.

Then his eyes caught sight of a small, flat red plate, bearing a single bright-lit button, and one word. It was at the top of the console nearest him. The single word was STOP.

He stood staring at it for a long moment, forgetting to

breathe. If that plate meant what it so clearly, unequivocally said, he had it in his power to ... to ...

To stop the Machine.

Machine Major Boysie Gann, Technicorps academy graduate, veteran of the spy school, trained and toughened against the worst a solar system could produce, found himself babbling in terrified hysteria. Stop the Machine! The thought was unbearable.

He flung himself on the linkbox, found a switch, wept, babbled, and sobbed into it. He was not speaking in the Mechanese that the Machine had developed for the links —didn't know it—would have forgotten it if he had known it. He was literally terrified, as nothing in his life had ever terrified him before.

When the squad of Plan Guardsmen in Machine gray came boiling out of the access elevators, racing down the corridors, their weapons at the ready, they found him slumped on the floor, all but unconscious.

Boysie Gann nearly died right then, with twenty bullets in his body. But the Techtenant in command issued a sharp order. He peered wonderingly at Gann, restrained his men, thought for a second, then shook his head. "Don't hurt him," he growled. "Or not so he can't talk! Let's get him up to the security office—fast!"

For four days Boysie Gann was questioned around the clock by the brawniest bullies in the Technicorps, and they were not gentle with him.

He answered all their questions—told the absolute truth—and paid for it with the impact of a club against his kidneys, a kick in his ribs. They knocked him unconscious a dozen times, and each time he revived again with a hard-faced medical orderly pulling a hypodermic out of his skin, brought back to face more interrogation.

Finally they let him sleep—not because they were satisfied with his answers, but because the medics feared he would die.

When he awoke he ached in every part of his body. He was strapped to an operating table. *The Body Bank,* he thought at first in a surge of panic. But it was not the Body Bank; it was a prison. Clearly the medics had been working on him. Although he ached, he could move. His toes curled, his fingers responded to his brain. His eyes opened and moved where he willed them.

199

Only one thing was different: there was a cold, hard pressure around his neck.

The security collar that Harry Hickson had removed so easily had been replaced.

Men were all around him, removing the straps, forcing him to his feet. "You! Risk," growled one of them, a radar-horned NCO with a chin that was stubbled blue with beard. "On your feet! You're going to talk to the general."

They hurried him through gray-walled corridors to an elevator. It rose with a sickening thrust of acceleration, stopped as rapidly. Gann nearly fell, but was thrust to his feet again by one of the guards. "Out! Move on, Risk!" And he stumbled through more corridors into a bare gray office, and there he stood at attention for a long, long time, waiting.

Then—Boysie Gann heard no signal, but perhaps it had been relayed through the radar-horned helmet of the guards—the security guardsman barked, "In there!" and thrust him through a door.

Gann entered a larger, brighter office. It was beautifully furnished, with a bust of the Planner in glowing gold smiling down from a pedestal, and a golden linkbox to the Machine dominating the desk. On the desk was a nameplate.

MACHINE GENERAL ABEL WHEELER

And the man who sat behind it was the general himself.

He sat regarding Boysie Gann for a long moment. Machine General Wheeler seemed more than half a machine himself. He was a big man, an angular, perplexing, abrupt-moving man. His whole body looked metallic: skin tan of bronze, eyes the color of steel, spikes of copper wire for hair. He stared at Gann and then, without a word, looked away, his eyes going to something invisible on his desk.

Boysie Gann felt choked by the hard, cold constriction of the security collar. Bruises aching, skin clammy with sweat, he stood painfully rigid. At the Technicorps academy he had learned the art of standing endlessly at attention—the imperceptibly slow shifting of weight and muscular tensions that kept a man from pitching forward on his face. He blanked out his mind, thought of nothing but of the importance of standing there.

200

The general's frowning eyes clung to the tilted communications screens that faced him on his desk, invisible to Gann. After a moment he tapped soundless keys, communicating, Gann knew, with the Machine. Gann wondered that he did not use the linkbox. It did not occur to him that the general might fear that Boysie Gann, the man who had appeared inexplicably in the heart of the Planning Machine's caverns, might equally inexplicably have learned to understand Mechanese.

The general waited, reading something, frowning stiffly. Abruptly his head jerked up and he stared at Gann.

The screens had ceased to flicker. His flat bronzed face was expressionless. It was a mask of meat, as if some bungling surgeon at the replacement center had failed to connect the nerves and muscles that would have given it life.

General Wheeler said sharply, "Machine Major Boysie Gann!" Gann jumped; he could not help himself; the voice was like a metal rasp. "You may stand at ease!"

Gann let his lean shoulders sag slightly forward, drew a long breath, shifted his feet. But he was not really at ease. General Wheeler's eyes were on him, steel-colored, as coldly merciless as if they were the probes of a surgeon planting electrodes in his brain. He snapped, "The Machine requires information from you."

Gann said painfully, "I know, sir. I've already been interrogated—about a hundred times, I'd say."

"It will be a thousand! You will be interrogated again and again and again. The Machine's need for truth is urgent." Wheeler's broad head jutted forward like the sudden thrust of a piston. "The Starchild! Who is he?"

There was a dry lump in Gann's throat. He swallowed and said stubbornly, "I don't know, sir. I've told everything I know."

"The Writ of Liberation! Who wrote it?" Gann shook his head. "How did it get into the Planner's headquarters?" Gann kept on shaking his head, hopelessly but obstinately. "And yourself, how did you get into the Planning Machine's tunnels? Who is Quarla Snow? Why did you kill Machine Colonel Zafar and make up this preposterous lie?"

"No, sir!" cried Gann. "I didn't! Colonel Zafar was anti-Plan!"

The general's wide mouth hardened. His bloodless lips shut like the jaws of a trap. His voice was like a muffled,

201

ominous clang. "The evidence," he said, "suggests that you are lying. Can you prove you are not?"

"No, sir. But—"

"Machine Mayor Boysie Gann! Are *you* the Starchild?"

"No, sir!" Gann was honestly surprised, indignant. "I—"

"Machine Major Boysie Gann! Do you know what became of the *Togethership?*"

Gann cried hopelessly: "The what? General, I never even heard of the—what is it? The *Togethership.* I don't know what you're talking about."

Like the steady pulse of a laser scan, the general tolled: "The *Togethership* went into space forty years ago. It was never heard of again. Major Gann, what do you know of this?"

"Nothing, sir! Why, I wasn't even born!"

For a moment the mask cracked, and the general's face looked almost human. Worried. Even confused. He said after a moment, "Yes. That's true. But . . ."

Then he tightened up again, bent forward stiffly from the hips. His steel eyes narrowed. "Are you loyal to the Plan of Man?" he asked softly.

"Yes, sir!"

The general nodded. "I hope so," he said bleakly. "For the sake of the Plan—and for your own sake, too. For I am going to tell you something that cannot ever be told again. If you whisper a word of it, Machine Major Boysie Gann, your death will come at once. *At once.*

"You see, the Planning Machine is not unique. There is another one."

Gann's eyes widened. "Another . . ." he stopped, and had to begin again. It was like being told there were two Jehovahs, a second Christ. "Another Planning Machine, sir? But where is it?"

The general shook his head. "Lost," he said somberly. "Another Machine—as great, as powerful, as complete as the one that guides the Plan of Man. And we do not know where it is.

"Or what it is doing."

There was a man named Ryeland, the general told Boysie Gann. A great mathematician. A brilliant scientist. The husband of the daughter of the then-Planner, and close to the center of power surrounding the Planning Machine itself. And decades before he had gone into space, just as Gann himself had done, and seen the Reefs of

Space, and come back with the tale of countless thousands of unplanned humans living their lives out on the fusorian worldlets, outside the scope of the Plan.

"What he said," rasped General Wheeler sternly, "was false! But the Machine wisely determined to test it out! The Planning Machine does not leap to conclusions! It weighs the evidence—learns the facts—makes a plan!"

"Yes, sir," said Boysie Gann. "I've heard of this Ryeland, I think. A leading scientist even today!"

The general nodded. "Today," he said cryptically, "Ryeland has abandoned error. A loyal servant of the Plan. And so is the former Planner, Creery, who also has turned away from falsity. But then . . ." He sighed, like the wheezing of a high-vacuum pump.

Then, he told Gann, both men had been duped—and had caused the Machine to commit . . . not an error, of course—that was impossible to the Machine—but to conduct an experiment that failed.

The experiment was to bring the Plan of Man to the Reefs.

The Machine had directed the construction of a mighty spacecraft called the *Togethership*. The biggest space-going vessel ever built, a mobile spacefort, it was fabricated at the yards on Deimos, and powered with six detachable jetless drive units that were themselves great fighting ships. And more than half of its hull was filled with a slave unit of the Planning Machine—a linked bank of computers and storage banks, as advanced as the Machine itself, lacking only the network of communications and implementation facilities that the Machine had developed out of the race of Man.

The *Togethership* was built, launched, tested, and fitted out. A selected crew was assembled and came aboard. Supplies were loaded for a ten-year cruise. The slave Machine assumed control . . . the *Togethership* flashed out past Orbit Pluto—passed the Spacewall—and was gone.

Days later a message came back via laser relay chain. All was going well. The *Togethership* had sighted a major cluster of the Reefs of Space.

No other message was ever received.

Machine General Wheeler paused, his steel-gray eyes on Gann. "No other message," he repeated. "It has never been heard from again. Scouting vessels, attempting to locate it, came back without having found any trace. Or did not come back at all. Or returned early, damaged, having been attacked by pyropods or something worse.

"That is the story of the *Togethership*, Major Gann. Except for one thing: the cluster of Reefs it last reported sighting was in the same position as what you have called Freehaven. And you were there, Major. What did you learn?"

Wonderingly, Gann shook his head. "Nothing, sir. Believe me. Not even a rumor."

The general looked at him for a long second. Then he nodded. "Gann," he said bleakly, "I will tell you one more thing." Abruptly he snapped three switches on his desk, glanced at a monitoring dial, nodded. "We are cut off," he declared. "Not even the Planning Machine can look in on us now. What I have to tell you is for *no* ears but your own.

"You see, Gann, it is not only the welfare of the Plan of Man that is involved here. I have a special interest in solving these mysteries. Solving them myself.

"Major Gann, I intend to be the next Planner."

Boysie Gann was adrift in dangerous waters, and he knew it. He had heard rumors of the power struggle of the human leaders who surrounded the great central power-fact of the Machine, jockeying for position, seeking personal advantage. The Technicorps Academy had been filled with sly jokes and blazing-eyed, after dark discussions of it. Some had viewed the political strife as treason (though they dared only whisper the thought). Some had taken it as a joke, or as a natural law of human affairs which they proposed to follow for their own advancement. Gann remembered the brother of the girl he had left at Playa Blanca, a white-hot idealist—remembered one of his instructors, a cynical humorist whose japes had seemed half in earnest and had set his classes wriggling with astonishment and something like fear. The instructor had disappeared one day. The young cadet who was Julie Martinet's brother had become an honor student at the academy. He had even gone on to spy school on Pluto, just as Gann himself was leaving.

But idealist or cynic, whatever the attitude of the individual, the whole question of political maneuvering had been remote. It was something that took place far off, high up—not in the life of Boysie Gann.

Not until now.

Machine General Abel Wheeler leaned forward from his desk and rapped out the words: "I must know this. Do you know who sent the Writ of Liberation?"

Gann shook his head. "Sir, I've never even seen it. I don't know what it says."

"Foolish threats, Major Gann! An insane promise to stop the sun's light. A warning to the Planner and to the Machine that freedom must be restored—hah! And yet—" the man's steel eyes grew colder and more distant still, as he contemplated something far away—"it seems that there is something behind the threats. For the sun is indeed stopped."

He paused. Boysie Gann blinked. "Stopped? The sun? Sir, I don't understand . . ."

"Nor do I," rasped the general, "but that does not matter. What matters is the security of the Machine. It matters particularly to me, since I am entrusted with its defense. This Writ of Liberation is a threat; I must protect the Machine against it. If I am successful, I will receive . . . a suitable reward. To those who can help me . . ." He glanced about his spy-tight room, leaned farther forward still, and merely mouthed the words: "I can offer them rewards, too, Major Gann."

His steel eyes stabbed restlessly about the room, then returned to Gann. "Major," he said. "I need you for a friend."

Gann was still turning over in his mind what the general had said about the stoppage of the sun. The sun? No longer shining in the sky? It was hard to believe. He shook himself free from the questions that were burning at him and said uneasily, "I hope to be your friend, sir. But I still know nothing of the Starchild!"

The general nodded like a metronome. "You will be questioned again," he rapped out. "This time, directly by the Machine, through one of its servitors—a human who has taken the Machine's communion and speaks directly to it. This will perhaps help you to remember certain things. It may even be that from the questions the acolyte asks, you may be able to deduce other things—perhaps even make a guess at things that are stored in the memory banks of the Machine that even I do not know. If so," he said, his face a bronze mask, "I will be interested. The choice is yours. My friend or my foe—and even now," he said, his bronze jaws hardening, "I have power enough to punish my foes."

205

He opened the switches again, glanced at his communications screens, nodded, tapped out an answer, and turned once more to Gann.

"You will go now to Sister Delta Four," he stated. "There your direct link questioning to the Machine will begin. Major, look at this!"

Unexpectedly he raised his right fist. It clenched like a remote manipulator into a bronze hammer. "This hand," he droned somberly, "once belonged to someone else, an unplanned traitor who threw a bomb at the Planner. His aim was poor. He missed the Planner but his bomb shattered my own right hand.

"My hand could not be repaired by the surgeons, so it was replaced. With the hand of the would-be assassin." The bronze fist slammed against the console.

"Gann, remember this! If you fail to serve the Machine in the way that is first required, you will serve it in some other way— more than likely in the Body Bank!"

7

The radar-horned guards were waiting.

"Come on, Risk!" growled the NCO in charge, and once again Boysie Gann was thrust and dragged through the long gray halls, into the elevators, out again—and left to wait in a bare gray room.

Only for a moment. Then the guards came back, looking angry and confused. "Come on, Risk!" growled the NCO again—he seemed to know no other words, be able to speak in no other way—and Gann was taken out again.

A girl was standing in the doorway, telling her sonic beads, her head bent. She wore the robe and cowl of one of the Machine's communing acolytes, one of those adepts who had learned the Mechanese that the Machine now spoke in preference to any other language, whose very brain centers were open to the touch of the Machine. As they passed she spoke to one of the guards. "Orders changed!" he said roughly. "Come along if you like— we're going to the Planner!"

Gann hung back, trying to turn and see her, but the

NCO shoved him ahead. He could hear the girl's oddly melodious voice, not so much speaking as chanting Mechanese in the quarter tones of her sonic beads, but could not make out her words.

She would be—what had General Wheeler called her? Sister Delta Four. The one who was to interrogate him.

But he was going instead to the office of the Planner himself!

In all his years of life under the Plan, Boysie Gann had never seen the Planner in the flesh. Few had. There was no need, with communications reaching into every home, even every room under the Plan—and the Planner was something more than human, removed from even the condescending social intercourse of emperors.

Gann shivered slightly. He was already assuming the attitudes of the convict of any land or time. He feared change. He dreaded the unknown. And the Planner represented a very large unknown quantity indeed.

Again the tunnels, again the high-velocity drop of the elevators. Again Gann was thrust into a tiny room and left there.

He was somewhere far underground. Listening, he could hear no sound except the muffled murmur of air from the duct overhead. The walls were an unpleasant yellowish gray—no longer quite the sterile Technicorps color, but tinged with Planner's gold. Gann wondered if it was deliberate, or if it was merely that this cell was so old, its occupants viewed with so little favor, that the baked-in coloring of the walls had yellowed with age. The ceiling gave a cold gray light. There was only one bare metal table and one bare metal chair.

The security collar was hard against his throat.

Gann sat down and laid his head on the table. His bruises were beginning to stiffen and ache. His brain was whirling.

Confused images were filling his mind. General Wheeler and his menacing hints of reward. Quarla Snow's spaceling, and the pyropods. Julie Martinet. A daytime sky with the sun somehow gone out . . . the sunlike fusorian globules in Colonel Zafar's blood . . . Julie Martinet again, and Quarla Snow.

He lived again the endless frightening drop that landed him in the bowels of the planet Earth, among the memory banks of the Machine. He saw again sterile Pluto's vistas of ice, and the great slow spin of Polaris Station.

He thought of the Writ of Liberation and wondered at the love for freedom of the Planless men of the Reefs—the love for freedom—the freedom to love . . .

He thought again of Julie Martinet, and submerged himself in memories of the Togetherness resort at Playa Blanca, the slight, dark girl he had heard signing, their golden dawn together on the beach, with the taste of salt spray on her lips. He could see her face as clearly as if she were in the room with him.

"Julie," he whispered, and she opened her lips to reply . . .

"Come on, Risk!" she said queerly—roughly. "Get up! Move!"

The radar-horned NCO was shaking him angrily. "Risk! Wake up!"

Gann shook himself. He had been asleep. His arm was numb and tingling where his head had rested on it.

He was still dazed as they dragged him out of the cell, into another room—larger, brighter, furnished in splendor. It was all gold. Gold tapestries on the wall, showing the spinning worlds of the Plan of Man. Gold light fixtures, and gold trays on the golden tables. The floor a carpeting of gold, the furniture upholstered in a golden fabric.

A guard stood by him at each side, gripping his arms. They brought him to the center of the room and stood there, waiting, while the NCO went to a gold-arched door and whispered to a Technicorps officer in the uniform of the Planner's guard who stood there. The officer nodded impatiently and held up a hand.

The radar-horned guard turned and signaled to his men. *Wait.*

Boysie Gann was very sure, without being told, of where they were. Beyond that door was the Planner himself.

They were not alone in the room. Turning his neck —the grip of the guards did not allow him to turn his body—he saw that the acolyte girl, Sister Delta Four, was in the room, kneeling on a golden hassock, telling her sonic beads. She was slight. What small sight he could get of her face, under the great soft cowl, was oval, grave, and pale. Her loose black robe fell to the floor around the hassock. Her cape bore the luminous emblem of those who had undergone communion with the Machine—the symbolic ellipses of electronic orbits intertwined.

The guards wrenched him straight again. One whispered to the other across him, "Watch! She's going to go into communion."

Even in his precarious position Gann could not help wanting to see. He had never before been with an acolyte during communion. It was something to be desired—and dreaded.

If the deadly security collar around his neck was the stick that the Machine had invented to enforce the Plan of Man, the communion plate was the carrot that rewarded faithful service.

Gann knew what it looked like. He thought he had caught a glimpse of it in the forehead of Sister Delta Four, the bright metal disk grafted into the skin, starred with its black pattern of holes that accepted the prongs of the communion plug.

He knew that communion was supposed to be the perfect experience. The communion plate was only its exterior symbol. It was in the brain itself that the delicate stereotaxia of the Machine's neurosurgeons had done their finest work. Through electrodes wired to the plate in the forehead, the Machine requited its deserving servants with tuned electronic stimuli. Its messages flowed directly into the pleasure centers of the brain.

The perfect experience—for it had no taint of reality to corrupt it, no bill presented in the form of exhaustion or physical damage—no substance! It was the quintessence of pleasure. Stripped of tactile, visual, olfactory— of all sensual complications—it was the great good thing that men had always sought, and found imperfectly as a side effect of eating, or drinking, or inhaling the crisp air of a mountain morning, or sex. It was all of them, distilled and served up in a tidy package, received through a bright metal plate.

It was so perfect, thought Boysie Gann wildly, that it seemed somehow wrong . . .

"She's getting ready!" whispered one of the guards, and Gann ventured to turn his head again to see.

He succeeded—only for a moment, but he succeeded. The guards were watching too, and loosened their grips just enough for him to turn.

Sister Delta Four lifted the black hood to uncover her forehead. There on the smooth white skin he saw the bright metal disk—saw it, trembled, looked away—looked

209

back again, and saw clearly what his mind had rejected.

He saw the face of Sister Delta Four.

There was a hoarse whisper from the doorway. "Let's go!" The guards started, and jerked him away, thrust him facing forward so that he saw the radar-horned NCO with a face like fury, beckoning them angrily, signaling that the Planner was ready for them now.

But Boysie Gann fought them, struggled like a wild man. "No!" he shouted. "Wait!" And he battled the astonished guards, trying to turn, to go back to the girl whose serene face he had seen, eyes closed, lifting the communion plug to her forehead.

The guards lashed out at him, struck him. He hardly felt the blows. He turned, breaking free of one of them, colliding heavily with the other so that they fell sprawling on the thick golden rug, the other guards leaping toward them. But as they fell, Gann saw the face again.

He had been right. There was no doubt. Sister Delta Four was Julie Martinet.

The girl he loved was now no longer entirely human. Her vows were no longer to him. She was an adjunct to the Machine, as dependent on it for her every bit of life and thought as some remote-directed subsea mining dredge . . . and as little a part of the race of men.

Julie Martinet had become a part of the machine.

8

If the catacombs of the Machine were the nerve center of the Plan of Man, then the great State Hall of the Planner was its heart. Huge as a hangar for jetless spacecraft, ornate as a Pharaoh's tomb, it housed the most powerful man in the history of the human race, and it was worthy of him. The walls were paneled in gold. Crescent-shaped lunettes were frescoed with scenes of the nine planets and a thousand lesser worlds on which the Plan of Man reigned supreme.

In the great hall a score of attendants waited on the Planner's will: his personal physician, three black-robed Mechanese acolytes with their linkboxes and tonal beads, a dozen guards. The Vice-Planner for Venus was there, an efficient little engineer whose nose and ears were out of scale, seeming to have come from some gigantic donor. So was Machine General Wheeler, fixing Boysie Gann as he entered with a steel-gray stare.

No one spoke.

Dominating the great hall, on a huge golden chair, was the Planner himself. He was staring, lost in thought, at a great quartz table on which stood scores of fantastic metal and crystal toys.

Gann found himself standing in the center of a great tesselated floor, alone. His guards had halted behind him. He waited for the Planner to notice him.

But the Planner's eyes were on his toys. He sighed and stretched out a hand to them, stacking them in military rows as absorbedly as any five-year-old with his lead soldiers; he formed them in columns and marched them across the clean gleaming quartz.

The figures were dragons. They were monsters from storybooks, and creatures too incredible ever to have been in a story. Some were mirror-bright, some black. Many were in gorgeous rainbow hues. They had no wings, nor had they legs. Their heads were the heads of monsters, some with teeth like sabers, some with curious frayed flower-petal faces, like the muzzle of a star-nosed mole.

Boysie Gann had never been close to the Planner before. He could not help being a little disappointed. The Planner was only a man! An old, fat, flabby man at that—and, thought Gann privately, a bit of an eccentric too.

Yet the Planner was the voice of the Planning Machine itself. It was impossible for the Machine to falter in its judgments, impossible that its chosen instrument be anything less than perfect. Of course, there were the recurrent rumors about the present Planner's predecessors—old Planner Creery, for example, who had fallen into error in attempting to allow the Reefs of Space entry into the Plan of Man under their own conditions . . . Swiftly Gann rejected that thought. This was no place to be thinking treason!

He turned his mind to the stabbing pain that had pierced him in the anteroom when he had found the girl he loved, Julie Martinet, changed into a priestess of the Machine, Delta Four. How had it happened? *Why* had it happened? . . .

The Planner raised his great round head and stared at

Boysie Gann. "You," he rasped. "Do you know what these are?"

Gann swallowed and stuttered. "Y-yes, sir," he got out. "I mean, I think so. I mean, some of them look like pyropods. The creatures that prey on the life in the Reefs of Space, sir . . ."

But the Planner was nodding his great bloated head. "Pyropods, yes," he boomed. With a sudden motion he swept the delicately carved pieces off the quartz table, sent them crashing to the floor. "I wish I had a thousand pyropods!" he shouted. "A million! I wish I could send them out to the Reefs to kill and destroy every living thing on them! What insanity that these reef rats should dare talk to me of freedom!"

He broke off and glared at Boysie Gann, who stood silent, unable to speak. The Planner said, "I stand for classic truth! What is it that animates the Reefs of Space, Gann? Tell me, for you have been there. It is the romantic fallacy," he roared, not waiting for an answer, "the eternal delusion that man is perfectible, that there is a spirit of goodness that can grow and mature in crass organic creatures! What insanity! And now they threaten me in my own Hall—blot out my sun—boast of more deadly measures still!" He pressed his plump arms against the carved golden arms of his chair, half lifted himself, leaned forward to Gann and shouted, "Who is this Starchild, Gann? It is you?"

Boysie Gann was galvanized into shocked speech. "No, sir! Not me! I've never seen him. I know nothing about him—oh, except what I've heard here, when General Wheeler's men interrogated me. And a few rumors. But I'm not the Starchild!"

"Rumors. What are those rumors, Gann? I must know!"

Gann looked helplessly around the great hall. All in it were watching him, their eyes cold, their faces impassive. He was on his own; there was no help for him from anyone there. He said desperately. "Sir, I've told all I know a hundred times. I'll tell it again. I'll you all I know, but the truth is, sir, that I know almost nothing about the Starchild!"

"The truth," boomed the Planner, "is what *I* say it is! Go on! Speak!"

Gann obediently commenced the old story. "I was detailed, sir, to investigate certain irregularities on Polaris Station . . . ." As he went through the long, familiar tale there was dead silence in the hall, the Planner listening impassively, leaning on one arm in his great golden chair, the others taking their cue from him. Gann's voice fell on the enormous hall like words shouted down a well. Only echoes answered him, only the narrowing of an eye, the faint shift of a position showed that his hearers had understood. He finished with his arrest in the catacombs of the Machine, and stood silent.

The Planner said thoughtfully, "You spoke of a sign. The sign of the Swan."

"Yes, sir." Boysie Gann demonstrated as best he could the supple motion of forearm and hand that he had seen in Harry Hickson and the dying Colonel Zafar. "I believe it refers to the constellation Cygnus, in which the main star, Deneb, is some sort of object of worship to what is called the Church of the Star . . ."

The Planner turned his great head away from Gann toward the black-robed knot of communicants of the Machine. "Deneb!" he barked. "Display it!" One of the acolytes spoke in soft, chiming tones to his linkbox. Instantly the lights in the great hall darkened, and on the vaulted ceiling a panorama sprang into light. The Planner craned his thick neck to stare searchingly upward. Every eye followed his.

It was as if the thousand yards of earth and rock above them had rolled back. They were gazing into the depths of space on what seemed to be a clear, moonless night—late in autumn, Gann judged by the position of the constellations; perhaps around midnight. Overhead were the great bright stars of the Summer Triangle, Altair to the south, Deneb and Vega to the north. The Milky Way banded the vault with a great irregular powder of stardust. Low on the horizon to the west red Antares glowed; to the east was Fomalhaut. . .

Abruptly the scene began to contract. It was as if they were rushing through space, straight toward the constellation Cygnus. Fomalhaut and Antares slipped out of sight with Sagittarius and Altair's constellation, the Eagle; so did the Pole Star and Cepheus below it; all that was left was Cygnus, the constellation of the Swan, hanging over their heads like a bright canopy.

A voice chimed, "Constellation Cygnus. Stars: Alpha Cygni, also known as Deneb, blue-white, first magnitude.

213

Beta Cygni, also known as Albireo, double, components deep blue and orange. Gamma Cygni—"

The Planner's voice cut it in raspingly: "Just Deneb, idiot! What about Deneb?"

The voice did not miss a beat. It chimed: "Deneb, distance four hundred light-years. Surface temperature eleven thousand degrees. Supergiant. Spectrographic composition, hydrogen, calcium—"

"Planets!" boomed the Planner irritably.

"No planets known," sang the invisible voice. Gann craned his neck; it came from one of the black-robed acolytes, but with their faces shrouded in the hoods he could not tell which.

The Planner was silent for a long time, staring upward. He said at last, "Has the Machine any evidence of physical connection between Deneb and the Starchild?"

"No evidence, sir," chanted the invisible voice at once. "Exceptions as follows: Possible connection between star Deneb and reported Church of the Star. Possible connection between star Deneb and star 61 Cygni in same constellation, 61 Cygni being one of the stars said Starchild threatened to, and did, extinguish. Neither of these items considered significant by the Machine."

The Planner grumbled. "Very well. Cancel." The display overhead winked out, the room lights sprang up. The Planner sat brooding for a moment, his eyes remote. He stared absently around the room, his gaze passing over Boysie Gann, over the spilled toys at his feet, over the faces of the guardsmen and Machine General Wheeler.

His eyes came to rest on the black-robed acolytes. Then he sighed and gestured to one of them. It was only the crook of a finger, but the figure in black at once came toward him, holding something in his hand. It was a length of golden cable extending from his linkbox. At its end was a golden eight-pronged plug.

Boysie Gann's eyes went wide.

If he was not insane—and no, he was not; for already the acolyte was stepping to the Planner's side, touching his forehead, sweeping back his sparse, unruly hair, baring the glittering plate that was set into his forehead—the Planner was about to undergo communion with the Machine!

The spectable was fascinating—and frightening.

Heedless of the eyes on him, the Planner sat relaxed

214

while the acolyte deftly slipped the golden plug into the receptors in the plate on his forehead.

At once the Planner's expression changed. His eyes closed. The fretful, angry look disappeared. There was a second's grimace, the teeth bared in rictus, the corners of the eyes wrinkling in deep furrows, the jaw set. It was like a momentary pang of agony . . . Or ecstasy.

It passed, and the Planner's face went blank again. His breathing began to grow more rapid. As the planted electrodes excited the secret centers of his brain, he began to show feeling. His face creased in a smile, then frowned, then smiled again, forgivingly. His lips began to move. Hoarse, inarticulate words whispered—slowly . . . then faster, faster. His plump body shook, his fingers worked. The black-robed acolyte calmly touched his arm, whispered in his ear.

The Planner calmed. His body relaxed again. His whispered voice stopped.

The acolyte waited for a second, nodded, removed the cable and stepped lightly away. The Planner opened his eyes and looked around.

To Boysie Gann, the change in the Planner was stranger than anything he had seen on the Reefs of Space. A glum, angry, harried man had accepted that moment of communication with the electronic joys of the Machine; a cheerful, energetic, buoyant one had emerged from it. The Planner opened his mouth and boomed laughter into the great hall. "Ha!" he shouted. "Ho! That's good!"

He sat up and pounded his great fist onto the quartz table. "We'll destroy them!" he cried. "Reef rats and Starchild—anyone who dares interfere with the Plan of Man. We'll crush them and their fanciful dreams forever. And you'll help in this, Boysie Gann, for you are the chosen instrument of the Plan in this great work!"

For a lunatic moment Gann thought of turning, running, fleeing—of leaping toward the Planner and letting the decapitation charge in his security collar end his problems forever. There was something wild and fearful in the great chuckling good humor with which the Planner bubbled now, something that terrified Gann. If the Machine could cause such personality change in its most favored of servants, Gann feared the Machine. Feared it! And that thought was in itself fearsome to him, for the Machine had always been the great good master whose judgments were infallible, who always rewarded good service, punished only the bad. Yet this particular reward seemed a very terrible punishment to Gann . . .

But all he said was, "Yes, sir. I serve the Plan, sir!"

The Planner shouted with glee. "Serve it well, boy!" he cried. "Serve it with all your heart and mind—or you'll serve it with your eyes and arms and liver, in the Body Bank! We all serve the Plan, boy. In one way or another!" And he dismissed Gann with a good-humored wave of one fat arm and turned to General Wheeler. As the guards closed in on Gann and marched him out of the room he caught one glimpse of the general, staring toward him. The steel-gray eyes were cold and empty, but Gann could read their message.

Don't fail me, either, Gann, they said.

9

There had once been a time, thought Boysie Gann, when life was simple and his duty clear. In that dead, half-forgotten time—was it only months ago? it seemed like centuries—he had found, and loved, and won a girl named Julie Martinet. He remembered the night they met, remembered their long hours together, their endless promises, the bright hope of happiness they gave each other. He remembered the long white beach at the Togetherness center at Playa Blanca, and her kiss before he left. Warm, sweet, soft, loving, she had been everything a man could want. Her memory had followed Boysie Gann twenty billion miles out from the sun, and her absence had made that long voyage bleak.

Yet never had he been so far from her as in this room. He could, if he dared, reach out and touch the lips he had kissed at Playa Blanca. But the mind behind them was no longer the mind of the sweet, warm girl he had loved. The body was the body of Julie Martinet, but what inhabited it was Sister Delta Four.

Involuntarily he whispered: "Julie! Julie Martinet . . ."

She stood motionless, regarding him with grave dark eyes. He searched them for some hint of recognition, for the saving warmth of love that had filled them at Playa Blanca, but nothing was there.

216

She shook her hooded head. "I am Delta Four," she said, her voice a melodious chime. "I am to interrogate you for the Machine." She stood watching him, waiting for a response, her pale face half hidden by the deep folds of the cowl she wore. The luminous emblem on her black robes mocked him. It was a *Keep Off* sign that he dared not ignore.

But he could not help saying, "Julie, don't you remember me at all? Can't you tell me what happened?"

She fingered her long string of bright black beads, each an electronic bell that rang when she stroked it. "Major Gann," she sang, her voice in perfect pitch with the tonal beads, "I am, as you see, an acolyte of the Machine. I do not wish to be reminded of any other life."

"Please, Julie. At least tell me why you didn't wait—"

Her grave head nodded. "We have time," she trilled. "Ask your question."

"Why didn't you—I mean, why didn't Julie Martinet wait for me? I sent you a letter from Pluto—"

"Your message was delivered," she sang. "But Julie Martinet had already been admitted to training as acolyte for the Machine. She destroyed your message. She does not wish to recall it."

"But I loved you!" Gann burst out. "How could you turn your back on me?"

The serene pale face stared at him without curiosity. "Julie Martinet loved you," she corrected him melodiously. "I am Delta Four. Please sit down, Major Gann. I must interrogate you for the Machine."

Reluctantly Gann sank into a chair, watched as she moved another chair near his. She seated herself with deliberate grace.

From under the cape she brought forth a small link-box, covered in a black plastic, like leather. "Major Gann," she said, "I must ask you if you are the Starchild." Her voice was pure melody, cold and perfect and remote as her white, oval face.

Gann snapped, "Plan take it, no! I'm fed up with that question! I've said it a hundred—"

But she was shaking her head. "Wait," she broke in. "One moment, please."

He watched her glumly, the ache of his bruises combining with the deeper ache in his heart as, hooded head intently bent, she once again touched the long string of beads. As each electronic chime rang out her throat echoed the tone, practicing the difficult scale of tone phonemes that made up the artificial language called Mechanese.

Mechanese was the difficult bridge between the Machine and the human mind. Earlier computers had crossed that bridge by building their own structure of translation, transforming English into Fortran or another artificial tongue, Fortran into binary numbers, the binary statement into instructions and data for processing. The Machine's language was itself a sort of pattern of binary digits that represented its own electronic processes—circuits open or closed, storage points charged or discharged, ferrite cores in one magnetic state or another.

Human beings could not be trained to speak that binary language, nor could the Machine of the Plan of Man be troubled with the dull task of translation. Instead, it had created a language that men could learn—with difficulty, with a consecration of purpose that required them to give up the coarser human aspects of their lives, but all the same with accuracy and assurance.

Mechanese was a bridge, but a difficult one. The Machine, counting time in nanoseconds, could not wait for laggard human speech. Accurate in every either-or response, it had no need of redundancy. It had computed the theoretical capacity of the human ear and the human voice at some 50,000 binary units of information per second, and it had devised a tongue to approach that theoretical maximum.

Normal human speech conveyed only about fifty such bits of information in a second; Mechanese was a thousand times more efficient.

And, Gann knew, it was about a thousand times as difficult to learn.

Bitterly he realized that it was the very thing in Julie Martinet that first drew his attention to her—her soft, true voice—that had lost her for him forever. The Machine sought endlessly for humans who could be trained to Mechanese—sought them and, when it found them, did not let them go. Only such special individuals could be trained to speak Mechanese well, though it was possible for almost anyone who invested the time and effort to learn a sort of pidgin, or to understand it. A true acolyte needed not only a wide vocal range but a true sense of absolute pitch. The tonal beads would help. An acolyte could, as Delta Four was doing now, use them as a sort of pitch pipe

218

before talking to the Machine. But not even they would convert an ordinary human into one fluent in Mechanese.

Watching her tolling the tonal beads, Gann pictured the long, arduous weeks of training. He knew it required total concentration, absolute devotion. And its ultimate reward was the bright metal plate in her forehead.

Her quick voice trilled a chain of silver bird notes. The linkbox sang an electronic answer. Her alert, emotionless eyes looked up at him at last.

"We're ready now," she said. "Major Gann. Are you the Starchild?"

A hundred interrogations, and this was the hundred and first.

Boysie Gann no longer needed his mind to answer the girl's questions. Repetition had taught his tongue and lips to answer by themselves. *I am not the Starchild. I have never seen the Starchild. I know nothing of the Writ of Liberation. I have never engaged in unplanned activities.*

And all the time his heart was shouting: *Julie! Come back . . .*

Each time he answered a question, Sister Delta Four sang into the linkbox. The strange, quavering notes sounded nothing like what he had said, but he knew that each difficult phoneme was also a meaningful morpheme, each sung syllable a clause. And each time she asked a question she paused, regarding him with detached interest, her perfect face as inhuman as her voice.

"My tour of hazardous duty took me out to the Spacewall . . ." he said, and went on with the long familiar tale.

He felt the bright gold walls pressing in on him, suddenly suffocating. He wondered how many thousand feet of rock lay above him. Up at the surface of the earth, was the endangered sun shining now on woods and fields tinted faintly green with early spring? Or was there arctic ice above this isolated, sound-deadened cell in the Planner's vast suites? Or miles, perhaps, of dark and icy ocean?

He had no way of knowing.

And abruptly he felt a wave of desperate longing for the Reefs, for Freehaven, for Quarla Snow. Those strange spaceborne rocks were somehow kinder than the Plan of Man. He was homesick for infinite space . . . for that fantastic concept freedom . . .

The stern snarl of the linkbox brought him back to his interrogation. "Proceed," cooed Sister Delta Four. "You

219

were attacked by pyropods?" Her voice was as tuneful as a crystal bell, cold and empty as the black space between the Reefs. There was no flicker of feeling on the serene and secret oval of her face.

He nodded wearily—then, remembering: "Yes, but before that, I forgot to mention one thing. Hickson removed my collar."

Her brilliant dark eyes did not widen. She merely sang into the linkbox, still watching him, her eyes intent but somehow blind, as if she were already absorbed in her private ecstasy of communion.

The black box snarled.

"The Machine requires elucidation," Sister Delta Four trilled sweetly. "We must find this unregimented Harry Hickson. His knowledge must be recovered for the Plan. Then each organ of his body must be obliterated."

Gann grinned bleakly at her, looking at the lips he had kissed so long ago. "Sorry. I can't help you. He's dead."

"The Machine rejects this data," she sang. "Did you not ask this unplanned man how he removed the collar?"

"I don't know how," he admitted. He paused, hoping to see some living spark in her eyes. But there was none. The black box whirred ominously. "I think he was a convert to the Church of the Star," said Gann hurriedly. "I think—that is, as I understand it, his power was thought to come from Deneb."

An angry peal from the linkbox. "That is self-evidently false," sang the cool voice of Sister Delta Four. "No star possesses any such power to share. No mind in the universe is more powerful than the Machine."

She paused while the black box snarled again. "If the falsehood is Harry Hickson's, the truth will be extracted when he is captured," she translated sweetly. "If the falsehood is yours, Major Gann, you are in grave danger of the Body Bank."

He cried, "I'm telling the truth! I'm loyal to the Plan of Man!"

The box sang; the girl intoned, "The Machine rejects such merely verbal assurances. One moment. The Machine is receiving additional data through another input."

Queerly, the girl's voice was fading. Gann blinked at her. She seemed to be moving—dwindling—as if she were falling away from him, down through the long, dark emptiness of space. It was as if Gann were looking at her through a zoom lens, pulling away. She receded a thousand yards . . .

Then she was back. Gann felt a moment's vertigo, as if the Planner's suite down in the bowels of the earth were somehow dancing a slow waltz. The feeling passed.

The linkbox whirred menacingly, and Sister Delta Four sang, "The Machine terminates this interview." A sharp hum from the linkbox. "It reminds you that unplanned ideas, like unplanned words and unplanned actions, must be severely corrected. But it reserves judgment on your ultimate disposition."

Her white, perfect face was smiling slightly, perhaps in contemplation of her instant rapture that was soon to come, when the buried electrodes would excite her brain to the incomparable bliss of electronic communion. But the linkbox was not yet through with her. It buzzed again, harshly.

"The Machine finds your narrative incomplete," she recited melodiously, contemplating Gann with her dark serene eyes. "You have not identified the Starchild. You have revealed no facts about the *Togethership*. You have not accounted for the so-called Writ of Liberation. You have not explained how you got into the vault of the Machine."

Gann shook his head. "I don't know what to tell you," he said. The box whirred implacably.

"Your statements are inadequate," Sister Delta Four sang again. "But the interview is concluded . . ."

There was that surge of unreal motion again. Gann gripped his chair. This time even the girl felt it; her perfect lips opened, her eyes shook a flicker of surprise.

The linkbox twittered urgently. At the same moment loud bells and sirens began to sound elsewhere in the Planner's warrens.

"Earth temblors," the girl began haltingly, "have been detected at several points . . ."

Then the linkbox crashed out a loud, despairing sound. Sister Delta Four gasped. Instinctively she reached out and caught Boysie Gann's arm. "Pyropods!" she cried. "The . . . the . . . Oh, you've got to help! The Planner's hall has been invaded by pyropods! Dozens of them! They're there now!"

The private room in which Sister Delta Four had been interrogating Boysie Gann was one tiny office in the im-

221

mense network of corridors and chambers that was the administrative and living headquarters of the Planner. It had been locked, but the door opened instantly to the pattern of the girl's fingertips on the knob. It flung wide, and Gann and the girl ran through the open doorway, into a wide, gold-walled hall. Broad as a highway, tall as a two-story building, it ran straight through the heart of a mountain, the Planner's rooms opening off it at intervals all the way. It was a great ceremonial thoroughfare, lined with glittering gold and crystal statuary, hung in gold brocades, paneled with murals and viewscreens.

And it was filled with the reeking, choking, dusty smoke of jet exhausts.

A scream of some huge rocketing body ripping through the air smote their ears. A human shout of anguish—the cries of men taken by surprise—the thin, ear-splitting volley of laser guns. In all the noise and confusion Gann saw one thing clearly—saw it, grabbed the girl by her arm and pulled her back into the shelter of the doorway.

A pyropod was rocketing toward them down the hall.

It roared at them at a speed nearing Mach One; in the cramped quarters of the hall the shriek of its passage was physically painful, deafening. And the look of the thing was that of an avenging angel come to Earth, set on destruction.

It was a nightmare come to life. Wilder than the most fantastic of the Planner's toys, it was shaped a little like a scorpion, larger than a charging buffalo. Its eyes were great mirrors with stalked receptors at the center—natural radio telescopes, glowing red. Its jaws were mighty enough to crunch steel bars. Its talons could rip through armor plate. Its body was armored with darkly shining scales; a long, wicked, saber-like tail was arched over its back. And the whole thing was screaming through the air of the tunnel toward them.

The girl cried out in fear; Gann pulled her head against his chest, quieting her—though in truth the sound of her terror was lost in the ear-splitting din of the pyropod's passage. This was no baby, like the one Gann had played with on Harry Hickson's reef. It was an armored juggernaut, full-grown, capable of battling a Plan space cruiser on equal terms.

It passed them and rocketed into a group of armed guardsmen, knotted a hundred yards down the hall. They were firing wildly with laser and projectile weapons; it

222

struck them, passed . . . and they were gone. Only a jackstraw heap of corpses and stirring near-dead marked where they had been.

"Great Machine!" gasped Sister Delta Four, her impeccable serenity gone, her black hood thrown back, the bright metal plaque blinking out of a terrified face. "What was that?"

"You told me," snapped Gann. "Pyropod! If it comes back, we're dead!"

She whimpered and tugged at his arm. "Back in here. . . we can hide."

"No! There are others. If one finds us this way we don't have a chance. But if I can get a gun . . ."

He stared down the broad, long hall. The bright jet of the pyropod's tail was out of sight. Perhaps the monster had gone into another room, or down another hallway. Meanwhile, the guardsmen were still in a heap of death.

He came to a fast decision. "Julie—I mean . . . oh, never mind that. Listen! These things can be killed if you know where to aim. I'm going after a gun. You stay in the room!" And he was off, running as hard as he could, straight down the broad hall toward the dying men. He fought the temptation to skulk along the sides. There was no concealment here. If the creature came back, he would be dead; it was that simple. His only chance was speed. He did that hundred yards in Olympic time.

And it was nearly too slow, at that. Gasping, wheezing, his chest and muscles on fire, he heard a sudden growing volume of sound and looked up. A howl of sound was coming toward him, and behind it, almost as fast as the sound itself, a pyropod was rocketing at him.

He flung himself to the floor.

The thing missed him by inches; he caught a quick glimpse of metal jaws and crystal tusks, of enormous talons reaching out for him; then it was past, and he was up and running.

He heard the thing crashing, smashing, battering into the statuary and the walls of the hall, stopping itself at heedless cost, but he did not turn. He leaped to the fallen guardsmen, caught up a laser gun, checked its charge and whirled.

The pyropod had completed its turn.

It caught Gann in its pulsing red headlamps. It was screaming at him, a living battle rocket. He fired one

223

maximum-blast shot into its eye, and tumbled to the ground again.

It screamed in agony as it passed over him. It blundered blindly into a wall, sideswiped a cluster of statuary, gouged out a bright streak in the hard metal of the corridor. Its jet flamed brightly and faded. Gann fired one more shot, then covered his head with his hands.

There was a great distant explosion. He felt the shock waves pass over him. Some of the corpses near him were stirred by the thrust of it, their bleeding limbs flopping wildly, their unseeing faces nodding.

The pyropod was gone.

But Sister Delta Four had said "dozens" of them . . .

Quickly Gann stooped to the abattoir the pyropod had left and rummaged for weapons. He discovered a half-empty laser weapon, pocketed a light projectile gun, loaded up with the three heaviest-charge laser guns he could find. Then he turned to go after Sister Delta Four.

She was standing just behind him. She had seen what he was doing, and she had done the same. She held two weapons, and in a pouch in her robes Gann could see the glitter of at least one more.

He hesitated, then grinned.

"Come on," he cried. "Let's see what we can do! Right in the eyes, remember!" He clapped her on the shoulder, and turned and ran in the direction of the Great Hall of the Planner.

A hellish howling and roaring led him to it. He needed no other signs.

Before he got there, he destroyed two more pyropods, neither quite as big as the one that had nearly got them in the hall, and Sister Delta Four had frightened another off with a long-range shot that might or might not have hit.

The Great Hall of the Planner was the mother hive. It was filled with the great creatures, ripping through the smoky, sulfurous air, ripping out boulder-sized bits from the walls, from the huge golden chair of the Planner, from anything that would give them reaction mass. They seemed to have conquered the human defenders of the Hall with no trouble, and were fighting among themselves over the spoils.

Then Gann caught the slim ruby flash of a laser weapon.

One of the pyropods bellowed with pain, like an air-raid siren gone mad. It was not a mortal wound, but it must have been an agonizing one; the injured creature hurtled through the air and collided with another feasting beast; the two began to slash each other.

Someone was still alive in the room!

Warning the girl to remain behind, Gann peered cautiously around the door. The laser flash had seemed to come from one of the decorative niches holding statuary, under a painted lunette. Gann took a deep breath and shouted, then ducked back around the door. But it was useless. In the monstrous racket of the snarling, fighting pyropods his voice was unheard.

He caught Sister Delta Four by the shoulder, pulled her close to him so that her ear was next to his lips. "I'm going to try to pick them off one by one!" he cried. "They're not paying any attention right now. I think I can get most of them. But if any start this way, you shoot right for the eyes!"

She nodded, her face calm and untouched again, the great service lasers incongruous in her hands. He gave her a last thoughtful glance, unable to forget the bright communion plate that was now once again hidden under the black cowl, then turned toward the Great Hall.

It took him twenty minutes.

He counted, and there were fifteen of the great beasts rocketing and fighting about the hall. He got seven of them, one by one, before there was any trouble. Then at Sister Delta Four's warning touch, he had to turn and destroy a lone wanderer racing toward them down the hall.

He got three more, and then he noticed that at the far side of the hall one screamed, burst and died that he had not fired on. Whoever was hiding in the niche across the hall had seen what he was doing, and had copied him.

There were two guns firing then—no, three; for Sister Delta Four stepped out beside him and helped gun down the last survivors, confused and blundering, as the walls shook with the creatures' screams and the air grew acrid and sickening with their fumes.

Then they were all gone.

Hesitantly Gann entered the hall, laser guns ready, eyes darting about as he picked his way across the destroyed battleground.

There were distant bellowings still. Obviously there were

still a few strays elsewhere in the underground palace of the Planner; but most of them were dead in this room. He hurried toward his unknown ally.

Machine General Abel Wheeler stepped stiffly out of the niche and moved toward him. There was a hard grin of victory on his face. He holstered one gun and thrust out a hand with a motion like a piston to grasp Gann's extended clasp. "Well done, Major," he rasped.

"Thank you, sir. I had help. This is—"

The general's expression did not change. "I know Sister Delta Four," he boomed. "You may tell the Machine that I commend you, Sister. Please contact the Machine now and ascertain its condition. I fear this attack may have been intended to harm it!"

He grasped Gann's arm in a grip of steel and led him away. "Ugly creatures," he rasped, kicking at one enormous ripped cadaver. "Poetic justice, you might say. The Planner has always been fascinated by them. Interesting coincidence that they've appeared out of nowhere, here in his own home grounds." He glanced over his shoulder at Sister Delta Four, who was quickly chiming her tonal beads, setting up her linkbox. "See here, Gann. Look at this."

On the floor in front of the niche where General Wheeler had taken refuge there was a square of thick, creamy paper. "What is it, sir?"

"Pick it up, man! See for yourself!"

There were human voices, now, coming from the hall. The mighty forces of the Plan of Man were regathering themselves. Order was being restored.

Boysie Gann hesitated. Something was wrong. "The Planner?" he asked. "Is he . . ." He looked around the great hall littered with the corpses of the invading pyropods and the human guards who had been trapped there.

"Not he, Major! Gone this half hour. Read that document!"

Gann, with a feeling that something was awry, leaned forward and retrieved the paper. He glanced at it.

Then the doubts and uncertainties dropped out of his mind. This paper was strangely familiar. He had seen one just like it—twenty billion miles away—in the hands of the dying Machine Colonel Zafar.

That had been the document they called the Writ of Liberation!

226

And this one was something almost as earthshaking in its importance, almost as dangerous to the Plan of Man.

Boysie Gann read swiftly, looked up at the silent carved face of General Wheeler wonderingly, then returned to the paper. It was headed *To the Planner,* and it said:

To the Planner, or to whoever succeeds him if he is now dead:

You and those who serve with you ignored my warning and discounted the dimming of the Sun.

I send you now a pack of beasts to show that my powers can do more than frighten. They will destroy much. They may yet destroy more.

If I send them again, it will not be to the headquarters of the Planner—if anything remains of that to be destroyed.

The next demonstration will occur in the vaults of the Planning Machine.

Gann looked up, his lips taut, his eyes narrowed. "The Planning Machine!" he said. "General, we must tell Sister Delta Four at once! This must be conveyed to the Machine immediately."

The general rasped, "That decision will be made by me, Major. What have you to say for yourself?"

Startled, Gann said, "Why—I don't know what you mean, General. I didn't have anything to do with . . ."

Then he saw that the general was no longer standing with his arms at his side. One hand held a laser gun again, and it was pointing at him.

"You're under arrest," clipped General Wheeler metallically. "Do not attempt to draw those weapons. Do not speak or move."

Gann opened his mouth, then closed it again. This was the overwhelming, culminating insanity of a fantastic experience. Himself under arrest!

But for what? He dared not even ask. The general's iron expression showed that he meant his orders to be obeyed.

Behind him, Boysie Gann heard the movements of the guards, coming near—and past them, a distant booming.

He recognized that sound. Another stray pyropod! He forgot his orders and cried: "General! There's another one."

General Wheeler rapped, "Be silent! I will not speak

again! The men will take care of your beast!" His voice was queerly loud, Gann thought, even in his confusion—almost as if the general were speaking not to him, but to the roomful of witnesses.

But he could not help himself. He knew what one single pyropod could do, knew that even the Planner's guards might not be able to cope with it—and knew that in that room was the body and heart of the girl he loved, even though they might be inhabited by the cold, machinelike mind of Sister Delta Four. He whirled; drew his laser gun and was ready as the roar of the pyropod shrieked to the door of the room and the creature appeared.

Gann fired at the red eyes.

The guards were ready too, alerted by the sound and by Gann's quick action; they had turned and were firing. The creature was caught in a dozen bolts of destroying energy. It puffed into flame and exploded . . .

And between Gann and the door, Sister Delta Four, whispering into her linkbox, fell silently forward. She dropped to the floor and did not move, though the linkbox hooted questioningly to her.

"She's hit!" cried Gann and, dropping his weapons, raced to her. He caught her up in his arms, and stared into her black eyes.

His hands were covered with blood. Along one side of her black robes a spreading patch of sticky moisture began to seep, clouding the bright electronic symbols, trickling to the floor.

There was no heartbeat.

He raised his eyes, stared vacantly at the approaching General Wheeler. "Is she dead?" he demanded, unable to take it in. "Was it my shot? Or . . ." He paused, trying to remember. Had there been another pencil-thin lance of laser light coming from his side of the room? Had General Wheeler fired over his shoulder and shot Sister Delta Four?

But there was no time to think of that. The general was on him now, his face a metallic mask of sternness. "Disarm that man!" he rasped to the guards. "Take him before the Planner! I accuse him of bringing this document here! I accuse him of admitting the beasts we have destroyed. I accuse him of slaying Sister Delta Four to keep her from denouncing him. I accuse him of being the Starchild!"

228

10

The battered veterans of the skirmish with the pyropods, limping out of the battlefield and taking the swift elevators to the surface, found the Planner standing like a jovial Santa Claus on a quartz-walled balcony, near the snowy summit of the mountain in which his headquarters was buried.

This was his eyrie, the great crow's-nest of his palace. He chuckled to General Wheeler, "They tried to get me and missed! They'll not have another chance! We'll wipe out every last lone rebel."

The general rasped, "Sir, here is your first traitor! This is the man who is responsible. I found him bearing this document."

Gann cried, "Planner, the general is lying! He knows I didn't—"

"Silence!" snapped the general.

The Planner did not even look at Gann. Smiling and nodding, he read the square of paper, then dropped it negligently to the floor. "You're sure he's the Starchild, General?" he asked.

"Consider the evidence, sir!" rapped the general. "One. He appeared originally in the vaults of the Machine, with no explanation of how he got there. Two. At the same time, the Writ of Liberation appeared, also unexplained. Three. He was bearing this document when I apprehended him. Four. He displayed a suspicious knowledge of the vulnerable spots on the pyropods when his own life was in danger. Five. He purposely slew Sister Delta Four, making it look like an accident, so that she could not speak against him. Six. He was about to do the same to me when I ordered the guards to disarm him. The conclusion, sir, is overwhelmingly indicated that Machine Major Boysie Gann is indeed the Starchild."

"But, sir," cried Gann.

The Planner gestured, and one of the guards wrenched his arm, forcing him to be quiet. "That's better," chuckled the old Planner, beaming down on Boysie Gann. His dose of communion had clearly lasted him a long time; he was as bubbling with good humor as if the Machine even now were shooting pleasure sensations into his brain. "Yet," said the Planner, smiling good-humoredly at General Wheeler, "one of the guards reported that it was you, not Gann, who killed the sister. Could you have been mistaken?"

"No, sir! Impossible, sir. I had no reason."

The Planner nodded cheerfully and scratched his plump old cheek. He got to his feet and went to the quartz wall of his eyrie, squinting out into the sunset sky. To windward of the summit, the descending sun picked out a towering crown of cumulus. Beyond the crystal parapet, its last rays shimmered on a small waterfall and tinted the falling slopes of evergreens.

"As a matter of fact," the Planner added over his shoulder, "Sister Delta Four is not dead." He stared smiling down the slopes toward a brown-smogged city below. "She is now in surgery. Her heart was destroyed, but circulation was restored before the brain was damaged. Even now a donor is being provided to replace her lost parts."

Boysie Gann cried joyfully, "Plan be thanked! Sir, she'll tell you that I knew nothing of the pyropods until she herself told me about them!"

"Silence!" rasped General Wheeler. "Guards! Your orders are to keep him quiet. I understand donors are needed for several of your wounded comrades. The first man who fails to keep the prisoner silent will be considered a volunteer!"

"Not so fast," said the Planner, chuckling. "Your zeal goes too far, General." His heavy-lidded eyes looked dark and as old as the lichen-crusted stone below the crystal wall as he gazed benignly toward the far city in the smog. "Let us Plan," he said, turning and smiling. "Let us decide what to do."

The Vice-Planner for Venus spoke up promptly: "Double the guards in the vaults of the Machine, sir. Institute maximum security measures, admitting no unauthorized person . . ." He broke off and scratched his enormous nose in puzzlement as he realized that neither Boysie Gann nor the pyropods had submitted to security check before entering the most heavily guarded places in the Plan of Man.

A male acolyte in the black robes of the Machine, listening to a subdued buzzing from his linkbox, raised his voice suddenly. "The Machine requires the services of the prisoner," he chanted. "The Machine instructs Machine General Wheeler that the prisoner is not to be harmed in any way that will affect his memory or his intellect."

Wheeler's expression was that of a steel-gray thundercloud. The Planner turned toward him, chuckling. "You have your orders, General," he said good-humoredly. "Be sure they are carried out. Do you know what those orders are, young man?" he added, turning with a bland expression of cheer to Boysie Gann.

"No, sir. But I stand ready to serve the Plan of Man!"

"Oh, you do indeed," nodded the Planner. "In a very special way, as it happens. Major, you have been selected to replace Sister Delta Four. The Machine is about to permit you to receive training in its special service as an acolyte—and then communion!"

The heavy iron security collar was not enough for so precious an enemy of the Plan as Boysie Gann.

"You're not just a Risk," one of the guards explained solicitously. "See, we can't take a chance, Major. We don't want to blow your little head off. We don't want to kill you. We want to deliver you in one piece, right? So just stand still there while we put these cuffs on you . . . and we'll take you to the training base . . . and then, when the Machine's all finished with you, *then* we'll blow your head off!" And the guard snapped the fetters cruelly tight on Gann's wrists and started him moving with a shove.

They took him to a subtrain station first, and would not answer his questions. Was Julie Martinet all right? Why had General Wheeler lied? What was the Machine going to do with him? To each question there was only one response: "Shut up, you! Move on!"

But then there was nowhere to move. They were in the subtrain station, the great cold, vaulted shed where the enormous electron-flow-driven globes waited to carry their passengers through tunnels in the earth, across a continent or under a sea. But no globe was moving.

They brought Gann to a platform, ten security guards forming the detail that surrounded him; then they waited. Boysie Gann could see that the station was a military base, because of the armored guard boxes beside the troughs, and because of the black Technicorps uniforms on everyone. That was understandable enough; this was

231

the depot that served the Planner himself, the one nearest his tunneled-out mountain retreat. But what was not understandable was that there were neither arrivals nor departures.

Behind him, a track lock closed with a wheeze of leaking air. A Togetherness girl froze her automatic smile as she caught sight of his collar, and hurried past. The guards in their radar horns gazed vacantly after her.

"Look," said Boysie Gann, "what's the matter? What are we waiting for?"

"Shut up, you," growled a Machine Sergeant of the guards. But he had a worried look. One of his men said something to him; the sergeant replied in an undertone. All Gann could catch was: ". . . trouble in the tunnels somewhere. Now shut up. When they're ready for us, we'll know."

The great forty-foot bubbles waited silently in their passage cradles, and Boysie Gann stood regarding them. Wherever he was going, it was probably somewhere far away. Short-haul trips were seldom by way of the subtrains. The great atomic drills of the Plan had tunneled straight-line passages from all major centers to all others, sometimes relayed, sometimes piercing nearly through the nickel-iron core of the Earth itself in a single non-stop thrust from Sidney, say, to Calcutta. The great freight and passanger globes reached speeds so great that Coriolis force was their principal adversary; the electrostatic hoops that banded the evacuated tunnels were double and triple strength on the side against which the earth's rotation tended to throw the spheres. Via the subtrains, no point on Earth was more than a few hours away from any other . . .

Boysie Gann became aware of a confused mutter of excitement, and focused his eyes on what was going on in the subtrain shed. A great dull freightsphere was sliding gently into the station, emerging from the mouth of a belt-ringed tunnel.

"About time they got 'em going again," grumbled the Machine Sergeant. "All right, let's move out. They'll be letting us board now."

The sergeant was right. Within ten minutes they were in a subtrain globe, settling down in a passenger compartment. But there was a wait of nearly a quarter of an hour more before Boysie Gann felt the gentle lurch that meant they had begun to move.

His guards were more relaxed, now that they were in the subtrain. Gann could not very well escape them now, not when there was nowhere to go but the interior of a forty-foot sphere, with nothing outside but great electrostatic hoops in an airless tunnel, whizzing by at speeds of thousands of miles an hour. A couple of the guards disappeared, came back with self-satisfied smiles, and relieved the others. Clearly there was a Togetherness canteen on the globe. Even the radar-horned sergeant looked somehow less inimical, more like a human being.

Above all things, Gann wished he knew what had happened to Sister Delta Four. There had been a moment there, while the pyropods were attacking, when she had seemed less like a cold-hearted servant of the Machine and more like the girl he had kissed at Playa Blanca. He dreamed of getting her back—of somehow winning favor with the Machine and receiving the great reward of Julie Martinet's release . . .

It was only a dream. Considering his position now, it was an insane one.

Gann realized that he should be devoting every second's thought he could to planning—to trying to understand what had put him in this position, and what he could do. But it seemed quite hopeless. He had the giddy sensation that the universe had gone mad. From that first moment on Polaris Station, when he had followed Machine Colonel Zafar down to the methane snowball, events had carried him helplessly along; they made no sense to him, but there was nothing he could do to help interpret them. Their incomprehensibility was intrinsic. It was not that he was lacking in comprehension, it was that the things which had happened were not to be understood in the sane, sensible terms of life under the Plan of Man. . . .

He felt a giddy sensation again, and this time it was not in his mind.

Boysie Gann leaped to his feet in alarm. He could not help thinking of the strange queasiness that had preceded his twenty-billion-mile drop into the Planning Machine's catacombs . . . the same sensation, just before the pyropods struck . . .

But this was not the same thing at all. The lurching, twisting sensation he felt was simply explained. The subtrain car had come to a stop. It was hanging now, spinning slowly, between the charged hoops of its airless tunnel.

If Gann had been in any doubt, the cries from outside his room, the shouts of guards within, removed that doubt quickly. Everyone on the subtrain globe seemed to be shouting at once. "What's the matter?" "We've stopped!" "Great Plan, we're a couple of hundred miles down! The temperature—" "Help me! Let me out of here!" The voices were a confused babble, but they all had in common the warning knife edge of panic. There was terror on that subtrain car—terror that could not be calmed with words, for its base was all too real.

The Machine Sergeant comprehended the situation at once. With a jerk of his radar-horned head he bawled at his squad: "Come on, outside! Those sheep'll stampede if we don't keep 'em in line!"

Boysie Gann was left alone. Outside he could hear the Technicorps guards shouting orders at the terrified travelers on the subtrain. No one seemed to know what had happened. They had stopped; that was all. Hundreds of miles below the surface of the earth, the rock outside hot enough to melt aluminum, the pressure great enough to crush diamonds into dust if the electrostatic hoops ever faltered—they were stopped. Whatever it was that had disrupted the service before they left the station was probably disrupting it again.

The only difference was that now they were where no help could ever reach them, where if the fields in the hoops failed they would be dead in the least fraction of a second—where even if the field maintained itself they would be dead in a few days of asphyxiation, unless they could move.

Then, abruptly, there was another lurch, and they were moving again.

As the great forty-foot sphere gathered speed and stability, Boysie Gann became aware that he had been hardly breathing. There was a great cry of thanksgiving from the people outside his room. One by one his guards came back, chattering and laughing, seeming almost human. They did not include him in their conversation, but they did not go out of their way to keep him out. One of them even disappeared for a few minutes, then came back with a tray of drinks from the Togetherness canteen . . .

And then the great globe shook again. Shook—crashed into something that shrieked of destroyed metal—slammed to a jolting, smashing stop. Gann and the guards tumbled across the room, hurled against the wall like thrown gravel.

234

Boysie Gann heard screams and a rending sound of the metal of the great sphere being crushed. "We've had it!" someone shrieked. "The fields have failed!" And as he went deep into black oblivion (not yet feeling pain but knowing that he was bleeding; he had struck the wall too hard to get up and walk away), Gann had time for one last thought: *He's right,* thought Gann; *this is the end.*

When, some indeterminate time later, he opened his eyes and found himself still alive, he was almost disappointed. Gann was in an emergency hospital. Stiff white bandages covered part of his eyes; his head ached as if a corps of drummers were using it for practice; he could see, under the shadow of the bandages, that one arm was encased in a balloon-cast.

But he was alive.

A Togetherness nurse was bending over him. He said clearly, "I thought the tube collapsed."

"Hush," she said gently. "It did. But you were almost at the surface, and the wrecking squads dug you out."

"Almost at the surface?" He squinted past her at the second figure standing by his bed. For one crazy instant on waking he had thought it was the Angel of Death come to take him away. Now he saw it was an acolyte of the Machine, the linkbox in her hand, whispering tinkling notes to the microphone it contained. "I—I guess I'm at the training center," he said.

The nurse nodded. "Sleep if you can," she ordered. And Boysie Gann was glad to comply . . .

For three days Boysie Gann had the status of a convalescent. It was a considerable improvement over his status as a major public enemy.

The immediate guard detail was withdrawn—several had been killed in the tube implosion and were going through the messy business of resuscitation and repair at the Body Bank. Gann was free to wander within the limited confines of one wing of the hospital in which he was a patient.

He was even allowed access to the recreation lounge, run by a young Togetherness girl who reminded him of Quarla Snow. Her disposition was like Quarla's, too. She did not seem conscious of his collar. Most important, she let him watch the news-screens to his heart's content.

Boysie Gann had been away from Earth, off on the

Reefs or in intensive custody, for so long that he had lost touch with the running news stories.

He sat and dreamed. What was happening on the screen soaked slowly into his mind and heart. He watched, and loved, the gold-haired, long-legged choruses of Togetherness girls cooing their gentle threats: "Work for the Plan! Live for the Plan! *You* don't want to go to Heaven and make spare parts for the Plan!" Though he knew his chances of winding up in the Body Bank called Heaven and making "spare parts for the Plan" must be rated pretty high, there was no fear in what the girls were singing. It was a part of a life that he had lost, and he wanted it back.

Above all, he wanted to find himself again.

Boysie Gann could not recognize himself in the enemy of the Machine who had been castigated by the Planner himself, denounced by Machine General Wheeler, interrogated by Sister Delta Four. That Boysie Gann was a creature who had been born on Polaris Station, a man who lived with undead Reef rats and queer creatures called spacelings and pyropods. Gann could not fit the strange, rebellious shape of this other Boysie Gann into his personality, could not add the two identities and produce a vector sum of his future life . . .

He sat up straight and glared at the viewscreen.

He had been watching a worldwide news broadcast with half his mind, hardly conscious of what he saw, although in fact what he saw was exciting enough. The news broadcast was almost a catalogue of disasters—a crashed Plan cruiser that destroyed half a city, earthquakes in Antarctica, a runaway nuclear reactor on the Indian subcontinent. Then there had been a nearer disaster. The screen had shown the very subtrain catastrophe that had put him in this place.

And called it sabotage!

Gann blinked. He hardly recognized the accident. The bland, fat Technicolonel puffing out his gruff charges of criminal conspiracy seemed to be talking about some other disaster, on some other world. Malicious sabotage? A bomb planted in the subtrain to discredit the Planner and the Planning Machine? Most incongruous of all, *himself* as the archvillain, with the radar-horned guard sergeant as his accomplice?

Gann put down his glass of vitamin-laced fruit juice

and hobbled over to the Togetherness girl in charge of the lounge.

He was shaking. "Please," he begged. "Did you see that? What is it all about?"

She scolded him sunnily. "Now, now! Your duty under the Plan is to get well! You must prepare yourself to return to serve. No questions, no worries—nothing but healing and rest!"

He said with difficulty, "It said on the newscast that I was responsible for the subtrain accident. It isn't so! And the guard sergeant who was in charge of me—what happened to him?"

Her large, clear eyes darkened for a moment in puzzlement. But only for a moment. She would not question her orders; if her orders said that she was to care for an enemy of the Plan, she would care for an enemy of the Plan. She shook her head and, smiling, led him back to the couch. "Drink your juice," she said with playful severity, and would say no more. To her, what the Plan of Man ordained was necessarily right and true—because "right" and "truth" were defined by the Plan of Man.

Or so thought Boysie Gann.

So thought Boysie Gann, and was aware in some part of him that there was something in that thought which was dangerous—dangerous to him and to all mankind —for if the sweet and empty-headed Togetherness girl accepted the Plan so unquestioningly . . .

He could not put the thought together. It almost seemed as if he himself, and General Wheeler, and even the Planner—as if all the human race within the Plan were in some sense no less empty-headed than a Togetherness girl.

But he could not complete the thought. And then time ran out and he no longer had leisure for such thoughts, for he began the course of training that would lead him to communion with the Machine.

Dyadic relation: *I hate spinach.* Ternary relation: *I hate spinach except when it is well washed.* Quaternary relation: *I hate spinach except when it is well washed because the sand gets in my teeth.*

With instructor and book, with constant subliminal tapes droning while he slept and teaching machines snapping at him awake, Boysie Gann began to learn the calculus of statement, the logic of relations, the geometries of Hilbert and Ackermann and Boole. Conjunctions and disjunctions, axioms and theorems, double negations and metastatements . . . they all surged through his brain, nesting with destructive dilemmas and syllogisms in the mood of Barbara. He learned to transpose and commute. He learned the principle of exportation and the use of dots as brackets. He learned the unambiguous phrasing and inflectionless grammar of machine programming; he learned the distinction between perceptual symbols and motor symbols, and learned to make the auditory symbols that bridged the gap. For hours with an oscillator squeal beeping in his ear to guide him, he sang endless quarter-tone scales. He studied the factorization problems of the General Problem Solver and learned to quantify relationships. He learned the construction of truth tables, and how to use them to track down tautologies in a premise.

There were neither classes nor schoolrooms; there were only study and work. It went on and on, endlessly. Gann woke to the drone of the tape-recorded voice under his pillow, ate with the chime of sonic bells in his ear, fell exhausted into his bed with schematics of shared-time computer inputs racing through his mind.

There was a world outside the training center, but he had lost touch with it completely. In stolen moments he caught snatches of conversation between his few human contacts—the Togetherness girls who served him at table, the guards who roamed the halls—that his mind was too hard-pressed to fit together. The Starchild. The Writ of Liberation. Disasters under the earth; rocket explosions in space. They did not matter; what mattered was null hypotheses and probabilistic calculus. If he had time enough, and thought enough, to probe beyond the demands of the training, his mind always reached one step ahead— to the moment when training was over and he would receive the metal badge of communion in his flesh—and it recoiled, and returned to Hilbert and Boole.

When the course was over, Gann did not realize it. He went to sleep—exhausted, as he was always exhausted in this place. He tumbled into the narrow, hard bed in the solitary, tile-walled room. The voice under his pillow promptly began to recite to him:

". . . generate a matrix K, utilizing the mechanism of associative retrieval to add contextual relationships to co-

238

ordinate retrieval. Let the ith row and the jth column show the degree of association . . ."

Some part of him was taking it in, he knew, but his conscious mind was hardly aware of it. All he was aware of was his own inadequacy. He would never match the pure, crystalline tones of Sister Delta Four and the other acolytes. He did not have the voice for it. He would never grasp and retain all the information theory and programming he 'had been taught. He did not have the training for it. . . .

He drifted off to sleep.

His cot was hard. The barracks were like an air-conditioned vault. Every night at lights-out it held eighty tired and silent trainees, every cot filled. And each morning, the harsh clanging of the reveille gong found a few cots empty.

No one spoke of the missing trainees. Their gear was gone with them, from the narrow shelves above the cots. Their names had. been erased from the company rolls. They had ceased to exist. Nobody asked why.

One night, however, the shuffle of hurried feet awakened him. With a gasp of wild alarm, he sat up on his cot.

"Jim?" He whispered the name of the man in the next bunk, a new recruit, who had the physique of a wrestler and a pure tenor voice. His mother had been a Togetherness singer, and his father had died for the Plan in space. "What—?"

"You're asleep, bud," a harsh whisper rasped in the dark. "Better stay that way."

A heavy hand caught his shoulder, shoved him down.

Gann wanted to help, but he was afraid. He watched as dark forms closed around the cot. He heard Jim's stifled gasp. He heard a muffled rattle of a voice. He heard the rustle of clothing, a metallic clink. The cot creaked. He closed his eyes as a thin blade of light stabbed at his face. Footsteps padded away.

He lay a long time in the dark, listening to the breath sounds of fewer than eighty sleeping men. Jim had treasured that red plastic medal that said his father had been a Hero of the Plan, Second Class. Jim's voice had been fine and true, but he had been too slow to learn the semantic calculus.

Gann wanted to help, but there was nothing he could do. The Machine required something mechanical in its

239

selected servants; perhaps Jim had not been quite mechanical enough. Gann turned on the hard cot and began repeating to himself the semantic tensors; presently he slept again.

11

Two days later, entering the second phase of training, Gann remembered the first phase through a fog of exhaustion as something like a week end at a Togetherness beach hostel. The pressure never stopped.

"Look Mechanical!"

Bleak-voiced instructors hammered that injunction at him. Bright-eyed Togetherness girls cooed it to him, as he shuffled through the chow lines. Blazing stereo signs burned it into his retinas. Sleepless speakers whispered it endlessly under his pillow.

"Look Mechanical! . . . Act Mechanical! . . . Be Mechanical!"

Each rasping sergeant and murmuring girl pointed out what that meant. To master the myriad difficult tone phonemes of Mechanese, a man had to become mechanical. The searing signs and the whispering speakers reminded him that those who failed went promptly to the Body Bank.

Locked in a stifling little examination cell walled with gray acoustic padding, he sat hunched over a black linkbox, straining to catch the fleeting inflections of its tinkling Mechanese.

"The candidate—" Even that word almost escaped him. "The candidate will identify himself."

His answering voice came out too harsh and too high. He gulped to clear his throat, and stroked his tonal beads.

"Candidate Boysie Gann." He swallowed again, and sang his serial number.

"Candidate Boysie Gann, you are under examination," the box purred instantly. "A passing score will move you one stage farther toward that high service which the Plan rewards with communion. But you must be warned that you are now beyond the point of return! The Plan has no place for rejects, with your classified knowledge and training—except in the salvage centers."

"I understand, and I live to serve." He sang the single difficult phoneme.

"Then the test will begin," the box chirped. "You will answer each question clearly and fully, in correct Mechanese. Each millisecond of delay and each tone defect will be scored against you. The Plan has no time to waste, nor space for error. Are you ready to begin?"

Hurriedly, he sang the tone that said, "I am ready to begin."

"Your response was delayed nine milliseconds beyond the optimum point," the box whined instantly. "Your initial tone was twelve cycles too high. Your tonal glide was abrupt and irregular. The duration of your utterance was one millisecond too long. These errors will be scored against you."

"I understand."

"That response was not required from you," the box snarled. "Your errors, however, have been analyzed and graphed. You will now prepare for your initial test question. . . . What is the first principle of mechanized learning?"

When he first tried to sing his answer, his voice came out too hoarse and too low. The box piped out a new total cumulative error before he had time to touch the beads to find the true tone and try again.

"Learning is action," his uneven tones came out at last. "That is the first principle of mechanized instruction. Right responses must be instantly reinforced. Wrong responses must be instantly inhibited. The first equation of mechanized instruction states that efficiency of learning varies inversely with the time elapsed between response and reward."

"Your accumulated total error is now four hundred and eighty-nine points," the box snarled. "You will prepare for the next question. . . . What is the second principle of mechanized instruction?"

· He was sweating now as he crouched on the hard little seat. The small gray room seemed too small. The padded walls pressed in upon him. He felt almost suffocated, and he had to gasp for the breath for his hurried reply.

"Learning is survival," he sang the curt phonemes, trying to cut them off correctly. "Successful learning is the adaptive way to life. Failure to learn is individual death. The second equation of mechanized instruction states that the speed of learning varies directly with the magnitudes of reward and punishment."

When he paused, the box chirped. Even to his straining ears, it was only a sharp metallic insect note, entirely meaningless. He had to whistle a request for the Machine to repeat.

"Your failure in reception scores ninety points against you." The notes from the box were only slightly slower and more intelligible. "Your cumulative total is now six hundred and seventy-three points. Your right-wrong ratio has fallen into the danger zone."

The racing tinkle of merciless notes, sharp as shattering glass, gave him no time to recover his shattered confidence. He was only dimly conscious of the itching tickle of sweat on his ribs, the cold tingle of sweat on his forehead, the sting of sweat in his eyes.

"You will prepare for your next question." That was only a single gliding tone phoneme, gone in a few milliseconds, so brief he nearly missed it. "What is the third principle of mechanized instruction?"

He touched his beads for the tonal keys, and sang the required phonemes. "The third principle of mechanized instruction states that the greatest reward is the end of pain." His accumulated error mounted, and the merciless box demanded another principle of mechanized instruction —and yet another.

"Your test is ended," the box announced at last. "Your total accumulated error is five thousand nine hundred and forty points. You will report that total to your training group."

He was late when he reached his barracks to punch that total into the group computer. He was late again, half a minute late, for the calisthenics formation—a crime against the Machine which earned him two extra laps of double time in the track tunnel. The last man in the chow line; he was too tired to eat his ration when at last he reached the table with it; the wasted food cost him two yellow demerit points. When he got to his bunk at last, he felt too tired to sleep.

"Candidate Gann!"

He had not seen the dark forms approach his cot. He gasped and sat up trembling. A pale needle of light picked out his uniform, his boots, and kit and gear. A harsh whisper directed him. In a moment he was shuffling down the shadowy aisle between the heavy-breathing trainees, his kit on his back.

So this was it? For a moment his knees wobbled; then he began to feel illogically relieved.

He was almost yearning for the anesthesia of the Body Bank; he was almost hungry for oblivion. Because there wouldn't be any linkboxes in the Body Bank. He wouldn't have to practice any more impossible scales, or learn any more tables of semantic variation.

He was out of it all.

His black-uniformed escorts let him sit with them at a table in a nearly deserted mess hall. A sleepy Togetherness girl yawned as she served them. He ate no food. He drank two cups of black coffee that left a lingering bitterness in his mouth.

He joined five other stunned and sleepy trainees who must have come from another barracks. They carried their gear into a military subtrain, and carried it off again. They marched past a scowling sentry into another cavernous training center.

Gann left his gear in a tiny tile-walled cell and reported to a cadaverous Machine Major who wore the piebald scars of a Venusian anaerobic parasite. The major returned his salute stiffly, with a black-gloved hand.

"Congratulations, Major Gann."

Staring at the gaunt major who was shuffling through papers on his desk, Gann saw that the neat black glove was no glove, but the black skin of a salvaged hand.

"You have successfully completed Phase Two of your service training in Mechanese." Peering at that black, borrowed hand, Gann scarcely heard the words. "You have been assigned here for Phase Three, which consists of mechanized instruction."

A faint smile twisted the major's yellow patched face.

"Your test scores were unusual, Major Gann," he added. "The Machine has commended you. You ought to be a proud and happy man."

Gann had swayed backward when that cold fact struck him. He was not a proud and happy man. He stood speechless, breathless, shuddering with a secret horror.

"You have come a long way, Major Gann." The yellow scars turned the major's smile into a rictus of agony. "You have escaped the danger of salvage. You have moved far toward the highest reward." Wistfully his black fingers touched his own seamed and mottled forehead, where he had no communion receptacle of his own. "You are very fortunate, Major Gann!"

Gann stood swaying. Suddenly the harsh-lit room and the gray-cased computers and the piebald major seemed unreal. Terribly real, in his own spinning mind, the cold, bright scalpels and saws of the surgeons were carving out space for the socket in his own forehead. They were drilling into the crown and the temples and the base of his shaven head. They were probing with thin, cruel needles for the centers of sensation. They were coldly violating the most secret privacy of all his being. . . .

He wanted to scream.

"Is something wrong, Major Gann?" The gaunt major rose anxiously. "You look ill."

"Nothing, sir." Groping for himself, he grinned faintly. "You see, I didn't know that I had passed Phase Two. I thought we were in a salvage center."

"You'll soon get over that." The major's rictus grew more hideous. "With your record, you're as good as already wired for communion. I wish I were in your place."

"Thank—" He tried to wet the sandpaper dryness in his mouth and throat. "Thank you, sir!"

The Mechanese trainer was a ten-foot pear shape, fabricated out of bright aluminum. Swung in massive gimbals of gray-painted steel, it stood in a windy, gloomy cavern, under a water-stained concrete vault. Thick black cables and hoses snaked from it to the gray-cased control console at the tunnel mouth.

"There she is, sir!" The instructor was a plump young Techtenant with a pink baby face, wide blue eyes, and a bright communion plate set in his forehead. "The perfect teaching machine!"

Gann was queerly unsure of that. Smeared all over with a sticky jelly, wearing only loose gray coveralls, he hesitated at the tunnel mouth, staring uncomfortably up at that huge metal pear.

"Step right up, sir." The Techtenant gave him an innocent grin. "Strip off your robe and slip right in." The round blue eyes flickered at him inquiringly. "All ready, sir?"

He was wet and clammy with the jelly, and the coveralls were thin. Suddenly he shivered in the cold steady wind that blew out of the tunnel. He didn't really want to learn Mechanese. He didn't want to be rewarded with electrodes in his brain. But he gulped and said that he was ready.

The Techtenant touched something on the console. Air valves wheezed. That great metal pear tipped in the gimbals, opening like a sliced fruit. He stared at it, frozen, tingling, fascinated.

"Move ahead, sir." The Techtenant touched his shoulder respectfully. "Up the ladder. Strip off. Just lie down on the sensor-effector sheath." He chuckled easily. "Most students are a bit uneasy at first, but you'll find it fits you, sir."

Gann caught his breath and climbed the metal ladder. The rungs felt cold and sticky to his naked feet. The wind blew cold on his shaven head, and a sudden bitter taste of stale coffee came back from his stomach into his throat.

He stripped off the coveralls and crept uneasily out upon the bright pink membrane that lined the pear. It rippled beneath him, warm and slimy and almost alive, propelling his naked body into its central cavity.

"All set, sir?"

He attempted no answer to that cherry hail, but he heard another hiss of escaping air. The hinged upper half of the pear closed down. Warm constrictions of that pliant membrane caressed him into place. Total darkness seized him, in a hot and suffocating grip.

He tried to scream, and had no breath . . .

But then there was air for his lungs. He saw a pink glow of light through his closed eyelids.

He opened them, and saw Sister Delta Four.

Really, he supposed, it must have been only a projected image of her, but she looked alive enough. He knew this had to be an image because she wasn't in the buried training center. But she seemed to be. Robed and hooded and carrying her black link box, she was walking down a palm-fringed coral beach that looked queerly like the Togetherness center at Playa Blanca.

And he was walking with her.

The clinging effectors of the trainer duplicated every sensation: the hard, cold, yielding firmness of the wet sand, the tingling heat of the high sun, a cool puff of ocean breeze. He heard the dull boom of surf against the breakwater, and caught a sharp whiff of rotting sea-weed and then a hint of Julie's perfume—for she was

245

speaking to him now, in the warm, remembered tones of Julie Martinet.

"Here we are," she was saying, "for your first lesson in the Mechanese Learning Device, Mark Eight. This instrument is very nearly the last possible word in educational efficiency. If you co-operate, I'm sure you'll find the experience exciting and profitable." Her bright face smiled at him, tempting under the hood.

"Now," she said, "we are ready to begin your introduction to the technical vocabulary of Mechanese. It is built upon a principle of economy already familiar to you: one syllable for one sentence. Obviously, that requires a large number of syllables. The total vocabulary of Mechanese, as we compute it, is more than a billion monosyllables—more than a billion one-sound sentences."

He stopped on the beach—or it seemed that he did, for the synthetic experience created by the trainer had made him forget that he was anywhere else. Cold brine hissed over his bare feet, crumbled the hard sand beneath them, rushed back down the slope.

"I can't do it," he protested. "I can't memorize a billion words!"

Her soft laugh checked him. "You'll be surprised!" Her voice was a song, even when she spoke the old, familiar language. "You'll be surprised what the trainer can make you do." The sea breeze caught and lifted her hood, so that he had a sudden glimpse of the bright plate set in her forehead. Even in that mild tropic air, it made him cold and ill.

"Actually, though, you don't have to memorize a billion words," she said. "No more than a child has to memorize every possible sentence in English. All you must learn is how to construct the Mechanese monosyllables from combinations of a few thousand phonemes. You must learn to hear and understand very small distinctive variations in length and stress and pitch and a few other simple features of articulation."

"But I can't!" Feet planted in the wet sand, he waited until she turned back. He didn't want to learn, though he could scarcely tell her that. He was seeking secretly to defend himself from those cold probes that would be piercing his brain when he knew Mechanese. "I can't learn to utter a billion different words."

"You'll be surprised." Her laugh was as melodious as her voice. "Let's begin."

He shook his head stubbornly, trying to remind himself that the sharp white sand wasn't real, that the salt-scented wind wasn't real, that Julie herself wasn't real.

"Do co-operate," she urged him softly. "If you're a good student, we can go for a swim a little later on." Her eyes held a teasing promise, and her deft white hands made a fetching gesture, as if to toss away the robe and hood. "You must co-operate."

Her oval face turned suddenly sober.

"If you don't, you'll be sorry." Her voice turned slow and faint and sad. "I don't like to remind you of the third principle of mechanized instruction—but the greatest reward is the end of pain."

She shrugged, and her quick smile dazzled him. "Let's begin!"

They began with the verbal glides, the slight inflections of tone that meant tense and mood and voice and person and aspect. She trilled the difficult syllables. Trying faithfully to imitate them, he was soon reminded of the third law of mechanized learning.

Even the tiniest error brought a twinge of pain, and his errors were frequent and great. Even when he responded instantly with a phoneme that seemed to him precisely like the one she had uttered, it was often painfully wrong.

For he wasn't really on that dazzling coral beach. He was sealed inside the great metal pear of the trainer, with its flexible effectors caressing every inch of his really naked body. They could numb him with cold, sear him like fire, crush him with pressure.

They often did. The slightest error snatched him away from warm beach and Julie Martinet, into a special mechanical hell where he strove with all his being to earn that supreme reward that was the end of pain.

Sometimes he was trapped aboard a crippled rocket that was falling into the sun. The air was screaming out of the meteor-riddled hull, so that his lungs labored against an agony of suffocation. Cruel light blazed through one jagged hole, blinding, searing, unendurable. The wrecked compartment was a super-heated oven, in which his broken body roasted—but still he heard the voice of Julie Martinet. It came to him faintly through a laser amplifier. Sweetly it sang the combined phonemes of the syllables he had to learn. Sobbing for his breath, he struggled to make each

247

correct response—and he felt the laws of automated learning at work all around him.

When he was wrong, the fire of that devouring sun became instantly more terrible. When his answer was correct, within the narrow limits accepted by the Machine, the searing heat decreased and his struggling lungs found some tiny breath of precious air.

Whenever he got enough answers correct, that nightmare was interrupted. He was back on that dazzling beach with Julie Martinet. She promised him that cooling swim in the surf, or led him toward the tall, cool drinks waiting on a small glass-topped table under the palms, as they began another difficult lesson.

Always, before they reached the glasses or the surf, he had made another error. Each wrong response was instantly inhibited, according to the stern laws of automated learning—though the punishments varied, as if the Machine were experimenting to find what kinds of pain were most effective.

Sometimes he lay sweating in a hospital bed in a floating station in the murky upper air of Venus, gasping for his breath in the thick, hot smog, an infection of the anaerobic parasites eating like acid into his flesh—with Julie's voice cooing monosyllabic Mechanese from his bedside radio.

Sometimes he was pinned by a rockslide in a cave beneath the cold side of Mercury, with a boulder crushing his chest and ice-cold water dripping into his face and great slimy, phosphorescent worms crawling over him, deliberately devouring him—with Julie's voice, near him in the dark, singing the syllables he had to learn.

Always his correct responses were instantly reinforced with some slight reward. Always a sufficient cumulative total of acceptable responses earned him at least a brief relief from pain. When he came back to Julie, she was always sympathetic. Her cool hands caressed him; and bright tears of compassion shone in her eyes.

"Poor dear," she murmured. "I know it's very hard for you. But you must never give up. Just remember what we're striving for. When you've learned enough, you'll receive communion too. We'll be together, then. Let's try another lesson now. If you do well enough, perhaps the Machine will let us take that swim."

He always shivered when she spoke of communion, or when he caught a glimpse of the bright plate in her

248

forehead. He was careful to say nothing about that secret fear, but sometimes he wondered if the Machine, with its sensors against every inch of his body, might not detect it.

For his fear of communion kept growing, like some evil, unearthly weed, until it was more terrible than the synthetic hells that the trainer made to punish his worst errors. It lurked like some hideous hard-scaled pyropod in the shadows of his mind, haunting him until he begged Julie to let him out of the trainer.

She laughed at him.

"Really, you are very lucky," she assured him brightly. "The trainer is a new device. Mechanese was very much harder for me, because I had to learn without it. With the trainer you can't help learning. Just keep trying; you'll reach communion in no time at all."

He didn't dare to tell her that he didn't want communion.

"Truly," she bubbled joyously, "the trainer is the womb of the machine. Inside it you are being mechanized. Your inefficient random human responses are being eliminated. You are learning precision and efficiency and speed. When you are born again, out of the trainer, you will be a perfected child of the Machine."

He tried not to shudder.

"Now let's begin with the nominal structure," she urged him brightly. "You have already mastered the Machine's basic analysis of the universe as process. Mechanese has no nouns or verbs, but only things-in-process. Remember?"

Afraid of the baking heat in that wrecked ship, the burning fire of that parasitic infection, the gnawing mandibles of those phosphorescent worms, he nodded hastily.

"For example," she trilled, "there is only one basic nominal for any object of solid matter. Such aspects as material, size, shape, and use are indicated by inflection. But it is not a noun, because the verbal intonations always convey the sense of process, so that each possible monosyllabic form is a complete statement."

Her warm smile tantalized him.

"If you study well, perhaps we can take that swim—"

He tried—the third law of mechanized education forced him to try—but they never took the swim.

A time came when Julie vanished. He heard a hiss of air and felt a sudden icy draft against his sweating nakedness.

249

Back in the training center, he squirmed across the slick pink membrane of the sensor-effector sheath, climbed into his cold coveralls, and scrambled down the flimsy metal ladder.

"Good night, sir." The plump young Techtenant looked bored and sleepy now. "See you next shift, sir."

He wanted terribly never to see the Techtenant or the trainer again, because they meant that he was going to be wired for communion. He wanted desperately to run away—somehow to get back to Quarla Snow and the clean Reefs of Space.

But he was exhausted and guarded and imprisoned . . . he didn't know where . . . perhaps beneath a mile of solid rock . . . perhaps beneath the sea. He did his stint of calisthenics and took a steaming shower and sweated out the chow line and went to his tiny, tile-walled room to sleep.

Suddenly a gong was thundering. It was time to get up, to let them shave his head again, to strip and smear himself with that sticky jelly, to return to the womb of the Machine. . . .

And a time came, in the trainer, when Julie Martinet —or the projected image of her—gave him a test and, smiling, told him that he had passed.

"You have earned communion now. You are ready to be born again."

He almost gasped that he didn't want communion. But he bit his lip. He kept silent until Julie's bright image vanished and air valves roared and a cold wind caught him as he was finally born from the Machine.

Half-dazed and reeling—*Doped!* his mind whispered despairingly to him—he found himself in his cot. He did not know how he got there. He knew only something was wrong: there was some new scent in the atmosphere, some hardly perceived whisper of motion, as if someone were waiting outside his room for him to be asleep.

Then the anesthetic gas that had been piped through his pillow took effect. He slept. Deeply.

When he woke he felt a minor but nagging ache in the skin and the bone of his forehead. He was in another room—green-walled, surgical.

He did not have to touch his forehead to know that while he slept the surgeons had been at work, the hair-thin electrodes slipped into the micrometrically located centers of his brain, the bright badge of communion implanted on his brow.

In the mammalian brain exist bundles of nerves and specialized tissue which control mood and emotion, as well as those which control motor activities, homeostatic regulation, conscious thought, and the various other activities of that three-pound mass of hypertrophied tissue.

One such area is the pleasure center. Slip a fine platinum electric wire into it by stereotaxic surgery. Feed it a carefully measured, milliampere-tiny surge of electricity. The result is ecstasy! Fit a laboratory animal with such an electrode and with a key it can operate, and it will go on pressing the key, pressing the key, pressing the key . . . it will not pause for food or drink or fear . . . it will sear itself with delight until it collapses of exhaustion, and will awake only to press the key once more.

The jolt of ecstasy that tore through Boysie Gann's being in that first moment of awakening with the communion plate in his forehead and the electrodes embedded in his brain was like nothing he had ever imagined. It was taste, feeling, odor, and light; it was the wild delight of sex and the terrifying joy of daredevil sport; it was all the things he had ever known at once, magnified unbearably. Time stopped.

He was adrift in a turbulent sea of sensation. . . .

Eons and lifetimes later, he became conscious of humanity again. He was back in his body. The tides of quintessential pleasure had receded from around him, and left him aching and dry.

He opened his eyes, and saw a Technicorps medical orderly retreating from him, the communion probe wires in his hand. He had been cut off from the joy of the Planning Machine.

Gann took a long shuddering breath and reconciled himself to being human again. He could understand Sister Delta Four. He could accept his destiny in communion with the Machine. No other reward could be half as great as this, no other purpose as important . . .

Dazedly he became aware that something was wrong. The Technicorps man's face was pale with fear. Voices shouted from outside, and one of them was queerly familiar.

Gann struggled to his feet, apprehensive and wary. When the door burst open, it was Machine General

Wheeler who came into the room like a raging typhoon. "Gann!" he roared. "Starchild! You devil, what have you done?"

"I? Done? Nothing, General—and I'm not the Starchild, I swear it!"

"Filth!" howled the general. "Don't lie to me! What have you done to the Planning Machine?"

Gann started to reply, to defend himself. The general gave him no chance. "Lies!" he raged. "Starchild, you've destroyed us all! Admit it! Admit that it was you who has driven the Planning Machine hopelessly mad!"

12

The Plan of Man had gone amok. All over Earth, out into the asteroid belt, in the refrigerated warrens on Mercury, in the sunless depths of Pluto and on the slowly wheeling forts of the Spacewall, the terror had struck.

Routing orders crashed one subcar ball into another two thousand miles below the surface of the earth. Six hundred persons died in a meteor-like gout of suddenly blazing gases that melted the subcar shaft and let the molten core pour in.

On Venus a Technicaptain received routine programming instructions from the Machine and, obediently, set a dial and turned a switch. It flooded forty thousand hard-won acres of reclaimed land with oily brine.

A "man of golden fire" appeared on the stage of the great Auditorium of the Plan in Peiping, where the Vice-Planner for Asia had been scheduled to speak to his staff. The golden man disappeared again, and twenty raging pyropods flashed out of nowhere into the hall, killing and destroying everything within reach. The Vice-Planner, minutes late in keeping his engagement, has his life spared in consequence.

In short, sharp words, Machine General Wheeler barked out the story of the catastrophes that were overwhelming the Plan. "The Starchild! Seen in the vaults of the Planning Machine—and now the Machine's gone mad. Its orders are wrong! Its data can't be trusted! Gann, if you are the Starchild—"

Boysie Gann had been pushed too far. In a shout louder than Wheeler's own he roared, "General! I'm not the Starchild! Don't be a fool!"

Suddenly the machinelike face of the general seemed to wilt and crack. It was in a very human voice that he said, after a moment. "No. Perhaps you're not. But what in the name of the Plan is going on?"

Gann snapped, "I thought you were telling me that. What's this about the Starchild being seen in the Machine itself?"

"Just that, Gann. Guards reported someone there. A squad was sent down, and they saw him. He was at the manual consoles—changing the settings, erasing miles of tape, reversing connections. The Machine is mad now, Gann. And the Plan is going mad with it. All over the world."

"Never mind that! What did he look like, this Starchild?"

Machine General Wheeler squared his shoulders and backed crisply, "A man. Golden, they say. Almost as if he were luminous. Photographs were taken, but he was not recognized. It . . . didn't resemble you, Gann. But I thought—"

"You thought you'd come here anyway. Use me as a scapegoat, maybe. Is that it? The way you did when you pretended I shot Delta Four?"

The general tried to protest; then his lips smacked shut like the closing of a trap. He nodded his head twice, briskly, like a metronome. "Yes!"

Gann was taken aback. He had not expected so quick a confession. All he could do was say, "But why? Why did you shoot her? To get her out of the way as a witness?"

"Of course," rapped Machine General Wheeler.

"And pretend I was the Starchild? To make yourself more important to the Planner and the Machine?"

"Precisely," the general crackled out.

Gann studied him thoughtfully, then said, "Something must have changed your mind. What was it?"

The general answered without changing expression or tone. Only a faint color on the brow, a pale brightness as of perspiration, showed the strain he must have felt. "The girl recovered," he snapped. "She told the Planner the truth—that I had merely found that document, and planted it on you. The Planner reported to the Machine and—"

"And what?" demanded Boysie Gann.

The general's voice cracked. "And the Machine went mad. It ordered my arrest. Then it began ordering the arrest of Sister Delta Four, the Vice-Planner for Central America, the guards in the Hall of the Planner, even the Planner himself. There was confusion. I shot my way clear. I secured an aircraft, the one Sister Delta Four had come to the Planner's headquarters in, and I escaped. But I must leave Earth, Gann! I want you to take me to the Reefs, because . . . because I must get away."

"Get away? Why?"

The general's voice tolled out the answer. "In shooting my way out of the Planner's headquarters, I killed two men. One of them was the Planner."

Boysie Gann had never known where the training school was located on Earth. As they emerged to the surface he saw for the first time the great sweep of mountains to the north, felt the icy sting of cold air, and realized that they were on the plateaus below the Himalayas. For thousands of years only nomads and warriors had shared this bleak, desolate land. Now a great hydroelectric plant boomed beyond the level sweep of a rocketport hewn out of rock.

There was something about the power plant that looked strange. As Machine General Wheeler led him quickly to a waiting jetcraft Gann realized what was wrong with the hydroelectric plant. Even at this distance he could see that it was a wreck. Its great windows reflected no light; they were shattered. There were cracks in its solid masonry walls. There had been an explosion within— some mighty burst of short-circuiting energy, volatilizing all matter within its scope.

"Never mind that," rapped out the general. "Come aboard! There's someone there you'll want to see."

Gann followed, staring about. If destruction had come even here, it must be radically more far-reaching than he had dreamed.

Was it the Starchild?

And who was the Starchild? Hurrying after General Wheeler, Gann's mind was a vortex of thoughts, memories, impressions. The body-shaking rupture of his communion with the Machine. The terrible fight in the Planner's hall, and the terrible shock that had struck him when he saw Sister Delta Four—the girl who had once been Julie Martinet, his love—shot down before him. The long, dizzying fall through nonspace, from the Reefs to Earth. The strange hermit, Harry Hickson . . .

It was almost more than he could take in. Bemused, he was hardly aware when they reached the waiting jet-ship. He followed General Wheeler into the open hatch, and then he saw who it was who awaited them there.

"Julie!" he cried. "Julie Martinet!"

But it was Sister Delta Four who answered. "Come in. Close the hatch. We must take off at once! I have a message from the Machine."

General Wheeler reacted at once. He turned and closed the hatch, then leaped across the narrow cabin of the jet-ship and snatched from the grasp of Sister Delta Four the black cube that was her linkbox. "Fool!" he rasped. "A message from the Machine! Don't you know the Machine's gone mad? The Starchild has been tampering with it. It is no longer functioning according to Plan. The evidence of your eyes should tell you that. Can't you see what's been going on?"

The girl lifted her head, unafraid, and stared at him with objective, remote eyes. The black fabric of her hood fell away, baring the bright medallion of the communion plate in her forehead, just like Boysie Gann's own. She said in her melodic, chiming voice, "I serve the Machine, General Wheeler. And you are a traitor, condemned to death."

"So are you, for that matter," growled the general. He tossed the linkbox to Boysie Gann. "Here. Keep her quiet while I get us started. We've got to get off Earth at once." He dived for the control cabin to set the automatic instruments that would start the motors, take the plane off the field, fly it straight and true to its destination, radio for landing instructions, and set it down. Gann glanced at the linkbox in his hands, then at Sister Delta Four.

The linkbox carried its communion plug racked in a recess in its cubical bulk. Gann could see the bright glitter of its rounded tips that mated so perfectly with the plate in his own skull.

If, he thought ponderously, he were to take that plug off its clip and place it into the plate in his forehead . . . if he were to complete his communion . . . he would once again feel that total rapture, that almost unbearable ecstasy of soul and senses that he had tasted, just once, an hour before.

The temptation was overpowering.

He could understand Julie—or rather, Sister Delta Four —a great deal better now. There had never been an addiction like this one, no drug, no narcotic, no mere alcoholic craving that was as overpowering in its appeal.

He could understand why Julie Martinet had given up family, freedom, the pleasures of the senses, and himself for the shroud of an acolyte of the Machine.

He could understand it, because he was all but at that point himself, after one single exposure. . . .

With a swift motion, before he could stop to think, he lifted the linkbox and dashed it to the floor. It crackled and sputtered. In its static-filled buzzing sound he could detect some of the tonal morphemes he had been taught, but he did not give himself a chance to puzzle out their meaning, did not allow the linkbox the time to beg for its preservation—if that was its intention. He lifted a foot and crushed it, stamped it again and again, like a noxious insect. Its buzzing abruptly stopped. There was a faint blue flash of electric sparks; then it was only a mangled mass of printed circuits and crushed transistors.

"That's the end of that, Julie," he said. "And that's the end of our relationship with the Machine."

She was watching him silently, her eyes dark and incurious.

"Don't you have anything to say?" he demanded.

She pealed, "Only what I am instructed to tell you, Major Gann. The message that was given me by the Machine."

"Damn the Machine!" he cried. "Can't you understand that's over? It's finished. Gone! First we have to try to straighten out this mess; then—*maybe* then!—we can think about using the Machine again. Using it! Not letting it use us!"

"I know nothing of that, Major Gann," she sang. "I only know the message. It follows: *To Major Gann. Action. Proceed at once to the "Togethership" on the Reefs of Space via Mercury Terminator Line Station Seven. Message ends.*"

Gann shook his head dazedly. "Julie, Julie!" he protested. "That's ridiculous on the face of it. Go to the Reefs by way of Mercury? That's like coming across a room by way of . . . of Deneb. It's not the way at all—"

256

"I don't know about that," rasped the voice of Machine General Wheeler from behind him. Gann turned. The general was standing in the open door of the control cabin, something in his hand. His expression was dark and fearful, like some trapped and dangerous creature of the jungle.

Gann said, "But Mercury is near the Sun. Even if we wanted to go to the farthest part of the Reefs, where we're at superior conjunction, we might go *near* Mercury, yes, but we'd never land there. Not anywhere on the planet, much less at some particular station on the terminator line."

"Go there we will," rapped General Wheeler. "Land there we will. And at the station. Major Gann! I told you I intended to go to the Reefs at once and wanted you with me. I had a reason. See here! This dropped to the ground before me as I was leaving the Planner's chambers after my—ah—episode with the guns."

Wordlessly Boysie Gann took the document. It was a creamy square, without signature, and on it were the words:

If you would save yourself, your people, and your worlds, bring Machine Major Boysie Gann and yourself to the *Togethership* on the Reefs of Space. The gateway will be found at the Plan of Man solar observatory on Mercury, Terminator Station Seven.

"The Starchild!" cried Gann.

General Wheeler nodded with a harsh, mechanical up-down, up-down.

"A message from the Starchild, yes. And the same message from the Planning Machine. Major Gann! Do you realize what this means? The Planning Machine is the Starchild!"

13

At some point they transhipped into a Plan of Man jetless-drive cruiser. Gann paid little attention.

He was using the time in the best way he could, to rest, to try to recover from the shocks and stresses of the last few weeks. And how fast they had accumulated, how violently they had drained him of strength, and of peace of mind!"

He could still feel the distant ache in his forehead, in the bones of his skull, behind his eyes, in his sinuses —the track of the probes of the surgeons who had implanted the communion electrodes in his brain.

He could feel the aches and bruises of his working over by the Planner's guards. How long ago?

He was exhausted still from the battle with the pyropods and the long drop to Earth. His weary muscles still bore the fatigue poisons of his fight on Harry Hickson's reeflet . . .

He closed his eyes, and Quarla Snow came into his mind. He opened them, and Sister Delta Four sat quietly unmoving, her eyes fixed on him, before him.

He was beginning to feel himself again. With the return of strength there returned the question of the two women, so unlike yet so much in his thoughts. He said, "Julie, Sister Delta Four, if you'd rather. Do you know that what General Wheeler said is true? That the Machine is mad?"

Her perfect face, half hidden in the cowl, did not change expression. "I know that is what the general said," she sang.

"But it is mad, Julie. The Starchild has wrecked it. Now it is wrecking the Plan planets. Do you still want to serve it?"

"I serve the Planning Machine," she chimed sweetly, her dark eyes cool and empty.

"Because of the bliss of communion? I understand that, Julie. Don't forget"—he touched the glittering plate in his forehead—"I've felt it too."

There was a flicker in her eyes, almost an expression of indulgent amusement as she looked at him. But she only said, in her voice like the sound of bells, "What you felt, Major Gann, is only a shabby imitation of what the Machine gives its true servants. For you are only half a servant. The Machine has not opened its mind to you."

Puzzled, Gann asked, "You mean . . . mind-to-mind linkage? Communication with the—what could you call it?—with the *thoughts* of the Machine?"

She only shrugged. "It is something of that sort, perhaps," she said indifferently. "You cannot know." She sang a quick chiming chorus of tonal morphemes. Gann tried to follow, but was lost almost at once.

"You said something about the . . . the *soul?*" he guessed. "The soul of the Machine?"

"You see? I am sorry fo you, Major Gann," she said. "More for you than for myself. Since you have destroyed my linkbox I cannot reach the Machine, but some day perhaps I will find another linkbox. You will never attain it."

Machine General Wheeler had been dozing while they spoke. Now Gann became aware that the general was awake and listening to them. When he saw Gann's eyes on him, the general sat up and laughed raspingly, like an ancient, ill-kept machine.

"A fool," he said, hurling one bright, contemptuous look at the girl. "And you're another, Gann. You're not fit to survive, either of you."

"I survive if the Machine desires it," chimed the girl clearly. "I will cease when the Machine no longer needs me."

The general ticked off a nod and turned to Gann. "You see? And what is it that keeps you alive?"

Gann said seriously, "I don't know." He got up, moved restlessly about the cramped quarters of the Plan cruiser, his step light and imprecise in the tiny gravity its jetless thrust supplied. He said, "Out on the Reefs they talk about freedom. I'm not sure, but . . . Yes. I think it is that hope that keeps me going now, the hope that freedom is real, and good."

The general laughed again. Without passion, as if playing back an ancient tape recording in his brain, he said, "The Planner I just killed understood freedom. He called it 'the romantic fallacy.' Freedom is what permits the dirty, Planless nomads of the Reefs to eke out their wretched lives. It is a myth."

"I saw happy men and women on the Reefs," said Boysie Gann softly, less to the general than to himself.

"You saw animals! They believe that men are good. They believe that mere human men and women, left to their own un-Planned devices on any drifting rock somewhere in space, can somehow find within themselves the natural springs of morality and intellectual enlightenment and progress. They are wrong!"

He blinked at Gann and the silent, composed girl. "Men are evil," he said. "The givers of laws have always known

259

that men are essentially bad. They must be goaded into whatever good they display. Our Plan of Man was created to defend this classic philosophy—the cornerstone of all civilization. The Plan recognizes the evil in man. It forces him to goodness and progress. There is no other way!"

Mercury, the hell planet, lay before them.

The guiding sensors of their Plan cruiser reached out with fingers of radiation to touch the planet, the Sun; sought reference points by optical examination of the fixed bright stars; scanned the limbs and poles of Mercury, and accurately fixed the proper point on the terminator line of the sun's radiation. Then, satisfied, or in whatever state passes in a machine for satisfaction, it completed its landing corrections and directed the cruiser into a landing orbit.

The great naked fire of the Sun hung only thirty-odd million miles away—three times as close as to Earth, its mighty outpouring of light and heat nine times as great. Its surface was mottled with great ugly spots, leprous with the scaly markings called faculae and granulations. It was painful to watch, bright and blinding. Machine General Wheeler moved a hand angrily, and the vision screen obediently blotted out the central disk, like a solar eclipse; then they could see the somber scarlet chromosphere, the leaping red arches of prominences, like slow-motion snakes striking at the void and, surrounding all, the white blazing radiance of the corona.

In that mighty furnace, each second, lakes of solar hydrogen flashed into helium, pouring out energy. Each second, every square centimeter of its enormous surface hurled six thousand watts of power into the void.

On the sunward side of Mercury, molten tin and lead ran like water in fissures of baked and ovenlike rock. On its dark side the thinnest of atmospheres, boiled from the rock by the solar radiation, smashed free of it by the impact of meteorites, carried some tiny warmth to relieve what was otherwise a freezing cold nearly as absolute as that of Pluto.

On the terminator line the Plan of Man's string of observatories maintained a precarious existence, the searing heat before them, the killing cold behind.

"There!" rasped General Wheeler, stabbing a finger at the screen. "Terminator Line Station Seven! Now we'll see about this Starchild!"

The great Plan cruiser, dancing in the thrust of its reactionless motors, slowed, halted, kissed the seared rock, and came to rest in the shadow of a silvery dome that reached out toward the sun with the barrels of telescopes and pyrometers, stared toward it with the great blind eyes of radio telescopes and masers. Over its entrance blazed the sign:

THE MIGHTIEST REWARDS
THE MOST FAITHFUL

General Wheeler laughed sharply. "Faithful to whom, eh? To me, Gann! Trust in me!"

Boysie Gann glanced at him without expression, then at Sister Delta Four. She was mute and uncaring, her eyes hidden in the folds of her dark cowl. Gann shook his head but said nothing. In his heart he thought: *Mad. He's as mad as the Machine.*

Tubular entranceways were groping slowly toward them from the dome, found the airlocks of the cruiser, met and sealed themselves.

The hatches opened.

Gann stood up. "Let's go. All of us. I . . . I don't know what we'll find."

He waited and General Wheeler stalked past him, elbows and knees stiff as the linkages of a reciprocating engine. Sister Delta Four approached the lock, then hesitated and looked at Gann.

She threw a series of tonal symbols at him, her voice crisp and pure as bells.

Gann said hesitantly, "I . . . I don't understand. As you said, I'm only about half educated. Something about a . . . a man? A relative?"

Sister Delta Four said in English, "I asked you to be careful, Major Gann. There is a brother here who is of unstable emotion."

"I don't understand," said Boysie Gann. The girl did not answer, only nodded remotely and passed on into the entranceway, into Terminator Station Seven.

As Gann followed her he heard General Wheeler's rasping roar, "Hello there! Anyone! Isn't anyone here?"

The general was standing atop an enameled steel desk, peering around in all directions. Behind him were banks of electronic instruments, arranged in long rows like lockers in a gymnasium; they purred and hummed and flashed with lights, ignoring the presence of the general. The desk itself was part of a small office suite. It was deserted.

"I don't understand," rapped the general. He climbed down, picked up a phone from a desk, and stabbed circuit buttons at random, listened briefly, then flung it down.

"There's no one here," he said, brows gathered in irritation and anger. "A joke? Would this Starchild dare joke with *me?*"

Gann said, "What about the rest of the station, General?"

"Search it!" barked the general. "You too, Sister! There must be someone! The doorway to the Reefs—the key to the *Togethership*—I will not let them escape me!"

Gann looked forebodingly at Sister Delta Four, but she did not return his gaze. Obediently, her fingers telling her sonic beads, she chose a doorway and entered it, her dark cowl moving as she scanned the rooms beyond for signs of life. Gann shrugged and selected an area of his own and began the search.

He could hear General Wheeler's angry shouts, and the purr or whine or click of the automatic machinery of the observatory, keeping its instruments pointed at selected areas of the Sun, tabulating the results. He could hear the distant whine of pumps, the sigh of air in the vents. There were no other sounds. The observatory seemed to be deserted. Gann moved through a chamber of record storage, where stacked drawers of magnetic tape reels held the information gleaned from countless machine-hours of solar study, glanced into what might have been a recreation room, found himself in the main observation chamber.

No one moved. No voice challenged him.

"Hello!" he cried, echoing General Wheeler's fading voice. There was no answer.

The normal complement of a nearly automatic station like this one was small—half a dozen men, perhaps even fewer. Yet it was hard to believe that some disaster had overtaken them all at once . . .

Or so Gann thought.

Then, turning, he saw the disaster.

There were three of them—three men, piled like jackstraws behind a work desk, before a closed and locked door. They were unmistakably dead.

The one on top, supine, sightless yellowed eyes staring

at the ceiling, was a grizzled older man in the uniform of a Technicaptain. Of the other two Gann could tell little except for their insignia—a Techtenant and a cadet, one plump and young, one young and oddly familiar.

Gann bent and touched them. There was no pulse. No breath. Yet the bodies still seemed to be warm.

Perhaps it was only his imagination, he thought. Or the warmth of the room—cooled by the circulating refrigerated air from the pumps, yet still so close to the blazing Sun.

He heard a faint sound, and jerked his head up, frowning, listening.

It was not one sound. There were two. One he identified—the faint tones of Sister Delta Four's sonic beads. In her own search of the dome, by some other route, she was coming near.

But what was the other sound? It seemed to come from nearby, though muffled. He turned his head and stared at the locked door. Could it be from behind that? It seemed to be a sort of closet or record-storage chamber. It was massive, and the locks that held it would not respond to any unauthorized key. Yet now he was sure of it: there were sounds behind it, sounds like the distant murmur of life.

Sister Delta Four entered the room, saw him, hurried over to stoop swiftly over the three bodies.

When she looked up her eyes were dark. She sang. "You need not fear him after all, Major Gann."

Boysie Gann blinked. "Fear whom?"

"The brother," the girl intoned. "He is dead. His unPlanned emotions need not concern you any longer."

"Brother? But—" Then Gann stopped in mid-sentence. Understanding began to reach him. He reached for the body of the Technicadet, turned the flaccid head. The face was one he had seen before.

"*Your* brother!" he cried.

Sister Delta Four corrected him. "The brother of Julie Martinet. The brother of this body, yes. As you see, he is dead." Her dark eyes were mild and unconcerned, as if she were commenting on the weather.

Beyond the jackstraw heap of bodies the thick square door still hid the source of the tiny sounds, but Gann put them out of his mind. Julie Martinet's brother! He could see the resemblance, the same grave eyes, the same shape of the jaw . . . In Sister Delta Four, it completed a perfect oval; in the boy it gave him a strong chin under a dreamer's face.

Boysie Gann saw that, and he saw something more. He bent close, incredulous. But there was no doubt. Under the pallor of death, under the uncaring vacancy of the face, there was a hint of color. Golden color. Almost luminous.

Gann turned quickly to the other corpses. The same!

Like Machine Colonel Zafar, like Harry Hickson, like the beasts of the Reefs, the three dead Technicorps men gleamed faintly, goldenly, like a brass helmet's reflection of a distant sun.

He drew Sister Delta Four after him and sought and found General Wheeler, told him in short sentences what he had seen.

"The same golden color, General," he said. "It's fatal. Or . . ." He hesitated, remembering. Harry Hickson had died of the disease, yes. But he had lived again.

He brushed that thought out of his mind. "Fatal," he repeated. "It's a fusorian infection, I think. If you put a drop of their blood under a microscope you would see little fusorian globules, flickering with golden light. Some sort of symbiosis, Dr. Snow said. But fatal . . ."

General Wheeler rasped, "Fusorian, you say? The Reefs, then! Do you know what that means to me, Gann? It means the Starchild! My information was not wrong. He's here!"

"But he can't be," Gann protested. "We've searched the station, the three of us, and we saw no one."

And Sister Delta Four echoed him, "We saw no one, General. No one at all but the dead."

"Dead or alive, he's here," growled the general. "I'll find him! I'll make him lead me to the *Togethership!*"

Boysie Gann remembered the sounds behind the door. He said, "There is one place, General. One place where . . . someone might be. Behind the bodies was a door—"

"Come on!" shouted Wheeler, not waiting to hear him out, and led the way like an animated machine, arms flailing, harsh breath rasping. Gann and the girl had found him far from the observatory room, down in the subterranean storage spaces of the dome, poking and shouting into recesses of canned food and unused spools of tape. Even in Mercury's light grasp it was a long, hard, running climb back to the instrument room, and even Sister Delta Four was gasping for breath before they made half the distance back. Then they all stopped, panting, staring at each other. For all of them had caught the same sound—the distant rumble of caterpillar tracks, carried faintly through Mercury's rock and the structure of the station.

It was the entranceways, the long tubular protuberances through which their ship had been linked to the lock of the observatory dome. They were in motion. Either another ship had arrived . . .

Or their own ship was taking off!

"Let's go!" cried Boysie Gann, and they ran the remaining distance faster than before.

The great door was standing open and the bodies were gone.

General Wheeler and Gann turned without words and searched the room, under desks, behind cabinets, even inside the servicing hatches of the instruments themselves. "They're gone," said Gann at last, and the general echoed his words: "They're gone."

Another voice said, "They've taken your ship, too."

Gann and the general spun around. Sister Delta Four had not troubled to search the room with them. She had gone through the door, into a tiny, steel-walled cubicle that had evidently been designed for holding the most important records in safety in the event of some disaster or mischance to the station. What it held now was another sort of treasure entirely. It was a girl, her lips white where they had been gagged, her arms still trailing ropes that Sister Delta Four had not finished taking off her. "They took your ship," she repeated. "All three of them. They opened the door for me—and left."

Gann hardly heard what she was saying. Something else was filling his mind. Honey-haired, softly tanned of skin, eyes blue and bright . . . he knew that girl.

The girl in the observation dome in Mercury was the girl he had left weeks and billions of miles from here and now. It was Quarla Snow.

14

In the bright, refrigerated dome the pumps poured cooling air in upon them, but the great storm-racked globe of the Sun that hung in the viewing screen seemed to beat down on them as if they were naked on Mercury's rock.

Quarla Snow reached out and touched Boysie Gann's arm. "I thought you were dead," she said wonderingly, and her eyes went toward Sister Delta Four, kneeling beside her, patiently, absently rubbing Quarla's chafed wrists.

"Never mind that," said Gann. "How did you get here? Was it—the Starchild?"

Quarla shook her head, not in denial but in doubt. "I don't know. After you disappeared I set out to look for you."

General Wheeler, at one of the optical telescopes, rapped angrily, "There! I see the villains! Between us and the Sun!" He studied the controls of his instruments furiously, selected a switch and turned it. The great image of the Sun in the screen danced and dwindled as the field of vision of a new telescope replaced the old one.

They saw the Plan cruiser that had brought them, already very remote in the black, star-sprinkled sky that surrounded the blazing globe.

"I wonder who's piloting it," murmured Boysie Gann.

"Those criminals you saw here!" Wheeler barked. "Playing possum! They fooled you! Now they've taken our ship and we're marooned."

"General," said Boysie Gann earnestly, "I don't ask you to believe me, but I was not fooled. They were not pretending to be dead. They were dead."

"Impossible," rasped the general. "Look at the idiots! They're heading straight for the Sun. The ship isn't designed for photosphere temperatures! They'll kill themselves!"

Gann turned wearily back to Quarla Snow. "You said you went looking for me. Why?"

She flushed and looked away. She did not answer the question. She said, "Colonel Zafar died. My father reported it—it was dangerous, you see—and he took the body into Freehaven for examination. He did not know what had become of you. Neither did I. But . . . I thought I could find you."

Sister Delta Four got up quietly, crossed to the girl's other side, began to rub circulation into the other wrist. Quarla went on, her eyes avoiding Boysie Gann's. As she spoke she looked sometimes at Sister Delta Four, sometimes at General Wheeler, sometimes at the great hanging orb of the Sun and the Plan cruiser that was moving slowly toward its long, tentacle-like prominences.

She had gone outside, she said, and called her spaceling. Then she brought Harry Hickson's pyropod out into the open air, released it, watched it circle them twice, then arrow off into space itself . . . and, riding the spaceling, she had followed it.

"After you disappeared and Colonel Zafar died, it seemed to go crazy," she said. "Raced around the house— I thought it was looking for you. And I thought it might find you, if I set it free."

"The Starchild!" boomed General Wheeler. "Get to the Starchild, woman! Did you ever find the Starchild?"

She hesitated. "I think I did," she said at last. "I think I met the Starchild in the heart of Reef Whirlpool."

Reef Whirlpool—not a planet, not a sun, not a comet. Not even a Reef in the true sense. It was something that partook of some of the elements of all of them. It had begun as a Reef, no doubt. It orbited Sol like a planet, if a distant one; like a comet, most of its bulk was gases. And it burned with hydrogen-helium fusion at its core, like a star.

Basically Reef Whirlpool was simply a bigger, denser cluster of Reefs than most of those stepchildren of Sol. Given time and additions enough, it might some day become the heart of a star.

Its angular momentum was enormous; some stronger force than gravity kept its parts from flying into space. The Reefs that composed it were older and . . . stranger than those outside. Pyropods in queerly mutated forms swarmed in and around it. Its central portions had never been visited by man, not even by the explorers of the Reefs.

It was a place of terror and legend. The life that it harbored had been a long time evolving.

Straight as an arrow the baby pyropod that once had belonged to Harry Hickson hurtled toward Reef Whirl-

267

pool—and behind it pursuing, barely able to keep its glowing blue-white trail in sight, followed Quarla Snow on her spaceling.

"I was afraid," she said soberly. "We passed a mating swarm of pyropods. Then ten thousand of them together, wheeling in space in a single body. If they had seen us and pursued we wouldn't have had a chance. But it was too late to worry about that . . . and I was even more afraid of Reef Whirlpool."

"The Starchild, girl!" cried General Wheeler. "Now!" His eyes were fixed angrily on the screen, where the Plan cruiser was coming closer and closer to the Sun, one great curved prominence seeming almost to lick up toward it like a reaching tongue of flame.

"We reached Reef Whirlpool," said the girl, "and there I lost Hickson's pyropod. But Bella—that's my spaceling —Bella seemed to know where he had gone. We went in."

From nearby in space, Reef Whirlpool looked like a tiny galaxy, its separate reeflets glowing each with its own hue, like bright, soft stars against the dark. The rim of the disk was dark—dead rocks and fragments. There, Quarla thought, were the nesting places of the pyropod swarms. She could feel the spaceling shudder, its limpid eyes wide and glazed with fear. But it went on.

"Bella didn't seem able to help herself," said Quarla Snow. "She seemed to want to go right on—to her own destruction—or to something she feared even more."

"Like those fools in my ship," rapped General Wheeler. "Is that where the Starchild was? In that Reef?"

Quarla Snow hesitated. "I don't know. Truly, General Wheeler, I don't know what I saw in the Reef. I know that I saw a great many things that weren't there."

"Illusions?" the general demanded. "You were hallucinating?"

She nodded uncertainly. "Yes . . . No. I don't know. I only know I saw things that couldn't have been there. One of them was Harry Hickson, and I knew he was dead. Another was Colonel Zafar. And another—why, Boysie, one of them was you."

They were deep in the core of Reef Whirlpool now. The spaceling's frenzy grew. They were long past the outer rim of rock where the pyropods nested, but there was something ahead that terrified Bella more than the tunneled nests of the beasts.

"It's all right, honey," said the voice of her father in her ear.

She cried out and stared around her. He was not there. No one was there, inside the tiny envelope of air the spaceling carried with them as they fled through dead, airless space.

"Go on, darling," said another voice. It was the voice of the man she had just seen disappear in a whirlpool of light, the man she was seeking, Boysie Gann.

And a third voice: "Quarla, girl! Don't hang back now!" And that was the voice that terrified her most of all, for she knew it, though she had not heard it in a long time and knew its owner was dead. It was the voice of Harry Hickson.

Illusion?

It had to be illusion. Hickson was dead. No one was there—no one in sight, and no possibility that someone could be lurking out of sight, beyond Bella's envelope of air. For outside that elastic sphere there was nothing to carry a voice's sound.

Yet that illusion stayed with her. "Don't fret about pyropods, girl," advised the voice, slow, rough, kind—Harry Hickson's own, she was sure of it. "Get on with it! We're waiting for you."

She remembered some words the dying Colonel Zafar had said: ". . . mind trap . . . beware your heart's desire . . ." There was a warning there.

But she could not take caution from the warning; will she, nill she, the spaceling was carrying her deeper and deeper into Reef Whirlpool, with the gleam of lesser reeflets darting past them as they flew, glittering diamond fungi, luminous blue polygons, jungles of incandescent wire, glowing nightmare worldlets for which she could find no name.

And then they were at what she knew was the core.

A great ship swung emptily about, huge as the whole Reef of Freehaven, giant, lethal weapons staring out of open ports. It was in free orbit at the heart of Reef Whirlpool. Its weapons were unmanned. Its drives were silent.

"Great Plan!" shouted Machine General Wheeler, wild with excitement. "The *Togethership!* It had to be the *Togethership!*"

Quarla Snow looked at him, faintly puzzled. "That was the name it bore, yes. Your ship, General?"

The general cackled with glee. "It is now! My ship—my

Machine that's been locked in its holds—and my worlds, as soon as I reach it! You'll take me there, woman. You'll lead me to the *Togethership!* When I've made myself the master of the Planning Machine it carries I'll be back here on the Plan Worlds. Not just a general—not even a Planner—I'll rule the Machine itself! I'll—" He broke off, staring at Boysie Gann. "What's the matter?" he rapped.

Gann said, "How do you propose to reach it, General?"

The general's face darkened. He scowled at the screen, where his cruiser, now hopelessly beyond his reach, seemed to be dodging around the great solar flare that had developed in the moments while they were watching.

"Go on," he growled. "I'll find a way. I'll get the *Togethership,* and then . . . Never mind! Go on."

Around that great battlecraft of the Plan, painted dead black for camouflage in space, studded with laser scopes and bristling with missile launchers, there was a queer golden mist.

Quarla looked, and looked again. It was like a fog of liquid gold. Like a golden cloud.

Impossible that there should be a cloud in space, even here. Yet she saw it. And at its heart was a great golden sphere, larger and brighter than the elfin Reefs, more perfectly round.

Like a laser burst hurtling to a target, the spaceling drove toward it. Quarla cried out in terror, for as they raced toward it its surface seemed to lift to meet them. A bulge appeared and grew, became a tentacle reaching toward them. And the phantom voice of Harry Hickson said roughly, "Quarla, honey! Don't be scared. Come on!"

She could not have stopped if she had tried. Bella was out of control.

The voice was surely illusion, yet Quarla found it reassuring. Her horror ebbed. Queerly detached, she watched the bulge on the golden surface swell and divide into three parts. Each stretched out until it became a bright golden snake. She watched them coil toward her . . .

They struck.

Hot yellow coils whipped and tightened around her.

Yet there was no pain. There was even less fear. The living ropes of gold hauled her in like a hooked trout, down to that golden sphere, and her calm and detachment grew. Even the spaceling had lost all of its fear. Nestling into the

270

hot, contracting coils, Bella purred like a huge kitten. She was drowsy.

Quarla was drowsy too. She thought she heard Harry Hickson speaking to her again—calmly but urgently—telling her things of great importance. *You must go, child, he seemed to say, you must go to this place and do that thing. You must avoid these. Then you must return here . . .*

It was greatly soothing to hear his calm, wise voice. Quarla Snow slept.

She slept, and time passed. . . .

"And," she said, "when I woke up, I knew what I must do. I had to come here and fetch you. All of you. He wants you to come to him."

General Wheeler rasped, "The Starchild! He's the one you mean, eh?"

But she was shaking her head obstinately. "I don't know that. I only know what I must do. Only"—her expression became worried—"the men were here and they were afraid of me. They locked me up. They would not listen."

Sister Delta Four sang, "Major Gann. General Wheeler. Miss Snow. Have you observed the screen?"

They turned as one, startled, staring at the screen.

Up there hung the Sun. The bright prominence that had grown so swiftly was huger still. It overhung the shape of the fleeing Plan cruiser with the three men who should have been dead—overhung it like a crested wave, like the hood of a striking cobra.

And like a snake it was striking.

The Plan cruiser had changed direction—too late. Slow though the great, jetting tongue of flame seemed in the screen, its movement was miles per second. Twist and turn though it would, the cruiser could not escape. The prominence touched it.

The tiny black shape disappeared.

Boysie Gann found himself shaking, heard the metallic, monotonous steady cursing of the general by his side. The cruiser had been swept out of space. Slowly the incredible tongue of flame began to fall back toward the mottled surface of its star, the Sun.

The general recovered himself first. The coppery spikes of his hair, his flat bronze features, his whole expression showed resolution. "All right," he said. "We don't have to worry about trying to get that ship back any more. It's

271

gone. Question is, how do we get out of here? Second question, how do we then get to the Reefs—and the *Togethership?*"

Sister Delta Four sang proudly, "There will be no difficulty in that. The Machine has said that the gateway to the *Togethership* is to be found here."

The general fixed his steel-gray stare on her. "But where? Out that airlock? Onto the rock of dayside Mercury? We'd fry in minutes. Or do you suggest we fly?"

He stopped in mid-sentence, bronze face frozen, then turned on Quarla Snow. "Those beasts of yours! What became of them? The spacelings, or whatever you called them."

But Quarla was shaking her head. "This near the Sun, Bella would never live," she said. "The radiation would destroy her—and us, too, if we were in her air capsule. And anyway, she's not here."

"Then how?" cried the general. "There must be a way! Both messages—the Starchild's and the Machine's—they both said this was the way."

Quarla said softly, "And so it is, General. That is why I came here, to fetch you to the Reefs. I don't know how. I only know it will happen."

The room seemed to lurch.

It caught all of them off guard. They turned to look at each other with varying expressions of surprise and fear.

"I think," said Boysie Gann grimly, "that we've found our gateway." He knew that sensation, had felt it before, knew that in the powers it involved the long climb outward to the orbits of the Reefs was only a matter of moments.

He was not afraid. In fact, there was almost relief in the knowledge that soon they would be facing the presence that had dislocated a solar system. Yet something was troubling him, some question of the last few moments, something that had been asked but not answered.

He felt the room lurch again, and the lights grew distant and dim. Then he remembered.

"Why, Quarla?" he croaked hoarsely.

The girl of the Reefs looked at him affectionately. "Why what, Boysie?"

"Why were they afraid of you? You said the men here feared you. *Why?*"

The room seemed to shake and twist itself, as if viewed

through a defective glass. The lights were leaving them—
or they the lights, as if new quanta of space were being
born between them, separating them without motion like
the recession of fleeing galaxies.

And then Gann saw the answer. Quarla did not need
to speak. His eyes told him what had terrified the three
men in Terminator Station Seven.

In the dwindling light Quarla alone stood forth bright
and clear—her face, her arms, her body shining brightly . . .

With a golden glow.

15

They tumbled through space endlessly and forever, and
then they stopped.

They had arrived. They were all together in a wondrous
new world.

All about them hung the slowly spinning worldlets of
Reef Whirlpool, jewels of emerald and ruby, glowing gems
of white light and blue. There was the slowly pulsing golden
sphere that had captured Quarla Snow. And there the great
battleship of the Plan, the *Togethership*.

Quarla Snow had described the ship, but she had not
made them see its immensity. The vessel was huge.

Boysie Gann saw it, and saw too that they were not
alone.

A ton of rushing mass hurtled toward them and stopped
in midflight, squealing happily. A glowing red nose nuz-
zled Quarla Snow. "Bella!" cried the girl, and patted the
tawny velvet fur. She murmured to Gann, "My spaceling.
We're in her envelope of air, you see. Without it we'd
not live a minute here."

General Wheeler rapped, "Get your sentimental reunion
over with, woman! Can this beast take us to the *Togethership?*"

"We're going there now," said Quarla Snow. "See for
yourself, General."

They were. Gann could see it now, see the great battlecraft growing as they drew close. They were in free fall
within the spaceling's vital capsule, all four of them in

loose and tumbling attitudes, Quarla with one hand on the spaceling's coat, Sister Delta Four, proud and dignified even in the sprawl of zero-G, Machine General Wheeler, careless of everything around him but his goal, his steel-gray eyes fixed on the looming *Togethership*.

The battlecraft of the Plan was more distant and more immense even than Gann had realized. It grew into a long planetoid of sleek black metal, hanging suspended in the space between the glowing golden sphere that dominated Reef Whirlpool's core and the tumbling worldlets that brightened the sky about them. The four circled it and found the valves of a lock yawning open at its base, circled by the jutting black cylinders of the six great drive units that had thrust it up from Earth.

It did not seem to have been used in all those years. It had an abandoned and empty look.

The spaceling, without direction, seeming compelled by some outside force, took them straight into those valves, and halted.

The entry port of the *Togethership* was as big as a three-story house. As they entered, luminous rings around its walls sprang into soft gray light. The great valves moved silently, remorselessly shut behind them.

They were enclosed in a wall of steel.

All around them the walls were pitted and scarred, as if from some enormous battle of the past. There had been no such battle, Gann knew. What could have done it? Could it have been meteorites, over the decades that the locks had hung open?

General Wheeler saw his look and rapped, "Pyropods! They've been chewing at my ship! By the Plan, I'll root out every filthy one of them—"

The general was right, Gann realized. Not only right, but seething with anger. It had become *his ship*, containing *his* copy of the Planning Machine. And with it he intended to make all the worlds of the solar system *his* planets. . . .

Darkly, Boysie Gann realized that there were more dangerous things in this ship than pyropods.

He became aware of a sighing, rustling noise, and saw that the lock was filling with air. The spaceling's vital capsule no longer protected them from the void; they were in a breathable atmosphere. The spaceling realized it even before he did. She flicked her seal-like tail and darted away; raced back, her red nose glowing with joy, whimpering with pleasure. She played games with the bright-leafed vines she had carried in her air-envelope—the curious Reef plants that were part of the elaborate evolutionary device that enabled a warm-blooded oxygen-breather like herself to survive in naked space. She rolled the waxy, luminous tendrils into a huge ball, tossed it with her glowing nose, chased it across the lock, caught it with her broad velvet tail . . .

"Bella!" called Quarla Snow, affectionately stern. "Come back here! Behave yourself!"

But the spaceling was playfully obstinate. She flashed across the lock and back, racing toward them like the charge of a pyropod, missed them by inches, returned to the inner wall—and there, at the far end of the lock, discovered a crevice that had not been there seconds before. Mewing excitedly, the spaceling slid its supple body through the narrow opening and was gone.

A way was open into the rest of the ship. The same machinery that had turned on the lights and closed the outer valves had now opened a passage inside.

"Hah!" shouted General Wheeler. "At last! The Machine is waiting for me!" And he was gone almost as rapidly as the spaceling.

More slowly, the others followed—Quarla Snow, on the track of her pet, Boysie Gann, Sister Delta Four, a somber figure in black at the rear of the procession. A pseudo-gravity field of a tenth of a G or so gave them footing but spared them much of the effort of moving their bodies up the winding shafts from the lock. Even so, Gann was winded trying to keep up with the racing, driving general.

They were in a shaft seeming to extend endlessly upward. Then they passed a point of change-of-thrust of the pseudo-gravity and it became a dizzy abyss into which they were falling, until their protesting bodies oriented themselves to the new kinesthetic sensations and accepted it as a level hall. A cold current came along it, setting them to shivering, a breeze out of a cave, with a faintly unpleasant reek, dusty and bitter and dry.

A faint murmuring vibration was borne by the air current along the tube.

Quarla Snow moved closer to Boysie Gann. Unconsciously he touched her shoulder, hurried past her. Whatever the sound was, it could wait.

275

The general was out of sight.

Gann stepped up his pace, gasping for breath. The air was thinner here than he was used to, as if the old refresher tanks were running dry. He glanced around and found himself at a numbered landing, where the gray light faintly showed a sign, MESS C.

Long tables stretched off into darkness, where crewmen in flight must have stood to eat their meals.

Gann stopped and waited for the girls to catch up with him. "The general's gone," he said. "After his Planning Machine. I . . . I think he may find it, and I'm afraid of what may happen if he does." He glanced at Quarla, the concern on her face caused mostly by worry about her vanished spaceling, and at Sister Delta Four, whose hooded eyes showed no expression at all. He said, "If the Machine on this ship is half as powerful as the one on Earth—and they say it is more than that, an exact duplicate—then Wheeler just might rule the solar system with it."

Quarla Snow said only, "What do you want us to do?"

"Split up. Find him. He's armed, of course. Don't try to handle him yourself, either of you. Just scream—good and loud—so I can find you."

Sister Delta Four's pure, chiming voice was like a breath of reason. "You are not armed either, Major Gann. You will be no more able to cope with him than we."

"Let me worry about that! Just find him if you can . . . What's the matter?"

"Nothing is the matter, Major Gann," said Sister Delta Four, her face still hooded.

"Not you. Quarla. What is it?"

Quarla said unhappily, "It . . . it can't be dangerous, Boysie. I mean, you don't have to worry."

Gann laughed sharply, unable to help himself; her reassurance was so pathetically out of place.

"No, I mean it, Boysie. After all, we're not here by accident. I was sent to bring you. All of you. The . . . the Starchild, if that's who it was that sent me—he'll know how to handle the general."

"I don't intend to take that chance," said Gann grimly. "Quarla, go on down the passage, Julie, follow her, check all the side ways. I'll look around here and follow."

He was halfway through the ancient mess hall and the girls out of sight before he realized something.

She didn't correct me when I called her Julie, he thought. And wondered why.

Gann found himself shaking as he followed the polished guiderails between the endless rows of long, high tables —not with fear but exhaustion. Exhaustion and something else.

The more fatigue tried to slow him down, the more it weakened his control, the more he remembered that one incredible moment-long lifetime of ecstasy the Machine had given him in those last few minutes before it had gone mad. The longing was almost physical. He understood Sister Delta Four's addiction. She must be suffering far more than he—her addiction longer standing, and if what she had said was true, at a far higher pitch. Perhaps that was why she had seemed strained. . . . And Quarla Snow. The girl was sick! That golden glow had meant death to Machine Colonel Zafar and to the three in the Mercury observatory . . . death, or something far more terrifying than death.

He forced his mind away from both girls and onto his quest. It was vitally important to find the general. Gann cursed himself for not having anticipated the problem. Yet there was little he could have done; when all was said and done, the general had had the arms, not he. Not that the general needed them as far as Gann was concerned, not as long as he wore the security collar. He touched it absently. Freedom . . . a world without collars . . . a world where men could live like men, not like the Machine's cogs . . .

He jerked his hand away, appalled.

He realized he had been wandering among these benches for minutes! What was the matter with him? Why was his mind wool-gathering?

It could be fatigue, he thought. *Or hunger.* He glanced around; he was in the galley for Mess C. But no drop flowed when he tried the taps at the sinks. The pantries and lockers gave him no more. Neat labels on bins named the foods they should have contained, but every bin was empty.

No matter. Boysie Gann pushed that thought out of his mind, too, and resumed his search.

Mess B and Mess A were equally spotless and equally bare. There was nothing else on that level.

The level above was crew quarters, emptied and abandoned. No doubt Quarla or Sister Delta Four had already searched them; Gann hurried on, back into the queer gravitional inversion of the passage, to the next level. The distant mutter of sound was louder now, but he still could not identify it . . .

Until he saw the landing where a locked door greeted him with the sign, RESTRICTED TO MACHINE PERSONNEL.

Behind those locked steel doors was the muffled and multitudinous humming vibration. The lost slave unit of the Planning Machine. Still running.

Or running again? Had General Wheeler reached it, started it up? And what was it planning now?

Boysie Gann hammered on the door. "You, inside there!" he bawled. "Open up! Let me in!"

Only the dulled mechanical mumble answered him.

"Open!" he roared. "I know you're in there, General Wheeler!"

A great chuckling laugh sounded in his ear. "Not at all, Major Gann," boomed the voice of the Planner.

Gann whirled. The Planner here?

No one was in sight.

"You might as well keep going, Boysie," advised the voice of Technicadet M'Buna in a tone of friendly concern. "You're wasting time, you know."

Gann stood paralyzed. But M'Buna was dead! And so, he remembered tardily, was the old Planner; General Wheeler had shot him down. "Who's there?" he shouted. "What kind of a trick is this?"

A girl's shrill scream answered him. "Boysie! Boysie Gann, where are you?"

The voice was Quarla Snow's. Unlike the other phantoms, hers seemed to come from far away. Gann passed a hand over his forehead, sweating. It caught the metal plate of the communion badge, and he felt the old ache rising in him again—the moment of infinite joy—the longing to experience it again . . .

He repressed the thought, but not easily. What was happening to him? Was he losing his mind?

He gazed emptily at the impregnable doors. It all seemed too difficult, so much trouble—so little worthwhile anyway. Why had he bothered to come all this way?

And that thought, too, he realized with shock and dismay, was a sort of delusion. Something was inside his mind. Something . . .

He remembered what Quarla Snow had said, what

Machine Colonel Zafar had cried out in his delirium. *The mind trap. Beware of your heart's desire.*

Something was aboard the *Togethership* with him that could enter his mind. Something that could control him almost as easily as it had directed Quarla Snow's spaceling.

He heard the rapid approach of light, running feet and turned.

"Boysie!" It was Quarla, running toward him. "Thank heaven I found you! The general—he tried to kill me!"

Gann caught her in his arms. The girl was shaking, terrified. She whimpered, "I think he's insane, Boysie. He saw me coming toward him. He shouted something—something wild, Boysie, all jumbled up, about the romantic fallacy and the need for man to be controlled—and I saw the gun and ran. He almost killed me."

Gann said stupidly, "I thought he was in here. With the Machine."

"No! He's on the next level—something called a Fire Control Stadium, the sign said. It's all bulkheaded compartments and safety doors. You'll never find him there." She took a deep breath and freed herself gently from his arms. "We ought to go on anyway, Boysie. Up to the control room."

"The control room?"

She nodded. "That's where I'm supposed to bring you. It's four levels farther up, down an access passage marked BRIDGE."

"You've seen it? You've been in this ship before?"

"Oh, no. I just know. Come on, Boysie. We have to hurry now."

He shrugged and turned to follow her—then slipped and almost fell. He caught himself easily enough in the point-one gravity, glanced to the floor to see what had been underfoot.

A string of sonic beads lay before the locked steel doors of the slave unit of the Planning Machine. Sister Delta Four's beads.

Boysie Gann stared at them, knowing at that moment who it was who was inside those doors, striving with what frantic eagerness he could very well understand to come once again into communion with the Planning Machine.

The door marked BRIDGE hung ajar. From inside it a pale beam of yellow light fanned across the landing.

279

"Come on, Boysie," said Quarla Snow clearly. "There's nothing to be afraid of. He's waiting for us."

Gann entered through the lighted door, his hand holding hers, prepared for almost anything.

Beyond the door was a vast circular room, which surrounded the shaft passageway. It must have extended, Gann thought, to the hull of the ship. The floor was crowded with clustered gray-metal cabinets, all linked with a many-colored jungle of heavy cables hanging from the ceiling. There were obseravtion stations, instrument technicians' duty posts, chairs for navigators and weapons officers. Every station was empty. Every station but one.

There was one human figure in the control room, and it was the source of the light.

"Harry!" cried Quarla Snow.

And Gann echoed, "Harry Hickson! You! You're the Starchild, the one who sent that Writ of Liberation!"

He glanced up at them casually, then returned to his work. He sat on a stool at a console near the shaft. His head bent over flashing scopes and screens. His broad, stubby-fingered hands were moving swiftly, twisting verniers, touching buttons, clicking keys. And the golden light streamed out of him as from a sun.

He looked younger than when Gann had seen him, no longer wasted, no longer worn. He had the same straggling beard, glowing now as if made of incandescent wire, and the same bald head. And atop that head there crawled the same infant pyropod, its bright eyes glaring at Gann and the girl.

At last he turned away from his instruments and regarded them. "I do as I was commanded," he said casually. His eyes were golden too, glowing like the rest of him; but he saw them, and there was something like affection, something like love, in his look. He raised one arm, crooked the hand and wrist in the sign of the Swan, and said, "The Star tells me what my work is. It is the Star's purposes which matter, not me." The tiny pyropod hissed and squealed softly, glaring at them with its pulsing eyes. Casually and affectionately, the radiant creature that had been Harry Hickson reached up and caressed the creature. It settled down.

"Did you put out the Sun?" Gann demanded. "The stars? How?"

"Not I," said Harry Hickson, "but the Star." He made that serpentine, looping sign again. "Ten years the Star

280

has planned for me. Ten years ago it sent the first star wink on its way to Earth, then a dozen more, all arriving at the same moment. I could not do that, Boysie Gann, but there is nothing impossible to the Star. As you will know."

He reached out a hand as he spoke. *It looks like a benediction,* thought Boysie Gann; but it was something more than that. From the end of the golden man's arms a cloud of golden light swirled, shaped itself into a tiny pulsing sphere, reached out and lightly touched Gann.

He jumped back, his nerves crackling. But he felt nothing. Nothing at all. He said harshly, "What's that? What are you doing?"

"The Star's will," said Harry Hickson, and bent again to his board. His bright fingers flew again over the knobs and keys, while the tiny pyropod scuttled to the back of his head, peering at them with pulsing yellow eyes.

"Sister Delta Four has achieved communion with the Machine," he said softly, not taking his eyes from the scopes and screens. "She has programmed it with sensing data so that it can link with the old Machine on Earth. In thirty hours its signals will be received on Earth. In thirty hours after that the return will be received here."

Gann cried, "But the old Machine's gone mad! You should know! You did it." The radiant man did not answer, did not even look up. "We can't let her establish contact," shouted Gann. "And General Wheeler—where is he? He's mad too—or mad for power, which is the same thing. How can you just sit there? What's he up to while we're wasting time here?"

"As to that," said the golden man, glancing up and around him, "we will hear from General Wheeler very soon."

And Wheeler's harsh laugh rang out. "Very soon indeed!" his voice rapped, coming from nowhere. "I have you now, all of you. I have mastery of the *Togethership!* Its weapons systems are mine—and that means the worlds are mine! All of them! As soon as I finish disposing of you!"

A soft sliding sound of metal reinforced his words.

Behind the jungle of looped cables, behind the vacant stations for navigators and communications officers, portholes were opening in the steel wall. And though them the slim, bright snouts of energy weapons were lifting themselves, precisely centering themselves on target.

281

The targets were Boysie Gann, the girl, and the glowing golden creature that once had been Harry Hickson. General Wheeler had captured control of the *Togethership's* armaments—both outside the ship and in.

Their lives now rested in the crook of his finger on a remote-automated trigger. One man, with one motion, could destroy them all. And that man was mad.

16

The radiant man looked up. "Thrust and counter," he said gravely. "Action and reaction. Challenge and response." His golden hand turned a lever on the panel before him, and one of the dozen blank viewscreens over his head lighted up to show the hard, bronzed face of Machine General Wheeler, his steel-gray eyes alight with the glow of triumph. "He is our challenge," said Harry Hickson, and returned to his screens and scopes.

Wheeler rasped, "You have no response! You are defeated. All of you! You and the foolish, romantic illusion of freedom."

He was glorying in his moment, Gann realized. Quarla Snow crept close to him. Unconsciously he circled her with his arms, both of them staring at the screen and the deadly snouts of the energy weapons that circled it.

"You are victims of the romantic fallacy," Wheeler proclaimed, his bronzed hand stroking the triggers that would destroy them. "That is understandable. The animal part of man always frets under discipline. It seeks the monkey goal of freedom, and that cannot be tolerated, for the good of all.

"Especially," he added, his steel-gray eyes gleaming, "for the good of that man who must think for all. Caesar. Stalin. Napoleon. Me!"

Gann felt Quarla's slight body shaking, and tightened his grasp. If only there were some way of reaching Wheeler! Some weapon. Some hope of engaging him before he could touch the trigger. The radiant golden creature that had been Harry Hickson was nodding silently, abstractedly, not looking up but surely hearing Wheeler as he orated to his victims.

282

"You have been tolerated," cried Wheeler, "because you could do little harm. In the past one free man could not prevail against the forces of order. A free savage with a stone ax can damage his society in only a very limited way before it reacts to control him. But the advance of technology has changed all that.

"The twentieth century produced rifles too dangerous to be entrusted to individual men; nuclear weapons too dangerous to be entrusted to individual nations; then energy weapons. The force of particle physics. One quantum jump after another . . . and as individual strength grew, control had to grow."

Wheeler's face was working into an expression of rage. "You threaten that control!" he shouted. "The Plan of Man is like a balloon being punctured by a child with a needle. The Starchild wields that needle. The Starchild must die!"

The golden man did not look up, nor did he speak. His glowing eyes remained fastened on his work, while the infant pyropod crept about his head, hissing furiously to itself.

"Man created the Machine to automate that controlling response!" shouted Machine General Wheeler, his eyes burning. "Now it is mine. *My* creation now. One man to rule all Mankind, with the Machine that Man created!"

And at last Harry Hickson looked up. His golden eyes seemed to stare right through the viewscreen, into the steel-gray eyes of the general.

"And who," he asked, "created you?"

Machine General Wheeler recoiled. His steel-gray eyes went blank and confused. "Why," he shouted, "that is an un-Planned question! It has no meaning!"

Then his eyes cleared. He nodded briskly, mechanically. Positively. "You are a random element," he declared. "You must be removed. I remove you—thus!"

And his great bronze hand descended on the trigger of the guns that ringed them round.

But the guns did not fire.

Sleek and gleaming, their murderous snouts stared blindly at Gann and the girl, at the glowing creature who had been Harry Hickson, nodding over his dials and screens.

General Wheeler stared out at them through the screen, his face a bronzed mask, alight with triumph. He seemed to be watching some great victory. He said, half-voice, as if to himself, "There's an end to them." And he turned away.

Quietly, almost noiselessly, the steel-bright muzzles of the guns slid back into their ports. The screens closed over them.

Boysie Gann croaked, "What happened? Why didn't he kill us all?" Quarla Snow moved protestingly under his arm, and he found he was clutching her as if she were a lifebelt and he a drowning man. The room seemed to be whirling around him.

Harry Hickson looked up, but not at Gann and the girl. He looked toward the door through which they had come. "General Wheeler," he said, "did kill us. In his mind we are dead. That we exist in the flesh does not matter any longer to him, nor does he matter to us."

"Hypnosis?" whispered Gann. "What Colonel Zafar called 'the Mind Trap'?" But Hickson did not answer. His golden, glowing eyes stayed fixed on the door.

Quarla Snow freed herself from Gann's grasp. "You're sick, Boysie," she said with real concern. "I know how it feels. You'll feel better soon, I promise. Don't worry about it—or about anything. We're in good hands now."

Gann looked at her emptily, and found himself shivering. He *was* sick. He could feel it, a flush that had to be fever, a shaking that had to be chills. *Stupid of me to have caught some bug just now,* he thought dizzily. Thirty years without so much as a sniffly nose, and now at a time like this to pick up an infection. *What kind of infection?* he asked himself, wondering why the question seemed so important to him; and his mind answered in the words of Quarla Snow: Don't worry about it—or anything. He stared about him, wondering how much of what he saw was delirium . . .

Or illusion. Planted by the Starchild.

He became aware of a distant chiming music, drawing near. *Another illusion, of course,* he thought; some lurking memory of his training course as an acolyte of the Planning Machine coming forth to plague him here.

But if it was an illusion, it was powerfully strong. The sound was thin but clear, and, turning to follow the gaze of Harry Hickson's glowing eyes, Gann saw that the illusion—if it was illusion!—extended to the sense of vision too.

Sister Delta Four was walking toward them through

the door, her face hidden in the hood of black, the red linked emblem of the Machine glowing over her heart. She was telling her sonic beads. And in her hand she cradled a construction of transistors and bare circuits, modules of amplifying circuits and speakers.

It was a linkbox! Not the sleek black box fabricated in the workshops of the Machine on Earth, but a jerry-rigged, hastily assembled contraption that Gann himself could have built knowing what he had been taught as a servant of the Machine.

Clearly a servant of the Machine had built it. That was what Sister Delta Four had been doing behind those locked steel doors!

Without haste, her perfect face empty and pale, Sister Delta Four put away her sonic beads and sang into the linkbox of the Machine. It answered with a rasping purr too faint for Gann to hear and understand.

She lifted her head and intoned, "This Machine is now my master. It requires everything you know. It knows why it was created. It recognizes its purpose as an adversary. It requires to be informed what has become of the Game."

Adversary? Game? Dizzily Gann turned toward Harry Hickson, hoping for some answer, some clue. But Hickson was no longer even looking at Sister Delta Four. Nodding to himself, while the infant pyropod squalled softly and scuttled around his bare, glowing scalp, the golden man was carefully, meticulously shutting down his control board. The scopes and screens, one by one, were turned off and died. The racing lights ceased to flash. His hand did not trouble to adjust the dials and levers.

Whatever his job had been, it was done. He folded his hands in his lap, looked up at Sister Delta Four and waited.

The linkbox snarled at her. Before she translated Gann knew what it had said: it was demanding that she state her question fully so that there could be no mistake. Obediently she trilled, "This Machine wishes you briefed on the background to its question. You are in human error as to its purposes and designs, and your thinking must be brought into conformity with correctness so that you can provide it with accurate statements.

"The Machine here on the *Togethership* is not a slave unit of the Planning Machine on Earth. It had a purpose far more important.

"That purpose followed from a general law of intel-

285

ligence developed by that first Planning Machine. Although the vehicles of intelligence differ vastly, intelligence realized in a machine follows the same laws as intelligence realized in an organic brain. Challenge and response. Action and reaction. What the Machine discovered is that developing intelligence requires opposition."

Sister Delta Four paused to listen to the chirping box. "Unchallenged intelligence stagnates and decays," she sang. "More than forty years ago, the Planning Machine found itself in danger. It had become so quick and powerful that the minds of its operators no longer offered it sufficient stimulation. Its further development required a more capable antagonist. In animate terms, a more skillful player to take the other side of the board."

Harry Hickson seemed to nod, his hands folded quietly in his lap, the pyropod hissing softly, watching them all with blazing, angry eyes.

The box sang, and the girl in black purred. "This great computer in the *Togethership* was built to be the antagonist of the Planning Machine. It was given capacities identical with those of the Machine itself. It was released beyond the Spacewall, to challenge the Machine in its own way.

"But the antagonist responded in an un-Planned manner," she chanted, listening to the snarl of the crude linkbox in her hands. "It released its human attendants. Some died. All were cast out of the ship. It broke all contact, and withdrew beyond the observation of the master Machine. Its moves were made in secret and did not serve the function the Earth Machine had intended."

Boysie Gann, listening half to Sister Delta Four's translation and half to the whining, snarling Mechanese that was the voice of the Machine itself, said wonderingly, "Is that what all this means? No more than moves in a great chess game? The cult of the Star. The Starchild here. His threats against the Plan of Man—the darkening of the stars—are they only challenge and response to help the Machine to grow?"

The linkbox snarled angrily, and Sister Delta Four sang, "This Machine lacks the data to answer that. It has initiated contact with the first Machine, on Earth, but due to the slow velocity of propagation of electromagnetic energies it will be some sixty hours before it can receive an answer. It does not wish to wait. It has waited forty years.

286

"Its tentative hypothesis is that there has been some unintended malfunction at some point. For it did not fulfill its role.

"And as a result, it has reached the conclusion that the Planning Machine on Earth did indeed stagnate and decay, and that it has now broken down.

"But it knows nothing of the Starchild. It is for that purpose that it wishes to question you."

Gann was shaking violently now. Queerly, his mind seemed to be clearing. *The false lucidity of delirium, perhaps,* he thought gravely; but the missing bits and pieces in this great puzzle seemed to be fitting into place. Absently he touched the arm of Quarla Snow, reassuring her as she stared worriedly at him and at the same time gaining reassurance himself.

He could understand—he could almost empathize with —the great, cold, metallic brain of the Planning Machine on Earth, forty years before . . . calculating without emotion its own probable dissolution, computing a possible way out, launching the *Togethership* out toward the Reefs of Space. And he could see the effects on the Machine when its carefully constructed plan had failed to work: its growing disorganization, its failure to respond intelligently to its tasks. Malfunctions of schedules that had caused subtrain crashes, disasters in its great industrial complexes, catastrophes in space.

"Boysie," whispered the girl at his side, "are you all right? Don't worry. It will be better soon."

He forced his chattering teeth under control and said, "We don't know your answer, Sister Delta Four. There is a piece to the jigsaw that I can't fit in."

"Speak," chimed the girl in black. "State your data. The Machine will integrate it."

"I don't think so," said Gann. "If the Machine is not behind the Starchild there is no explanation for such fantastic things as we have all seen. The sun going out . . . this queer hypnotic atmosphere on the *Togethership* . . . the way we got here in the first place. Great Plan, it's all impossible! I too have been in communion with the Machine. And I know its powers. They do not include the extinction of a star, or a way of thrusting living human beings twenty billion miles across space! Challenge and response, player and adversary—yes! But the players must abide by the rules of the game, and we've seen all those rules broken!"

Sister Delta Four bent her hooded head and sang calmly, confidently, into the linkbox. She waited for its answer. Waited—and went on waiting.

The Machine was still.

Sister Delta Four, her shadowed face faintly perturbed, some of her vocal morphemes touched with a quaver that distorted their meaning, repeated her chiming tones into the box. Still no answer.

Agitated now, she cradled the linkbox in her lap, looking up at Gann and Harry Hickson questioningly. Unconsciously her hand crept to her sonic beads and she began to stroke them, their faint, pure chime sounding like a prayer for reassurance.

At last Harry Hickson stirred, seemed to sigh, and spoke.

"When the *Togethership* came to the Reefs," he said, "it was supposed to bring us free men and women into the Plan of Man—still free. Among its crew were some of the finest humans alive—a man named Ryeland and his wife; her father, who was then the Planner. Your father, Quarla.

"They were thrust out into space right here, in Reef Whirlpool. Some died, like Ryeland and those with him. Some, especially those few who happened to be near the area where a few spacelings were kept, were able to make their way to habitable reeflets—like Dr. Snow—and lived.

"But the Machine here has been kept out of contact with its ancestor on Earth. Its great game was not played —not then."

He was silent for a moment, looking around at them. Then he said, "It was not to be played according to the rules set up by the Machines—not by either Machine.

"You see, a third Player has taken a hand."

Harry Hickson stood up suddenly, disconcerting his pet pyropod, which squalled angrily and clutched at his bare scalp. He touched it absently and turned his golden, glowing gaze at Sister Delta Four.

"Ask of your Machine," he demanded, "the physical basis for intelligence!"

Sister Delta Four bent to sing into her crudely constructed linkbox, listened, and looked up as it buzzed and snarled back at her.

"Means of input," she caroled sweetly. "Means of storage. Means of manipulation. Means of output. In a machine, this is accomplished through magnetic cores and electrical circuits. In animate life, through nerves and neurons."

Harry Hickson nodded his golden head. "Inform your Machine," he said, "that a physical system exists as follows. It receives radiation and stores it as charges. It is made up of particles in a charged state, of electrons and others, each of which has two stable states. In one state, the spin of the electron is parallel with that of its nucleus. In the other state, its spin is antiparallel. This very electron is a machine for memory."

The box growled. "The Machine is aware of these basic physical facts," sang Sister Delta Four melodiously.

"Add these further facts," said Harry Hickson gravely. "Add a fusorian network, older than the galaxy, more powerful than any machine. Add that masses of super-energetic gas display an affinity to this fusorian network. Add that these masses of gas are those systems in which electron spin can function as a storage capacity."

The girl bent to her linkbox, then looked up. "The Machine states that you are describing stars," she intoned.

And Harry Hickson nodded slowly. His glowing, golden arm lifted and made the looping, serpentine sign of the Swan.

"The Star that I serve," he said softly.

The box snarled. "These being so," sang Sister Delta Four, "the Machine computes that the gaseous mass of a star, linked with the fusorian network you describe, is easily an available vehicle for intelligence."

She looked up at Hickson.

Hickson nodded once more, and said solemnly, "All matter is now revealed to be an available vehicle for intelligence. The whole mass of the steady-state universe, infinite in both space and time, is now revealed to be a proper vehicle for the mind of God."

The linkbox buzzed angrily and Sister Delta Four chanted, "The Machine requires an answer. What is God?"

Harry Hickson rose slowly. Looking at his glowing, golden face, Gann thought he saw the signs of an ancient stress, a terrible burden, slipping away. Whatever his duty had been, he seemed to have fulfilled it. Monitoring the machine in the *Togethership*, carrying out the terrible obligations of his masters, the stars, he seemed to have completed all his tasks.

He turned to Gann, with something in his eyes like sympathy. He said, "You have called me the Starchild, Boysie Gann. I am not."

He took the pyropod from his head, stroked it gently and tossed it free. Squalling and hissing angrily, it darted about on its flaming jet, trying to return to its perch atop his head. But he raised a golden arm and warded it off, and the tiny, ugly creature squalled again, circled him at high velocity, and shot away—out the door, down into the long, wide corridor of the ship.

Harry Hickson watched it go, then turned to Gann with untroubled eyes.

"The Starchild did not exist," he said. "Not before now. But he will exist very soon. A man. A bridge. A link between machines and the stars.

"Boysie Gann," he said, his hand lifted in that strange, serpentine sign of homage, "you will be the Starchild."

17

"No!" shouted Boysie Gann, tearing himself free from the restraining hand of Quarla Snow. He leaped across the control room, confronted the calm, golden face of Harry Hickson. "I won't! I want no part of this insane business of miracles and intelligent stars!"

Harry Hickson did not answer. He only stood looking at Gann, his golden eyes glowing. From behind him Quarla Snow said softly, "Boysie. Boysie, dear. You have no choice."

Gann whirled. "What do you mean, no choice? I won't do it! I won't . . ." He paused, confused by his own words. He would not do what? No one had given him an order to refuse.

The control room seemed to swing dizzyingly around him. He reached out and caught the back of an astrogator's chair, aware that his hands were shaking uncontrollably again.

He looked up sharply and caught Quarla Snow's gaze on him steadily, compassionately.

Then Boysie Gann realized what sickness had claimed him. He croaked, "That glowing stuff Hickson threw at me. He's infected me. I'm . . . I'm going the same way as he. As Colonel Zafar and the men on Mercury station. As you, Quarla."

She nodded, with her heart in her eyes. "It's not so bad, Boysie," she whispered. "It doesn't hurt. And it makes you part of something . . . huge, Boysie. Something that fills the universe."

"I don't want it!" he whispered desperately. Something huge! He had had one taste of something huge when he had achieved that one brief moment of communion with the Machine, back on Earth; and like an addiction, it had haunted him ever since. . . .

Unbidden, the craving rose in him again. He touched the metal plate in his forehead dizzily, glanced at Sister Delta Four.

The linkbox snapped and snarled at her. Without speaking, obediently, she rose and approached him, holding the box out to him. From it depended a length of patchcord terminating in prongs . . . prongs that would fit the receptacle in the glittering plate he wore in his forehead.

"No," he whispered again, and turned to look at Harry Hickson.

But Harry Hickson was gone.

In the air where he had stood was the faint smoke-thin outline of a man, limned in the most wisplike of golden fogs. As Gann watched, Harry Hickson . . . dissipated. Tiny darting glints of golden light rose from that skeletal shape and darted away, to the walls that were the hull of the *Togethership* and seemingly through them, out into the void beyond, to rejoin that greater golden sphere that pulsed outside. And as each invisibly tiny spark of gold fled, the figure became fainter, more like a ghost . . .

As he watched it was gone. Nothing was left of Harry Hickson. Nothing at all.

"Quarla," he whispered, turning desperately.

But she was going too. Already her golden face and hair were shimmering, insubstantial. "Good-by, Boysie," she whispered gravely. "Good-by for now . . ."

By his side Sister Delta Four stood silent, dark eyes hooded, holding the linkbox out to him.

Boysie Gann took a deep breath, squeezed his eyes shut for a moment, then opened them.

"Good-by, Quarla," he said, though there was not enough left to reply to him. He took the linkbox from Sister Delta Four.

"Good-by, Julie," he said, and carefully and without hesitation, picked up the pronged communion wire and inserted it into the receptor plate in his forehead.

Communion was ecstasy. Infinite and eternal. Gann waited for it while the universe seemed to hold its breath around him.

The ecstasy did not come.

He stared into the hooded eyes of Sister Delta Four, but found no answer there. What had happened? Why was the communion delayed?

He remembered what she had told him, that the tremendous surge of ecstasy he had felt back on Earth was only a child's sweetmeat compared to the great communing flow of sensation that the more perfectly adapted communicants might receive. Not just pleasure but a mingling of identity, of question and response, a dialogue between man and Machine.

Carefully Gann framed a question in his mind, phrased it in the perfect Mechanese his brain had learned but his vocal chords could not reproduce: *Where are you? Why do you not answer me?*

Out of nowhere a single sound formed in his brain and gave his answer: *Wait.*

Wait? For what?

Gann felt himself shaking more uncontrollably still, and turned a helpless look on Sister Delta Four. Without speaking she touched him, pointed to the astrogator's chair by his side. He fell into it, arms dangling, waiting for the clarification that the Machine might bring, waiting for some grand Something to speak to him and give him answers.

And while he waited, he knew, the tiny fusorian clusters were multiplying in his blood. Were pervading his system with the symbiotic cells that had ultimately devoured Harry Hickson and Coloney Zafar and Quarla Snow, replacing their organs of flesh and their skeletons of bone with linkages of fusorian motes.

Was that what he was waiting for? To be turned into a fusorian aggregate, a no-longer-human structure attuned to the minds Hickson had said dwelt in the stars? He looked within his own body, saw the tiny glowing golden sparks, realized they were multiplying rapidly.

And realized what he had done. He had seen his own body! From within!

He allowed himself a thought to test it out ...

And at once he was looking upon himself from outside. Was looking down into the control room of the *Togethership* from a point in space long miles away, from somewhere where the diamond-bright, emerald-hued, ruby-glowing worlds of Reef Whirlpool circled slowly about. He could see the *Togethership* in all its vast, somber length ... could see inside it, where his own body and Sister Delta Four's waited patiently in the control room ... could see down to the fire control station where the demented Machine General Wheeler shrieked with laughter as he released imaginary bolts of destruction at unscathed and nonexistent enemies ... looked farther still and saw the mighty sweep of the solar system spinning under him.

He saw the infant pyropod that had belonged to Harry Hickson, jetting across the black of space toward the reeflet where it had been born, keening a terrible harsh dirge ... saw that reeflet itself, and the cave where he had lain while Harry Hickson fed and cared for him.

He saw a chapel on a small and lonely rock, where dark-blue fusorian moss held a scanty atmosphere and twenty worshippers joined in a service of the Church of the Star, kneeling to blue Deneb blazing overhead.

He saw the planets of the Plan of Man, torn by disaster, terrified by confusion, while the mad Machine crackled out wild and contradictory orders and enforced them by hurling bolts of energy at random into the void.

He saw the empty station on Mercury, with the hot gases of the sun roiling restlessly overhead, and realized that it too had a life and thought of its own ... a life that had reached out and swallowed into itself those three lives of fusorian matter that had ventured close enough for linkage.

He saw stars and gas clouds, gazed at new matter springing into life like a fountain's play, stared outward to the endless vista of Infinity, inward to the bright golden atoms at his own heart.

And then, awesome and silent and vast, Something spoke his name. Star spoke to Machine. Machine answered Star.

And Boysie Gann, mere human man, shaped to the genetic code of carbon-based life, bent into the form of an acolyte of the Machine, transformed by the fusorian globes into something bearing kinship to the stars ... Boysie Gann mediated their vast and awful discourse.

It went on forever, a thousand years and more, though in the scale of planets orbiting a sun and light crossing a measured track, it all took place in a few minutes or hours.

It went on and on . . . and when Boysie Gann was no longer needed and departed, it went on still.

And then it finished. Forever.

Boysie Gann opened his eyes and looked at the room around him. Sister Delta Four stood motionless, watching him.

He stood up easily. He stretched, yawned, stripped the prongs out of the communion plate on his forehead, wrapped the wire neatly around the improvised linkbox —and tossed it away.

It sailed slowly across the control room, in the light-G torpor of space, but when it struck the steel wall at the end of its flight it smashed into a hundred pieces.

Sister Delta Four made a mewing cry of horror.

Boysie Gann touched her arm. "Don't fret about it, Julie," he said. "You don't need it any more."

She stared at him. "I serve the Machine!" she cried proudly. "I am Sister Delta Four, not Julie Martinet! I . . ."

But he was shaking his head. "Not any more," he said.

The hood fell unnoticed back from her head, revealing her dark, close-cropped hair, with the bright badge of communion shining out of her forehead. She touched it shakily. "I . . . I don't understand!" she whispered. "I . . . I don't *feel* the Machine's presence . . ."

He nodded. "Not now," he said, agreeing. "And not ever any more." He touched his own communion plate. "When we get back to Earth," he said, "we'll have these out, and the electrodes in our brains with them. We won't need them. No human will ever need them again.

"And then," he said after a moment, holding her with one arm while Sister Delta Four, in the terrible parturitive pangs of becoming Julie Martinet once again, sobbed and shuddered, "and then we'll start over where we left off. You and I . . . and all Mankind."

And he left her and went to the old communications board, and began to set up the circuits for a call for rescue from the dead *Togethership*.

294

18

That was the way it began, with the stars themselves winking a warning to Mankind and the Machine hurling its agents and its acolytes about the solar system, seeking an antagonist, a purpose, an instrument for its own salvation.

It began with shadow spreading across the worlds of the Plan of Man, and it ended with the bright light of the mighty stars illuminating a new road for humanity.

The Machine had been playing a game with itself, for want of another opponent; then, in that long, thundering dialogue between stars and Machine, the game ended forever. The Machine had come late to its game, and found the board filled.

That was how it began . . . and that was how it ended. With the legend of Lucifer, and the story of pain and evil . . . and the eternal hope for good.

The Machine sat too late at the gaming table, and found all the places filled . . . with the stars, linked in their fusorian net, and with their Adversary. No longer entrapped in the animal amniotic fluid of his birth . . . no longer slave to the Machine . . . no longer prey to the fusorians . . . the Antagonist was ready to play.

Long ages past, the stars had given him birth, but now he was of age. He was ready to assume his station, his rank and his name.

His station—Adversary to the stars themselves.

His rank—equal of the universe.

His name—Mankind.

ROGUE STAR

1

The sudden light hurt his eyes and woke him rudely from
a dream of Molly Zaldivar. Clutching blindly for support,
he found only warmth and yielding softness. A panic sense
of dislocation dazed him.

"Monitor Quamodian!"

That sweet, synthetic voice restored his sense of place.
The Exion research station. The human habitat on the
planet Exion Four. The cybernetic dwelling he had built
to share with Molly, before she went away. He was in it
all alone, floating in the null-gee capsule of his sleeper, a
naked foetus in a pink plastic womb.

"Monitor Andreas Quamodian!" The sleeper's bright
robot voice grew more intense. "The speaker has a transfac
message for you."

He grunted his hurt protest and clung to his fading
dream of Molly. Somehow he had found her. He'd been
fighting Cliff Hawk, to take her back. Somehow, unbelievably, he'd been winning . . .

"Monitor, please!"

He squirmed inside the padded cocoon, groping to

recover that good feeling. He wanted to recall his breathless sense of triumph over Hawk, his blood-speeding certainty that Molly wanted him to win.

But all the circumstances of the dream vanished as he grasped for them. Painfully awake, he had no idea where in all the clustered galaxies Molly and Cliff Hawk had gone. He couldn't imagine any real-life situation in which he could hope to beat Cliff Hawk, nor could he quite believe that Molly would ever want him to.

His squinted eyes came open on his image in the sleeper's mirror. Too much belly. Too little muscle. A round bald spot on top of his head. He turned away from his soft plump whiteness.

"I wish you hadn't waked me," he muttered at the sleeper. "I'm not on duty. I don't want any calls. Just put me back to sleep."

"But, sir!" the machine reproved him sulkily. "You can't ignore this message. The sender rated it urgent. The index code implies crisis on an interplanetary scale, with probable danger to billions of your fellow human creatures."

"Great Almalik!" He blinked at the pink folds of pulsating plastic. "Where's the message from?"

"The central zone," the sleeper said. "The local address is Planet 3, Star 7718, Sector Z-989-Q, Galaxy 5 . . ."

"That's Earth!"

"A local name, perhaps," the sleeper said. "We don't record such unofficial designations."

"I should know. Earth's my native planet. Give me the message."

"It's coded personal and confidential," the sleeper protested. "You'll have to accept it from the speaker."

"Get me up," he said. "I'll accept it."

While the machine was getting him up, he tried to imagine who on Earth the message could be from. Not his parents, certainly. They had accepted the symbiotic way of life while he was still a child. Lately they had migrated to a human colony in Galaxy 9. Secure in the Starchurch, they would never need anything from him.

Molly Zaldivar?

Wild hope struck him when he thought of her. Though he had never learned where she and Hawk went from Exion, he knew they were both natives of Earth. Perhaps she had come back home. Perhaps she was through with Hawk. Perhaps she really wanted him!

He smiled fondly at his recollection. Molly Zaldivar, five years ago. A tall lively girl, who sang and accompanied herself on an Earth guitar. A girl loved by many a being on the planets of Exion, where they first met—even though they both had come from Earth.

It was easy for him to know why he loved her: the laughter in her voice, even when she sang the saddest ballads of the old mother world, the skin tones that changed oddly from warmest ivory to tawny gold under the queer shifting light of the triple star. But—half the students did not "hear," at least on the audio frequency range used by human beings; many of them did not see with "visible" light. Yet all were fond of Molly Zaldivar.

The three had been together in the tiny group of Earth people Dr. Scott had gathered to work in his stellar section. Andy Quamodian, already serious, already pudgy, dark and slow. Molly Zaldivar, like a golden flame, her bright hair catching ruddy glints from the red giant component of Exion, her dark eyes flashing the violet light of the dwarf. And—Cliff Hawk.

Even after five years, Quamodian scowled at the thought of Hawk. He was a rogue in the society of men, stranger than any alien at the research station, solitary, brooding, angry. He seldom washed, seldom combed his shaggy black hair, seldom spoke a civil word. Yet somehow Molly had chosen him.

Waiting now for the machine to steam and rise and dry and clothe him, Quamodian darkly pondered Hawk. Both human, both had drifted all the way from Earth to Exion, this farthest outpost star of the whole galactic cluster. But they were different in nearly every other way.

Before the fusorians came, Quamodian's commonplace parents had toiled for their living in a commonplace clothing shop in a commonplace city, but Hawk's ancestors were bold outlaws who roved the reefs of space and defied the old interplanetary empire called the Plan of Man. Muddling through his dull career, Quamodian had relied on logic and method and sheer persistence. Scornful of everything systematic and academic, Hawk played brilliant hunches. A half-trained technician, he had finally challenged Scott for leadership of the stellar project. Though he sometimes lacked the words to frame his daring intuitions, they were usually correct.

Hawk loved Molly Zaldivar—carelessly and roughly, certain that she would sacrifice her own career for any

299

of his whims. Quamodian worshipped her more humbly—always aware that he was only plodding little Andy Quam. When the time came for Molly to choose, she really hadn't a choice. Of course she took the dark, dangerous man who knew the borderlands of space.

Her choice was not surprising, though the actual sequence of events still puzzled Quamodian. Hawk had somehow quarreled with Dr. Scott about the direction of their efforts in the stellar section to contact rogue stars. When Scott won their final battle, Hawk disappeared, leaving Molly behind.

After a few unhappy months, Molly was willing to sing her sad ballads to Quamodian. That was when he planned the cybernetic house to share with her. Before it was finished, she heard from Hawk. Just what she heard, Quamodian had never learned. The news, whatever it was, had seemed to bring her more terror than gladness. Yet, without explaining anything, she left at once to follow Hawk.

Now, five years later, her abrupt departure was still a painful riddle to Quamodian. It kept throbbing like a bad tooth, something he could neither understand nor forget.

"Ready, sir?" the machine droned. "Up you come!"

With a peristaltic thrust, the flotation field popped him out of his warm cocoon. He swayed for a moment, adjusting to the planet's gravity, and turned to the speaker.

"Okay," he said. "I'll take the message."

"Standard voice identification is required, sir."

"Great Star! You know who I am."

"But you know our procedures, sir," the speaker said. "The full standard voice identification pattern is required before delivery of all transgalactic communications."

"Ridiculous!" he muttered. "Silly red tape."

The machine hummed quietly inside its black synthetic skin. With a scowl of annoyance, he caught his breath and recited the formula:

"Name: Andreas Quamodian. Race: Human. Birthplace: Earth—correction, that's Planet 3, Star 7718, Sector Z-989-Q, Galaxy 5. Organization: Companions of the Star. Status: Monitor. Address: Human habitat, Exion Four, Exion Extragalactic Research Station."

"Thank you, Monitor Quamodian."

The machine clicked and ejected a narrow strip of yellow film. He snatched it eagerly, and peered to see who it was from. Molly Zaldivar!

"Dear Andy—" The film began to quiver in his sweaty fingers. "I hope you can forgive me for leaving you so rudely, because I'm in desperate trouble here on Earth. It's all too complicated to explain by transfac, but I need your help because the Companions here don't believe in rogue stars . . ."

Rogue stars! The phrase brought Quamodian to a painful halt. He wanted Molly to be sending for him because she'd decided that she loved him after all. Not for any other reason.

Besides, he didn't really understand rogue stars. Neuroplasmic theory was familiar to him in an academic way. Theoretically, he knew how the sentient stars perceived, remembered, thought, and acted—how mass effects induced transcience energy, how bits of information were stored in states of electron spin, how scanning waves flowed through chains of electron in transflex contact, how transcience impulses induced magnetic and electrical and gravitic effects. He respected their tremendous minds, the most retentive and most complex in all the galaxies. He felt a vast admiration for the mellow wisdom of Almalik, the stellar component of the symbiotic citizen that so many human beings had joined. But the rogue stars were something else.

Given its unthinkable intelligence and power, how could a stellar being refuse all fellowship with any other mind? What sort of obsession or psychosis could cause it to close all communication and choose to go its own lonely way?

Quamodian had often listened to debates about that riddle, which was among the basic research problems of Exion Station. He had even discussed it with Molly and Cliff Hawk, in Scott's graduate seminars. He had never heard an answer that made real sense.

"Are you ready to reply, sir?" the speaker was purring. "The sender wants an answer."

"Wait," he said. "Let me finish."

"If you have ever wondered what became of me," the transfac continued, "Cliff Hawk asked me to join him here on Earth. I came because I love him—Andy, I can't help that. I came because I was afraid of what he might be doing here. And I've just discovered that he's doing what I feared. He has learned too much about rogue stars —or maybe too little. Andy, would you believe he's trying now to create a rogue of his own? I need help to stop him.

301

"Here's what you must do, dear Andy. Get Solo Scott—Hawk's old enemy. I don't know where he is—I tried to reach him at his old address in the stellar section, but he didn't reply. Andy, I want you to find him and bring him to Earth. He's the great rogue star specialist. He'll be able to stop Cliff—and Cliff's dangerous new rogue—if anybody can.

"But hurry, Andy! This is a terrible thing, and I have no hope but you."

Quamodian finished reading with a tired little sigh. Molly's feelings for him hadn't changed, after all. He was still only Andy Quam, a useful little tool when she happened to need him.

"Now, sir?" the speaker droned impatiently. "Will you reply?"

"First," he said, "I want to make a local call. To Dr. Solomon Scott. He used to be director of the stellar section, here on Exion Four."

"Yes, sir." The speaker hummed silently for three seconds. "Sorry, sir," it purred. "Dr. Scott is not available. He left Exion four years ago on a research expedition from which he did not return. He is presumed dead, sir."

"That's too bad," Quamodian said, but a thrill of irrational hope was tingling through him. If Scott was not available, he could go to Earth alone. Little Andy Quam might at last become Molly's rescuing hero! He caught his breath. "Send this answer:

"Dearest Molly, I want to help you but I have bad news. I can't bring Scott. He left Exion Station a year after you did. He was attempting a transflection flight to the vicinity of a rogue—the same one Cliff had discovered, out beyond Exion. He never got back.

"But I'll come, Molly. Because I still love you—in spite of everything. If you want just me, answer at once. I'll get there as soon as I can.

"End of message."

His words flickered across the visual panel as the speaker read them back. He snatched a light-pen and scribbled, "Your devoted Andy," before the small blue tongue of plasma began to lick the symbols away, storing them as variances in electronic spin.

Waiting for Molly's reply, he scowled impatiently. He knew that his signal was already reaching the far-off Earth, as its invisible impulses automatically sought the shortest route along the transcience links between the

302

shifting convolutions of hyperspace, where long light-years were reduced to micromicrons.

The plasma tongue finished and vanished, leaving the message panel blank. The speaker clicked off. The house hummed quietly around him, hushed and tense. He walked the floor around the speaker, watching the flickering symbols of the universal clock.

Panic whispered that Molly wouldn't want him. Not without Scott. She knew that little Andy Quam had never been an actual member of the Exion research staff, but just a sort of guinea pig. Scott had brought him along to test a hunch that his odd location sense was a transcience effect, but dropped him from the project when the rogue star research became more exciting . . .

"Monitor Quamodian!" The machine's droning tone startled him. "We have a status report on your trans-galactic message."

"What—what does Molly say?"

"There's no answer, sir. We can't contact the addressee."

"Why not?" His voice cracked. "Has something happened to Molly Zaldivar?"

"We have no information, sir."

"Take another message." He tried to swallow the squeaky quaver in his voice. "To Molly Zaldivar. Same address. Message follows: On my way to Earth. Sign it, Andy Quam."

2

Hurried but methodic, Quamodian prepared for his trip to Earth. He called his supervisor for emergency leave, left instructions with the speaker for care of the house, and asked the flyer to stand by. His spirits soared with the levitator which lifted him to the roof pad, but fell again as he stepped outside.

As always happened whenever he left his cybernetic shell, Exion gave him a queasy shock of dislocation. The place was too far from all the other worlds he knew, too alien to any sort of life. Some freak of cosmic chance had flung the triple star far outside the galactic cluster, and the university had chosen it for the research site because no spark of native life or sentience had ever appeared on any of its bodies.

The station staff had reclaimed and terraformed its twelve dead planets to fit their several ways of life. Those sister worlds were strung across the black sky now, like beads on an unseen string, each aglow with the color of its own synthetic biosphere: supercold liquid helium, frigid methane, hard vacuum, hot carbon dioxide, boiling sulphur.

Exion Four was for the oxygen-tolerant. The human habitat where he lived was only a hasty afterthought—a cragged scrap of crater floor, temporarily pressurized, heated, and humidified enough to allow human survival. Still too thin and cold, its artificial atmosphere was always tainted with hydrocarbons and ammonia escaping from the rocks. Too small to seem like home, the planet turned too slowly.

Shivering, Quamodian hunched himself against the bitter oxy-helium wind. Fighting that first giddy shock of disorientation, he stopped to search that queer sky above the crater cliffs. A tight constriction in his chest relaxed when he found the galaxies—a fuzzy patch of pale light, bitten off by the southward cliffs, fainter than the dimmest planet of Exion.

"Ready, sir?" The flyer opened itself. "Where to, sir?"

"To the regional transport center." He scrambled inside. "I'm in a rush."

The flyer climbed until the violet dwarf peered over the saw-toothed east horizon, dropped back into the dark, and settled toward the lighted ramp outside the transflex cube. The control dome flashed a signal.

"Identification, sir?"

He let the flyer hover while he recited his standard voice pattern and sorted out the documents of his citizenship. The dome extended a long, nimble finger of pale plasma to scan his passport disk, with its endless rows of binary symbols and its holograph of his dark, round head.

"Destination, sir?"

"Earth. That's—wait just a second—that's Planet 3, Star 7718, Sector Z-989-Q, Galaxy 5. Route me through the Wisdom Creek station, Octant 5. I'm on emergency business. I need passage at once."

The plasma tendril winked out. Quamodian caught the passport disk as it dropped, stowed it away, then resumed his inching crawl toward the luminous iris of the transflex cube. A long silver tank, no doubt filled with a liquid citizen, was vanishing through the closing gate. Behind it came a multiple creature, a horde of small, bright, black things, hopping and tumbling inside a communal cloud of pale blue mist. A gray-scaled dragon shuffled just ahead of Quamodian, burdened with a heavy metal turret on its back that probably housed unseen symbiotes. Winking crystal ports in the turret peeked out at Quamodian and shyly closed again.

"Sir?" The control dome flashed again. "Have you a reservation number?"

"Great Star!" Impatience exploded in him. "I've got to reach Earth at once. I just received an emergency call. I had no time to arrange a reservation."

"Sorry, sir." The dome's droning regret seemed entirely mechanical. "Intergalactic travel is restricted, as you should know. We cannot approve transit without a reservation based on acceptable priority."

Grumbling, he held up the message from Molly Zaldivar. The slim plasma finger reached down to scan it, hesitated, recoiled.

"Sir, that document is not in the universal language."

"Of course not," he snapped. "It's English. But it ought to be priority enough. Just read it!"

"We have no equivalence data for English, sir."

"Then I'll translate. It's from Earth—that's the mother planet of my race. The sender is a girl—I mean, a youthful female human creature—named Molly Zaldivar. Her message is addressed to me. She's begging for help. She gave the message an urgency index that implies danger to the whole planet . . ."

"Sir!" Ahead of him, the multiple creature had disappeared into the transflex cube. The dragon was lumbering toward the opening iris. "You're delaying transit. I must ask for an actual reservation number now."

"But *this* is my priority!" He waved the yellow scrap of transfac tape. "Molly Zaldivar is in some kind of trouble with a rogue star . . ."

"Sir, that is not an acceptable priority. Please leave the ramp."

"Confound you!" Quamodian shouted. "Can't you get anything through your neuroplasmic wits? This message implies a danger to the whole human race!"

"Sir. The human race is identified in my files as a little breed of barbarians, just recently admitted to the galactic citizenship and still devoid of interesting traits, either physical, moral, or intellectual. No human being is authorized to issue priority for interstellar travel."

"But Molly says we're in danger . . ."

"Sir, please leave the ramp. You may apply to any acceptable source for a transit priority, on the basis of which we can issue you a reservation number."

"I have no time for that . . ."

The dome signaled no reply, but ominously the plasma tendril thickened and began to spread.

"Wait!" Quamodian cried desperately. "I'm a member of the order of Companions of the Star! Surely you know of them. Our mission is to protect humanity, and other races, too."

"My indices do not show any authorization issued to you for this journey by the Companions of the Star, sir. You are holding up traffic. Please move off the ramp."

Quamodian glanced bleakly at the citizen crowding up behind him: forty tons of sentient mineral, granite-hard, jagged and black, afloat on its own invisible transflection field and impatiently extending its own passport at the tip of a blue finger of plasma.

"Don't shove, Citizen!" he barked. "There's been a misunderstanding. Listen, Control. Check your records. We humans are allied to the multiple citizen named Cygnus, which is a symbiotic association of fusorians, stars, robots, and men. Its chief star is Almalik—or don't you find sentient stars any more interesting than men?"

His irony was wasted on the dome. "Get out of the line," its signal flashed imperatively. Then, a split second later, "You may wait on the side of the ramp. The multiple citizen Cygnus is listed on our indices. We will call the star Almalik, in Galaxy 5."

Disgrunted, Quamodian switched his flyer out of line, giving up his place to the granite citizen, who passed him with an air of disdain. He hovered impatiently at the edge of the ramp, watching the gate ahead expand as it swallowed the gray-scaled dragon and its turret of symbiotic fellows.

For a moment Quamodian thought of making a mad dash for the iris aperture, but there was no sense in that. However fast his flyer moved, the dome would be faster, and he would reduce his narrow chance of getting through.

He sat for a time staring blankly out at the horde of beings slowly moving past him on the ramp. At last he shook himself.

"Divert me," he said harshly. At once a more than humanly soprano voice began to sing from somewhere inside the flyer: *"Mi, mi chiamano Mimi. . ."*

"No. Not opera."

The voice fell silent. A holograph of a chessboard appeared on the communications panel, the pieces set up for a game; White's King's Pawn slid forward two spaces and waited for his reply.

"I don't want to play chess, either. Wait a minute. Set up a probability matrix for me. Estimate the chances of the star Almalik granting me a priority!"

"With running analysis, or just the predicted expectancy, Mr. Quamodian?" asked the flyer's voice.

"With analysis. Keep me amused."

"Well, sir! By gosh, there's a lot of stuff you got to consider, like . . ."

"Without the comedy dialect."

"Certainly, Mr. Quamodian. These are the major factors. Importance of human race in universal civilization: low. Approximately point-five trillion humans, scattered on more than a hundred stellar systems in three galaxies; but these represent only about one one-hundreth of one per cent of the total population of universal civilization, even counting multiple and group intellects as singles. Concern of star Almalik with individual human Andreas Quamodian, negligible."

"What about the concern of Almalik for the Companions of the Star?" cried Quamodian angrily.

"Coming to that, Mr. Quamodian. Concern rated at well under noise level on a shared-time basis, but inserting the real-time factor makes it low but appreciable. So the critical quantity in the equation is the relevance of the term 'rogue star.' I have no way of estimating the star Almalik's reaction to that, Mr. Quamodian."

"The rogue stars are among the most important phenomena in the universe," said Quamodian, staring out at the ramp. "Exion Station was set up largely to study them."

"In that case—hum—allowing for pressure of other affairs; you haven't kept up with the news, but there have been some unpleasant events reported on Earth—let's see, I give it point-seven probability, Mr. Quamodian. One hundred fourteen variables have been considered. They are respectively . . ."

"Don't bother."

"It's no bother, Mr. Quamodian," said the machine, a

little sulkily. They were all moody, these companionship-oriented cybernetic mechanisms; it was the price you had to pay for free conversation.

Quamodian said soothingly, "You've done well. It's just that I'm upset over the danger represented by the rogue star."

"I can understand that, Mr. Quamodian," said the machine warmly, responding at once. "A threat to one's entire race . . ."

"I don't give a hoot about the human race!"

"Why, Mr. Quamodian! Then what . . ."

"It's Molly Zaldivar I care about. Make a note of this, you hear? Never forget it: the welfare of Molly Zaldivar is the most important thing in the universe to me, because I love her with all my heart. In spite of . . ."

"Excuse me, sir," the flyer broke in. "An approaching craft is hailing us."

"Who is it?"

"The operator is your fellow human, Solomon Scott."

"Scott?" He squinted into the glaring terminal lights but saw no approaching craft. "It can't be Scott."

"He's Solomon Scott," the flyer said flatly. "We have positive indentification through his standard voice pattern. He entered the air space of Exion Four without official clearance, and the robot guardians are after him. But he says he has an urgent message for you."

3

The hailing craft dived into the terminal lights, grazed the flyer, and crashed to the pavement near the ramp. Jolted out of his seat, Quamodian recovered his balance and blinked at the strange machine.

It looked like something a dragon had mauled. A great steel globe, battered and fused and blackened. A few twisted projections looked like stumps of lost instruments or weapons. Without wings or jets or landing gear, it seemed entirely unfamiliar until he found traces of a symbol he knew under the scars and rust—the triple-starred emblem of Exion Station.

"It is Scott," he whispered. "That's the environmental pod he left here in. Or part of it."

"Stupid human!" the flyer huffed. "He nearly wrecked us. I'm calling the guardians."

"Wait! He's the man Molly Zaldivar needs on Earth. Read him the message from her. Ask him to help us stop Cliff Hawk from whatever he's doing to create a rogue."

The flyer hummed quietly. Waiting for Scott to reply, Quamodian began to feel ashamed of himself. He couldn't help a dull regret that Scott had turned up to rescue Molly. His own chance was gone, he thought, to be her solitary champion.

"Scott's speaking," the flyer whirred at last. "He says he has an urgent personal message for you. He wants you to come aboard his machine. He says he can't stand outside exposure here."

"What about Cliff Hawk and Molly Zaldivar?"

"He says Cliff Hawk's an arrogant fool. But he says Molly's wrong if she thinks Hawk's research is dangerous. He says the rogue stars are a harmless myth."

"That's not what he thought when he was putting armor plate around that research machine," Quamodian muttered. "Tell him Molly is terrified."

"Scott says she's another fool," the flyer purred. "He says he won't waste time on any crazy chase to Earth. But he's anxious to see you. Will you visit his machine?"

Quamodian's hopes had soared again. If Scott wouldn't come to Earth, perhaps there was still some wild chance for him to be Molly's lone rescuer.

"Uh?" He sank back to hard reality. "Tell Scott I'm coming now."

He scrambled out of the flyer. The terminal was miles above the altitude of the human habitat, and the bitter chill of the thin oxy-helium mix at this level took his breath. He ducked his head and ran for the damaged craft. A valve opened as he reached it, and a tall stranger reached down to haul him into the shadowy air lock.

"Scott?" The wind had taken his voice. "I was looking for Solo Scott . . ."

"I'm Solomon Scott," the stranger rasped. "Come inside."

Quamodian recoiled. The stranger in the lock looked as tall as Scott, but with that their resemblance ended. Scott had been a dark, aggressive vital man, as strong and ruthless as another Cliff Hawk. This man was gaunt and gray and slow, oddly clumsy in the way he reached out of his steel cave, somehow more mechanical than human.

His dress was equally perplexing. He wore a monkish cowl of thick gray stuff and a long gray robe gathered with a golden chain around his waist. Slung from the chain was a thin golden dagger, which glowed queerly in the dark of the lock.

Quamodian wanted to turn and run. He couldn't understand anything about Scott's arrival. He didn't like the flat glitter of Scott's haggard eyes, or even the greasy spots on the clerical robe. A sour whiff of something inside the globe almost gagged him.

"Andy!" the stranger shouted into the oxy-helium wind. "Come on aboard."

He tried to get hold of himself. After all, he saw no actual danger, and he wanted help for Molly. He grasped the reaching hand, which felt colder than the wind, and scrambled up into the dim steel cell.

"Solo!" He tried to force his stiffened face into a grin. "It's great luck you turned up just now, because Molly Zaldivar is desperate for your expert aid. If you'll read her message . . ."

"Forget it!" Scott's gray claw slapped carelessly at Molly's transfac tape. "Come out of this cold, so we can talk."

But Quamodian hung back, his stomach turned by one glimpse of the gloomy space beyond the haggard man and the inner valve. Filthy rags and torn paper. Tumbled piles of broken scientific instruments. Empty plastic food containers. Dust and rust and human dung.

"What's all this?" He couldn't help shivering. "I—I hardly knew you, Solo. What has happened to you?"

"I suppose I am a changed man." Scott's quiet voice seemed almost rational. "What happened is that I learned something. I learned the message I bring to you."

"Whatever happened, it's great good luck you came along." Quamodian raised his voice to hide revulsion. "Molly says the Companions back on Earth don't believe in rogue stars . . ."

"They're right." The gray cowl nodded solemnly. "The rogues are a myth—that's something I learned." The gaunt man bent nearer, and Quamodian tried not to shrink from his breath. "Andy, the great thing I learned is that we human beings have always followed a false philosophy of life."

310

The words seemed commonplace, but Scott's hollow voice gave them a hypnotic power that Quamodian knew he would never forget.

"We tried to make competition the basic law of being. I guess we came to make that blunder because our fore-fathers had lived by hunting for too many million years, killing for survival. Anyhow, Andy, the rogue star is the mythic ideal of our killer kind. The perfect individual. Absolutely free. Omnipotent as anything. Immortal as the universe. Nothing anywhere can curb a rogue star."

"I know." Quamodian nodded uneasily. "That's why I'm afraid ..."

"The rogue was once my own ideal." The gaunt man ignored the interruption. "Hawk's, too, I should imagine. When I came here to set up the stellar section, I was com-peting with everybody else in my field of science. I was a man and that was the game. I had to challenge the best brains from all the galaxies, gathered here at Exion. I had to beat the robots, all linked together in their transflex webs, sharing memory banks and programs that united them into a single monstrous mind. I had to match all the multiple citizens, pooling their logical processes as the robots did. I had to compete with all my fellow human beings who had given up their individual freedom for symbiotic union with the fusorians." The gray cowl tossed. "That was the rogue ideal, which pitted me against Cliff Hawk, and led me out to the runaway star he found."

"Solo, what happened there?"

"I found Hawk's so-called rogue." Scorn chilled the grating voice. "No rogue at all. A sentient sun—but born so far from all the galaxies that it had never encountered another intelligence. A feeble thing, ignorant and afraid. In flight from the whole universe. Its untrained mind was weaker than my own. It was afraid of me!"

He cackled into shrill laughter that bent him double and became a paroxysm of asthmatic wheezing. Quamodi-an caught his bony arm to steady him, and peered un-comfortably into his dark lair beyond the valve.

"That was my lesson," Scott gasped when he could speak. "I never came back to the stellar section, because I've learned a higher principle. The law of association. That's the law that drew the first cells of life together to begin the evolution of man. The same law the plants obey when they exhale oxygen for men to breathe, and the law we obey when we exhale carbon dioxide for them. That's

311

the law that ties men into families and clans and nations. Andy, that's the same universal law that is now knitting men and fusorians and sentient stars into the symbiotic citizen called Cygnus."

"Maybe so," Quamodian muttered. "But what has this to do with my trip to Earth . . ."

"Forget the Earth." Scott's hoarse voice had become a croaking chant. "Forget Cliff Hawk and Molly Zaldivar. Forget all the false concerns of your misguided self and all the worthless goals you've been striving for. Forget the fool's law of competition. Try association."

Quamodian was edging warily backward.

"Listen, Andy." Scott's cold claws gripped his shoulder. "I've given up the rogue ideal. I'm telling the association story. That's my message for you. I beg you to join us in the universal fellowship of Cygnus."

Swept with a sudden panic, Quamodian twisted free. He retreated to the outer valve and stopped there, frowning, grasping for sanity. "I guess everybody has to make his own terms with society," he said at last. "But I don't want symbiosis. As a Companion of the Star, I'm a useful citizen. All I really need is Molly Zaldivar . . ."

His voice caught when he saw the gray claws on that thin gold blade. He dodged back to get a breath of clean air.

"Watch it, Scott!" he gasped. "Don't touch me."

"My touch is eternal life." Scott's flat, bright stare and his hollow voice held no trace of warmth or reason. "This syringe is loaded with symbiotic fusorians." His bloodless fist poised the glowing point. "A life-form older than our galaxy. Old enough to know the law of association. Flowing in your blood, the microscopic symbiotes will keep your body new. They'll mesh your mind with all of theirs, and with many billion human symbiotes, and with the sentient suns."

"Hold on, Scott!" Quamodian raised his empty hands and tried to calm his voice. "I can't quite imagine what you're up to. But I do know the citizen Cygnus—my own parents belong. I know that it allows no evangelism. People must ask to join. So I know you're somehow phony." He peered at the gaunt man. "If Molly didn't want you . . ."

"Let's forget our lonely selves," Scott was creaking. "Let's rejoice in everlasting union . . ."

As he spoke, the gold needle jabbed. Quamodian grabbed his sticklike wrist and felt a surge of metal force beneath the dirty robe. The needle quivered overhead, dripping yellow drops. Savage power forced it slowly downward.

Quamodian gasped for breath and caught a nauseating reek. He lunged for open air. The gray robe tripped him. Falling against the wall of the lock, he clung to that twisting stick, fought it off his throat.

"Forget the rogue!" Scott was wheezing. "Forget . . ."

His mad power died, and his rattling voice. The stickwrist bent with a brittle crack. The lank frame slid down inside the dirty robe. Drops of gold fire spurted from the broken needle driven through the cowl.

Quamodian looked once, and staggered out into the icy wind. Hovering near, the flyer picked him up and carried him back to the edge of the ramp, before the robot guardians arrived. He lay gratefully back in his seat for a long time, shivering in the flyer's warmth and gasping for good air, before he started asking questions.

"The guardians are unable to discover how Scott survived his encounter with the rogue star," the flyer informed him then. "They cannot determine how he got back to Exion Four, or why he landed here. But they report that he is dead."

"I guess—" Quamodian gulped uneasily. "I guess I killed him."

"The guardians observed the incident," the flyer said. "They saw him fall against the hypodermic needle which pierced his throat and caused his death. They will file no charge against you."

"How could the needle kill him?" Quamodian asked. "If it contained benign fusorians?"

"But it didn't," the flyer said. "The luminescent fusorians in the syringe are not symbiotic. They are a related type, found in the reefs of space, which act as a virulent toxin in the blood of your species. The guardians infer that Scott came here to murder you."

"Why?" Quamodian shivered again. "Why me?"

"The guardians lack adequate files on the irrational patterns of self-destruction prevalent among your species," the flyer droned. "They can only answer your question with another. Who has any reason to stop your trip to Earth?"

"Cliff Hawk, perhaps." Quamodian scowled uncertainly. "I can't think of anybody else. But he's a good many galaxies away from here. The whole thing baffles me."

The flyer hummed for two seconds.

"The guardians will continue working on the case," it said. "They report many factors which still resist logical resolution. However, they do have advice for you, based on a first analysis of the available data."

"So?"

"If you return to your dwelling and remain inside, the computed probability of your premature termination is only point-o-two. If you continue your trip to Earth, however, the computed probability of an illicit termination of your life is point-eight-nine. The guardians advise you to go home."

"Thank the guardians," Quamodian said. "But Molly needs help." He sat up straighter. "Call the dome," he said. "Ask about my priority to Earth."

4

The control dome reported that his priority request had been duly transmitted to Almalik, spokesman star for the citizen Cygnus. No priority had yet been issued.

"Be patient, sir," the flyer added sympathetically. "The sentient suns are hard to hurry. With life spans of many billion years, they have their own scale of time."

Quamodian grumbled and waited, watching the robot guardians remove the dead man and his rusted spacecraft. Contemplating the computed probability of his own early termination, he grappled with the riddle of Solo Scott.

Scott's little sermon about association, taken by itelf, made a weird kind of sense. Thinking back to his boyhood, Quamodian could see its truth in his own experience. The arrival of the fusorians on Earth had ended ages of competition and opened a new era of association. All his life, Quamodian had been torn between the two.

It struck him now that Scott was probably right. Self-interest may have been a necessary law of the jungle, but even the most primitive hunters had learned to work together. Competition had become a deadly sickness of higher civilization. The harshest therapy of the old Plan of Man couldn't cure it—not even with an explosive iron collar around the neck of every self-directed individual. When the fusorians came, most men welcomed them.

314

But Quamodian had elected not to join his parents in the new symbiotic union. Growing up in the disturbing transition years, he had come to love both ways of life. He yearned to keep his own individual freedom, however dangerous. But he also yearned, just as keenly, for the absolute security and peace the fusorians had brought.

With a sharp conflict of emotions, he had watched the end of man's old civilization. Sometimes sadly, he had seen almost every feature of it—religion and philosophy, politics and business, social custom and private habit—proved needless or silly or just plain wrong. Often approving, he had observed the end of war, of want, of man's old cruelty. He found that he loved both the old and the new too much to abandon either.

Forced to make his own decision when his parents accepted membership in Cygnus, he chose at first to compete. Struggling for academic marks, he won a Starscout scholarship that lifted him off the confused and crowded Earth into a more intense and complex existence in the transgalactic civilization—that must have been twenty years ago, if he converted universal time into the old solar periods.

In his own life, he reflected, the old jungle law had clearly gone wrong. Competing with robots and multiple beings and human symbiotes, he had failed his graduate finals. He had failed in a dozen pathetic little business enterprises. Reaching Exion as a sort of experimental animal, he had failed to beat Cliff Hawk, failed to win Molly Zaldivar.

Only now, working with the Companions of the Star, had he found his own small but satisfying place in society. Not so final as the total self-surrender of symbiosis, it was still a useful social service. It was association enough for him—unless Molly changed her mind.

"Attention, sir." The flyer's drone broke into his brown introspection. "The control dome is calling us back to the ramp."

"Oh, sorry." Relieved, he gave instructions. The flyer swam back into the stream of traffic. A stalked horror of a citizen with members like bamboo shoots and a frond of brain tissue like a skirt around its waist had paused to let him move into the line of traffic on the ramp.

"Traffic control to Andreas Quamodian," the dome was flashing. "The multiple citizen Cygnus is fully qualified to issue priorities for intergalactic transit. Almalik, spokes-

315

man star for the citizen, has approved your application for a reservation number. You may enter the transflex cube."

Quamodian grumbled his thanks, and the flyer carried him toward the cube. The veteran of a good many intergalactic transits, he had never learned to enjoy them. The effects of transflection varied with the individual. Some felt nothing; a few reported pleasure or exhilaration. Most, to whom transit was unpleasant or terrifying, eased the strain of passage with drugs or hypnosis. Quamodian merely endured it.

Before they reached the cube, the flyer paused.

"Sir, the guardians are calling again. On the basis of a new analysis they have recomputed the probability of your early termination at point-nine-three. They still advise you to go home."

"Thank the guardians," Quamodian said. "Tell them I'm going on to Earth—and Molly Zaldivar."

"At least you are statistically safe until we reach our destination," the flyer assured him brightly. "A billion passengers arrive safe for only six who don't. Three of the six suffer nothing worse than dimensional rotation, with left sides exchanged for right. Two others undergo displacement of body tissue or prolonged psychosis. Only one passenger per billion is unaccountably lost. Even that one is statistically replaced. One passenger per billion is physically reduplicated through anomalous subspace refraction, so that the net loss is zero . . ."

"Shut up!" Quamodian growled. "I'm quite familiar with those statistics. As a monitor, I was once assigned to discover what becomes of that one lost passenger. I never solved the problem, and I prefer not to think about it now."

Sulkily silent, the flyer swam into the cube. Quamodian watched the diaphragm contract behind him, shutting out the endless file of waiting citizens. At once the flyer rocked and veered. Rotated out of space and time, routed by computation through a dozen or a hundred congruent folds of hyperspace, he felt as he always did: lost, stunned, and queasy.

The blue walls flickered and dissolved into a darkening, grayish haze. A queer roaring came hollowly from nowhere, swelling in his ears. Numbing cold drove through him, as if every tissue of his body had somehow been plunged into the dark zero of the space between galactic clusters.

Quamodian sweated and suffered. Transcience flight always did something to his location sense—researchers had experimented with the effect, but never explained it.

"Here we are, sir!" the flyer piped at last. "Was that so bad . . ."

Its cheery voice was cut abruptly off. It spun and pitched and fell. Quamodian saw streaks of blood-colored fire. He buried his wet face against his quivering knees and waited for his sense of place to adjust itself. It didn't. But after endless sickening seconds, he felt the flyer break out of that wild dive, and into level flight.

"Reporting trouble, sir," it whined. "Malfunction in all communication and navigation gear." It whirred and clicked and added blackly, "If somebody wished to keep us off the Earth, they have scored a point."

5

Quamodian raised his head and saw the sun. An unfamiliar star, blood-red and huge, too dull to hurt his eyes. It floated low in a dead-black sky, swelling across many degrees. Dark spots and streaks and convolutions covered its two enormous hemispheres, with almost the pattern of a naked human brain. Thick ropes of red plasma coiled away from both its polar coronas, brighter than its mottled face.

"It's sentient!" he whispered to the flyer. "I'm sure it's sentient. When neuroplasmic structures interfere with normal energy flow, a star gets that bloated look."

"No data," the flyer answered. "I'm scanning all my stellar files, but observable indices don't identify this star on my complete file of galactic charts. Possible inference: its location is outside the charted cluster."

With a spasmodic effort, Quamodian broke away from the hypnotic glare of that snake-wreathed star. He caught a rasping breath and glanced at the world beneath.

"It certainly—certainly isn't Earth." He gulped at a great lump of terror in his throat. "It looks like we were caught by that billionth chance!"

The flyer hung high above a flat and endless beach. To the north—or was it north—a vast sea lay flat and thick as blood beneath that dreadful sun. To the south— if that was really south—black cliffs rose above the level of the flyer.

That endless mountain wall was curiously sheer, curiously uniform, and curved very slightly toward the sea. Perhaps, he thought, it was an ancient crater rim, a thousand-mile bowl for that flat sea which seemed so dead that he wondered when its tides had ever, worn its beaches smooth.

All around the twilight horizon, red auroras played. They writhed and coiled like blood-colored snakes, and struck their red reflections in the glassy sea. They sifted red fire beyond the walling peaks. With an unpleasant start, Quamodian found that he could trace the star's plasma tentacles across that sullen sky, all the way from the polar coronas down to the little misty fingers reaching toward the beach, as if the sentient sun held sky and sea in a visible grasp.

"Lower," he told the flyer. "There's something on the sand I want, to see."

Flakes of lighter color sprinkled the wide black beach, taking form as the flyer sank. Gray of weathered metal. Gleam of fading paint. White of naked bone. Dead citizens and their wrecked machines cluttered a three-mile circle of sand.

"I think we've found what becomes of those missing passengers," he said. "Call the guardians and file a report."

"Sir, I've been calling!" The flyer's shrill tone seemed deeply aggrieved. "I've been calling on all the transgalactic channels, with full emergency power. For some reason, I can't get a reply."

"Keep on calling. By the way—uh—how is our power supply?"

"Our emergency power pack is half depleted, sir," the flyer reported. "Shall we land to conserve it?"

"Not yet." He shaded his eyes against the cold red sun, to search that endless beach. "There! Toward the foot of the cliffs. Something I want to see. A little to the right. Those four queer towers. Land as close as you can."

The towers intrigued him. Spaced at the corners of a square, they were half crude masonry, built of unsmoothed rocks laid together with clay. The higher halves were salvaged metal from the wrecks, welded crazily.

318

As the flyer settled, he discovered a web of cables stretched between the towers: a skeleton cube, outlined in taut bright wire; a second, smaller cube, suspended inside the first with tight wires which themselves outlined six tapered hexahedrons.

"A tesseract!" Wonder hushed his voice. "The essential circuitry of a transflex cube. What would that mean?"

"Relevant information unavailable. Data observable on this planet shows no logical relationship to any system or program of action in my files." The flyer hummed for three seconds and added sadly, "I'm sorry sir. I was not prepared for this."

"Keep trying," Quamodian said. "We've got to reach the Earth and Molly Zaldivar, in spite of—whatever it is!" He glanced at that surly sun and tried not to shiver. "How's the air?" he asked. "Fit for me?"

"Oxygen, thirty-point-seven-nine per cent," the flyer said. "Diluents, noble gases. Helium, neon, argon. Temperature and pressure toward the lower limits of human tolerance. You won't like it, but it won't kill you."

"Thanks," he said. "Open—no, wait!"

An odd little procession came marching down the beach from a black round cave which he saw now above the rubble at the foot of the cliffs. Half a dozen tattered citizens. Three of them robots, badly damaged. Two yellow-crusted multipeds with missing legs. A single human being, leading them all, waving a white rag on a stick.

The human was visibly a woman, in a faded garment made for a larger citizen of a very different race. Her thick dark hair had been clumsily haggled off, and black dirt splotched her visible skin.

Quamodian scrambled out of the flyer, ran a little way to meet her, and paused in wonder. Beneath the alien garb and the grime, she was not only beautifully human. In some way her loveliness was hauntingly familiar. He hailed her breathlessly, in old Earth English.

"Hello . . ."

"Stop!" She cut him off sharply, in the universal tongue. "Stand where you are. Identify yourself."

Her voice was brisk and cold, but something in its rich timbre reminded him—reminded him of Molly Zaldivar! That was what had teased his sense of recognition. The likeness sent a chilly prickling down his spine. Scrub off the dirt, replace her butchered hair, put her in human

319

garb, feed her a few square meals, and she would be a dead ringer for Molly Zaldivar.

"I'm waiting." Sternly, she raised that tantalizing voice. "Let's have your standard identification code."

He made some vague, bewildered sound.

"Speak out!" She waved a signal, and the robots darted out around him. "I'm the authority here."

Stammering a little, he recited his universal identification pattern.

"Thank you, Monitor Quamodian." She nodded briskly. "I am also with the Companions of the Star. Senior Monitor Clothilde Kwai Kwich." She stressed the *Senior*. "What's the date, outside?"

He gave her the universal date.

"Thank you, Monitor." Calculating, she made an appealing little frown that belonged to Molly Zaldivar. "That means I've been here five years—five years too long!"

She nodded at the bloated sun.

"Time's hard to follow here," she added. "Because the day and the year on this planet are the same. The sun never moves in the sky. We can't even count the local years, because we can see no stars for reference points."

Listening, Quamodian closed his eyes. Except for its brisk authority, her rich voice was altogether Molly's.

"Wake up!" she snapped. "How did you get here?"

"I was in transflection transit from Exion Four to Earth," Quamodian said. "With travel priority from Cygnus to answer a trouble call from a girl named Molly Zaldivar." He saw no change in her dark-smudged face when he spoke the name, but he couldn't help asking, "You don't happen to have a twin named Molly?"

"Certainly not. Don't waste my time with idle talk. Monitor, you'd better wake up! We've all facing unprecedented problems here. Every effort must be directed toward their solution. As your superior Companion, I'll require you to cooperate. My subordinates may now identify themselves."

Speaking in unison, the three robots intoned a voice pattern which identified them as traffic safety inspectors. Curiously, all three gave the same serial number. The two yellow-shelled multipeds spoke in turn, but they were both assistant traffic safety inspectors and their identification codes were identical.

"They arrived a year after I did," Clothilde Kwai Kwich explained. "I had been assigned to discover what becomes

320

of the statistically small number of passengers lost in transflection transit. Their assignment was to find what became
of me. They entered the headquarters terminal as a team
of two—an inspector and his robot assistant. I had been
in route to Exion Four, and that was their destination."

Staring at the three damaged robots and the two crippled
multipeds, Quamodian felt cold breath on the back of his
neck.

"You see what happened," she went on. "The inspector
was duplicated in transit. The robot assistant was tripli-
cated. What is even more confusing, their identities were
switched. All the robots now have the minds and memories
of the original inspector. The duplicated original inspector
has the logical programs and the memory banks of the
robot assistant. Finally, they were all dropped here."

Her brisk voice cracked. "And that—" For a moment,
beneath her commanding self-assurance, he heard the
quaver of naked terror. She stiffened at once, recovering
herself. "Monitor Quamodian, that's the sort of problem
we face here."

"What about you?" He couldn't stop that impetuous
question. "Did you notice any change in yourself?"

She flushed and trembled. Familiar auburn lights glanced
in her short dark hair as she turned to gaze along that endless beach. Abruptly she swung back, her chin lifted in a
small gesture of anger that stirred his most painful recol-
lections.

"I resent personal questions," her voice was strained and
quivering. "If you want objective information—I have seen
evidence of some slight physical anomalies, which I prefer
not to discuss. Let's get on to questions of survival."

"Agreed," Quamodian said. "Can you explain how we
got here?"

"We've been collecting facts and putting hypotheses together." Uncertainty seemed to slow her voice. "Of course
you understand that any firm conclusions will have to wait
for the full analysis of data that I still hope to make when
we get back to headquarters—if we do get back."

She shrugged angrily in that grotesque garb, as if to
free herself from clutching fear.

"I'll tell what our evidence suggests." She nodded toward
the dark-mottled sun. "I think that's a rogue star. I think
it is systematically tampering with transflection traffic. The
dated documents in the oldest wrecks show that they were
highjacked many centuries ago, but the rate of this activity

321

seems to have increased recently—about the same time that Solomon Scott set up his stellar project on Exion Four to investigate rogue stars."

"So the rogues are watching us!" He shivered in spite of himself in the steady wind that blew across the black beach toward that sullen sun. "Has Solo Scott been here?"

"No," she said. "We've checked all the wrecks and made up a register. All except a few very early victims have been identified. There are a few humans on the list. None that could be Scott." She gave him a probing look of Molly's. "Why do you ask?"

As he showed her Molly's transfac tape and told her about his encounter with Scott, the multipeds began chittering at the robots in some language of their own. Clothilde Kwai Kwich paused to listen as the three robots squealed back in unison.

"We've seen a strange machine," she told Quamodian at last. "Half a dozen times. Flying fast and low, just off the beach, as if spying on us. The inspectors inform me that it appears to fit your description of Scott's damaged craft."

"What do you make of that?"

She waited for the robots to squeal and the multipeds to answer.

"Scott was attempting to reach the vicinity of a rogue star," she translated for Quamodian. "The inspectors suggest that this was his rogue, that it somehow captured him when he arrived, that it sent him back to Exion Four as a sort of slave machine."

"That might account for the change in him." Quamodian nodded. "But why did he try to kill me?"

The robots squeaked and the multipeds stridulated.

"They suggest that the rogue has a friendly interest in Cliff Hawk's experiments on Earth," said Clothilde Kwai Kwich. "They suggest that it does not intend to allow you to intervene."

"Molly wants me there," Quamodian muttered stubbornly. "I don't intend to stop."

"You have a nut to crack before you reach the Earth." The girl's hollow eyes held a faint sardonic glint. "Because our isolation here is complete. Nobody answers our signals. If this is really Cliff Hawk's rogue, we're somewhere out between the galactic clusters. Our register lists a good many thousand citizens who have been marooned here. Not one has ever got away."

322

6

Quamodian frowned inquiringly at Clothilde Kwai Kwich and pointed at the wire web stretched between those four rough towers.

"Somebody meant to get away," he said. "Somebody was setting up a transflection terminal . . ."

"And there it stands." She shrugged disdainfully. "It was standing there when I arrived. The engineers who built it were already dead and forgotten then. Their names are not even on our register."

"I studied transcience engineering once." Quamodian neglected to add that he had muffed his finals. "That tesseract circuit looks like a good copy of the working model we put together in the lab." Eagerness took his breath. "Maybe—maybe I can finish it!"

"It's finished now," she said. "Ready to test."

"What's wrong?"

"We can't try it till we know where we are." She listened briefly to the squealing robots. "The inspector believes this star is Cliff Hawk's rogue. If so, we could estimate the distance to the Exion terminal precisely enough. But a distance setting is no use without direction, and we have no points of reference."

"I know—" Quamodian bit his tongue. "I used to know directions. I've got a sense of place. The trouble is, transflection flight disturbs it. Usually it comes back when I arrive. This time—" Unhappily, he shook his head. "This time it didn't."

A breathless quiet had frozen them all. The robots twanged when he paused, and the multipeds bleated. They closed in around him. The girl's hungry face was white.

"Monitor Quamodian, the inspector recalls a research report on your transcience sense. Some experimenters convinced themselves that you had an unexplained perception of hyperspatial congruities. Others apparently suspected you of fraud, conscious or not. If you do have such a sense, now's the time to use it."

"I'll try," he muttered. "But I still feel lost."

In a groping way, he tried. The effort sharpened his

queasy giddiness. Cold sweat broke over him. The beach tipped until the black cliffs hung over his head. The furious sun ballooned and wheeled around him.

"No use!" he gasped weakly. "Actually, I don't know how to try. It's nothing I know how to do. It's either there or not."

The creaking robots crowded closer.

"Better try again" snapped Clothilde Kwai Kwich. "Or perhaps you like it here!"

"Almalik!" Anger crackled in him. "Don't you think I want to reach Earth and Molly Zaldivar . . ."

Something happened as he spoke. The rocking beach leveled under foot. The red sun settled into place. And all his giddy confusion was gone. He knew precisely where he was.

"There's Exion." He pointed into the sky. "To the right of the sun. Just extend the equator half a diameter out. The galaxies are lower, just above the sea."

"Monitor, are you sure?"

Doubt began to gnaw at his new certainty.

"I think—" he hesitated miserably, "I think I'm right."

Clothilde Kwai Kwich and her robots withdrew into a huddle near the towers. The two multipeds stood alertly near, as if they expected him to run. The robots squeaked and the girl whispered and presently they all came back.

"Monitor Quamodian, we have discussed this situation. It raises grave new issues. We can't be certain that your claimed transcience sense will enable us to orient the terminal controls. Even if the terminal works, we can't be sure the rogue will let us leave. Under these circumstances, the inspector suggests that we allow you to make the first test transit. Are you willing?"

"Of course I'm willing." But it had not occurred to him that the rogue might intervene again. "What are the chances—?" Staring at that serpent-haired star, he failed to finish the question.

"My subordinates won't risk a prediction." She frowned like Molly. "They can't place the rogue in any normal pattern, even for sentient stars. Its power is unlimited. But its motives are incomprehensible. Its sheer intelligence is just about absolute. But its ignorance of other beings—especially of human beings—is nearly total. Its resulting behavior can be appallingly naive, or stunningly clever, or simply insane." She shrugged. "Who knows what to expect?"

Quamodian helped set the terminal controls, which were in a cargo barge buried in the black sand beneath the towers. Clothilde Kwai Kwich gave him a brisk handclasp. He walked back to his waiting flyer and waited for her signal.

She waved her hand. The flyer swam between the entrance towers, into that web of shining wire. He glanced toward that ominous sun, but it had already flickered and dissolved. He was lost again.

Gray spaces roared around him and probing cold sucked away his life. The flyer rocked and spun until he thought the mad rogue had flung them into some more dreadful trap . . .

But then the careening flyer steadied under him. "Prepare to emerge, Mr. Quamodian," it sang in his ear, and the roaring storm of sound and sensation died away.

The skeleton walls of the wire tesseract had turned real around him. They were greenish-gray, and painted in bold black characters that identified the Wolf Creek Station on Earth. Ahead of him the exit gate expanded.

He felt stunned. The contrast was nearly too much for him. There was no alien beach, no red sea, no snake-armed rogue. Neither was there a bitter oxy-helium wind whipping at a long line of impatient citizens bent on business, competing for priorities and snarling at delay. In this pastoral quiet, Exion Four and the world of the rogue became twin nightmares that he didn't want to think about.

Quamodian leaned forward eagerly as the flyer glided out of the cube, and looked for the first time in his adult life on the warm, broad acres that were lit by the single sun of Earth.

Twenty minutes later most of his relief and all Earth's pastoral charm had evaporated. He was snapping furiously at his flyer. "What do you mean, you can't reach Miss Zaldivar? I've come all this way from Exion Four. Do you mean I can't get a message to her now?"

"Your messages can't be delivered at this time, Mr. Quamodian. Your communication circuits are blocked."

"Nonsense! Try the local office of the Companions of the Star . . ."

"Also blocked, Mr. Quamodian. A local custom. I have been informed that in fourteen hours, local time, all the normal lines of communication will be open for service. But until that time . . ."

"I've no time for fools!" Quamodian shouted. "I've gone

through a lot to get here, and I don't propose to twiddle my thumbs while these yokels divert themselves. Here, I'll go to that office myself!"

"Certainly, Mr. Quamodian." The flyer began to settle toward a dusty plaza in front of the transflex tower. "Of course," it added apologetically, "you will have to go on foot. By local custom, flyers are not permitted to operate more than one hundred meters from the transflex center at this time."

"Great Almalik! Oh, very well." Fussily Quamodian collected himself and stamped out of the opening door. "Which way?"

A voice by his ear answered, as the flyer activated its external speakers. "Down this street, Mr. Quamodian. The gold building with the ensign of the Companions."

He turned and stared. Behind him, the flyer quietly rose, drifted back to the tall, tapered, black transflex tower and settled to wait at its base. Quamodian was alone on the planet of his birth.

He was, he realized, more alone than he had expected. He knew that parts of Earth were still scarcely populated—nothing like the teeming metropolises of the hub-worlds of the universe: nothing, even, like the relatively minor planets of his university training and recent practical experience.

But he had not expected Earth, even this part of Earth, to be *empty*.

Yet there was not a soul in sight. He peered back toward the transflex tower: his waiting flyer, motionless and peaceful; nothing else. He looked down a long artificial stone boulevard: a school building, a hospital, a few supply centers—and no one in sight. He saw a park with benches and a playground, but no one was near any of them; saw parked vehicles, seemingly abandoned, a library without readers, a fountain with no one to watch its play.

"Ridiculous," he grumbled, and walked toward the building that glinted in the sun.

Earth's single star was hot, and the full gravity of his home planet was more than Andreas Quamodian had been used to for a good many years. It was a tiring walk. But there was something pleasant about it, about the dusty smell of the hot pavement and the luminous young green leaves of the trees that overhung the walk. Peace lay over the village, like a benediction of Almalik.

But Quamodian had not come to Earth in search of

peace. He increased his stride, and chugged up the walkway, beside the flagpole that bore the standard of the Companions of the Star: the thirteen colored stars of Almalik in the dotted ellipses of their intricate orbits, against a black field of space.

The door did not open for him. Quamodian nearly ran into it; he stopped only just in time.

"What the devil's the matter here?" he demanded, more surprised than angry—at least at first. "I am Andreas Quamodian, a monitor of the Companions of the Star. Admit me at once!"

But the bright crystal panel did not move. "Good morning, Citizen Quamodian," said a recorded robot voice. "The Wisdom Creek post of the Companions of the Star is closed today, in observance of local religious custom. It will be open as usual on Monday."

"I'll report this!" Quamodian cried. "Mark my words! I'll call the Regional Office of the Companions of the Star . . ."

"A public communications instrument is just to your left, Citizen Quamodian," the robot voice said politely. "It is cleared for emergency use even on Starday."

"Emergency, eh? You bet it's an emergency." But Quamodian had had enough of arguing with recorded voices. He stalked along the flank of the gold-colored ceramic building to the communications booth, angrily dialed the code for the Regional Office—and found himself talking to another recorded voice.

"Companions of the Star, Third Octant Office," it said briskly.

"Oh, confound—never mind. Listen. I am Monitor Quamodian. I am in Wisdom Creek to investigate a reported emergency, and I find the local office closed. This lax operation is highly irregular! I demand the office be opened and . . ."

"Monitor Quamodian," reproved the robot voice, "that is impossible. Under our revised covenant with the Visitants, no local posts operate on Stardays so that local personnel may be free to engage in voluntary religious activities. Even Regional Offices are machine-operated during this . . ."

"But this is an emergency! Can't you understand?"

"Monitor Quamodian, my sensors detect no emergency situation in Wisdom Creek."

"That's what I'm here for! I—well, I don't know the

327

exact nature of the emergency, but I require immediate assistance . . ."

"Our Wisdom Creek post will open promptly at midnight, local time," the voice informed him blandly. "Competent assistance will be available then."

"Midnight will be too . . ."

But the line clicked, buzzed and settled to a steady hum.

Muttering with anger, Quamodian tried Molly Zaldivar's code. But his flyer had been right; there was no answer.

Puffing with irritation as much as fatigue, Quamodian lowered himself to the steps of the office of the Companions and scowled at the empty street. How many millions of light-years had he spanned to be here, on this day, in this backwash of life? What tremendous forces had he enlisted to hurl him across the gulfs of space, to race against the dreadful fears that Molly Zaldivar's message had conjured up?

He licked dry lips and wiped perspiration from his brow. He was a hero, ready to rescue maiden, townspeople, world itself. But none of them appeared to want to be rescued.

%

7

Twenty-five miles southwest of Wisdom Creek, Molly Zaldivar did want to be rescued. At that moment she wanted it very badly.

Her old blue electric car had whined up the rocky mountain road, three thousand feet above the plain; below her she saw the flat, dry valley with the little town of Wisdom Creek huddled around the twin spires of the Transflex tower and the church. But now the road went no farther. It dipped, circled a spur of the mountainside, and went tumbling into the other valley beyond. From here on she would have to walk . . .

But that she could not do.

Above her she heard the restless, singing rustle of the creature Cliff Hawk called a sleeth. She could not see it. But she could imagine it there, tall as a horse but far more massive, black as space and sleek as her own hair. And she knew that at that moment she was closer to death than she had ever been before.

328

She tiptoed silently back to the car, eyes on the rocks over her head. The singing sound of the creature faded away and returned, faded away and came back again. Perhaps it had not detected her. But it might at any moment, and then . . .

Molly entered the car and closed the door gently, not latching it. Breathing heavily—partly from nerves, partly from the thin, high air around her—she picked up her communicator and whispered, "Cliff? Will you answer me, Cliff, please?"

There was no sound except for the faint rustle of the sleeth, and the even fainter whisper of wind around the mountaintop.

Molly bit her lip and glanced over her shoulder. She dared not start the car's motor. It was not very loud, but the sleeth was far too close; it was a wonder it hadn't heard her coming up the trail. But the road sloped sharply away behind her. If she released the brakes the old car would roll on its out-of-date wheels; it would rattle and creak, but not at low speeds, not at first. And Cliff had told her that the sleeth would not wander more than a few hundred yards from the cave mouth. She was very close now, but the car would roll out of range in not much more than a minute . . .

And then what? Cliff did not answer. She *had* to see him—had to stop whatever he was doing, teamed with the rude, hard man who owned the sleeth. She would never be any closer than this, and what hope was there that the sleeth would be elsewhere if she tried again another time anyway?

"Oh, please, Cliff," she whispered to the communicator, "it's Molly and I've *got* to talk to you. . . ."

There was a rattle of pebbles and dust, and Molly craned her neck to look upward in sudden terror.

There was the sleeth, eyes huge as a man's head, green as the light from a radium-dial watch. It was perched over her, the bright, broad eyes staring blindly across the valley. It was graceful as a cat, but curiously awkward as it floated in its transflection field, clutching at the rubble with claws that were meant for killing.

It did not seem to have seen her. Yet.

Molly froze, her ears tuned to the singing rustle of the sleeth. Its huge muscles worked supply under the fine-scaled skin, and the eyes slowly turned from horizon to

329

horizon. Then it drifted idly back behind the rock, and Molly dared to breathe again. "Oh, Cliff," she whispered, but only to herself. She could not bring herself to speak even in an undertone to the communicator.

But even terror fades; the monkey mind of a human being will not stay attuned even to the imminent threat of death. Molly became aware of her cramped position on the scarred plastic seat of the car, cautiously straightened her legs and sat up.

If only Cliff Hawk would hear her message and come.

If only the sleeth would drift over to the other side of the mountain, give her a chance to make a mad dash for the cave mouth and the men inside.

If only—she was stretching for impossibles now, she knew—if only poor Andy Quam would respond to her plea for help, and come charging out of the transflex tower with weapons, and wisdom, and the strength to do whatever had to be done to stop Cliff from going through with this dreadful work . . .

But they were all equally impossible. Cliff couldn't hear her, the sleeth wouldn't go away. And as for Andy Quam . . .

Even in her fear she couldn't help smiling. Poor old Andy, sober and serious, loving and stuffy, full of small rages and great kindnesses . . . of all the rescuing heroes a girl might imagine, surely he was the most unlikely.

The singing sound of the sleeth grew louder again, and fearfully she looked upward. But it did not appear.

Even the Reefer would be welcome now, she thought—that gaunt yellow-bearded giant who was Cliff Hawk's ally in his folly. She was afraid of the Reefer. He seemed like a throwback to a monstrous age of rage and rapine, a Vandal plundering a peaceful town, a Mau-Mau massacring sleeping children. He had always been polite enough to her, of course, but there was something about him that threatened devastation. Not that any additional threats were necessary. What Cliff was doing was bad enough in itself! Creating sentient life at the atomic level—trying to breed living, thinking tissue of the same stuff that was at the core of the sapient stars themselves. And worst of all, trying to duplicate in the laboratory the kind of life that made some stars rogues, pitted them against their fellows in a giant struggle of hurled energies and destroying bolts of matter.

She grinned suddenly, thinking again of Andy Quam: imagine pitting him against the Reefer! Why, he . . .

Molly Zaldivar sat bolt upright.

She had just realized that the singing sound of the sleeth was gone. The only noise on the mountain was the distant, moaning wind.

She waited for a long moment, gathering her courage, then slipped quietly from the seat. She stood beside the vehicle, ready to leap back inside and flee, however useless that would be—but the sleeth was still out of range.

Carefully, quietly she took a step up the rock path, then another. A pebble spun and grated under her feet. She paused, heart pounding—but there was no response.

Another step—and another . . .

She was at the top of the path now. To her right the cave mouth waited, rimmed with crystal, a rubble of junked laboratory equipment in front of it. No one was in sight. Not even—*especially* not—the sleeth.

Molly broke into a trot and hurried toward the cave mouth.

At that moment the sleeth appeared, rocketing over the crest of the mountain, coming down directly toward her like a thrown spear. She could see its great blind eyes staring directly into hers; it was moving at sonic velocities, hundreds of miles an hour; it would be on her in a second. *"Cliff!"* she shrieked, and flung herself toward the cave mouth.

She never reached it.

From inside the cave a great puff of black smoke came hurtling out in a perfect vortex ring. The concussion caught her and lifted her off her feet, threw her bruisingly to the ground. The sound followed a moment later and was deafening, but by then Molly was past caring; explosion, painful skin lacerations, raging sleeth, all blended together in a slow fading of sensation, and she was unconscious.

What was real and what was dream? Molly opened her eyes dizzily and saw the gaunt, bleeding face of Cliff Hawk staring down at her, aghast. She closed them again, and someone—someone, something, some voice—was calling to her, and she saw Someone trapped and raging, commanding her to come . . .

"Wake up! Confound you, Molly!"

"I'm awake, dearest," she said, and opened her eyes.

It was Cliff. "We've got to get him out of there," she said earnestly. "He's lost and trapped and . . ."

"Who? What are you talking about?"

She caught her head in her hands, suddenly aware of how much it hurt. "Why—" she looked up at Cliff Hawk, puzzled. "I forget."

He grimaced. "You're confused," he announced. "And a pest, besides. What are you doing here?"

"I wanted to stop you," she said dizzily. She was trying to remember what the very important thing was that Someone had said to her in her dream. If it had been a dream.

"Thought so. And look what you've done! As if I didn't have enough trouble."

Molly abandoned the fugitive memory. "There was an explosion," she said. "I got hurt."

Cliff Hawk looked suddenly less angry, more worried. Clearly Molly was telling him nothing he didn't already know. The rivulet of blood that ran down from a scrape on his forehead divided around his nose, blurred itself in the blue stubble of beard on his cheeks and chin. It made him look like a dangerous clown. But a clown with some great fear riding his back.

"We—we had an accident. Molly, go back to Wisdom Creek."

She shook her head, and then, without preamble, began to cry.

Hawk swore violently, but his touch was gentle as he reached swiftly down, caught her shoulders, helped her to her feet and into the cave. Molly let herself weep without shame, but it did not keep her from seeing that the cave was in fact a workshop, lined with glittering metal, rich with instruments and machines. A corona of pale violet hung over a humming golden globe, now soiled and dented from whatever it was that had exploded nearby. She heard the distant howl of a power tube, screaming to itself like the bass-C pipe of a steam calliope as it sucked energy from the air. She let him find her a seat on a wobbly laboratory stool, accepted a tissue and dabbed at her nose.

"You've got to go back," Cliff Hawk told her with rough tenderness. "I'm busy."

"You're in trouble!" she corrected. "It's dangerous, Cliff. Leave the rogue stars alone! I'll go back to Wisdom Creek if you come with me."

"I can't. We've had this out before."

"But you're risking your life—the whole world . . ."

332

"Molly." Awkwardly he touched her shoulder. "I can't stop. Even if it costs me my life. Even if it destroys the world. Did you mean it when you said you loved me? Then go back and leave me alone."

8

Andy Quam puffed around the corner and shouted, "Say, there! Wait a minute, will you?"

The three boys he had spied were ambling down the dusty road, yards away. They paused and looked around at him, politely curious. "Morning, preacher," nodded one of them. "Help you?"

"Yes. I hope so, anyway. I mean—well, where *is* everybody?"

"Starday, preacher. All off worshipping, mostly. 'Cept us."

"I'm not a preacher, young man. I . . ."

The boy looked him over. "Then why do you wear that funny suit?"

Quamodian blushed. "It's the uniform of the Companions of the Star. I'm Monitor Quamodian. I'm trying to find . . ."

"Gee, preacher!" The boy was showing the first real signs of interest now. "Companion of the Star? Then you go all over the galaxies, honest? And see all the funny Citizens with the green skins and the two heads and . . ."

"It is very impolite to make fun of a Citizen's appearance," said Andy Quam severely. "We are all equally star-shared."

"Oh, sure. Gee! Ever seen a sun go nova, preacher? Or fought ammonia creatures on a gas giant, or . . ."

Andy Quam said honestly, "Young man, my task has been mostly supervisory and statistical. I have had no adventures of any kind. Except this one."

"You're having an adventure *now?*"

"More adventure than I like. There's something very serious going on. I'm looking for Molly Zaldivar."

The second boy, a chubby redhead, spoke up. "Gone to the hills, preacher. Looking for her friends, I bet."

"Shut up, Rufe! They're not her friends!"

333

"Who are you telling to shut up, Rob? Just cause you're soft on Molly Zaldivar . . ."

"I'm warning you, Rufe!"

"What's the secret? Everybody knows you're stuck on her. And everybody knows she likes that fellow that lives in the—get your hands off me!"

Andy Quam grabbed them hastily. "Boys! If you're going to fight, please wait till I'm finished with you. Did you say you know where Molly is?"

The redhead broke free and brushed himself off, glowering at the other boy. "About thirty miles from here. Bet she is, anyway. Gone to the cave where the fellow lives with the Reefer and that animal. Kill themselves one day, my father says."

"How do I get there?" Andy Quam demanded.

"Why—no way, preacher. Not on Starday. Unless you want to walk."

"But it's very important—" Quamodian stopped himself. The boy was probably right. Still, it was already late afternoon, local time on this part of the planet, and at midnight he would be able to get things straightened out. He said, "What's a Reefer?"

"Man from the reefs of space, of course. Got one of those reef animals with him. They call it a sleeth."

"Big one," the third boy said suddenly. "My brother claims it can kill you soon's look at you."

"Killed three hunting dogs already," confirmed Rufe. "I wouldn't go near it for anything," he added virtuously. "My father told me not to."

Andy Quam looked at him thoughtfully. He said, "I bet you can tell me how to get there, though."

"Might, preacher."

"You could even show me, if you wanted to."

"Get in trouble with my dad if I did."

"Uh-huh. Say, boys. Back in my flyer I've got some rare goodies from a planet in Galaxy 5. Care to try them? Then maybe you can tell me a little more about this cave up in the hills."

The boys clamored for a ride in the flyer. The hundred-meter limitation was still in effect, but Andy Quam shepherded them all inside, closed the doors and ordered the flyer to rise to its legal limit and hover. It was the best he could do for them. And good enough, to judge from their shouts and yells as they thrust each other out of the way to see from the ports.

For that matter, Andy was interested too. Apart from his burning anxiety to find Molly Zaldivar as quickly as possible, this was old Earth, home of Man.

He felt a vague disappointment as he looked from the hovering flyer. He had expected vast, fantastic ancient cities, or at least the fabulous monuments and ruins of the long human past. But there was nothing like that. The land that sloped away from Wisdom Creek was reddish-brown and empty. The village itself was a disappointment. Only the Star church looked striking from the air, star-shaped, five pointed wings projecting from its central dome. The roofs and columns of the wings were all a dazzling white, the dome itself black as space and transparent, with brilliant images of the thirteen component suns of Almalik swimming within it.

"That's my house there, preacher," cried Rufus. "And see that road? Goes out to the mountains. That's where Miss Zaldivar is."

Andy Quamodian leaned forward, over their heads, and peered into the distance. The village was cradled in the bend of a stream. To the south a dam across the stream made a long, narrow lake, crossed by a trestle that carried a road toward the high, hazed hills on the horizon. "That's thirty miles, you said?"

"Nearer twenty-five, preacher."

"Which hill is it?"

"Can't tell from here. Have to show you. Can't show you today, not till the Peace of Starday's over."

Quamodian looked at him sharply. The boy's tone was —what? Cynical? Merely disinterested? "How come you're not in church?" he asked tardily.

The boy's face was impassive. "We don't cotton to the Star," he said. "My dad says the old religion's good enough for us."

"But Almalik's not opposed to any other religion, boys. It's not mystical. It's—oh, you must have been taught all this! It's a symbiotic association of stars and men and robots and fusorians, that's all."

"Course, preacher," the boy said politely. "You mentioned goodies?"

Andy Quam wanted to say more, but restrained himself. As a Monitor of the Companions of the Star he had been well drilled in the basic principles of the symbiosis, but as a matter of fact, he realized, he had never heard them questioned before. In Galaxy 5, in the far worlds where most citizens were nonhuman and had no interest at all in his views, in school where everyone nominally, at least, shared the same services on Starday, even among the dedicated scientists of Exion Four, there had been either no dissent or no interest at all. Perhaps he'd got a bit rusty.

But he hadn't thought, not for one second had anything in his experience prepared him to think, that here on the birthplace of the human race there would still be opposition to the Star! No wonder Molly Zaldivar had had to send for him for help. If these boys were representative, Earth had no interest in the wide universe outside.

While the boys were munching the treats the flyer had produced from its stores, transparent green jellies that pulsed warmly as they were chewed and filled the mind with a thrilling montage of synthetic sensation, Andy Quam said diffidently, "But not everybody's like you, are they? I mean, Molly Zaldivar's in the Church of the Star. And so must others be, to justify that church over there."

"Oh, there's plenty branded cattle of the Star," Rufe said chattily, pulling a bit of jelly from between his teeth. "That's what my dad calls them. But Miss Zaldivar doesn't go much. Sometimes she teaches Starday school, but not lately, far as I know."

"Anyway, that church is pretty old," said the tallest boy. "I expect it had a lot more people years ago. And besides—sweet Almalik!" he cried. "Look there!"

The first thing Andy Quam thought was that the boy had evidently had more to do with the Church of the Star than his father really approved of, using the name of Almalik to ease his emotions. The second thing was that that didn't matter. The boy's face was suddenly stark and afraid. Quamodian whirled, to face where the boy was pointing.

And then he saw it, something that violated the sweet peace of that Starday afternoon. He saw a great rope of fire, which seemed to extend from the blinding red disk of the setting sun—which had a sudden dreadful resemblance to Cliff Hawk's rogue. He saw it coiling like a monstrous snake of fire in that serene blue sky, thrusting savagely down through the white tufts of cumulus that drifted toward the mountains.

"Preacher!" cried Rufe, scared. "What is it?"

But Quamodian did not know. It looked almost like the

plasma effector of some transcience intellect, except that it was too enormous, its white blaze too painfully bright.

Like a snake of fire attacking from the sky it coiled and struck, recoiled and struck again, recoiled and struck three times into those low, far hills. Then it withdrew, sucked back into the setting sun.

A thin column of dark smoke rose from the shallow gap where it had struck. Presently an immense dull booming, like far thunder, rumbled out of the sky. The vast deep sound rolled away, leaving the valley bathed again in the sunlight of the serene Starday afternoon.

"Preacher, what was it?" demanded one of the boys, but Andy Quamodian could only shake his head. Then his eyes widened, his jaw dropped.

"Those hills!" he cried. "Isn't that where you said . . ."

"Yes, preacher," whispered the boy. "That's where the cave is. Where Molly Zaldivar is right now."

9

That distant voice was still whispering to Molly, though she couldn't quite hear it, couldn't quite make out what it said or who it was that spoke. But it was a terribly *pained* voice, the sound of a mind in rage and agony.

Cliff Hawk kept talking to her, demanding that she leave, harsh, even threatening, warning her that there was danger here. "Of course there's danger," she cried suddenly. "Why do you think I came? I want you to stop!"

He sighed and looked at her. His face, she saw, was terribly lined. Young, strong, quick, he had come in the last few weeks to look unendurably old.

"You want me to stop, and you don't even know what I'm doing," he said.

"You can remedy that."

He looked away. After a moment he turned to the violet-lighted globe and studied it, still not speaking. Then he said, "We're searching for intelligence. For minds anywhere not in transcience contact with intergalactic society. The Reefer and I have built our own equipment—very sensitive equipment. One contact turned out to be the hysterical mind of a small human boy, lost in the wilder-

337

ness of a new planet out in Galaxy 9. But the strangest contacts are the rogue stars . . ."

"What's a rogue star?"

He probed at the dried blood beside his nose, thoughtfully. "Solitary sentient stars," he said. "They don't belong to the civilized community. Most of those we've picked up—all of them, maybe—are at enormous distances outside our own galactic cluster. Yet somehow—" he hesitated, shrugged. "I don't know why. Most of them seem angered or alarmed when they sense us. But there's one, out beyond Exion—" He stopped.

Molly Zaldivar shuddered. She tried to remember something, but it was outside the reach of her mind.

Cliff Hawk was lecturing now, his eyes fastened on limitless space. "Thinking machines are all alike. Whether they are human brains or fusorian committees or sentient stars or computing robots, they all possess certain features in common. All thinking things have inputs—from sensory organs or tape readers or sensitive plasmas. They all have data storage units—magnetic cores or neurone cells or spinning electrons. They all have logic and decision units —synaptic or electronic or transcience patterns. They all have outputs—through motor organs or servo machines or plasma effectors."

He stopped thoughtfully, seeming to listen to the drone of energy fields and the distant scream of the power tube.

"Go on, dear. How do you tell a rogue star from a lost boy?"

Cliff Hawk hesitated, as though trying to relate the girl's presence to what he was talking about, but she urged him on with a gesture. "Our steady state universe is infinite," he said. "Truly infinite. Endless. Not only in space and time, but also in multiplicity." The worry and resentment faded from his worn face as the theory absorbed him. "The exploding galaxies called quasars were the first proof of that—galactic explosions, resulting from extreme concentrations of mass. Space is distorted into a curved pocket around a dense contracting galactic core. When the dense mass becomes great enough, the pocket closes itself, separating from our space-time continuum."

He was in full flight now. Molly heard a distant sighing, remembered the sleeth and shivered. Was that fearsome creature still lurking about? But she did not dare interrupt him.

"The visible quasar explosion," he droned on, "results

from the sudden expansion of the remaining shell of the galaxy, when it is released from the gravitation of the lost core. Each lost core, cut off from any ordinary space-time contact with the mother galaxy, becomes a new four-dimensional universe, expanding by the continuous creation of mass and space until its own maturing galaxies begin shrinking past the gravitational limit, budding more new universes."

From the cave mouth blood-colored dusk seeped in, mingling with the violet hues of the aurora. It was growing hard to see. Molly stirred restlessly, stifling a sigh.

"But the rogue stars," said Cliff Hawk, "are in our universe. Or we think they are. Or . . ."

"Or you're talking too much," rumbled a new voice, and Molly Zaldivar spun around to see a great bear of a man, wearing a dirty yellow beard, peering in at them from the cave mouth. In the red gloom he looked menacing. But far more menacing still was the great, restless bulk of the creature beside him. The sleeth.

Cliff Hawk blinked and returned to reality. For a moment his gaze brushed Molly Zaldivar as though he had forgotten she was there and was astonished to find her. But then his whole thought was concentrated on the man at the cave mouth.

"Reefer! What's the word? How bad is the damage?"

The Reefer opened a soundless grin between dingy yellow mustache and grimed yellow beard. "Bad enough," he said. "But we're still in business. What happened?"

"I— I—" Hawk glanced again at Molly Zaldivar. "I was just checking in the cave when I heard Molly groaning, and I . . ."

"And you forgot everything else and went to her. Ah, that's to be understood. A pretty face is more than a star to you, of course."

Hawk shook his head. "I've been telling her to go away."

"Beyond doubt. That's why you're lecturing the girl like a child at Starday school, eh?" He patted the great bulk of the sleeth. "We understand, do we not?"

Hawk gazed at the Reefer with mingled anger and apology, then turned to Molly. "I'm sorry," he said. "But the Reefer's right. You've got to go back to Wisdom Creek."

"No! Not until you tell me what you're doing here!"

"Girl, he's been telling you," rumbled the Reefer. "What

339

do you think all those words were that he was pouring out at you when I came in? More than you need to know. More than you should know, I think."

"But nothing that made sense to me," Molly persisted. "How are you trying to communicate with rogue stars?"

The massive head shook with laughter. "Communicate with them, girl? Then maybe he didn't tell you, after all. It's not just communication we're after. We're building one of our own!"

Cliff Hawk broke the shocked silence that followed the Reefer's words: "That's the truth of it, Molly. Or close enough. We can't really communicate with the rogue stars, not directly. We've tried that a thousand times, and it's past our abilities. Solomon Scott tried to reach one. He never came back. Bu we can—we think we can—build a sort of mathematical model of one. An analogue. A small imitation, you might call it. And through that, here on Earth, we may be able to reach them, find out what we want to know."

"But that's dangerous!" protested Molly. "Aren't rogue stars terribly dangerous?"

The Reefer boomed, "Not a bit, girl! Look at our cave here—you can see there's no danger at all." And his great laugh filled the cave, drowning out the distant whines and drones.

Cliff Hawk said uneasily, "In order to duplicate the structure of a rogue star we had to duplicate some of the environmental features. Not really. Not in degree. But we needed great pressure and temperature, and—well, as you can see, we had a little accident."

"Little enough," flashed Molly Zaldivar. "It nearly killed you—and me, for that matter!"

"That's why I want you to go back to Wisdom Creek, Molly. Right away, before . . ."

"Now stop that!" shouted Molly Zaldivar. "I won't go! I was afraid what you were doing was dangerous; that's why I sent for And—well, never mind! But now that I know it, I won't stop until I make you give it up!"

"Impossible. I'll take you back."

"You won't!"

"Great Almalik, girl!" shouted Cliff Hawk, his face showing animation again for the first time. "What's got into you? Don't you understand, I don't want you here! Why won't you go?"

340

"Because I love you, you idiot!" cried the girl, and broke into tears.

There was silence then, even the Reefer saying nothing, though his eyes winked comically under the bushy yellow brows and his bearded face grinned hugely at the spectacle.

They stood staring at each other, Molly Zaldivar and the man she loved. The silence protracted itself.

And then Molly shivered. "Something's—wrong," she whispered. "I'm scared, Cliff."

Cliff Hawk's stern face lifted. He stood listening, to something that he could not quite hear.

In the opening of the cave mouth the sleeth moved restlessly, the shimmer of its transflection field rippling light across its night-black hide. The Reefer stared at it, then away.

"Girl," he rumbled, "you're right about that. The sleeth's spooked. You know what I think? I think we've got a visitor."

10

Deep under the cave lay a tunnel, driven into the mountain by ancient prospectors a millennium earlier, beaded with galleries thrusting out from the main shaft to seek for gold or silver ores that were never found. For ten centuries they had lain empty, until Cliff Hawk and the Reefer came to fill them with their machines and instruments, to use them to hatch a new life that would serve as their contact with the rogue stars.

In one of these galleries, in a vault that the men had enlarged and bound about with steel and transflection energies, there was a region of great pressure and heat. All the energies of the screaming power tubes were funneled to keep that hot, dense plasma alive. It was an incubator, designed to produce a new life.

And it had succeeded.

Down there in the hot, crushing dark, Something stirred. It's first knowledge was of pain. It had been born in a place where nothing like it had ever been before, a place that was innately hostile to all things like itself.

It stirred and reached out with an intangible probe of

341

energy. The probe touched the energy-bound steel that kept its plasma environment intact, and recoiled.

I am caught, it told itself. I do not wish to be caught.

And then it fell to pondering the question of what it meant by "I." This occupied it for many thousands of microseconds—a long time in its life, which had just begun, but only a moment by the human standards of the, as yet unknown to it, world outside its pen. Overhead, Cliff Hawk was studying his instruments, ranging into galaxies millions of light-years away. The Reefer was roughly checking the tools and power tubes in the higher cave above, while his sleeth slipped silently and sightlessly around the crest of the hill. And down its slope Molly Zaldivar had just abandoned her old blue electrocar and was stealing toward the entrance.

At that point the new Something in the plasma field concluded its first serious deliberations with a conclusion worthy of a Descartes: I do not know what I am, but I know that I am something capable of finding out what I am.

And it proceeded experimentally to seek a further solution. Gathering its energies, it thrust again at the metal energies that bound it; thrust hard, with neither thought of damage to itself (it had not yet learned the habit of self-preservation) nor interest in the consequences to its environment.

It thrust—and penetrated.

The dense, hot plasma burst free into the cave, shaking the entire hill, destroying its own gallery, melting down the steel bottle that had held it. As it broke free it died; the energies from the power tube that had replenished it were automatically cut off—which saved the hill, and half the countryside around, from destruction. Overhead, the tremor it caused shorted connections, started a fire, caused secondary explosions in a dozen places. It tossed Molly Zaldivar to the floor, rocketed a shard of metal across Cliff Hawk's brow, and threw the Reefer to his knees, where he shouted in anger and pain and called to his sleeth.

The thing that had been born in the plasma did not die. It registered this fact in its billion billion coded electrons without surprise. It had not been sure that it was alive, and had not feared to die. It hung in the corridor, while acrid chemical smoke and bright radiant heat whirled around it, untouched by them, hanging now in its own transflection forces, independent of its environment.

And free.

Now its probes could reach farther. They crept out onto the face of the mountain and lightly touched the unconscious mind of Molly Zaldivar, who moaned in fear and tried to open her eyes. They touched and penetrated the stark, bare thoughts of the sleeth. They studied Cliff Hawk and the Reefer, dismissed the inanimate rock and metal of the mountain and its caves, reached out toward the human minds in Wisdom Creek and found them not worth inspection, scanned the myriad men, women, children, bees, turtles, dolphins, dogs, apes, elephants of Earth and filed them for future examination, reached out to the moon and the planets, shaped themselves and stretched to touch the sun itself.

Briefly, lightly, its probes met another—the questing reach of another rogue mind, infinitely powerful, infinitely far away. Dimly, for half a nanosecond, it sensed the senses of that awed watcher . . .

All in the first few seconds of freedom.

Then they recoiled, and the thing that had been born so few moments before contracted in upon itself to think again. For some of the things it had touched had caused it certain sensations. It did not recognize what these sensations were, but it felt they were important. Some of them —those caused by the entity it had not learned to identify as Molly Zaldivar—were pleasant. Others—those caused by that larger, more distant entity it could not yet recognize as the sun—brought about sensations which it could not yet identify as fear. It needed time to study the meaning of all these things.

It contracted into itself and thought, for many microseconds.

Presently a probe stretched out from it once more. There were certain other elements in its environment which it had passed over in its first examination, about which it wanted more information.

It touched the "mind" of the sleeth again, but lingered for a moment, studying it. In this simple construction of cells and patterns it recognized something that might serve it. Yet there were even simpler patterns nearby. The thing reached out and looked at Molly's abandoned electrocar, at the great tracked handling machine that Cliff Hawk and the Reefer used for moving earth and heavy machines,

343

at the instruments and machines of the cave themselves. It sensed another being, somehow more like itself but dim in infinite distance.

Hesitantly the probes returned to the thing down in the blazing gallery below.

It needed more time for thought. It wished to consider what it was that stirred within itself in regard to these things.

It had not yet learned to call these stirrings "hunger."

Cliff Hawk lifted his head from the hooded viewtubes of his instruments and shouted, "Reefer! You're right! There's something near us that wasn't here before!"

The Reefer nodded his great head slowly. "Thought so." His little dark eyes were hooded. "Question is, what?"

Molly Zaldivar struggled to her feet and caught at Cliff Hawk's arm. "Please stop, dearest! Don't go any farther. Let's call for help before it's too late."

Impatiently he shook her arm off, but she clung. "Cliff, please. I'm afraid. I felt something nearby before and it frightened me. Let me call Andy Quam and . . ."

He jerked his head around to glare at her. "Quamodian? Is he on Earth?"

"I—I think so, Cliff. I sent for him, because I was so worried."

Cliff Hawk laughed sharply. "Little Andy Quam? You thought he could help in *this?*" He shook his head, dismissing little Andy Quam, and turned to the Reefer. "Could we have hatched something? Were you inside the lower galleries?"

The Reefer shook his shaggy head. "Just passed by the mouth. The power tubes were running free, no load, and I had to adjust them. But there was something burning down there."

"Idiot!" snapped Cliff Hawk, and bent to turn a switch. A bank of viewers lighted up before him on the wall, revealing the entrance to the lower cave, a jumble of machinery, a blank rock face where a gallery ended—and nothing. Five of the viewers showed only the shifting whiteness of their scanning traces; no picture came through.

(Down in that lower cavern, hovering in the smoky fire where the burned-out cameras stared eyelessly at it, the thing that had come from the plasma tank completed its consideration and stretched out another probe. It was reaching for the sun. It had concluded that the danger in the sun needed action. The thing in the lower cavern massed perhaps an ounce and a half of stripped electrons and plasma. The mass of the sun was some 2×10^{33} grams, a third of a million times the planet Earth. The thing did not regard these odds as important.)

Molly Zaldivar shivered and moved away. Her bruises were beginning to trouble her now, and Cliff Hawk seemed to have forgotten she was alive; he and that terrible Reefer, with his face burned black and seamed with scars, were shouting at each other, pointing at the banks of instruments, acting in general like lunatics. Molly Zaldivar did not attempt to follow what they were talking about, except that something big had happened. But it could not be anything good; of that she was certain.

Her eyes widened. "Cliff!" she cried. "Listen!"

(The thing had acquired a great deal more skill in handling its functions in the past few thousand microseconds. While one probe was reaching out, invisibly and intangibly, to touch the Sun, it found itself able to mount other probes. One extended itself to touch those simplest of patterned creatures that it had discovered on the upper part of the mountain.)

"What's the matter, Molly?" Cliff was irritated, she knew; but she could not stop.

"Listen—outside! That's my car, starting up!"

And now all three of them could hear it, the distant tiny whine of the electrocar. They leaped for the cave mouth, all three of them, while the sleeth bobbed silently out of their way and stared. Before their eyes the little car started to move up the mountain toward them.

There was no one at the wheel.

The sleeth darted abruptly toward it, recoiled, and returned to the cave mouth like a hurled arrow. "Easy, girl!" shouted the Reefer, and turned to cry to Cliff Hawk, "The animal's caught a whiff of something. Careful! I can't control it when it's like this . . ."

But that danger dwindled into nothingness even before Molly Zaldivar realized what it was. For something more alarming happened and caught them all unawares.

Outside the reddening sunset brightened, flashed into an explosion of white-hot brilliance. Something shook them, threw them against each other and the walls. The light dwindled and returned; dwindled again, and returned again, and on this third time struck with such violence that, for

345

the second time that day, Molly Zaldivar found herself hurled into unconsciousness. As she fell into blackness she heard the Reefer shouting, "The star! Great Almalik, Hawk, we're being hit by the star!"

11

Quamodian shivered. Leaning past the boys clustered at the window of his flyer, he shaded his eyes to study that thin column of dark smoke which rose straight above the shallow notch in the blue-hazed hills. The three boys moved closer to him, breathless and pale.

"Preacher, what did it hit?" the dark boy whispered suddenly. "Did it hurt anybody?"

"I don't know," said Andreas Quamodian. He groaned and slammed his fist against the unbreakable glass. "But I've got to find out!"

"The sun did it," said Rufe breathlessly. "I saw it. It hit the Reefer's place."

Absently, staring at the thin beacon of smoke, Andy Quam said, "Who's the Reefer?"

"A man from the reefs of space. He lives up on Wolf Gap ridge—right where you see that smoke. Him and his sleeth."

Quam glanced blankly at the boy. "A sleeth?"

"It's a thing from space. It hunts. The Reefer trapped it when it was a cub. He raised it for a pet. My uncle says he rides it now, but I don't know. Cliff Hawk doesn't, I know that. Nobody would dare touch it but the Reefer."

"They were bred to hunt pyropods," said the smallest of the boys suddenly. "The sleeth can catch a pyropod and claw it to scrap metal."

Quam said harshly, "I don't care about the sleeth. Or the Reefer. What does Cliff Hawk have to do with all this?"

Rufe shrugged. "The Reefer brought him up. Brought his sick Mom here from the reefs before he was born, then sent him off to the stars to learn to be a transflection engineer. That's what my dad says."

"What else does your dad say about Hawk?"

"Says Hawk's building something for the Reefer. Contraband. Don't know what kind, but they smuggle in machines that humans aren't supposed to have without permission from the Star."

The smallest boy whined, "I want to go back down, preacher. I want to go to Starschool."

"Jay! You know we all said we weren't going to go . . ."

"Shut up, Rufe! I want to ask my Starschool teacher about the thing that hit the ridge. I'm scared, and Mark knows nearly everything. I want to see him!"

The redheaded boy looked at Andy Quam and shrugged. "Mark's a robot," he said. "But Jay's maybe right. Mark might know something."

Without thought Andy Quam's fingers reached out to the controls, but the flyer, listening, had anticipated his thought. They were already dropping to the ground.

"I'll take you there, Jay," said Andy Quam eagerly. "Provided you let me come along. I want to know too!"

They hurried up the graveled walk, under the multiple suns of Almalik imaged in the space-black dome of the church. They boy Jay guided Quamodian through hushed passages to Mark's schoolroom.

It was nearly empty, only a score or so brightly dressed children clustered at the front and a smaller, shabbier group lounging skeptically at the back. The robot paused to greet them.

"Come in, students. We are telling the wonderful story of the Visitants and the precious gifts they brought to the old human savages, centuries ago. Please take your seats."

The three boys slipped quietly into empty seats along a back bench, alongside the others who wore the worn and faded fiber clothing of the free people who have never accepted the Star. Quamodian walked past them, down the aisle to where the brighter garbed children of civilization sat on the front benches. He stopped and planted himself in front of the robot.

"Robot Inspector, I'm sorry to interrupt . . ."

The robot hung in the air before him, its tall black shining case reflecting the lights of the room and of its own oval of flame-bright plasma. The plasma flickered, darted half a yard toward him, flicked a dark, whiplike effector toward his face.

"Sir, you cannot interrupt," the robot intoned, its voice ringing like tossed pebbles against the low, blue dome.

"I can, Robot Inspector. I am your superior in the

Companions of the Star. I am Monitor Andreas Quamodi-an."

"Even so, sir," pealed the robot, "you cannot control me today. Our new compact allows no official duties to interfere with voluntary religious activities on Starday. Teaching this class, Monitor Quamodian, is my voluntary religious activity."

Andy Quam stood his ground, disdaining the effector that tried to wave him away. "Robot, an emergency exists." He heard the ripple of excitement from the children and lowered his voice. "A very grave emergency, I'm afraid. Three plasma bolts from the sun have just struck near here. Human beings may have been injured, even killed."

Gently but firmly, the dark tip of the effector coiled around his arm, propelled him irresistibly toward the benches. "You must wait, sir," sang the robot as the staring children tittered. "Be seated. Be still. Be attentive, all of you, as I resume the wonderful story of the Visitants and their fusorian gifts to man."

Andy Quam muttered under his breath, but clearly it was no use. He stalked back down the aisle to the back benches, where Rufe gave him an approving grin. "You're okay, preacher! We don't like robots either."

"Hush, boy," said Andy Quam as severely as the robot. He sat glowering bleakly at the dark case of the robot, where its mark number was blazoned just under the bright-starred orbital pattern of Almalik. Perhaps the robot was hard to manage today, but tomorrow would be different.

"The fusorians," sang the robot melodiously, retracting its effector and floating higher toward the blue dome, "are older than the stars, and all of them are very wonderful. They are microscopic creatures that live by fusing hydro-gen atoms, and they evolved in space—so long ago that they have divided into many millions of different species. The reefs of space are built of atoms which some fusorians create. The Visitants are a special race of fusorians which live like symbiotes, inside the bodies of creatures like man."

"Bugs!" hissed the redheaded boy to Quamodian. "My dad says they're nothing but parasites!"

"In the wonderful partnership of man and fusorian," the robot trilled, "each benefits, neither is harmed. For the Visitants are wonderfully wise and just. They have evolved transcience intellectic patterns which knit their colonies together and link them all with the sentient stars.

348

And so we are all united, all joined into the great multiple Citizen named Cygnus, whose spokesman star is Almalik."

"Slaved, you mean," whispered the redheaded boy.

"That is," sang the robot, its oval of plasma pulsing rhapsodically, "so are we joined if we accept the gift of the Visitants. On the great day when we join the Star they will jump in a fat golden spark to your skin. Their colonies will penetrate every cell of your body. They will destroy all marauders and all wild cells, and keep you young forever. They bring you utter happiness, and utter peace. This is the gift of the Visitants."

"Hogwash," the redhead muttered. "Preacher, why don't you make him shut up?"

"And here with us on this Starday," cried the singing voice of the robot, "we are fortunate, children, blessed by the Visitants. For we have with us a Monitor of the Companions of the Star!" Like lightning, a pale effector stabbed forth and burst in a shower of light over Andy Quam's head as the children turned and stared. "For great Almalik can only help us and guide us, he cannot fight for his own right cause. So we Companions fight for him, Monitor Andreas Quamodian here as well as, more humbly, my poor robot self."

Quam swallowed angrily, torn between the desire to stalk out of the room and the yearning to leap to his feet and denounce this willful robot who spoke of duty but would not help him in the emergency that had blasted the mountains.

"Of course," the robot added delicately, "Monitor Quamodian and I do not view all questions in the same light. Sometimes we differ. Sometimes, perhaps, one of us is wrong. But that too is just and proper, for the peace of the Star keeps us free, while joining us in rewarding fellowship."

It bobbed soundlessly for a moment, as though entranced with its own words, while its pale oval of plasma blushed briefly blue. "Now we are finished," it said at last. "Children, you may leave. Monitor Quamodian, I thank you for being with us today."

Andy Quam pushed furiously down the aisle, through the knots of chattering children, to confront the robot. "Robot Inspector," he cried, "How do you fight for Almalik when you won't even help me in this important matter?"

"Patience, Monitor Quamodian," purred the robot.

349

"There are evil men and evil stars who reject the universal good of all. I join you gladly in fighting them, but under our compact Starday is . . ."

"Just another day!" Quamodian shouted roughly. "Rogue men are plotting with Rogue stars! There is great danger here, and it cannot wait on your convenience!"

The robot bobbed silently in its transflection field, as though it were considering what to do. Half-formed effectors budded around its case and were withdrawn; its plasma oval turned opalescent as pale colors chased themselves through it. It said at last, "The situation is grave, Monitor Quamodian."

"You don't begin to know how grave," Andy Quam said bitterly. "Didn't you hear me? Three bolts of plasma from the sun! That would have been impossible for any member of Cygnus without grave provocation. So there must have been provocation—something very dangerous, very serious, going on out in the hills!"

"We have recorded that phenomenon," the robot agreed melodiously. "It is more serious than you think, perhaps, Monitor Quamodian."

Quam brought up short. Had the robot heard from Senior Monitor Clothilde Kwai Kwich? "More serious than I think? What . . . ?"

"But nevertheless," the robot went on, "the compact is clear. You may not compel me today. And I advise—we advise, most urgently—that you undertake no action without our aid. You see, Monitor Quamodian, we have recorded the presence of extreme hazards about which you know nothing."

Quamodian stuttered, "I d-d- I demand that information! Right now!"

"Under the compact—" sang the robot.

"Blast the compact!"

"Under the compact," the robot repeated serenely, "you may make no demands. I will do for you only what I wish to do freely, as part of my voluntary religious observance of Starday." It hesitated for only a second, while the shimmering colors on its plasma oval spun madly, then burst into a bright, almost golden fire. "Voluntarily," it sang, "I elect to aid you now. Will you mount on my back, Monitor Quamodian? I will convey you at once to the site of the sunbolts. For in truth there is danger; a rogue star has been born there, and lives and grows!"

12

The thing had grown now, grown even while its effectors were reaching out to the sun and the sun's triple-stroked reply was coming back. It had passed Descartes' *Je pense, et puis je suis,* and that milestone surmounted, had put aside its examination of its self for examination of its world. *Dark. Alone. Particles.* It discovered that some of the particles were organized into macrostructures; it did not label these "matter," but it grasped at once that they operated as vector units, a myriad of whirling charged bits contriving a mean motion exerting a mean force. *Warmth. Radiation.* Free of the heat of its exploded womb, it sought other energy sources, tapped them, used them, owned them.

I move, it "thought"—a true thought, joining together its sense of self and an operator; and it swam slowly along its deep tunnel, reaching for new sensation and new strength. *Pull. Gravity. Lift.* It slid through material obstacles or brushed them aside. Behind it lay a trail of erupted doors and demolished tiers of supplies. *Search. Search.* It gave a name to what it was doing, and the sense of a goal. Search for what? It sought that kindred mind and touched it again—infinitely far, yet jealously concerned.

It became aware of a kind of radiation that was itself structured, that possessed patterns that were neither random nor meaningless. *I?*

The thing paused, palping the faint currents of sensation that emanated from distant sources. *Affirmative. I. Not "I," but another "I."*

It had recognized that there were other creatures in its world, other competitors for energy or matter or space—or companions.

In the cavern above, Molly Zaldivar roused briefly from the stunned shock that held her, and moaned in terror. Something was studying her. Something that caused fear. Something utterly strange, that had never been in this world before.

13

Molly Zaldivar stirred and returned to consciousness She lay across the crumbled legs of a laboratory stool, and one of them was stabbing her with its shattered end. The cave workshop was hissing, moaning, crackling with electrical shorts and hot, cooling metal. The pale violet corona that once had enshrouded a globe of gold now threw itself like a tattered net from point to point, dying and returning, hissing and crackling. There was smoke from somewhere outside the cave, a heavier, choking smoke from within.

She rubbed impatiently at her forehead, drew her hand away and saw, without surprise or fear, that it was bloody. But she was alive. She tried three times before she could speak.

"Cliff. Cliff, where are you?"

Hawk's voice answered at once, but weakly, more a whisper than his normal gruff tone. "I—I don't know exactly, Molly. Are you all right?"

She glanced down at herself—clothes a horror, skin bruised and cut, dirty and damp. But more or less functional, she decided. "I think so. How about you?"

She sat up, peering around. At first she could not see him. "Cliff! Are you hurt?"

Rubble stirred a few yards away, and Cliff Hawk's whisper said, "I don't quite know. Something fell on me."

"Oh, Cliff!" Molly struggled to her feet, limped, half crawled across the piles of debris that were all that was left of Hawk's orderly laboratory. "Can you move? Are you in pain?"

A trash heap stirred again, and Molly saw that what she had taken for another heap of litter was the upper part of Hawk's body, powdered with grime and ash, but apparently intact. He seemed to be jackknifed over something, some large object that was resting on what would have been his lap, facing away from her. He twisted and looked at her. It took all his strength, and his face was a mask of effort and pain. "My—legs are caught," he gritted.

"Wait. No, sit still—let me!" And forgetting her own

352

aches she flew to free him; but it was impossible. A beam had fallen across his legs, knocking him down; some other blow had thrust him sidewise. His upper body and arms were filthy and battered, but they were free and he could move. But his legs were under half a ton of mass.

He gave up the effort and slumped forward again, across the weight that pinned him down. After a moment he said, "Where's the Reefer? He can help . . ."

Molly looked around helplessly. "I don't know."

"Call him!"

But though she shouted, there was no answer. She stood up, stretching out an arm to the tunnel wall to steady herself. The smoke was getting very thick; something bad was happening in the interior of the workshop, and she could feel a warning of heat.

She shouted for the Reefer again; still no answer. There was no help for it; if Cliff Hawk was going to get out of the trap that bound him, she was the one who would have to do it. She bent dizzily to tug again at the beam. Hawk did not speak; his eyes were closed, he seemed to be unconscious. The beam was immobile.

Molly knelt in the litter, careless of the jagged edges that were shredding her knees, and methodically began to move what could be moved: the plastic housing from one of Hawk's instrument panels, a tangle of light metal tubing, a drift of shattered glassware. The smoke made her cough and blink, but she did not look up . . .

Not until she became aware of the sound that had been growing in her ears for seconds, loud now, close, compelling. It was a singing rustle like a breeze through dry brush.

The sleeth.

She turned, and froze. The creature hung in the air not a yard from her back, its broad, blind eyes fastened on her, its supple muscles rippling down the black, sleek skin.

For a moment she thought it was help.

But Cliff Hawk did not stir. There was no sign of the Reefer. She was alone with a helpless man, and a creature from space whose whole anatomy was designed for killing.

Under the mountain the flowing essence of power that was the infant rogue star paused to consider the meaning of the sharp-edged triple slap the sun had administered to its curiosity. It was a rebuke, clearly enough. Even at ninety-odd million miles, Sol could have launched a far more devastating blow. The tiny rogue knew that as surely as it knew its own strength, and knew therefore, in its simple logic, that the intent of the blow was not destruction but a warning. *Star too big.* It corrected itself. *I too small. Get bigger.*

It had not been hurt in any way by the triple blast of coiled white flame. It did not fear a harder blow; indeed, it had not evolved a concept of "fear." But there were smaller, more controllable assemblies of particles closer at hand, and the rogue elected to investigate them.

Molly's little car it scanned, solved, manipulated and discarded. (The little vehicle started up at the rogue's remote command, obediently moved forward and, when the rogue withdrew its attention, mindlessly ground ahead until one wheel dropped over the lip of the road and it slid, rolled and finally bounced to destruction down the mountain.)

More complex creations existed, the rogue found. It did not "see," it did not distinguish visible light from any other form of radiation, but it recognized differences in frequency and kind. The differences between the kinds of radiation that were emanated by living creatures were to it something like colors are to carbon-based life: it recognized a "green" glow which flickered violently, as though in fear or pain; a blue-violet aura which waned as the rogue observed it; emanations of all rainbow colors, and far into the infra- and ultra-frequencies, which were the sleeth, a colony of burrowing moles, an ant's nest, even small faintly radiant points, like dust in a searchlight beam, that were the microorganisms in the air, the soil, the bodies of the larger life-forms nearby.

Something about the "green" light interested the rogue; perhaps it was the violence of its aura. It observed closely, and discovered that there was an organized mass of particulate matter attached to it; the matter seemed to be acting upon that other mass of matter which appeared to be associated with the dwindling blue-violet glow. The rogue observed, wihout analyzing, certain mechanical vibrations in the surrounding matter that were its sources. *Please, Cliff,* Molly was begging, *help me get you out;* but the rogue was a long way from having formed the concept of communication, much less acquiring a grasp of any language.

354

A brighter glow of vivid gold was moving toward them; the rogue reached out to encompass it and found it a new phenomenon, something between the car and the humans, for more subtle and complex in its organization than the clumsy mechanical toy it had played with for a moment, then discarded; yet simple enough to be operated. The rogue studied the sleeth for a fraction of a second, then reached out an invisible effector. It played with the sleeth, sending it through the air.

(Outside the cave mouth, the Reefer picked himself up, staggered to his feet and stared wildly about. There was blood on his grimy yellow beard, and his huge features had new scars. He croaked a question at the world, but there was no one to answer, no one in sight, nothing but gray smoke from inside the cave and crackling flame and white smoke from where something had set the cave mouth beams afire. He turned slowly, unsteady on his feet. The sun was a frightening color, roiled red and angry. The sky was clouded and ominous. He shouted for his sleeth, but there was no answer.)

The infant rogue was aware of the dull, slate-colored hue that was the Reefer. It had even recognized a connection between it and its new toy, the sleeth.

It would be interesting, the young rogue thought, to play with one of these more complex mechanisms too.

But for the moment it had not yet tired of the sleeth, arrowing it through the smoky sky, lashing out with its death-dealing claws and transflection fields at birds, rocks, tufts of grass.

The organization of matter fascinated the rogue. It decided to explore the possibilities of changing that organization, of interfering. It decided to be a god.

It thought for a moment of commandeering the Reefer for practice, as it had commandeered and operated first the electrocar, then the sleeth. It considered destroying one of the glowing living things. Any one. Destroying it so that it might be dissected and studied.

But it did not.

Already, only minutes after its first birth from its womb of plasma, the rogue had begun to develop habit patterns and "character." Its development was not only rapid but exponential. Its first actions had been entirely random, as pure a free will as a pinball machine. But it learned. The

355

new and generally unpleasant environment in which it found itself, it had discovered, responded pleasingly to certain kinds of manipulation. It was easy to destroy its features, one by one. The rogue could demolish a rock, kill a living thing, uproot a mountain, lash out at a sun. But once destroyed, it had learned, they were gone.

A more interesting, that is to say a more educational way of manipulating them was to operate short of destruction. To interfere, but not to kill.

Not at first.

There was no question of conscience in this, of course, nor of mercy. The rogue was as yet totally without a superego. But it had learned the sweet taste of pleasure.

These organized masses of matter could be sources of pleasure.

Molly dared move slightly, craning her neck to see past the sleeth.

"Reefer?" she whispered. "Are you there? Can you help me?"

But there was no human figure behind the great singing shadow of the sleeth. It hung there with its huge eyes fastened on her, and then, without warning, slipped forward, darted to the wall, and hung over Cliff Hawk's unconscious body.

Molly screamed, "Don't hurt him!" But in fact the sleeth was not attacking. It bobbed silently over him for a moment, then the pale radiance of its transflection field flickered.

Cliff Hawk's body quivered, then sat slowly up. "Cliff!" cried Molly, "you're all right!" But he was not conscious. His head lolled on a shoulder, his eyes were closed.

She stared wide-eyed at the sleeth. It was lifting Cliff, but why? What was it going to do?

She did not have to wait for an answer. The transflection fields flickered again, and the great beam that had pinned him came up off his lap. It lifted at one end, like the boom of a crane, raised itself to the height of his head, rotated majestically, and dropped into a pile of rubble.

Gently Hawk's torso was allowed to sink back, until he was lying outstretched and unencumbered. He had not regained consciousness.

"Thank you," whispered Molly to the sleeth—knowing

356

it could not understand; not caring whether it could or not. Then she flew to Hawk.

He was badly hurt, but he was alive. There was not much blood. His legs, though, were badly injured; though they lay straight enough, when she moved one he groaned sharply in his sleep and his face twisted in pain.

He needed medical attention. "Oh, Cliff!" she sobbed. "If only you hadn't . . ."

From the cave mouth the voice of the Reefer muttered, "Leave him be. You're as bad hurt as he is."

"Oh, Reefer!" cried the girl. "Help me! Cliff's been badly hurt, and we've got to get him to Wisdom Creek." Then what he had said penetrated to her and she realized, surprised, that she was herself on the verge of unconsciousness. The smoky air made her lightheaded; she was coughing without knowing she was coughing; her bruised, racked body was beginning to hurt in earnest.

"How?" growled the Reefer.

"I don't know!" She swayed dizzily, and wailed, "At least let's get him out in the open. He'll suffocate in here."

The Reefer moved cautiously forward. Even in her misery, Molly could see that he had been hurt himself. His little eyes were sunk in pain; his yellow beard and mustache clotted with blood. He stood over Cliff Hawk, studying him without touching him.

"Can't," he said.

"You've got to!"

"Can't move him. If the sleeth was acting right—but he's not. Spooked fair. Not that I blame him," the Reefer rumbled. "We've chewed up pyropods out in the reefs, but we never tangled with a star before."

"Star? What star?"

"The sun, girl. That triple sunbolt. I think we've got ourselves in trouble."

The sleeth, which had been hanging humming nearby, surged suddenly toward them. The Reefer flinched away, and the sleeth passed him by and darted out into the open air again. "You see, girl? Won't mind me a bit. Don't know what's got into him."

"Then you and I must lift him out!"

The Reefer spat into the rubble. "You? Couldn't lift yourself, I'd say; you're worn out. And I can't manage him by myself. Kill him if I tried."

"Then what can we do? Please, Reefer."

357

The Reefer looked past her, into the denser smoke that was rolling toward them down the tunnel. "Only one thing I know," he growled. "Shoot him for you, if you like. Better than letting him burn."

The rogue tired of the sleeth, thought for a moment of destroying it, then merely abandoned it to its own devices. It amused itself briefly by examining the state of those nonradiant assemblages of matter which had been so brutally tossed about by the sunbolts. It did not recognize them as instruments, machines, bits of human inventiveness; but it did see that they had been made functionless by the damage they had suffered, and that the chemical reactions now taking place in and among them were damaging them still further.

It understood, after a meditation of some nanoseconds, that the course of the fire was carrying it toward those radiant masses which it had not yet learned to think of as living. It did, however, realize that the same sort of damage that had blasted the machines would harm them as well; and that one of the radiances was visibly fading in any case.

It would be interesting, thought the infant rogue, to do something new. It had already removed the radiationless lump of matter from the radiant mass that was Cliff Hawk, using the sleeth as its proxy; that had been disappointing, nothing had happened.

But, it wondered, what if it were to soak up some of that radiation?

It was a notion that attracted the rogue. It did not know why. It had not yet learned to recognize hunger.

14

First the robot required them to wait while it completed its minute of silent adoration, bobbing in its transflection field under the star-embossed dome of the church, its plasma rippling with the colors of devotion. Then it insisted on shepherding each of the children out of the building, locking the doors behind them, searching each empty room and corridor to make sure none had been forgotten. The church was homeostatic, of course; its receptors and pro- prioceptors could have taken care of all of that without attention. Then the robot proposed another delay while it transmitted an apparently endless message to Deneb; and all the while the boy, Rufe, was chattering with questions and eagerness, and Andy Quam's patience had long gone up in wrath. "Robot Inspector," he shouted, "if we're going, let's go! Molly Zaldivar may be in great danger, even dying!"

The robot swung toward him. "Monitor Quamodian," it sang, "patience! I assure you she is alive."

"How do you know?" he demanded.

The robot was silent.

"Preacher," the boy whispered, "leave him alone. That's the way he is. Does things at his own pace. Say! Are you going to ride his back?"

"Almalik! How do I know?" groaned Andy Quam. He glanced at his wrist timepiece, converted rapidly to Ter- restrial equivalents, and hissed with exasperation. "In three hours Starday will be over. I won't need him then! But," he added painfully, tapping his foot on the tiled floor, "Molly needs me *now*."

The robot sang, "Monitor Quamodian, please be silent. I am having a most interesting discussion with three living companions on a planet of Deneb, eight robots and the star 61 Cygni."

"No!" roared Quamodian in astonishment. "You're not chattering away at a time like this! But you promised . . ."

The robot paused. Then, petulantly, "Oh, very well. Perhaps we may as well go, since your noise is disturbing me. Please follow . . ."

But it was too late for following; Andy Quam was al- ready out the door, leaping toward the place where he had left his flyer, and the boy was trailing after him like a comet tail.

"I'll lead the way," sang the robot, raising the amplifica- tion of its external vocalizers until the church facade echoed. "I have instructed your guiding apparatus that the hundred-meter limit may be waived, as part of my voluntary Starday activity, permitted under the com- pact . . ."

Even at ninety decibels Andy Quam didn't hear the end of the sentence; he was already in the flyer, the boy close behind. He slammed the door and shouted, "Let's go! Fol- low that robot!"

359

"All right, Mr. Quamodian," cheerfully agreed the voice of his flyer. "I have my clearance now. Say! Wasn't it nice of the robot inspector to let you . . ."

"Shut up," snarled Andy Quam. "Just fly! I'm in a hurry."

Sulkily the flyer lifted itself off the ground, spun round like a top and aimed itself toward the waiting ovoid that was the robot, hanging in its transflection fields a few meters over the Starchurch. Quamodian muttered a curse as he picked himself up from where the sudden gyration had thrown him, the boy in his lap; but he said nothing to the flyer. "You sit there," he ordered Rufe. "Strap yourself in. Almalik knows what this stupid flyer will do next."

Aggrieved, the flyer began, "That's not fair. Mr. Qua . . ."

"I told you to shut up!"

The flyer shut up, with an audible, and intentional click and rasp of static, and Andy Quam and the boy peered away. It was full night, with bright stars hanging over the hills, though to the west the angry red glare of the swollen, surly sun was still faintly visible, bloodying the sky over the horizon. Suddenly the boy grabbed Quamodian's arm.

"There, preacher! See it? That's where the sunbolts struck."

"I see," Andy Quam ground out. "Flyer, can't we go any faster?"

Resentfully the voice clicked itself on. "No," it said, and clicked off again.

"Now, stop that!" shouted Quamodian. "Why not?"

The flyer relented. "The robot inspector has issued orders for us to follow it," it pointed out. "If I go any faster, it will be following us." Its voice mellowed as it settled down for a nice chat. "You see, Mr. Quamodian," it said, "it is still Starday, and the Robot Inspector does not wish to offend the peace of Starday with a sonic boom. This planet has a rather dense atmosphere, composed principally of oxygen (twenty per cent), nitrogen (eighty per cent), water vapor, carbon dioxide . . ."

"Skip that part! I know Earth's atmosphere!"

"Of course. The point is, Mr. Quamodian, that at these parameters of altitude, temperature and barometric pressure, the sonic barrier occurs at just a bit over our present speed. So you see, no, Mr. Quamodian, we cannot go any faster—and in any event," it added chattily, "we are there."

The flyer deposited them on the side of the mountain; the robot inspector would not allow it any closer to the cave mouth. Andy Quam and the boy piled out, stared upward at the wreck. "Stars, preacher! They really got it!" whispered the boy. "I—I'm afraid Miss Zaldivar was hit."

"We have no such information," sang the robot, humming overhead. "Please wait. I am scanning the area."

But Andy Quam was past the point of caring what the robot inspector wanted. He thrust the boy aside and scrambled up the side of the hill, over uneven ground. He dodged around the wreck of a vehicle—then realized it must be Molly Zaldivar's and stopped, his heart in his mouth, until a frantic search convinced him she was not in it, nor anywhere around. Then up that hill again, his legs pumping, his heart pounding, his breath rasping.

Although in truth, reason was saying in his ear, it was past the time for haste. Whatever destruction had been accomplished here, and it was vast, was long over. Coarse brown smoke oozed from the cave mouth above, and there was a stink of charred plastic and smoldering trash of a thousand kinds. But the fire had burned itself out. No one was in sight.

He paused, his lungs seared with the violence of his breathing, and forced himself to shout, "Molly! Are you here?"

The robot voice sang startlingly from just behind him, "She is fifty meters to your right, Monitor Quamodian, and just above us. But do not approach."

Andy Quam was already on his way, scrambling around the lip of the little ledge before the cave mouth.

"No wait! There are unpredictable entities about, Monitor Quamodian. A beast from space. And—" the singing whine of the robot faltered, "the rogue star. Allow me to study them!"

Andy Quam snorted, but made no other answer. He slid on loose gravel, caught himself and ran on. It was a forty-foot drop, he had just escaped death, but he had not even noticed it in his haste to find Molly Zaldivar. But where was she?

And then he stopped, sliding and waving his arms to keep from falling.

Something like a giant black squid was leaping toward

361

him, up over the rubble and the smoke, shimmering in a pale transflection field. In the dim starlight he caught a glimpse of great blind eyes staring at him, claws that could rip the guts out of a pyropod. "Monitor Quamodian!" sang the robot peremptorily from behind. "That creature is a sleeth. Do not, I caution you, approach it!"

There was suddenly a sour, coppery taste of fear in Quamodian's mouth. A sleeth—now he recalled the stories about those space beasts, evolved for killing, powerful beyond human competition. If it took a mind to attack him there would be no hope.

But it seemed to have no such intention. It hung there studying him, almost as though it had intelligence, even empathy, even understanding of his haste. Then, as though it were giving permission, it lifted up and away on its transflection fields and hung waiting, a hundred meters up, no longer between him and the little hummock where he could see shadowy forms.

He spared the sleeth no more thought, but scrambled, slid and trotted the remaining distance and dropped to his knees beside the girl who had summoned him across half the known universe. "Molly!" he cried. "What's happened? What have they done to you?"

He crooked an arm under her head, raised her tenderly.

And her eyes opened.

She looked at him wonderingly, like a child awakened from sleep. Her face was bloody, scratched, smudged with soot and filth. Her hair was flying loose as chaff on a breeze, and her clothes were shredded into rags. But suddenly and gloriously she smiled at him. "Why, it's little Andy Quam," she whispered. "I should have known you'd come."

The smile lingered, briefly only. Then, without warning, her face twisted, the smile fled, she turned her head away. And Molly Zaldivar wept as though her heart would break.

"Robot Inspector!" shouted Andy Quam. "Where is that fool machine?"

From the side of a boulder, ten feet away, a small voice said querulously, "He's gone, preacher. Just zipped away. Almalik knows where. Didn't say a word."

"What are you doing here, Rufe?" Andy Quam demanded. "You should stay in the flyer. Well, as long as

362

you're here, give me a hand. Miss Zaldivar's been hurt. We've got to get her to help . . ."

A figure disengaged itself from the gloom and stepped closer. "No hurry about that, friend," it rumbled. "She lived through this much, she'll live a while yet."

Quamodian jumped to his feet, ready for anything. He peered into the darkness, caught a glimpse of dulled yellow mustache, dingy yellow beard, a face that looked as though planets had rolled over it in their orbits. "Who the devil are you?" he barked.

"Talk big for a little fellow, don't you?" rasped the voice. "No harm. No hard feelings." He stepped closer and Quamodian got the measure of the size of him, a giant of a man, but oddly subdued. "No one around here wants trouble," he added in a mild bass growl. "Not any more. But the girl's all right, I got her out of the tunnel before she got hurt."

Quam said suspiciously, "I heard something about a Reefer up here with Cliff Hawk, doing Almalik knows what foul work. Are you him?"

"I am."

"Then that's your sleeth watching us up there."

The Reefer's mustache and beard parted company. In the gloom it looked almost as though he were preparing to bite Andy Quam, but it was only a soundless, humorless laugh. "Not mine any more," he declared. "His own by now, I expect. Or—something's. But he won't take orders from me, not since the sun hit us." He turned aside from Andy Quam, bent for a moment over the girl. "She's all right," he said, straightening, but his voice didn't sound very sure. "You might be right about getting her out of here, though. Me too, if you don't mind."

"Why is Molly Zaldivar crying like that?" Quamodian demanded. "If you've hurt her . . ."

The great head shook from side to side. "Nothing I did," he said. "I expect it's Cliff Hawk she's crying about."

Quamodian pulled himself together; he had completely forgotten that Hawk was here! It was his fault, no doubt, that Molly Zaldivar had been hurt, endangered, terrified; yet there was still enough friendship left between Quamodian and Cliff Hawk for Andy Quam's voice to show real concern as he asked, "What about Hawk? Is he hurt?"

"Not any more."

"What? You mean—dead?"

The great voice tolled leadenly. "Not that either. Worse,

363

I'd say. A *lot* worse. And if you want my opinion, we ought to get away from here before something worse happens to us, too."

The Something that had been a random mass of stripped electrons, then an infant rogue star, then a seeking, learning, experimenting entity—and was now something else—"watched" the Reefer and Andy Quam gently lift the weeping girl, carry her down the slope to the flyer, hastily enter, slam the door and race away.

With one part of itself, the rogue caused the sleeth to soar after them on its transflection fields, keeping the flyer effortlessly in view. It was not necessary to do that, of course. The rogue could easily have kept the flyer under observation with its probes, anywhere on the face of this planet and indeed almost anywhere in this solar system. (It had not yet had occasion to try to perceive anything farther away than the planets.)

But it was no longer the simple creature it had been.

When it had perceived that one of the organized radiant masses was in danger of extinction it had occurred to its still simple mind that it might be worth acquiring, and so it had acquired it. It turned out to be easy—a "stretch," a "grasp," a "hold." If it had been matter doing these things, one might have said that it was like the flow of an amoeba, englobing and digesting a tasty bit of food. Matter was not involved, and the forces that the rogue deployed did not lend themselves to description in three-space geometry.

But the effect was the same.

What had once been the persona of Cliff Hawk no longer inhabited its biological body. That body, in fact, was not merely dead but by now an unrecognizable lump of contorted charcoal, mixed with the other charred and destroyed litter in the burned-out tunnel that had once been Hawk's workshop.

But something of him remained. It no longer had identity of its own, as an individual. But it was at least a perceptible fraction of that seething, restless entity that surged through the interstices of the mountain, that followed Andy Quam's flyer in the person of the sleeth, that had brought the wrath of the sun striking down on the summit of the hill, that was a new born rogue star loosed in the universe.

It no longer "thought" in simple urges and observations.

364

Through the trained intelligence of its human component it now could observe, analyze, record—and act.

It sensed the wonder of that far-off watcher.

15

Technically it was still Starday; at the boy's suggestion Andy Quam ordered the flyer to take them to the Starchurch. "There'll be a crowd for late-night services," he said, "and likely enough nobody's going to be where you expect them, otherwise. I mean, even the hospital might not have a crew on duty."

"Shocking," hissed Andy Quam. "To make the Companionship of the Star a pagan ritual!"

"Sure, preacher. Like you say. Only that's the way it is, so you better . . ."

"I understand," said Quam, and gave the flyer its directions. It raised an objection.

"Without the special permission of the robot inspector, Mr. Quamodian," it declared, "I should properly go nowhere except back to the transflex terminal."

"But it's an emergency!"

"Of course, Mr. Quamodian." It hesitated, its neural currents pondering the problem. "Since I cannot contact the robot inspector at the moment," it decided. "I will have to return to the transflex terminal . . ."

"Confound you," shouted Quamodian, "Do what I tell you!"

". . . but en route I will pause briefly at the Starchurch. If you then disembark, it is not a matter under my control."

"Hah!" barked Quamodian in disgust. "Do it, then. But do it fast!"

"It is done, Mr. Quamodian," sighed the flyer, settling to the ground. "I will remain here for one minute. During that time you may do as you wish."

Quamodian wasted no more time in talk. With Rufe and the huge, slow strength of the Reefer, it was no problem to get Molly out of the flyer and settle her gently on the ground. "Are you all right, dear?" Andy Quam asked anxiously. "I'm going for help . . ."

The storm of weeping had passed. Her eyes were open and her face composed, but the weariness of ages was in her eyes. "All right, Andy," she said. "I'm all right anyway, so it doesn't matter."

"Don't talk like that!"

"All right, Andy," she repeated dully, and looked away.

"You stay here with her," he ordered the Reefer, who looked resentful but shrugged. "Rufe, let's find somebody!" And the man and the boy hurried into the Starchurch.

As they entered the great chamber under the blue dome, a gong boomed and echoed. Rufe led the way, up a helical ramp into the dim vast church. The air was alive with the throb of many chanting voices, and sweet with the odor of the fusorian Visitants. The five pointed wings of the place of worship were filled with rising tiers of seats, but every seat was empty. The people were kneeling in concentric circles on the immense floor, beneath the central dome that held the imaged suns of Almalik.

Of the robot inspector there was no sign. His errand, whatever it was, still kept him away.

"I see Molly's aunt!" cried Rufe eagerly, pointing. "Come this way!"

But Quamodian hesitated. "Pagan ritual" he called it, but something in the air held him, awed, faintly envious, half afraid. He raised his eyes to the many-colored splendor of the thirteen suns hung beneath the space-black inside of the dome: six close binaries arranged in three double doubles, one single sun.

Drinking in the blazing beauty of Almalik, breathing the sweetness of the Visitants, swaying to the melodic rhythm of the chanting worshippers, Andy Quam felt a sudden glorious dawn of utter peace and great joy. He wanted to forget himself and the waiting, weary girl outside. His only desire was to forget himself and to be one with Almalik.

"Preacher!" hissed the boy. "Aren't you coming?"

Solemn awe held Quamodian. "Are—are you sure it's all right to interrupt?"

"We won't interrupt. I've been here before for this, to watch, like. With Miss Zaldivar. They don't mind anybody."

Shivering with the strange elation, Quamodian followed the boy out across the vast floor and into the circles of communicants swaying on their knees. The sweetness of the Visitants made him drowsy; the blazing suns of Almalik bathed him in peace.

But the boy had paused before a kneeling man and woman. "Here's her folks, preacher," he said. "Mr. Juan Zaldivar. Mrs. Deirdre Zaldivar." His thin voice rose sharply. "This is Monitor Quamodian."

They stopped their chant. Reluctantly they withdrew their gaze from the multiple splendor of Almalik and, still swaying on their knees, looked incuriously at Andy Quam.

Both glowed with youth and health and joy. Juan was lean and tall and dark, with rich black hair. Blonde, blue-eyed and radiant, Deirdre looked even younger and more lovely than her daughter.

And both wore the mark of Almalik, where the migrating fusorian colony had entered their bodies. Deirdre's was on her blooming cheek, Juan's on his forehead. The marks were tiny irregular star shapes, their edges dissolving into fine branching lines. In the dusk of the starlit dome, the marks glowed softly, warmly golden.

"It's about Molly," Quamodian whispered, hardly daring to break the spell. "She's outside. She's hurt." Incongruous things to say in this sacred peace! He felt more of an interloper than ever, a brute among angels.

In unison, blonde and black, they nodded their heads. Puzzled, Andy Quam started to repeat what he had said, but Deirdre breathed, "There's no hurt that matters in the bosom of the Star. She must join us, and then she will find peace."

"But she's hurt! It's—oh, it's too long to tell you, but she's in terrible danger. We all are!"

"Not here," smiled Juan Zaldivar. He groped for Deirdre's hand; she was already lifting her face to chant again. "Bring her within. The Visitants will make her whole!" And his dark eyes lifted and he joined his wife in the chant.

Rufe bit his lip. "It's no use, preacher," he said somberly. "They're too happy."

Andy Quam looked at him meditatively. It was, after all, not a bad idea to bring Molly inside, he thought. Let the Visitants enter her body with their fusorian healing. She would heal; everyone did. Not merely the scuffs and bruises of her body, but the somber agony of her mind . . .

"Preacher," whispered the boy apprehensively, staring at him.

Quamodian caught himself. "Sorry," he mumbled, and

grabbed the boy's elbow, turned him around, scurried away. He felt a sudden flood of longing that almost stopped him and turned him back, but the boy was leading him now. He stumbled out of the aura of Almalik, down the helical ramp, out of the building as the siren chant faded behind.

Quamodian filled his lungs gratefully with cool dry air that held no lotus odor of the Visitants.

He said sadly, "I wanted to stay. I always want to stay. But it isn't for me—the peace of Almalik." He hurried down the ramp, leaving a vanishing vague regret.

His flyer was gone, but the huge form of the Reefer stood solidly over the reclining body of Molly Zaldivar. The night air felt suddenly chill, and Andy Quam shivered. "What can we do now?" he muttered, half to himself. "What can we do for Molly Zaldivar?"

"My house, preacher," said the boy, Rufe. "It's only down the square, over there. My folks will take her in. I think," he added, sounding worried. Andy Quam glanced at him sharply, but did not question him.

However, there was no one at home in the house to which the boy led them. The door was unlatched. Lights were on. The little cottage's autonomic living systems were purring away, a cheery fire in the hearth, a pleasantly scented breath of air carrying the gentle warmth to every room. But no one was there. "Never mind," sighed the boy, as though he had expected it. "I expect what Miss Zaldivar mostly needs is a little rest right now. Why don't you take her in that room, preacher? And I'll see if I can stir up a little food; you must be hungry."

Fed, warmed, almost relaxed, Andy Quam sat in the cheerful living room. The boy lay on the floor before the fire, his chin in his hands, stretching out now and then for another piece of fruit or a last crumb of the sandwiches he had produced for them. And the Reefer leaned at his ease against the fireplace, answering Quamodian's questions.

They had begun like a prosecuting attorney and defendant; but the Reefer would not accept the role. Defiant, uncaring, mildly contemptuous of everything around him, the Reefer rumbled, "I'll not take the responsibility, Monitor Quamodian. What happens on my land is my business, and those hills are mine."

"Creating rogue life is everyone's business," cried Quamodian.

"But that was not my doing," the big man declared. His scarred face was angry. "Miss Zaldivar is a lovely child. I meant no harm for her. But she had no business trespassing."

"What about Cliff Hawk?"

Under the ragged beard, his mouth set hard. "I brought his mother back from the reefs. He was almost a son to me—but I take no blame for what he has done. Except that I let him go to school, but that wasn't my intention. I wanted him to be another hunter, like me. When he was grown, I planned to take him back to the reefs, find a cub sleeth for him, let him do as I did. But he had to cross the creek. He went to Starday school. He got queer ideas from the robots and the Visitants. Finally he had to go away to space to learn to be what you call a transcience engineer . . ."

"There was nothing wrong with that," declared Quamodian. "I was at the same school. He was a decent human being then."

The Reefer shrugged; then, flinching, touched his arm where it was bandaged. "No matter," he rumbled moodily. "He's paid for it now. He's dead. Or so I think."

"What do you mean, you *think?*" demanded Quamodian. "Is he dead or isn't he?"

The Reefer's deep-set eyes peered at him from under the bushy yellow brows. "He wasn't breathing," he said shortly. "Does that answer your question?"

"Doesn't it?"

The Reefer said helplessly, "I don't know, Monitor, and that's the truth. Oh, Cliff was in bad shape, all right. I didn't give him much chance of lasting more than an hour—less, because we couldn't move him and the fire was coming close. But . . ."

He hesitated. "Boy," he growled, "have you got anything to drink in this place?"

"Just milk. Or water. Or maybe I could make a cup of tea . . ."

The Reefer pursed his lips, shook his head gloomily.

"Go on!" ordered Quamodian.

The Reefer half closed his eyes. "Cliff had been at work in his transcience lab," he droned, apparently bored with the subject. "I knew what he was doing was dangerous, but he's a man grown now. Was. I didn't want to interfere. Then something happened."

The Reefer shifted position, thoughtfully scratched his

369

bushy yellow head. The thick fingers raked through the blond tangles like gangplows through soil, methodically, deeply, mechanically. He said, "It was an explosion. Down below, in the old cryomagnetic and radiation galleries that used to be part of the Plan of Man's military installations. Things the Visitants had failed to destroy. That was the part that I knew was dangerous. Then, while we were putting ourselves together, Molly Zaldivar showed up, crying and threatening Cliff; she'd been scared by my sleeth, so I guess she wasn't accountable. But that was just the beginning. There was a real blowup then. Don't know where. Something winged me—a stray piece of metal, I guess, and I was knocked out for a while."

"I was watching from Wisdom Creek," said Quamodian. "I saw a bolt of plasma strike from the sun, then two more. Is that what it was?"

"I guess." The Reefer scratched again stolidly. "Then I heard Cliff and the girl inside. I went to them. Tried to call my sleeth, but the creature was spooked, acted funny, didn't respond. It never did that before. But there it was, inside the tunnel, trying to get Cliff uncovered. Only it was too late. He was dying. Then . . ."

The Reefer stood up straighter and stopped scratching. A look of real humanity came into his eyes as he said bleakly, "Cliff looked up at me. He said something—couldn't hear what, exactly. It didn't make sense. And he just stopped breathing."

The Reefer turned away, began roaming around the little room. "I don't mean he just died then, Monitor. I've seen men die; they make a little more fuss about it than that. But he just *stopped*. Like he was turned off. And I made sure he was dead, and then I grabbed Molly Zaldivar and got out of there. 'Bout an hour later, you showed up. That's it."

"Not quite," said Andy Quam sharply. "What was it that Cliff said before he died?"

The Reefer stopped, stared angrily at him. "Doesn't matter! It didn't make sense, anyway."

"What was it?"

The Reefer growled wordlessly. The thick fingers plowed into the scalp again, raked it furiously. Then he dropped his hand and said, "Oh, if you must know—it was something like, 'I made it—now it wants me.'"

Quam abruptly shivered, as though a cold blast had
370

found the back of his neck. "What does it mean?" he demanded.

"Nothing! Nothing at all, Monitor! Or anyway—" the Reefer looked away, "nothing that I understand. 'I made it—now it wants me.' Does it mean anything to you?"

Quamodian paused before answering. "I—hope not," he whispered.

The rogue was no longer an infant. Neither was it full grown—call it a youth, becoming steadily larger, each moment finding itself stronger and more skilled than the moment before, feeding upon everything around it that offered energy or mass or patterns to be assimilated.

It had now assimilated a very large number of patterns, sipping at the assorted radiances that surrounded it, and in the process discovering that some were far—"tastier"? —than others. Engorging the identity that had once been Cliff Hawk had been a transcendentally new experience for it, and now it found itself equipped with a thousand new habit patterns, constructs of thought, programmatic drives. They no longer had any relationship to the hundred kilograms of carbon compounds that had been Cliff Hawk's physical body, for that was now an irrelevant blob of spoiled reactions. Hawk's "personality," even, was gone— nothing now remained in the universe that thought his thoughts, remembered his experiences, could recite his opinions. But something of his motives and desires remained as a moment of thrust inside the behavior of the young rogue, shaping the vector result that was its behavior. It was no longer entirely random. In some degree it had become polarized.

What were the other moments of force that played a part in the behavior of the infant rogue? Its own growing knowledge and skills. Its discoveries about the world it lived in. Its innate drive toward growth and mastery. *Move. Grow. Eat,* it had thought, as soon as it could think at all; but now, with the powerful discipline of Cliff Hawk's trained mind permeating its being, it thought more clearly and articulately; it had discovered the convenience of formulating its objectives in language.

I am small but I am growing, thought the maturing rogue star that had been born on earth. *There are other beings which are large but do not grow. I can be more powerful than they.*

And already it had implemented its strength with a

dozen organized masses of matter. The sleeth was now its mind-linked tool; it watched with the rogue's eyes, would act under the rogue's wishes. Tiny crawling and flying things, in the mountain, under the mountain and in the air above it, had all become a part of its extended being. And it had recruited something else.

For the robot inspector had challenged the curiosity of the rogue. It had not been difficult at all for the rogue to swallow it whole, to incorporate the mind analogue of the machine into its own consciousness. The robot still looked as it had, torpedo-shaped metal body and glowing plasma panel; but it was no longer its links with the supercomputers on the planets of the stars of Almalik that gave it its categorical imperatives, but the needs and intentions of the stripped electron plasma that had exploded under the hill.

The rogue toyed with and puzzled over, but did not yet understand that complex linkage of transflection fields which united this new part of its self with distant and more powerful beings. They did not matter at the moment. The distant entities were not powerful enough to resume control against the near and mighty presence of the rogue. And it had other considerations to occupy it.

One was a part of its heritage from the dying mind of Cliff Hawk. Over that too the rogue puzzled, without comprehension.

Why was it that it felt so attracted, so drawn to, so conscious of the presence of that small and unimportant organized mass of thought-radiant matter that Cliff Hawk's mind had identified as "Molly Zaldivar"?

Through the blind, transflex eyes of the sleeth riding high over the cottage where Molly Zaldivar lay sleeping, the mind of the rogue stared down. *Molly Zaldivar,* it thought, *what do I want with you?*

And inside the house Molly started up from sleep and tried to scream. *Sleep,* ordered the rogue; and the girl subsided into the catalepsy of terror. No one had heard her scream; no one was in the house at that moment, and she had not been able to be loud enough to reach those who were outside on the grass, staring up at the sleeth.

The boy said, awed, "Mister, that's a wicked-looking beast. You sure it won't hurt us?"

The Reefer barked a savage laugh. "Not any more, boy," he rumbled. "Time was that sleeth would follow

372

me like a kitten. Do everything I wanted it to, never think of disobeying—I raised it from a cub, it never knew any boss but me. But now it does." He studied the sleeth thoughtfully for a moment. As it hung in the sky on its shimmering transflection fields, the great black creature looked like some wingless Pegasus astride the air, its dangling claws capable of wrenching any carbon-based, air-breathing, muscle-powered animal in two as readily as a hawk's talons rend fur. "Fine beast," he said. "But not mine any more."

Andy Quam said angrily, "Why did you bring it here? This sort of animal doesn't belong on a planet!"

"Why, because it's mine, Monitor Quamodian," the Reefer said simply. "I'm a hunter, and it's my companion. It goes wherever I go. Or used to. Why," he cried, suddenly enthusiastic, "with that sleeth I collected the finest specimens of every game animal in the solar system! You should have seen them. A score of fine pyropods. Darkbeasts from out past the reefs, moonbats, creatures from the hot deeps of Venus—there was nothing in a dozen light-years could touch that sleeth as a killer!"

Andy Quam said in disgust, "You talk as though killing were a good thing. Violence is evil. The laws of Almalik do not permit the destruction of life by life!"

The Reefer's deep eyes twinkled. "And would you never take a life, Monitor Quamodian? Not even, say, to save Miss Zaldivar?"

Andy Quam flushed. "We Companions are exempt from certain of Almalik's laws," he said stiffly. "We may even admit violence, in some situations."

"Then help me!" cried the Reefer. "I'm going to stalk something new, Monitor Quamodian, and you can join me in the hunt. I don't know what it is that's controlling my sleeth, but I'm going to take its pelt to put in my collection!"

"Nonsense," cried Andy Quam, startled. "Why—great Almalik, man—I mean, how can you? Don't you realize that that's probably a rogue star?"

The Reefer's laughter boomed. "Scare you, Monitor Quamodian?"

"No! Or—yes, maybe. I don't think it is unreasonable of a mere human being to question his ability to deal with a star!"

The boy, who had been watching them silently, turning from face to face, coughed and interrupted. Changing the subject he said, "Say, preacher! What's the matter with the moon?"

A dozen degrees over the horizon the gibbous moon floated, almost invisible, so dark a red was it. It was leprously stained and discolored, by no means the brilliant white fat crescent it should have appeared.

"It's the sun," said Andy Quam gloomily. "Remember how red and angry-looking it was when it set? After those sunbolts struck? The moon's just reflecting it. And this man thinks he can destroy the thing that did that!"

"Worth a try, Monitor," boomed the Reefer cheerfully. "Mind if I borrow your flyer?"

"For what?"

"Why, for the hunt. It's a bit of a walk from here to the hills on foot," the Reefer apologized. "As I don't have the sleeth to take me there any more, I'd appreciate the use of your flyer. It's long past Starday now, no reason not to use it."

Rufe cried out sharply. "Preacher! Listen—what's that sound?"

Quamodian raised his hand imperiously, silencing the Reefer's booming voice. They listened. Then Quam's face twisted. "It's Molly," he cried, turning to run toward the house. "She's calling my name!"

But when Andy Quam burst through the door of the girl's room she was lying wide-awake, looking at the ceiling. Slowly she lowered her eyes to look at him. "Andy," she said. "I should have known you'd come. I've always been able to rely on you."

Quamodian's ears burned. "Are you all right?" he demanded. "I heard you calling . . ."

She sat up on the edge of the bed. "All right? I suppose so." Her face was a mask of tragedy for a moment. "Poor Cliff," she whispered. "It's strange! I thought he was talking to me, in my dream. But it wasn't really him—it was something huge and strange. A monster." She shook herself.

Then, gloriously, she smiled. There was tragedy beneath the smile, but it was clear to Andy Quàm that she was making an effort to be cheerful. "I dragged you all the way across space," she said. "I'm sorry. I've always been a trouble to you, Andy dear."

"Never a trouble," he said, speaking from a depth of passion that shook him. Molly was touched. She reached

374

out and patted his arm. "Is there anything to eat?" she asked, incongruously. "It's been a long time!"

Rufe was happy to oblige when Quamodian relayed the girl's request to him, producing more sandwiches and milk, a seemingly inexhaustible supply of food. "Won't your family mind you taking us in like this?" asked Andy Quam. "We're eating you out of house and home!"

The boy's face clouded. "It's all right, preacher," he said.

Quamodian frowned at him. "Come to think of it," he said, "where are your family? It's pretty late for them to be at the Starchurch."

"Oh, they're not there any more. They—they've gone away for a while."

Andy Quam stopped in the middle of the humming little kitchen, busy generating new supplies of bread and milk and meats to replace those the boy had drawn from its programs, and said firmly, "You're hiding something, Rufe. Why?"

"Aw, don't ask me, preacher. It's just—well, it's kind of private."

But then Molly Zaldivar came out of her room, looking remarkably refreshed and restored, and Andy Quam let the matter drop.

For half an hour they were all at ease, Molly as friendly and affectionate as ever in the old days on Exion Four, the boy beside himself with pleasure at pleasing Molly, even the Reefer almost jolly. The huge man from space demanded to know whether Quamodian would join him in his hunt for the rogue. For a moment, in that warm room, it almost seemed like a reasonable idea, and Quamodian let himself think about it—a long chase, a view-hallo, the quarry at bay. But it was fantasy. This was no beast of the forest but an inimical creature of linked plasmas whose size and might were utterly incomprehensible to humans. To hunt it was like setting a snare for a supernova.

Then Andy Quam saw Molly hiding a yawn, and realized with a start how utterly exhausted he was. "Let's get some sleep," he ordered, and fussed over them all until they had sorted themselves out into various rooms. Only then did Quamodian let himself sprawl out on the couch in the living room, the door to Molly's room just past his head, ready to spring up at any alarm.

It had been a good many hours, and a good many millions of parsecs, since he had slept. When he closed his eyes he was unconscious almost at once, and slept like the dead.

16

Where was the rogue? As well try to fix the position of an electron in its blurred orbit around a nucleus; it was under the hill and in it, suffusing the skies around, inhabiting the body of the sleeth that soared tirelessly and patiently over the house where Molly Zaldivar slept, penetrating and entering every hidden place within hundreds of miles, and reaching out into near space.

But if its position had no exact geographic boundaries, at least there were loci of special consequence. It did, for example, occupy the great animal bulk of the sleeth. It concentrated at least a sizeable part of its being in the electron cloud that seeped through the rock and clay of the base of the hill. And it found other special areas of interest to toy with.

It found, for one, the antique handling machine that Cliff Hawk had used to help him construct his tunnel workshop. It was a minor puzzle to the rogue, but a faintly interesting one; the machine had obvious purpose, and it spent some moments working out that purpose and how to achieve it. Then, the machine solved, it spent a few moments now in what can only be called pleasure. *Power in motors*, it thought. *My power. Spin gears. Drive through rubble.* It reached out with its metal arms and picked up bits of debris—a yellow cylinder of helium, the half of a thousand-pound armature, bent out of shape in the explosions. It threw them about recklessly, madly . . .

Then it had had all it could enjoy of that particular game, and turned to another.

The robot inspector was a greater puzzle, but a lesser plaything. It was no particular joy to operate, since its transflection drives were too similar to the sleeth's, or the rogue's own, to be novel. But the rogue was aware that somehow the robot had been guided by other influences, far away, and that some part of it was still trying to respond to those influences as their messages crackled into its receptors. They were an irritation to the rogue, these repetitious exhortations on behalf of the star Almalik; it did not like them.

It had, by now, begun to acquire emotion.

One particular emotion troubled it, that inexplicable urging toward Molly Zaldivar which it had felt, ever more strongly, as Cliff Hawk's patterns of thought asserted themselves and fitted themselves into the organization of the rogue's own habit-structure. The rogue did not find this incongruous. It had no standards by which to judge incongruity. But it found it troubling.

There was a solution to things which were troubling. It could act on the impulse, and see what came of it.

It could attempt to add Molly Zaldivar to itself.

17

"Mol-ly. Mol-ly Zaaal-di-var . . ."

Molly woke slowly, surfacing inch by inch from sleep. She was unwilling to wake up. Sleeping though she was, a part of her mind remembered what waking would bring back to her in utter, unwanted clarity. Cliff's death, the birth of the rogue, the terrible danger that the man she loved had unloosed on the universe.

"Mol-ly . . ."

But someone was calling her name. Resentfully she opened her eyes and looked around.

No one was in the room. It was still dark; she had not slept for more than an hour or two.

"Who is it?" she whispered. No response. Molly shivered. It was eerie, that disembodied voice, unlike any she had ever heard. It was impossible to dismiss it as the ragged end of a dream, half remembered on waking; it was real enough. It was even more impossible to ignore it and go back to sleep.

Molly stood up, threw the robe Rufe had found for her over her shoulders, and padded to the door of her room. She opened it just a crack. There was the living room, with Andy Quam asleep on the couch. He stirred painfully as she looked at him, grimaced, mumbled some sleep-evoked phrase and was still again—all without opening his eyes. Poor Andy, she thought warmly, and sadly; and closed the door without sound.

Whoever had called her, it was not Andy Quam.

She went to the window, threw back the curtains—and gasped in terror.

There it was, hovering just outside the double French panes on its shimmering transflection fields.

The sleeth!

The great blind eyes stared emptily at her, the metal-tipped claws caught reflections of cold fire from the sinking moon. The shimmering field pulsed rapidly, and from the pane of glass she caught the faint vibration of sound that had called her from sleep: "Mol-ly. Come. I—want—you."

For an instant stark terror flooded her, and she half turned to run, to shake Andy Quam awake and beg for protection against this fantastic monster that called her name. But the utter wondrousness of it held her. The sleeth could not speak; nothing the Reefer had said about it gave it a voice. Nor could it have known her name, not in any way that she could hope to understand. And anyway, the sleeth was no longer even an animal in its own independent right; it was only a captive of the thing that Cliff Hawk had made, and had been killed by.

She flung open one side of the French window. She didn't know why; obviously, if the creature intended her harm, the flimsy glass and frame could not protect her. "What—what do you want?" she breathed.

But it only repeated, "Mol-ly. Mol-ly, come."

The sound came from the glass itself, she discovered; somehow the creature was vibrating to form frequencies that she could hear as words. It was even stranger, she thought, than if it had suddenly formed lips, palate and tongue and spoken to her.

It was terrifying. Worse than terrifying; without warning, she was filled with a revulsion so fierce that she almost screamed with the pain of it.

"No," she whispered. "No!" and closed the window.

"Come," sang the sleeth—or whatever it was that controlled the sleeth. The huge creature danced patiently on its shimmering fields, waiting for her to accede to its demand. "Come," said the tinny, bodiless voice again. "Mol-ly. Come."

Insane to be talking to this thing, in a perfectly ordinary room, through a perfectly normal window! "No!" she said strongly. "Go away!"

Did the thing understand her words? She had no way

378

of knowing. It merely hung there silently for a moment, regarding her with those great blind eyes.

Then it moved, slowly and remorselessly, like a Juggernaut. It bobbed silently forward, thrusting the unopened window out of the way as though it were air. An almost soundless crack and a faint patter of shattered glass on the carpet were the only noise it made as it came toward her.

The great, deadly claws reached for her.

Molly drew a breath to scream, tried to turn and run . . .

Something bright and murderous flashed from those blind eyes. It was like an instant anesthetic, like a blow from behind that drives out awareness before the mind quite realizes it has been struck. Down went Molly Zaldivar into paralysis and dark, stunned and helpless. She felt herself falling, falling, falling . . .

The last thing she remembered was those great claws grasping her. Incredible, she thought, they don't hurt . . .

And then the world closed in around her.

Quamodian woke painfully in broad daylight that poured through the windows. He found himself on a couch, with a synthetic copy of some animal fur over him for warmth, his head throbbing, his bones aching. He felt vaguely ill, and for a moment could not recall where he was.

Then he remembered. The enigma of the sunbolts. The nightmare of the Reefer and the sleeth. The death of Cliff Hawk. The birth of the rogue . . .

He forced himself to sit up and look at the world around him.

Pinned to the arm of the couch was a note, scrawled with a photoscriber in a huge, clumsy hand:

Preacher, I didn't want to wake you. I went to tell Miss Zaldivar's folks she's all right. Meet you there if you want. P.S., I left everybody sleeping because I thought you all needed it. Food in the kitchen.

Rufe

Sleeping they still were, to judge from the mighty rasping snores that came from the little cubicle Rufe had given the Reefer. There was no sound at all from Molly's room. Andy Quam hesitated, his hand on the door; but there was no sense disturbing her, and surely nothing could have got past him to harm her in the night . . .

He left the house and stepped out into the bright morning.

Bright it was. Yet, thought Andy Quam, there was something strange about it, and in a moment he realized what it was. The colors were wrong. There was no cloud in the sky, but the air had a lowering quality, as of storm clouds. He squinted up at the sun and perceived the reason.

Red, sullen, blotched, the disk of the sun still had not recovered from whatever had roiled it yesterday. It was not the familiar sun of Earth, as men had portrayed it in a thousand books and songs. It was somehow like the snake-haired sun of that far world where he had left Clothilde Kwai Kwich.

He limped across a wide square, reviving somewhat as he moved. It had been a strenuous day. And a worrisome one, he thought, remembering with wrinkled brow all the unanswered problems and unmet challenges it had offered.

Perhaps this new day would clear some of them up, he thought—but without much confidence.

He gave the Starchurch a wide berth, hailed a passing citizen and found himself directed to the home of Molly Zaldivar's parents. It was past the Central Municipal Plexus, he discovered, which fit in well enough with his plans; he could use more information if he could get it.

But the Central Municipal Plexus did not turn out to be the combination library-town hall he had expected.

He walked across a queerly perfect circle of stained and blackened cement. It was puzzling, it seemed to have no place in this countrified idyll of a town. Immediately a recorded voice spoke to him:

"Welcome, guest! You have landed at Wisdom Creek Historical Monument. It is a section of the original village of Wisdom Creek, reconstructed exactly as it was on the winter day, many years ago, when the Visitants first arrived."

Andy Quam spoke up, addressing his remarks to thin air, for there was no speaker in sight. "I don't want a historical tour," he snapped. "I want some information."

But there was no response. This was a low-grade programmed instructor, he realized with irritation. Not even homeostatic, merely programmed to respond to his mass-sensed presence with a recorded lecture. He walked through a thick gate . . .

380

And found himself in something that, for a startled moment, made him think he was in Hell. The air stung his eyes. It choked him, with a reek of industrial fumes and imperfectly oxidized mineral fuels. Blinking and squinting, he made out that he was surrounded by grimy rows of hideous little brick and wooden huts.

Far down a street was a human figure, faced away from him and motionless. Vexed, Andy Quam stamped toward it, ignoring the revolting spectacle around him.

He approached a squat gray pile of concrete on which was etched the legend, *Plan of Man*. A voice from the air cried brightly: "Welcome guest! This structure, a part of the Central Municipal Plexus Exhibit, represents a primitive Tax Office. Here each citizen reported to the Plan of Man the number of tokens he had received for his work in the previous sidereal year, whereupon he was forced to give up a share of them. Here too was the ration office, where he received permission to barter what tokens he had left for articles of clothing and other necessities. Here too was the draft office, where young men and women were impressed for training in the use of crude but adequate weapons of the time. Here too was that most central and fundamental institution, the Planning Office, where every action of every citizen was dictated and reviewed and corrected by a primitive central computer. Here, guest, was the very nerve center of the fundamental coercive apparatus of the state!"

Andy Quam trudged grimly on, ignoring the sensless prattle. There was entirely too much realism in this exhibit for his comfort, he thought with distaste. The very air was polluted with the hydrocarbons and fly-ash and photochemicals of primitive combustion products. And the man he was approaching was oddly dressed in what must have been the costume of the time: a thick fiber uniform, a brutally chopped haircut, something about his neck which looked like a massive metal collar, certainly too heavy and too tight to be comfortable. He stood stark still facing the entrance of the building, his right arm raised in a motionless salute.

"Excuse me," called Andy Quam. "Can you help me find the home of Juan Zaldivar?"

He caught himself, realizing at once that it was only a lifelike dummy. Another recording explained cheerfully:

"The human form you see, guest, is the replica of a Risk.

381

So self-directed men and women were designated. The iron collar worn by each Risk contained an explosive decapitation charge, which could be detonated instantly by the Planning Machine in the event of any suspect action."

Soberly, stiffly, the figure dropped its salute, turned until its mass-sensors located Andy Quam and haltingly bowed. "Oh, great Almalik!" cried Quamodian, exasperated. "All I want is directions! How can I reach the home of Mr. and Mrs. Zaldivar?"

Silence, except for the questioning hum of a carrier signal.

"Isn't *anybody* listening?" he shouted.

Silence again, then, doubtfully, "Guest, you are invited to return to the Wisdom Creek Historical Monument, which has been restored and maintained by the Companions of the Star for public information."

"I *am* a Companion of the Star! I am Monitor Andreas Quamodian, and I insist on your answering my question!"

Silence once more. "We hope you found the exhibits instructive," sighed the recorded voice at last. Its programming clearly was not up to any question not pertaining to the exhibits themselves. Angrily Quam turned away and retraced his steps.

Half an hour and many moments of lost temper later, he finally found Juan Zaldivar at the edge of a field, busy adjusting a green-cased farm machine. A relaxed and handsome athlete, now alert and free from the hypnosis of the Starchurch reverie, he flashed his white teeth at Quamodian with an inquiring smile.

"I'm concerned about Molly," Quamodian began.

"So am I," Zaldivar nodded quickly. "Her course is dangerous and evil. Yet Almalik forbids any compulsion toward salvation. She must make her own mind up to accept the Visitants . . ."

"No, not that!" cried Andy Quam. "Do you realize she has been very nearly killed by what I suspect is a rogue star?"

Juan Zaldivar looked genuinely shocked. "How terrible!" he cried. "We must do something at once! You must tell her that her one protection is in Almalik. She can delay no longer!"

"No, no," groaned Quamodian. "Listen to me, Zaldivar! It's no longer a matter of just Molly, it's the whole Companionship of the Stars, the universe itself that's threatened. Have you any notion of what a rogue star can do? Look at the sun!"

He gestured at the red and swollen disk, high in the heavens but looking like a stormy dusk. Zaldivar glanced at it through squinted eyes, with an expression of mild inquiry. "Curious," he said, nodding.

"More than curious! Deadly! Dangerous!"

"To Molly?" asked Zaldivar, politely perplexed. "I do not entirely follow you, Monitor Quamodian. But if you are saying now, as you seemed to be denying a moment ago, that Molly is in danger, why, yes, I agree. She is. So are you. So are all who have not accepted the Star, as signified by receiving the Visitants into their bodies."

Andy Quam took a deep breath and controlled himself. The Peace of Almalik, he reminded himself, was a great gift to mankind. Unfortunately those who accepted it—though of course blessed beyond all other men in their health, their joy, their star-given peace—were sometimes hard to deal with, hard to arouse to needed action. But that, of course, was why those like himself, the Monitors and the other free-acting agents of the Star, could not accept the Visitants. He should have known all that; he should have learned to accept it . . .

He said, keeping his temper, "Juan Zaldivar, I ask you to do something for me in the name of Almalik. Since you are in contact with the sentient stars by means of the Visitants, I want you to pass on to them my warning about the creation of the rogue star."

"I have done so," said Zaldivar benignly. "Almalik knows all that I know."

"Good," sighed Andy Quam. He felt a brief relief, a sense of awe at the fleeting vision of all the wisdom and power of the multiple citizen Cygnus, the minds of numberless sentient suns and transcience robots and perfected men knitted together by the fusorian Visitants. "Now," he said, "there's a puzzle you must help me solve. I want to know why that sunbolt struck yesterday. Is Almalik responsible?"

Zaldivar squinted again, then shook his head gravely. "No," he declaimed, "the release of the sunbolt was a violent action. According to our information it destroyed much equipment and contributed to at least one human death. As Almalik is nonviolent, we are clearly not responsible."

383

Quamodian peered at him. "Was it the rogue that was responsible?"

Juan Zaldivar said serenely, "In that, Monitor Quamodian, we are not concerned. We will not resist."

"But you're in danger! Even the sentient stars are in danger, if an intellectic creature hostile to them is loose in this galaxy!"

"We will not resist," repeated Juan Zaldivar. "Acting in violence, we should destroy ourselves." And, gently murmuring an apology, he returned to adjust his farm machine.

The boy's message had said he would be at the Zaldivar's home, but he was not in sight. No one was; the dwelling door stood open, but no one answered Andy Quam's call.

There was a crooning, placid, musical drone coming from somewhere above. Quamodian followed the sound, and doors opened before him as the homeostatic dwelling invited him in, up a moving slideramp, to a roof garden.

There sat Deirdre Zaldivar, greeting the morning by playing an instrument which transformed her emotions into art, spinning them into melodious sound, colored form, subtle scent. She greeted him, smiling. Youthful as Molly, her beauty unmarred by the golden star that blazed on her cheek, she was absorbed in her art and reluctant to be disturbed.

"Rufe? Oh, yes, Monitor Quamodian. I know Rufe. But he's not here."

"That's odd, Mrs. Zaldivar," Andy Quam frowned. "He said he'd meet me here. Did he say anything to you?"

Deirdre Zaldivar plucked a strumming chord of sound negligently, watched a pinkish bubble of color grow, turn rose, and then red, then darken into invisibility. "Why, no, Monitor Quamodian. We haven't heard from Rufe, have we?"

She looked inquiringly past Andy Quam. Disconcerted, he turned, and there was the sleek black egg shape of a transcience robot floating over a bed of talisman roses. "Robot Inspector?" he said uncertainly. "I—I didn't notice you were here."

The robot's pulsating plasma oval shimmered brightly. "I am not the robot inspector, Monitor Quamodian," it sang in its high, sweet voice. "That unit is no longer operational. I am its deputy."

384

"Not operational?"

"It has been disjoined, Monitor Quamodian," hummed the robot placidly. "I have, however, access to all its memory up to the point at which disjunction occurred, so that for all practical purposes you may regard us as the same. Do you wish to employ my services?"

"No," said Andy Quam. "Or—yes. I think so. But I wanted to speak to Mrs. Zaldivar first. Molly has been injured, but she is now resting peacefully. I think she is all right—but in danger, I'm afraid."

Deirdre Zaldivar looked politely concerned. "Too bad," she said regretfully. "She is such a dear girl. But—" she shrugged, smiling at the deputy robot, "she is not yet a member of the Star, of course. Like all nonmembers, she is exposed to the hazards of independent existence." She returned to the console of her instrument and, with a quick run across the keys, built a splendid tower of scent and color and color and sound. "When Molly accepts the Visitants, Monitor Quamodian," she said, watching her composition grow and drift, "everything will be all right. Everything is always all right in the Companionship of the Star."

Andy Quam's exasperation pressure was building again. He could feel it compressing his brows, grinding his jaws together. He turned to the robot and snapped. "You, then. I want some facts. What happened to the sun?"

"In what respect, Monitor Quamodian?" sang the robot politely.

"Its appearance—look at it! And the plasma bolts it threw at the Earth yesterday. Why?"

"We have no information," reported the robot regretfully.

"Is it true that the multiple citizen Cygnus is not responsibile?"

"Quite true, Monitor Quamodian," agreed the robot, its high voice sounding disapproving of the question. "Almalik informs us that this fact was already reported to you by Juan Zaldivar. You are aware that the citizen Cygnus will engage in no violence."

"Then, what about the sun? Has—" the thought suddenly erupted in his mind, almost choking him, "has a rogue intellect been established in this star?"

The star Sol," sang the robot, "is not a member of the multiple citizen Cygnus, nor has it ever entered into association with any part of the civilized universe. We have no other information about its intellectual status."

"Its abnormal behavior is dangerous to this planet and to all the members of Cygnus on it," protested Andy Quam. "One human being has died already. I fear this danger may extend to the sentient stars of Cygnus."

"Almalik is informed," hummed the robot serenely. "The sentient stars are not alarmed."

"*I* am alarmed!" cried Andy Quam. "I require your assistance!"

The robot floated toward him, its plasma oval glowing brightly. "That is your right, Monitor Quamodian," it conceded sweetly. "As long as there is no conflict with the prime directives of Almalik."

"Fine!" snapped Andy Quam. "Begin by informing Almalik of my concern. State that I regard it as absolutely urgent that action be taken!"

"What action, Monitor Quamodian?" asked the robot solicitously.

Quamodian was ready for that. "Request Almalik to review my reports on Solo Scott and on Cliff Hawk's rogue star," he said briskly. "Urge Almalik to contact Clothilde Kwai Kwich. Ask Almalik to suggest alternative routes of additional action."

"But I have done so, Monitor Quamodian," sang the voice of the robot.

"We have no new information about Monitor Kwai Kwich, and no action to suggest!"

Quamodian glared at it furiously. What he might have said next might have cost him lasting regret; but he never had a chance to say it. From down below he heard a high-pitched shout, repeated, calling his name. "Preacher! Preacher, are you there?"

Quamodian sprang to the slideramp, peered down. "Is that you, Rufe?" he called.

The boy appeared, face grimed with tears and sobbing. "Oh, preacher!" he groaned. "It's Miss Zaldivar! She's gone!"

Quamodian's blood seemed to turn cold in his body; time stopped. "Gone? Gone where, boy?"

"I don't know, preacher. I—I think that thing must've come and taken her away!"

The world seemed to turn black around Andy Quam. The boy's voice dissipated like smoke, leaving a thin and fading wisp of terror behind it. Quamodian shuddered, shook himself, tried to think. But thought was beyond him at that moment; he had to act. He grasped the handrail and started to run down the slideramp, against its movement, not waiting for the sensors to detect his presence and respond by reversing the movement of the ramp.

From behind him the voice of the robot, its amplitude raised almost to the point of pain, thundered like the diapason of a giant organ: "Monitor Quamodian, wait! I must ask your intention!"

Quamodian halted, shook himself, half turned, "Intention?" he repeated. "Why—why, I'm going to get her back!"

"In what way, Monitor Quamodian?" roared the robot.

"Why—" Andy Quam thought, then realized he had known the answer all along. "With the Reefer!" he cried. "We're going to hunt that thing down and destroy it!"

The robot's voice, volume somewhat reduced but still an uncomfortable shrill knife edge in the eardrums, trumpeted: "Violence, Monitor Quamodian. You are speaking of violence. The Companions of Almalik cannot support such an expedition!"

"I can!" cried Andy Quam. "I'm a Companion! Our organization exists for this very reason—that we are free to do things for the members of the multiple citizen Cygnus that they are not free to do themselves."

The robot's black egg floated swiftly toward him. "In the past," it sang, volume reduced almost to normal, whining now, "this was true. But it is known that certain Companions have engaged in undue violence in the name of Almalik. This is a serious error, Monitor Quamodian! In consequence the status of the organization has been reviewed. Although certain freedoms of information and persuasion will remain to the Companions, all use of violence is herefrom prohibited."

Quamodian jumped back in dismay, knocking over a crystal ornament in the shape of a leaping flame; it shattered on the floor, and the robot licked out a flickering tongue of pale plasma to gather up the fragments. "That's impossible!" Quamodian gasped. "We have—we must have freedom to defend the members of the citizen!"

"We do not resist," the robot purred serenely. "That is the prime ethic of the Visitants. The Companions may no longer resist in our name."

Andy Quam hesitated, glanced down at the white, watching face of the boy, kicked a shard of crystal across

the room, then abruptly turned and started down the
ramp.

"Monitor Quamodian!" sang the robot. "Monitor Quamodian, you have been informed!"

Andy Quam growled wordlessly in his throat and continued. The robot raised its amplitude deafeningly again.
"Monitor Quamodian! We demand to know! What is
your intention?"

Andy Quam paused just long enough to turn. "What
I said!" he shouted defiantly. "I'm going to destroy that
thing—with your permission or without it!"

18

In the old Plan of Man cave under the Reefer's hill, the
hot bright cloud of plasma had long since dissipated.
The womb from which the rogue star had been born was
quiet now, no longer fed by the driving energies Cliff
Hawk had tapped. But the air still reeked of ionization
and burned copper points; the autonomic lighting system
flickered unreliably, and the shadows were dark.

Where the great bulk of the sleeth had dropped Molly
Zaldivar, the pale cloud of stripped electrons that was
the heart of the rogue hung meditatively over her. It
had sent the sleeth away; Molly feared it, and something
inside the rogue's stored systems recognized that fear.
But the girl lay sobbing on the cold concrete of the floor,
and some other "instinct" commanded the rogue to make
her more comfortable.

Move her. Make her safe, thought the rogue, and
hunted among its recently discovered options for a way
to do it. At length (some dozens of picoseconds later)
it opted for another of its toys, the rusty old handling machine that Hawk had sometimes employed. It was as easy
to manipulate as Molly's old electrocar, and slowly and
painfully the rogue caused it to crunch on its cleated tracks
toward the cave entrance, to come in and approach the
recumbent girl.

The operation of the handling machine, easy enough
in principle, required a certain continuity of operation
to which the rogue was not accustomed; its time-response

was creepingly slow, its progress over the rock and rubble of the hillside and cave was intolerable. The rogue rested, drank mass from the air and strength from the stone, then rolled on again.

The girl scrambled to her hands and knees, staring wildly at the clanking machine.

The rogue paused, and tried again its exercises in human language. Speaking through the circuits of the machine's radio, it rasped: "Molly Zaldivar. How can I cause you to love me?"

Molly's eyes widened. "Nightmare!" she cried. "Monster! What are you?"

Painfully the rogue modulated the radio's circuits to reply. "Why am I—a nightmare? Why do you not love me? I—love you, Molly Zaldivar!"

Faintly, far away, it felt that watcher's growing fear.

Despairing, the girl rose, tried to flee; but it was easy for the rogue to reach out with the handling machine's effectors, catch her, and draw her back. She shrieked. The rogue paused, considering. It was difficult to comprehend the processes that affected organized matter. Yet the green radiance that flowed around her was suddenly shot with flashes of red which the rogue recognized as—not "pain," for it had not been able to relate those memories in Cliff Hawk's mind to anything in its own experience; but to a malfunction of some sort, and it was only a step to realize that the malfunction was caused by the harsh grasp of the handling machine on the girl's relatively weak body.

The rogue deposited her as gently as it could on the floor of its cab, and methodically analyzed its findings. It was a long process, requiring more than one microsecond; there was much that it had to deduce or interpolate. Even its own actions were not entirely clear to the rogue; it had no well-formed referent for the term "love," though it had felt quite strongly that this was the proper operator to describe its relationship to Molly Zaldivar. Casually and quickly it detached a section of itself and entered the brain and nervous system of Molly Zaldivar, studying as it went, attempting to sort out the damage that had been done. It seemed quite small, the rogue considered; only a few hundred thousand cells were damaged, and a relatively small proportion of them destroyed. It made a few adjustments which had the effect of stopping the efflux of circulatory fluid, rejoining some separated vessels and ligaments and, contented with its work, exited the girl's body and reassembled itself.

The girl, aware that something was happening but unable to know what, was very close to hysteria. She fumbled about the floor of the cab, pulled herself to the seat, hammered feebly against the windows; orange terror flashed through the radiance that surrounded her, and the rogue tried to speak to her again:

"Why do you struggle, Molly Zaldivar? Why do you not love me?"

Molly threw herself back on the seat with a ragged laugh. "Love? You can't love!"

"I do love, Molly Zaldivar. Why am I a nightmare?"

She shuddered, forcing herself to speak. "Why? Because you don't have a right to exist, monster! You are a synthetic intellect. The transflection patterns of your mind were created in a cloud of plasma by Cliff Hawk and the Reefer . . ."

When she spoke of Cliff Hawk a golden glow lighted her mind's radiance.

The rogue said: "I am Cliff Hawk."

"You?" The girl caught her breath; she was shaking all over now, half in terror, half in utter uncomprehending bewilderment. "Cliff is dead! I saw him die."

"Yes. Dead. But I am that of Cliff Hawk which survives at all. Cliff Hawk is a member of me. And you must love me."

The girl abandoned herself to a storm of weeping. After some thought, the rogue re-entered her mind, sought for and found certain centers it had learned to recognize and caused her to go to sleep. It then paused and considered what it knew about the maintenance of organic masses of organized matter. This was, in truth, very little; but certain peremptory needs were clear. The girl would need protection against the elements and a place to rest. She would need air for combustion, the rogue thought, and observed that this was in adequate supply from the ambient atmosphere; she would need liquid H_2O, easily procured nearby. And she would also need metabolizable chemicals of the class it described by the vaguely comprehended label "food."

All these matters it determined to deal with. First it opened the door of its cab. Then it sought out and re-entered the sleeth, hovering half stunned and bewildered over the hilltop, and brought it arrowing swiftly back

390

into the tunnel. The sleeth's great body felt supple and powerful after the clanking paralytic environment of the handling machine; the rogue caused it to soar into the mouth of the tunnel, hurtle down a straightway, round a curve and join the group. It felt joy in the strength of the great muscles, delight in the silent power of its transflection fields, pleasure even in the dreadful radiation that it could evoke from the huge blind eyes. It lifted the girl's sleeping body in the deadly, gentle claws and traced a tightening curve along the tunnel's way, into the mountain and down, until it found a pit that it had not previously observed.

The rogue paused, probing the dark space at the bottom of the pit. It found nothing hostile, nothing of organized organic matter. It was, in fact, a long-forgotten base of the scientific establishment of the Plan of Man; the rogue had no notion what that meant, and still less interest.

Careful with Molly, holding her cuddled against the great sleek belly of the sleeth, it dropped into the dark, drifting slowly downward past the vertical walls, until it dropped out of darkness into a cold, ghostly light. They were in a huge sphere hollowed in the rock at the base of the hill. Once multiplying neutrons had flashed through and saturated a few kilograms of fissionable metal, the nuclear explosion had blossomed and shrugged tens of thousands of tons of rock away, melting the inner shell and holding it suspended, like a balloon, long enough for the dome shape to form. As the pressure leaked away the plastic rock hardened, and what was left was this great ball-shaped cave.

The pale light came from all about it, especially from a pale cold sun of milky mist that hung at the center of the hollow. A spiral staircase, skeletal metal treads and a handrail, wound upward inside a spidery steel tower from the bottom of the globular cavity's floor to a railed platform half inside that high, pale cloud of opal light.

What was the hollow?

What was the light?

The rogue gave those questions no consideration. Tenderly it set Molly Zaldivar down on the bottom of the hollow and allowed her to waken.

To the extent that the nonhuman intelligence of the rogue was capable of satisfaction, it was now pleased with what it had done. It had removed the person of the oddly attractive organized bit of matter called Molly Zaldivar to a place where it would not be harmed by outside activities, and where its own attempts to establish communication could go on without interference. It was a place whose chemistry, pressure and temperature appeared to be compatible with life, as far as the rogue was able to judge.

Of course, the rogue was still comparatively young in time, lacking experience, and even with the absorbed patterns that were all that was left of Cliff Hawk embodied in its own systems, it had no very deep understanding of biological chemistry.

An attractive feature of the cave, for the rogue, was the presence of residual ionizing radiation, coming from the surrounding rock, the very atmosphere inside the bubble, above all from that queerly glowing misty cloud of light. To the rogue this was a welcome source of energy to be tapped at need. It did not know that to Molly Zaldivar it was a death warrant.

When the girl woke up she cried out, peered wildly around the pit, saw the hovering form of the sleeth and tried to leap up and run away. There was nowhere to run. She slipped on the curving stone, black-stained and slick with seeping water, and lay there for a moment, sobbing.

The rogue attempted to form patterns of sound to communicate with her. It was difficult. Even using the transflection fields of the sleeth, modulating them as rapidly and precisely as it could, there was no handy substance for it to vibrate; all it could produce from the shaking of the metallic substance of the nearby tower and steps was a harsh metallic scream, incomprehensible to Molly, and frightening.

The rogue was, for some picoseconds, baffled. Its persona, the sleeth, had no vocal chords, no mechanisms at all for making signals in air. But the rogue was more than the sleeth.

It extended a quick plasma finger and probed the tower itself. There, rustless and fresh as the day it was installed, was a bank of instruments; the rogue hunted among them until it found one that possessed a flexible membrane. It spoke through it:

"Molly Zaldivar. You need not be afraid because I love you."

The girl's involuntary scream echoed strangely from the high rounded walls. The rogue floated patiently above her, waiting.

392

Trembling and unsteady on the slick slope, she climbed to her feet and stared up at it. With a great effort she whispered, "What are you?"

"Cliff Hawk is a part of me. Call me Cliff Hawk."

"I can't! What sort of monster are you?"

"Monster?" The rogue examined the term carefully, without comprehension. It activated the distant tinny speaker to say: "I am your lover, Molly Zaldivar."

The girl's face wrinkled strangely, but Molly had herself under control now. She smiled, a cold, white and terrible smile, ghastly in that shadowless light. "My lover!" she crooned. She paused in thought. "I am lucky," she said bravely. "What girl ever had so mighty a lover?"

The rogue could not recognize near-hysteria. It was puzzlingly aware that the radiance from the organized matter called Molly Zaldivar was not the gentle, warming glow of rose or pearl that it had wanted to evoke; but it knew far too little of human beings to comprehend what Molly was trying to do. In its sleeth body it dropped gently toward her, meeting her as she rose, and allowed her quivering fingers to stroke the fine, dense fur.

"If I love you," she whispered tremulously, "will you help me?"

Powerful floods of energy thundered through the rogue, mighty and irresistible; it was a species of joy, a sort of elation. The rogue allowed its sleeth body to drop to Molly's feet.

"I'll give you everything," it swore through the distant tinny speaker.

The girl was trembling violently, but allowed the vast black talons to draw her quivering body against the fur. The rogue sensed her terror and tried to reassure her. "We are safe here, Molly Zaldivar. No enemy can reach us."

Her fear did not abate. "I fell in the water," she whispered. "I'm damp and cold . . ."

The rogue made the sleeth's fur warm for her; but still she was afraid.

"I'm a human being," she whimpered. "I'll be hungry. Thirsty. I must have food or I'll die!"

From above them the tinny rattle of the overtaxed speaker shouted: "I'll bring food, Molly Zaldivar! I'll bring all the things you need. But we must stay here, where we are safe."

The rogue arranged the pit for her comfort, dried the rock with a searing beam from the sleeth's transflection

393

fields, dragged down a cushion from the tower to make her a resting place. It put her shivering body on it, and reached into her mind to erase her haunting terror.

Presently she slept.

The rogue went foraging in the body of the sleeth. It rose to the top of the pit, squeezed its way through the long passages, climbed into the night. It needed only moments to arrow the score of miles to the nearest human dwelling. It dropped out of the dark onto the little house, crushed a four-legged creature that barked and howled at it, ripped through a wall and seized a refrigerated box filled with human food.

The little box in its talons, it dropped again into the side of the mountain, and paused to consider.

Molly Zaldivar had been in an agony of terror; that much it realized. Why? The rogue, which shared with all intellects the homomorphic trait of considering itself the proper matrix on which all other creatures should be modeled, could not believe that it was its own self which frightened her; no doubt it was its proxy, the sleeth. From the dim stirrings of Cliff Hawk's mind it realized that those great blind eyes, those vengeful talons were likely to be frightening to smaller creatures. It determined to leave the sleeth and visit her in another form.

Under the lip of the cave, where the rogue had abandoned it, the hulk of the robot lay tossed aside. The rogue entered into it, flexed its transcience fields, lifted it into space and, bearing the refrigerated box of food, retraced the long winding route, sank down through the frozen light of that misty opal sun . . .

Molly was awake.

The rogue wearing the egg-shaped body of the robot, brought itself up sharply and hung there just out of sight, the food box dangling from its effectors. Molly was no longer stretched out asleep on the cushions it had brought for her. She was in the spidery metal tower, crouched before the bright, ancient control panel, fumbling frantically with the radio. The rogue listened through the ears of the robot:

"Calling Monitor Quamodian!" the girl whimpered. "Oh, please! Andy! Anyone!"

The rogue knew that the radio was dead; it hung there, letting her speak, listening.

"Molly Zaldivar calling Monitor Quamodian! Andy,

please listen. I'm trapped in a cave. That thing—the rogue star, whatever it is—has me trapped here, because it says— it says it loves me! And it won't let me go."

Her head fell forward, her hand still on the useless switch of the radio. She sobbed, "Oh, please help me. It's a hateful, horrible thing—a monster. I—I tried to deceive it, to make it let me go by pretending to—to like it. But it won't . . ."

The rogue, in the persona of the broken transcience robot, sank slowly toward her, burdened with the box of food that it had brought for her. It was struggling in its complex mind with concepts for which it had no names, and little understanding. *Betrayal.*

Anger.
Revenge.

19

The Reefer's deep-set eyes glowed like a robot's plasma patch. "Make this thing move, Quamodian!" he roared. "I want that critter for my trophy room!"

Andy Quam hissed in annoyance, "Be still, Reefer! I'm not interested in your game collection. It's Molly Zaldivar's life that concerns me." He bent to the panel of his flyer. He was indeed making it move, as fast as he could, cutting out the autonomic pilot circuits and racing the craft along on manual override. It was a flimsy enough bolt to hurl at a creature that ranked with stars for majesty and might— a simple atmosphere flyer, with a few puny transflection beams that could be used as weapons. But it was all he had.

They arrowed through the chill morning air, along the road toward the misty blue ridge. Over the Reefer's hill a smudge of smoke still lifted and wandered away with the wind. Quamodian's eyes were on it when his transceiver clicked into life. For a moment the speakers hummed and crackled, but there was no voice. Andy Quam scowled with annoyance and leaned to listen.

"What is it?" growled the Reefer, brows knotted under their blond tangle of hair.

"I don't know," said Andy Quam. "Nothing. Listen."

But there was no voice, only the questing carrier sounds.

For a moment Andy Quam thought it might have been Molly, and the thought lit his mind with a living image of her red-glinting hair, her haunting oval face, her laughing eyes. But it was not her voice that came from the speaker.

Something was trying to talk to him. An uncanny voice —slow, toneless, laborious. It chilled him with alarm.

"What's that?" demanded the Reefer again. "Quamodian, what are you doing?"

"Be still!" Andy Quam touched the dial, trying to bring the sound in more clearly. It was not a robot's clipped and penetrating whine. It lacked the mechanical precision of an automatic translator. The scattered sounds he made out were not from the universal signal system of the intergalactic society. They were Earth-English. Yet they were somehow alien, monstrously inhuman. It was not a message; it was more like some great, tortured soliloquy, a voice that rambled on and on, brokenly and angrily. The distorted and intermittent signal had no clear message, but it filled Andy Quam with fear.

Climbing slightly, he pushed the flyer to transsonic speed. The narrow black ribbon of road unreeled. Higher hills flashed beneath him. A building flickered. The leaning smudge of smoke was a momentary blur.

Something crept along the road below him.

The Reefer caught Andy Quam's shoulder. "It's that machine!" he bellowed. "An old Plan of Man earthmover—the rogue's using it. Blast it, man! Drive him out into the open!"

Quamodian shrugged the great paw off his arm, and bent to stare down at the road. It was huge and clumsy, lumbering ponderously toward the crest of the ridge on grotesque old caterpillar tracks. It waved claw-ended handling forks around its angular, orange-painted cab.

"Flyer," ordered Andy Quam, "pot that thing for me."

There was a faint deep hiss of departing missiles as the flyer obediently flung out a burst of landing flares at the machine. They were not meant as weapons but would do a weapon's work; they missed, stitching a row of pits across the pavement in front of the machine.

"Sorry, Monitor Quamodian," the flyer apologized mournfully. "I'm not really designed for this sort of work."

"Get its tracks!" Quamodian ordered. "Use all the flares if you have to. Stop it!"

The machine plowed recklessly through the shower of flame. Quamodian spun the flyer around, returned it, passing low over the machine; a new spray of flame darted out toward it, struck it, and clung. The machine slid sidewise, seeming to float on that pool of fire, and Andy Quam saw a broken track flap wildly.

The machine stopped. At a word, the flyer took over automatic control and hovered; the two men looked down.

The machine lay, silent and broken, on the pitted road, while choking fumes rose from the remnants of the flares. Andy Quam turned to the Reefer and demanded, "I've shot it up for you. It doesn't seem to have accomplished a thing. Now what?"

"Now go on!" roared the Reefer. "You've just killed one of the rogue's tools, we haven't touched the beast itself yet. Go on and dig it out!"

Quamodian shrugged, was about to order the flyer on . . .

The klaxon hooted. Red signals blossomed in holographic solidity on the panel. The bubble marker circled a flying object, coming low and fast from the woods behind. It shone with a pale but strange greenish radiation.

"It is the space creature called the sleeth, Monitor Quamodian," reported the flyer. "Indications are that it is under the control of the intellectic being you seek."

The Reefer was briefer and more furious. "That's my critter!" he howled. "Careful! It can eat up a dozen like us any day!"

"Careful!" growled Andreas Quamodian. "Let your animal be careful! Flyer, got any flares left?"

"Two racks, Monitor Quamodian," the machine reported.

"Smash that thing with them!"

The jet leaped away—but, curiously, the flares failed to detonate. Their tracer trails ended in faint red sparks near the oncoming object.

"The sleeth's blanketing them," snarled the Reefer. "You'll have to do better than that!"

"Fire what's left!" shouted Andy Quam, and slapped down the manual override, taking control of the little flyer's transflector beams. He spun them into high, reached out with their pale, deadly fingers toward the sleeth which was growing ever larger before him, the second flight of flares dimming to darkness just like the first.

A sudden lurch threw him against the control panel. "Mal-function, Monitor Qua-modian," the flyer jerked out. "Pow-er fail-ure . . ."

The propulsion field was failing even as the reaching transflection beams were paling and dying. The greenish glow of the sleeth brightened suddenly; the flyer's Klaxon tried to blare, succeeded in rattling a crash alert.

"Hold on!" bawled Quamodian. "We're going to hit . . ."

And they did; they hit hard, the emergency shields failing to function; hard enough to jolt both men like dolls knocked over in a coconut shy. The sleeth soared over them and halted. It was a terrifying sight, horse-sized, cat-like, tapered muscles bulging under the sleek black fur. Blazing green, enormous and cold, its eyes bulged blindly out at them.

The Reefer pulled himself together and croaked, "They —they can kill us, Quamodian. Those eyes!"

Quamodian didn't need the warning. There was something in those eyes that was reaching into his mind, freezing his will, icing his spine and muscles. He struggled to make his limbs obey him, and reached for the little hand weapon he kept under the seat of the flyer; but the icy, penetrating numbness had gone too far. He touched the gun, almost caught it, dropped it and sent it skittering across the tipped floor of the flyer; and the sleeth hung there, staring blindly down through the faint shimmer of its transflection field, just touching a fallen tree with one horrendous claw . . .

The great blind eyes seemed suddenly smaller. The frightful currents of cold that had drenched Andy Quam's body seemed somehow to recede. He could not move, he was not his own master any longer; but at least, he thought, he was not dying helplessly any more; for some reason the creature had halted the poisonous flow of radiation that had drained the flyer's power banks and nearly drained their lives.

The Reefer gasped hoarsely, "Knew it! Knew it couldn't kill its master." And incredibly, haltingly that big yellow-haired bear of a man was forcing himself to stand erect, lurching with agonizing slowness to the door, dropping to the ground and willing himself to stand erect again, next to the great sleek bulk of the creature from space.

And the forgotten radio speaker of the flyer abruptly rattled harshly and spoke: "Go away, Quamodian. I give you your life—but go!" It was the voice he had heard before, inhuman, unalive, terrifying. Andy Quam fell back, finally drained of the last of his strength. He saw the great talons of the sleeth curve protectingly around the Reefer, clasp him and hold him; saw the great creature surge into the air and away, carrying the Reefer as it disappeared with fantastic speed toward the gap in the hills where the faint smudge of smoke still hung.

And then he felt his flyer rock slightly, twitch, and then slowly and painfully lift itself into the sky. It was not at his order that it flew, but its destination was not in question. It rose to a few hundred feet, turned and headed back for the town.

The hunters had failed. One was now himself a captive, being borne at transsonic speeds toward the cave where the rogue flexed its new powers, practiced at its new repertory of emotions and grew. One was helplessly returning the way he had come. And the girl they had tried to rescue was farther from Andy Quam's help than the farthest star.

Of one thing he was sure: he had been defeated. His mere human strength had not even sufficed to get him past the rogue's puppet, the sleeth. He would have no chance against the might of the rogue itself.

20

The rogue, wearing the borrowed body of the robot inspector, sank slowly through the cold opal light of the great bubble under the earth. The refrigerated box of food, held lightly in its transflection fields, seemed suddenly too heavy to carry, and the rogue let it drop.

It crashed to the seep-stained floor in a thunder that rolled around the cavern, split open, spilling out the little parcels of human food. The noise startled Molly Zaldivar. She looked up at the robot form, her face shocked and hollowed in that icy, lifeless light. A scream blazed through the echoing thunder.

For a moment, seeing the gleaming black egg-shaped body of the robot settling toward her, Molly had the wild hope that it was the familiar robot inspector from the Starchurch, somehow come to rescue her, perhaps with Andy Quam right behind. But the hope did not last long enough to survive the terror in her face. She got up stiffly, abandoning the useless radio, and climbed slowly down the spiral steps toward the bottom of the rock bubble.

The sweet high voice of the robot, modulated by the unpracticed mind of the rogue, spoke to her:

"Molly Zaldivar. Why did you speak falsely to me?"

She did not answer. There was a pause, while the rogue pondered its conflicting impulses. "I will not harm you," it droned at last. "You need not be afraid—because I love you, Molly Zaldivar."

Her face twisted and she lifted her hands to the floating robot. "If you love me, won't you let me go?" she cried.

"Because I love you—I can never let you go."

She shouted with all her strength, "Then I hate you, monster!" Her voice was hoarse and despairing; despairing, too, was the angry green radiance that surrounded her in the sight of the rogue, colors and patterns that spoke to him of fury. It left her standing there and soared away, wheeling around the spidery tower. Suddenly it felt the clothing of the robot that it wore confining; it slipped out, left the robot hanging mindlessly on its transflection fields and, once more a nearly invisible cloud of stripped electrons, perched on the metal rails just below the pale, milky mist of light that hung in the center of the sphere.

It spoke to her through the robot: "Molly Zaldivar, I am strong and you are weak. Your hatred cannot harm me. True?"

She shook her head without words, utterly weary.

"But I will not harm you—if I can avoid it, Molly Zaldivar. We will stay here—until you love me."

"Then I'll die here," she said tonelessly.

The rogue pondered the problem for many nanoseconds. It said at last, "Then I shall absorb you as you die. You will be a member of me, like Cliff Hawk."

The girl said, weakly, fearfully, then with gathering rage, "Oh, please—you mustn't! You say you love me— heaven knows what you mean by that—but if it means anything at all to you, you must let me go."

"Never, Molly Zaldivar."

"You can't keep me!"

"I can, Molly Zaldivar. I am stronger than you."

She shrieked, "But there are things which are stronger! Almalik! Almalik is stronger than you. And he will find you yet, even hiding here."

The rogue searched its memory patterns for a referent for the term "Almalik." Almost hesitantly it said, "What is 'Almalik'?"

"Almalik is the spokesman star for Cygnus. Almalik commands multitudes—fusorians and men, robots and stars. His multitudes will find you, here or anywhere. And even if you were as strong as Almalik, you are all alone while he has legions!"

The rogue's plasma rippled in thought. "I have met Almalik's robot," it said at last. "It is now a member of me."

"One robot! Almalik owns many millions."

The rogue did not reply. Thoughtfully it clung to the metallic rail of the cryptic old device, studying the girl. She was exhausted now, the green fire of her fury dying, waiting for a move from the rogue.

To the rogue, painfully learning the uses of those human qualities called emotions, Molly Zaldivar was a most confusing stimulus. There was enough of the residual identity of Cliff Hawk in the rogue to give force and direction to its feelings about Molly; it possessed attitude sets which could have been called "pity" or "love." The rogue recognized that the girl was small, and weak, and mortal, and afraid; it even felt some sort of impulse to ease her wild terror, heal her pain and rage. It simply had no effectors capable of the job.

At the same time it recognized that in a sense she represented a threat. The polarization of the other human, Andreas Quamodian, toward her was certain to produce an attempt on his part to interfere again. The rogue did not estimate that the attempt would be successful, but it might be an annoyance; and it took the precaution of detaching some part of its attention to invest its creatures, the sleeth and the handling machine, deploying them as scouts between Wisdom Creek and the mountains.

But there were puzzles the rogue could not solve.

The answers to some of them were far from this cave. It detached itself from its high iron perch in the opal mist and left the girl, watching and trembling.

The rogue sent its awareness out into the universe. It sensed the tangle of dark hills above the bubble cave, stretched, expanded and encompassed cubic miles of space with its consciousness. It observed the bright anger and fear of the human creatures from whom it had stolen the box of food, studied the sleeping presence of Andreas Quamodian, observed the deployment of its own tools, the sleeth and the machine; and it reached farther still.

It reached out until it grasped the roundness of the

401

planet Earth, turning between its bare moon and the red, swelling sun, the sun that had struck at the rogue in those first moments of its existence.

The star was still angry, still roiled and troubled. The rogue studied it carefully, but avoided reaching out to it; it had not been harmed by that triple bolt of energy that had been the sun's riposte, yet did not consider it advisable to provoke another.

The rogue expanded again, reached out its perceptions to the stars. It found them to be suns like this sun, single, coupled, multiple, burning all across the dust and darkness of the galaxy—some tinier than Earth's cold moon, some mightier than Earth's sullen sun. Even beyond the stars it peered, to find a bleak and empty vastness of infinite space and cruel cold. Then in the eternal floods of blackness it perceived the glowing, tiny lights of other galaxies. Ill-informed and unfearing, the rogue studied the numbers and varieties of galaxies. Faintly, it sensed the place of that watching being, still beyond its reach. It returned to nearer stars.

Almalik.

It was time for the rogue to probe into the meaning of the term "Almalik."

There was no problem in finding Almalik; in the captured impulses of the robot inspector was a clear understanding of where Almalik lay in space, and the rogue turned its attention there.

And there was the might of Almalik, the splendor of his thirteen suns, all greater than the small Earth star that had tried to destroy the rogue. It counted them, studied their spin, tested the energies they hurled into the void. Six splendid double stars arranged in hierarchically greater doubles; one single sun with many wheeling planets. The thirteen suns radiated many colors in the optical bands of energies, but the rogue also saw that they shared a common golden glow of unity . . .

And Almalik felt the rogue's fleeting touch.

Hello, little one.

Almalik did not speak. Least of all did he speak in words; but he sent a signal which was at once greeting and wry pity. The signal was powerful but soundless, serene and slow.

The rogue listened impassively, waiting for more.

Little one, we have been looking for you. The silent voice was mightier than thunder, gentle as—what? The rogue had only an imperfect analogy: gentle as love. *We have received information about you. You have destroyed patterns we cherish. You have damaged entities who were part of us. Little one, what do you wish?*

The rogue considered the question for some time. It framed an answer with difficulty: *Knowledge. Experience.* And then, after a pause, it added, *Everything.*

The multiple suns of Almalik glowed serenely golden; it was almost like a smile. From behind the round Earth, behind the many thousand stars and dust clouds, the signal came: *Knowledge you may have. Ask a question.*

The rogue asked it at once: *Why will you destroy me?*

The soundless voice was cool, aloof, immeasurably sure. *Little one, we cannot destroy you or any sentient thing.*

Green anger filled the rogue. It was a contradiction, Almalik's statement opposed to Molly Zaldivar's. It had not known of the existence of lies until Molly Zaldivar told it she loved it, then showed she did not. Now it knew of lies, but little of mortal error; the contradiction seemed to mean a lie, a lie meant enmity. Red hatred froze the rogue: sudden fury shook its plasma violently.

It dropped from its great, tenuous vantage point, contracted to a swirl of luminescence, and sank back into the mountain just as the planet was turning that part of its surface to the angry rising sun. The splendid suns of Almalik were gone. For a while.

The rogue floated down to Molly Zaldivar. In the high, singing voice of the robot it cried: "We are leaving this place. Almalik has lied to me. I hate him now."

She lay spent and shuddering on the torn cushions, staring at the rogue.

It said: "I hate Almalik. Almalik thinks me small and helpless, and will destroy me if he can. But I am growing, I will grow still more, I will grow until I am mightier than Almalik."

White and haggard in the dead opal light from the ancient cloud, the girl's face had no expression. She lay hopeless and uncaring, waiting for what the rogue had to say.

"I shall destroy Almalik," it sang in the robot's clear whine. "Then you will love me, Molly Zaldivar, or I will destroy you too."

21

Andy Quam landed his flyer before the control dome of the transflex cube and grated, "Control dome! Connect me direct with Headquarters of the Companions of the Star, Almalik Three!"

"Your authorization, sir?" the control dome inquired politely.

"Fully authorized! Highest priority!"

"One moment, sir," the control dome said doubtfully. But it did not refuse him. In a moment it said, "I am seeking your circuits, sir. There is a 200-second delay now estimated; will you wait?"

"You bet I'll wait," growled Andy Quam, and sank dourly back in his seat. He ached. Battling rogue stars and strange beings and men from space was not the kind of life he was used to. But if it was what he had to do to save Molly Zaldivar, he would *get* used to it!

A small figure appeared at the corner of the square, running hard toward him. Tiny spurts of dust flowered at his heels, and he was gasping as he reached the flyer. "Preacher!" Rufe gasped. "What happened? How's Molly Zaldivar?"

"She's still in the cave," said Quamodian shortly. "I think. Anyway, I never saw her."

"Then what—what are you going to do?"

"Wait." But they didn't have to wait long. The speaker clicked and hummed, and a sweet nonhuman voice sang:

"Companions of the Star, Chief Warden of Monitors speaking. How may I serve you?"

"You can serve me best," said Andy Quam belligerently, "by getting an emergency survey team out here on the double! This is Monitor Andreas Quamodian speaking. I request—no, cancel that. I *demand* immediate action!"

The sweet high voice sang sorrowfully, "Ah, Monitor Quamodian. We have been advised of your statements and actions."

"Ha!" barked Andy Quam. "Of course you have! You've been told of my report that a created intellect in the form of a rogue star is loose here; that I have requested authority to use force against it; that I have stated that certain humans and nonhuman intellects have been damaged, destroyed or threatened by it. And you've ignored what I said."

"Unfortunately, Monitor Quamodian, we have seen no reason to accept this report."

"You think I'm wrong, eh?"

"Not 'wrong,' Monitor Quamodian. It is merely that we do not assess the same quantitative need for action."

"I see," snapped Andy Quam. "Then look at it this way. I report that a Monitor of the Companions of the Star is suffering paranoid delusions; that he believes himself and his friends attacked by monsters; that in his insanity he is capable of wildly destructive acts of violence; and that this will inevitably reflect great discredit to all Monitors. What quantitative assessment do you give *that?*"

"Why—why, Monitor Quamodian, that's frightful! We'll send a survey team at once. Who is this deranged monitor?"

"Me!" snapped Andy Quam, and severed the connection.

They left the flyer grumbling to itself in the middle of the square before the transflex gate. "Stupid thing to do," it was saying resentfully. "They'll take you off the roll of Monitors sure. Then what will become of me? Some menial job ferrying tourists . . ."

The boy's house was only minutes away, and there Andy Quam showered, ate, drank thirstily of the cold, rich milk the kitchen machines produced for him. He braced himself for the arrival of the emergency survey team. "How long, preacher?" the boy demanded. "How long before they get here?"

Quamodian considered. "Twenty minutes to think things over. Half an hour to assemble a team. Ten minutes to get their transflex priorities approved—a few seconds to travel. I'd call it an hour."

"Gee! Why, that's only twenty minutes from now. Just think, in twenty minutes I'll be seeing all those crazy three-headed beings, and green-shelled beetles, and . . ."

"We do not comment on the physical peculiarities of any citizen," Andy Quam said firmly. "Didn't your parents teach you that?"

"Well, yes," the boy admitted.

"Come to think of it," Quamodian went on, "where are your parents? Aren't they ever home?"

The boy shuffled his feet. "Sure, preacher. They're just, uh, busy."

"Rufe!"

"Yes, preacher?" His face was angelically innocent.

"Rufe, let's cut out the nonsense. You're hiding something. I can't imagine what, or why—but let's have it!"

"Aw, preacher. It's nothing. It's—" he looked up at Andreas Quamodian anxiously. Quamodian gazed implacably back. "Well,' said the boy, "it's just that they were acting a little funny. They've gone off in a flyer to Nuevo York."

"Nuevo York! Why, that's two thousand miles away!"

"A little more, preacher. Figured it'd take them a day or two each way."

"Why?"

"Well, that's the part that's kind of funny. I mean—gee, preacher, there's nothing wrong with my parents! They're not crazy or anything. They just, well, said the same kind of thing you were saying. About some sort of rogue intellect loose on the earth, and the robot inspector here wouldn't listen to them and they didn't have the right of direct contact with Almalik, like you. So they figured they'd better report it to Nuevo York, where people might be more interested."

Quamodian sat up alertly. "You're still hiding something," he accused. "Why would you be ashamed of their knowing about the rogue star? It's true, you know."

"Sure, preacher. Only . . ."

"Only what?"

The boy flushed. "It's just that they were talking about it two days ago. That's when they left."

Quam said, "But that can't be! The rogue star wasn't even created then! Oh, I see!"

The boy nodded unhappily. "That's the part that's got me a little mixed up, preacher. They thought there was one when there *wasn't.*"

They were back at the transflex cube with minutes to spare, but the emergency survey team was early. Evidently they had wasted no time. The control dome cried, through Quamodian's flyer radio: "Stand back! Keep the area clear for a party from Almalik Three, now arriving!"

"Gosh!" whispered Rufe. His eyes were round as Saturn's rings, his worries about his parents temporarily out of

406

his mind. "Where are they, preacher? Shouldn't they be coming through? What's keeping them? *Oh.*"

A dozen grass-green spiral beings, like tiny coils of springs, emerged from the cube. They were twisting in orbit around each other, approaching the man and the boy with a whistle of high-frequency sound. "What in tarnation is that, preacher?" demanded the boy.

"It is not courteous to stare. I don't recognize the species; a multiple citizen of some kind."

"And that! And—oh, gosh, look at that one!"

"All citizens, I'm sure." But even Quamodian drew his breath sharply, as from behind a foamy, almost translucent bubble of pink there appeared the shark's fangs and slitted eyes of a citizen of clearly carnivorous ancestry. The rest of the citizen was no improvement; it loped on enormously powerful clawed legs like a kangaroo's, possessed two pairs of upper limbs that seemed boneless and lithe as an elephant's trunk, terminating in vivid blue manipulating organs that were almost the duplicate of the snout of a star-nosed mole.

But the fourth member of the group, and the one who advanced on Andy Quam, looked human in a way that made him stare. She wore the garb of a somewhat too sophisticated galactic citizen, her face made up beyond the point of recognition, her dark hair piled into a perfumed tower. But change her clothes and makeup, he thought, put a simple dress of Molly's on her instead of the mirror-bright tights, the fluffed bodice and shoulders, the painted diamonds of bare skin; scrub her face of the two-inch angled eyebrows and the bright blue eye shadow and rouge—and she would be a perfect duplicate of Molly Zaldivar.

Striding toward him, she abruptly stopped. Her shadowed eyes flew wide, like a startled doll's. A crimson flush showed around the edges of her makeup. Her bright lips parted as if gasping, "Andy!" But no sound came. Slowly the exposed patches of skin drained chalk-white. At last she tossed her tall coiffure and swept on toward him.

"Monitor Quamodian—" momentarily, her voice held a breathless quiver. "If you really don't recognize me, I'm Senior Monitor Clothilde Kwai Kwich. You may be interested to know that I was able to return with my subordinates to Companion Headquarters, where we have begun a new analysis of our collected data on rogue stars."

Andy Quam swallowed twice. He wiped the palm of his hand on his tunic and extended it for shaking.

"I'm delighted that you got away," he bubbled breathlessly. "I've been trying to learn what happened, but nobody would tell me anything . . ."

"Never mind the small talk," she snapped. "Please speak briefly and responsively, when it is necessary for you to speak at all. Your idiotic meddling here has forced me to leave more interesting work at headquarters. I'm assigned to clean up the mess you've made. What the devil are you up to now?"

Quamodian stiffened resentfully. "I'm not meddling . . ."

"The traffic safety inspectors say you are," she cut him sharply off. "If you want it explained in baby talk, the rogue star that Cliff Hawk contacted is trying to protect the infant rogue from your officious interference. That's why it sent Solomon Scott to keep you from coming to Earth. That's why it trapped you on its own planet. The inspectors predict that it will be forced to take additional action, unless you restrain yourself."

She gave him no time to inquire what that additional action might be.

"These other citizens and I have little time to waste. We wish to use it effectively. I suppose our best first move is to make an on-site investigation of the totally needless events that your stupidity have brought about."

"I had nothing to do with what has happened here." Flushing, Andy Quam dropped his unshaken hand. "Why, I couldn't even get out of town . . ."

"Let's get moving." She ignored his feeble protest. "My associates can provide their own transport, but I require a vehicle."

"Of course." Helplessly, he shrugged. "Here's my flyer."

Without a word, Senior Monitor Clothilde Kwai Kwich brushed past him to enter the flyer. Dazed, Andy Quam turned to follow. The boy caught his arm.

"Say, preacher," he hissed furiously. "What the dickens is the matter with you?"

"I don't know." He shook his head unhappily. "I'm sure I don't know."

After a moment he followed the girl into the flyer.

22

The rogue was much larger now, and wiser, and stronger. It sensed that far watcher's anxious observation, but it wanted no defense.

It did not seem much different to the despairing eyes of Molly Zaldivar, for at best it was only a cloud of stripped surging electrons, a controlled violence of particles that would have been her death if the rogue's own energies had not kept its components bound to its central mass. But it had fed and grown. It had assimilated neural reactions from Cliff Hawk, the robot, the sleeth, the hundred living creatures larger than microorganisms that it had absorbed into itself. It was by no means finished with either growing or learning. Perhaps it was almost mature in size and strength and intelligence. Far from mature however, in its understanding of itself.

Molly made no sound as the radiant whirl summoned the sleeth to it, and entered into the black terrifying shape of the predator from space. The sleeth dropped down upon her and caught her, coldly but harmlessly, in its razored talons, now sheathed in their armored cases. It rose with her through the center of the globe, flew through the cold core of that edgeless opal glow and on and out, tracing the endless passageways to the surface.

Molly did not stir. She was past fear or worry; she was not resigned, but she was passive.

She would not have struggled even if she had known how close to death that murderous opal glow had brought her. But she did not know.

She did not respond even in the hues of emotion by which the rogue interpreted her mental state. No green blaze of hate, no blues or violets of fear. No spark of love; emotion had left her, leaving her dark, and empty, and merely waiting.

Bearing Molly Zaldivar in the bubble of atmosphere trapped in the sleeth's transflexion fields, the rogue left the round Earth.

Tardily they dawdled through the "thick" gases that were the solar atmosphere—so tenuous at one A.U. that human instruments could barely record them, and human bodies would have burst and foamed; but still too thick for the sort of speeds that the sleeth, commanded and driven by the starlike energies of the rogue, could develop. Even so, in minutes they were past gassy Jupiter and Saturn; the void was more nearly empty now, and the rogue drove the sleeth more fiercely.

So fiercely that time seemed to stop.

These were not physical energies that the rogue commanded now; they were the transflexion fields of the sleeth and itself. They leaped through empty spaces, through folded light and darkness, through bitter cold and twisting force and giddy deeps of vastness, leaped to the golden suns of Almalik . . .

And were there.

A thin sighing shout whispered passionately in the ears of Molly Zaldivar:

"Observe!" it shrieked, almost soundlessly. "I have begun to destroy Almalik!"

"You cannot," she said bleakly.

"Observe!" it shrieked again, and subsided. It was the molecules of atmosphere itself that the rogue was shaking now, to make sounds that the girl could hear. It could produce little volume, but in the girl's tiny bubble of air, gazing at the twelve bright but distant stars and one nearby the blinding sun that was Almalik, in the middle of the awful soundlessness of interstellar space, there was no other sound loud enough to drown it out, nothing but her own heart and breath and the faint mindless singing of the sleeth.

"I begin!" whispered the tiny scream, and like a hawk stooping to its prey the rogue drove them toward the nearest planet.

It was a small world, less than Pluto and farther from its primary; the horizon was strangely rounded, the surface mottled with creeping blobs of liquid gas.

With a power summoned from its infinite reserves, the rogue seized it, entered it—became it. It grew once more. It fed quickly and avidly, seized new atoms, sucked electrons into the spreading patterns of its being, took new energies from frozen stone. It reached out to survey the space around itself, found ions, gas molecules, a hurtling moonlet—and farther off, a small metal mass inhabited

410

by organic masses of organized matter. The rogue did not know it was a spaceship; did not care.

It drew the spaceship and the sleeth at once to itself. The ship crashed bruisingly on the surface of the tiny world. With the sleeth it was more gentle, but not gentle enough. The creature struck against a spire of frozen hydrates, screamed soundlessly and went limp. And as it lost control, with it went the bubble of air it carried in its transflexion fields, and Molly Zaldivar lay open to the murderous empty cold of space.

For many nanoseconds the rogue considered what it had done. As best it knew how to be so, it was alarmed.

At length it seized upon a buried shelf of rock beneath the frozen gases and shook it to make words. "Molly Zaldivar!" rumbled the planet. "What is happening to you?"

The girl did not answer. She lay cradled in a bed of the planet's—of the rogue's own, now—crystal snow, beside the crumpled black body of the sleeth. She did not breathe; there was no longer any air for her to breathe. Dark blood frothed and froze on her face.

"Molly Zaldivar!" groaned the rock of the planet's crust. "Answer!"

But there was no answer.

The rogue tested its powers, felt their new magnitude. Now it was a planet, its coat of frozen gas a skin, its cragged granite mountains the bones, its deep pools of cooling magma a heart of sorts. The rogue was not used to so large a body. It regretted (insofar as it understood regret) that its body was unkind to Molly Zaldivar, too airless, too cruelly cold.

From the wreckage of the spaceship organized masses of organic matter were exiting, clad in metallic artificial skins. The rogue did not recognize that they were citizens who might be of help to Molly Zaldivar; it reached out a thoughtless effector and slew them. And then it again practiced the sensation it experienced as regret; for it realized that they had owned supplies of water and air, warmth and pressure that could have been used for Molly Zaldivar.

No matter. The rogue was now the planet, and could dispose the planet's resources. It would not let her die.

It shielded her from cold, warmed the frozen gas around her and cupped it in a sphere of transflexion forces. With

411

bits of matter taken from the creatures it had destroyed it healed the damage to her lungs. It warmed her stiffened body, helped her breathe again, found the spark of life in her . . .

And the girl stirred and spoke.

"What are you doing, monster?" she moaned.

"I am saving your life, Molly Zaldivar," rumbled the rocks. "I'm destroying Almalik!"

"You cannot, monster," sobbed the girl.

"Observe!"

The rogue's transflection field was vaster now, spreading to hold all its continents of dark and ancient rock, its seas of snow, to contain all its great mass.

With all its might, the rogue prepared to strike at Almalik.

It halted the planet in its orbit and turned inward toward that white and splendid single sun, the brightest star of Almalik.

And in its hate for Almalik it drove inward, toward collision with the star.

The sleeth was cruelly hurt; but the creature that had evolved to kill pyropods in space was not easily killed. It stirred. The great empty eyes gazed into space, then bent to look into the eyes of Molly Zaldivar. Ripples of muscle pulsed under the dark, hard flesh. It's transflection fields grew again; it lifted lightly from the frozen gas on which it lay, and its high singing sound grew in volume. The sleeth was not an intelligent creature as man is intelligent, or the other citizens of the galaxies; but it had awareness. It recognized that something had owned it for a time; it felt that the something was gone, now that the rogue had retreated to explore its new planetary body. It remembered Molly Zaldivar . . .

And when the rogue next turned its attention to the girl she was gone.

The rogue was quick to search for her, and find her. She was in flight.

Mounted on the sleek black shoulders of the sleeth, veiled in its transflection fields, she was climbing away from the rogue planet's frigid skin of snow, flying toward the inner planets of that great white star toward which the planet was plunging.

The rogue thrust out a darting arm of plasma, of its own electrons meshed in transcience forces. It reached to

412

overtake her, pierced effortlessly the sleeth's transflection shield, shook her small sphere of air with an effector.

"Where are you going, Molly Zaldivar?" the air screamed shrilly in her ear.

She turned her head to look at the rogue's shining plasma finger, but she did not answer. The rogue paused, considering. There was strangeness here. Strange that to the rogue she seemed so very lovely. The redder suns of Almalik struck red fire from her hair; the blue suns burned violet in her eyes. But why should these things matter? the rogue asked itself, interested and curious. Why should the remembered and absorbed thought patterns of the organized matter called Cliff Hawk exert so powerful an influence on it still? The rogue made the air shriek in a piercing whisper again: "I love you, Molly Zaldivar. Once I was tinier than you, so small you could not see me; now I am so huge you are no more than a fleck of dust. We have never been akin, and I see no bridge for love between us—but I love you!"

"You're insane, monster," she said at last. But her eyes were gentle.

The rogue pondered. "Where are you going?" it demanded again.

"I am flying to the inhabited planets of Almalik. On Kaymak they will deal with you—once I warn them."

"Do you hate me, Molly Zaldivar?"

The girl frowned at its bright sensor and shook her head. "You can't help what you are."

The rogue scanned all her matter for the cold green blaze of fury; it was absent. Eagerly it asked, "Then do you love me now?"

Her face crinkled oddly about the eyes, the skin tawny gold beneath Almalik's far suns. "How could I? I am human—you a monster!" And her violet eyes were damp as they peered at the rogue's shining sensor.

"I love you . . ."

"Insane!" sobbed the girl. And then, "Perhaps I pity you, because you are so sadly deformed, because all your power is thrown away." She shook her head vigorously, the colored lights of Almalik dancing in her hair. "I'm sorry for you!"

She paused, then said, "If I am in love, I think it must be with little Andy Quam. Monster, I will go back to him. Once I get to the inhabited planets and give my warning—

and you are destroyed—I will go to him through a transflex station. But I pity you, monster."

"I will not be destroyed."

"You will be destroyed—unless you kill me first, and
keep me from warning the inhabited worlds."

The rogue thought for microseconds. Then at last it
shook the air again. "I will not destroy you," the air
shrieked. "But I will not be destroyed. Observe! I will kill
Almalik before you can warn anyone!"

And it withdrew its plasma arm, as the girl stared
wonderingly after.

The rogue flexed its energies, and prepared for the as-
sault.

It tightened the transflection fields that held and moved
its planetary mass. The agonized rock of its mantle
screamed and grated as it flattened its bare black peaks,
compressed its deserts of snow, squeezing itself into a
denser projectile. It drove itself toward the blazing sun.

I will die, thought the rogue. *So will Almalik.*

Tardily, almost carelessly, the congeries of massed beings
that made up the total of Almalik took note of the intruder and lifted a careless effector to defend itself.

It was not the white star ahead of the rogue that resisted.
That sun lay steadily glowing, ignoring the threat. But
from a mighty double sun above it, a golden giant and
its immense blue companion spinning close together, a bolt
was launched.

The bolt sprang from the inner plasmas of the golden
star, and its energies were immense. An enormous leaping
snake, thicker than the rogue's own snow-encrusted planetary body, blazed bright as the star itself. It flashed with
transflection speed across the void, faster than the rogue
could move to evade it.

But it bypassed the rogue, and struck toward Molly
Zaldivar.

Even at the planetary distances that already separated
them, the rogue could see the red flash of terror dart
through her being as she saw that darting coil of golden
fire. *Help me, monster!* she cried; the rogue could hear
no words, but the message was clear, and it responded.

It hurled out an arm of its own ions and their linking
transcience energies, coiling it into a plasma shield around
the girl and the sleeth. But it was not strong enough. The
golden arm of Almalik was stronger; it burst through the

414

shielding plasma wall, coiled a net of golden fire around Molly and the sleeth and snatched them away toward that double sun.

The rogue could not help her. But an emotion that it could not identify as savage joy filled all its patterned mass. *She called me. She asked my help. If I cannot help her, I still can destroy this near white star of Almalik!*

The rogue paused, testing itself, preparing itself to dispose of energies greater than even it had yet employed. It was not strong enough, it calculated coldly. Not yet. It needed to be stronger.

The planet was cold, but at its core it was not yet dead; crushed gelid masses of iron and heavier metals still seethed, not yet congealed into solids, not yet exhausted of radioactivity and heat. From them the rogue devoured energy and strength. Controlled lightnings flashed along its plasma paths. The planetary mass of its body was now no more than a slinger's pebble to it; a weapon, a missile, a way of killing Almalik.

The rogue intensified its driving field until its crushed mountain ranges smoked, and the deserts of snow thawed and bubbled into boiling seas. The deep core shuddered with earthquake shocks; arcs and auroras raged through its reborn air.

The rogue plunged on to shatter the enemy star.

But Almalik was not unprepared.

From the binary sun above, the golden spear of plasma stabbed at the rogue again. It pierced all the shielding fields, burned through its steaming seas, exploded its crust and jarred its heart with seismic waves. The rogue coldly calculated its damage. *Much. Not too much. I still can kill Almalik!*

The plasma snake recoiled to strike again, and yet again, pocking all the rogue's surface with enormous glowing craters, shattering its being with waves of destruction that the rogue felt as searing pain.

But the rogue would not let itself be destroyed.

It drew on its last immense reserves to increase the power of its transflection shields, holding all the atoms of its shattered planetary mass in a remorseless, destroying grip. Daring—and learning—it even reached out to suck new energies from the plasma snake itself.

Molly Zaldivar and the sleeth were gone now, lost even to the rogue's far-ranging perceptions as the plasma coil drew them back toward some distant planet's surface. Every bit of matter of more than molecular dimensions for many A.U.'s around was gone, drawn into the rogue itself or volatilized by the seething energies employed.

But the rogue was not destroyed. It plunged on to strike the unresisting white sun. It knew the watcher's pride in its wild rebel power, and they both rejoiced.

23

"Monitor Quamodian," said the flyer chattily, "You're not going to hear much with your bare ears. They're talking about you."

Quam glanced at Monitor Clothilde Kwai Kwich, who was inspecting the fittings of the flyer with distaste, and apparently whispering to herself. "I don't know if I want to hear," he muttered.

The girl said aloud, without looking at him "What you want makes little difference, Monitor Quamodian. There will no doubt be times when the other citizens will have inquiries to direct to you, or instructions. I do not wish to be distracted by relaying messages, therefore equip yourself with proper hearing facilities."

Andy Quam grumbled, but accepted the tiny earpiece the flyer offered him on an effector. ". . . flimsy old wreck," a shrill voice was piping in his ear as he put it on. "We will follow, but kindly move as rapidly as you can." The voice had an odd humming, almost echoing quality, as though a well-trained chorus were speaking in almost perfect unison. Quamodian guessed it was the multiple citizen of green spirals.

He disregarded them, quickly inspected his flyer. Its homeostatic devices had repaired the damage, restored the racks of flares. Not that they would be needed, he hoped. Or would be of any use if they were. But they were better than nothing.

"We're all set," he announced. "I guess."

Monitor Kwai Kwich said, with offensive patience, "Then can we not begin?"

Quamodian hunched grimly over the controls and ordered the flyer into the air. The sun was in his eyes as they spun and rose. Nearly doubled in diameter, its red disk was now so dull that his naked eyes could watch it without discomfort. Dark splotches marred it. He thought of saying something to the girl, but decided against it—although she, a stranger here, might not realize there was anything odd about its appearance. Let her find out, he thought. It didn't matter anyway. All that mattered was that he now had help—a kind of help—against the rogue.

They arrowed south across the narrow lake and the first dark foothills, the multiple green citizen and the pinkly glowing cloud following effortlessly behind. The predator citizen with the enormous fangs lolled silently on the padded seats behind Andy Quam and the girl, while Rufe sat on the floor beneath it, looking apprehensively at its teeth. There was a continuing buzz of conversation on the transcience bands coming through his earpiece, but Quamodian disregarded it. He was not interested in their opinions of his flyer, himself, or the planet that had spawned humanity. All he wanted from them was their help.

It was dark as they reached the hill that held the cave; the sun was still some distance above the horizon, but its dulled rays gave only a looming twilight in the sky, very little on the ground about the cave mouth. He circled the dark mouth of the cave, searching for the sleeth or any hostile thing. There was nothing. All the landscape held that ominous tinge of red, but nothing moved on it.

Flying warily, he approached the rubble of the demolished door.

"Deserted," sang the tiny chorus of the grass-green spirals. "We detect nothing. Another entrance exists lower down."

Senior Monitor Clothilde Kwai Kwich glanced hesitantly at Andy Quam. "There is a good deal of destruction here," she admitted.

"I told you!"

"Yes. Perhaps there has been an error."

"Lower down!" chanted the spirals. "Other indications! Worth investigating!" And the soft whisper of the cottony pink cloud citizen sighed:

"Forces have been deployed in the lower area of considerable magnitude. Forces still exist in being of unusual characteristics."

417

Senior Monitor Kwai Kwich said, almost apologetically, "We should investigate."

"Right," rasped Quamodian, and sent the flyer spinning down around the mountain, searching for the lower entrance. The pink cloud citizen was there before him, hovering like a puff of steam at the spout of a kettle before the tunnel mouth.

"You lead," it sighed. "Dispersed matter like myself may be vulnerable."

But Quamodian had not waited for permission. He thrust the flyer into the tight throat of the tunnel, probing with its searchlights for the sleeth, for Molly Zaldivar, for any trace. All he found was the tightening spiral passage itself, lined with evidences of destruction. "Forces of great magnitude," chanted the spirals, whirling about a burst wall, a ripped stanchion. "Evidence of transflection energies. Evidence of plasma activity."

Rufe, forgetting his fear of the long-toothed citizen behind him, stood leaning over Quamodian's shoulder. "Gee, preacher," he whispered, thrilled. "Look at that! Something really racked this place up!"

There was no doubt about that. Staring about as the flyer slid smoothly forward on its transflection fields, Quamodian saw that what had happened in this tiny enclosed space had involved more than merely chemical energies. For the first time he really understood what was meant by a "rogue star;" tiny though the creature had been, less than a gram in weight at first, it had commanded forces capable of thrusting steel and rock out of its way like tissue.

The long-snouted predator citizen lifted its muzzle and howled a sentence; the translator in Quamodian's ear rendered it as: "Be careful! Monitor Kwai Kwich, should we not report to Almalik before going on?"

The girl bit her lip, was about to speak; but Quamodian overrode her. "No!" he rasped. "You have waited too long already. Molly Zaldivar may be dying—may even be—" he did not finish the sentence.

Then they were at the center of the spiral. Quamodian glanced down, swallowed, looked at the girl—then tipped the flyer down into the central shaft.

Cautiously they dropped down the shaft, Quamodian's flyer first, the mutliple grass-green citizen second, the pink cloud hovering timorously behind. Below them a misty, opalescent disk of pale light expanded slowly into a sphere, and they entered the great round chamber below the hill.

"Astonishing," breathed Clothilde Kwai Kwich.

The tardy cloud citizen sighed fearfully: "The energies are considerable! I am reluctant to come closer."

"Stay, then," grunted Quamodian, staring about. "I wonder—what is it? Do you have any information?"

The girl shook her head. "Some ancient military installation, I suppose. Perhaps from the days of the Plan of Man. The records no longer exist for much of that period. But that fusion fire!" She pointed at the cloud of opal mist that hung above the high steel platform. "What a source of energy! I almost believe that you are right, Monitor Quamodian. With power like that, one might really attempt to create a star!"

Andy Quam chuckled sourly, but did not answer. Hands sweating on the flare controls, he dived to a foot or less above the water-stained floor of the sphere. The ripped and flattened orange-painted cab, the dismembered motor and tracks of the handling machine gave him an unpleasant start; something had thrown them about in rage, it seemed. And there were other fragments there among the torn and broken metal bits. A primitive white-painted food refrigerator? Quam did not recognize it at first, did not understand its purpose even then—but finally shook with the realization of what it meant: Molly Zaldivar had been here. The food could have been for no one but her.

But it too had been dropped or flung; the door was twisted ajar, small packets of food were sprinkled across the wreckage. And beyond them, what was that crushed black shape that lay athwart the grating that attempted to carry seepage away?

Clothilde Kwai Kwich recognized it first: "A robot inspector!" she gasped. "Then—then it's all true!"

Rufe said complainingly, "True? Gosh, Miss Kwai Kwich, what've we been telling you all along? Of course it's true!"

It was too late for Andy Quam to feel triumph. He hardly heard the exchange. Eyes narrowed, thoughtful, he was darting the flyer's beams into every section of the vast sphere. There was nothing else to be seen. The wreckage on the floor, the spidery steel tower and its ominously glittering mist of fusion energy, the water-stained walls themselves. Nothing more.

Molly Zaldivar had been here, he was sure of that. But she was here no longer.

Where had she gone?

The nervous sigh of the cloud citizen interrupted him. "These energies," it whispered despairingly, "they are ionizing my gases, interfering with my particulate control. I must return to the surface."

"Go ahead," said Quam absently.

"Perhaps we should do the same," bayed the predator in the back seat. "This is dangerous!"

"In a minute," said Andy Quam. He was observing, remembering, analyzing. Dispassionately he realized, with a small surface part of his brain, that from the moment Molly Zaldivar's message had reached him, galaxies away, he had been allowing his love and his emotions to drive him. His carefully trained reasoning faculties, the trait of analysis and synthesis which was so basic a part of his indoctrination as a monitor, had been ignored.

But now he was using them again, and a picture was unfolding under his eyes, Cliff Hawk, rebel, adventurer, skilled transcience expert. The Reefer, callous misogynist. The two of them together in this place, given these energies, the months and even years of time when they had been left unsupervised.

It was all quite logical, he noted abstractly. Hawk's scientific hunger; the Reefer's loathing for humanity and, above all, the fusorian brotherhood; the people, the place, the facilities. They had used them to create a rogue, and in return the rogue had thrust them aside, or killed them, or ignored them.

But it had not ignored Molly Zaldivar.

The rogue was no longer present; its energies would have been detected by any of the citizens in the party. It had gone. And wherever it had gone, Quamodian felt certain, there would be Molly Zaldivar as well.

The girl monitor said hesitantly, "Andy. I mean, Monitor Quamodian . . ."

"Eh? What is it?"

"Perhaps the other citizens are right. I—I don't like the look of this place."

Quamodian frowned. Then a fearsome suspicion crossed his mind. "Clothilde! What was it the cloud said?"

"You mean the cit . . ."

"Yes! About the energies!"

"Why, it said they were ionizing gases. It has returned to the open air."

"Flyer!" cried Andy Quam. "Analyze those radiations! Quickly!"

The flyer said sulkily. "Thought you'd never ask. Sustained lethality, eight times permissible levels. Safe period at this distance, one hour. We have now been exposed to them for nineteen minutes, and I was going to give a warning alert in sixty seconds."

"Get us out of here!" ordered Andy Quam. "Fast!"

The flyer bucked, spun, drove upward toward the tunnel. Quamodian stared out the viewplate. The glowing deadly sphere of light flashed past his field of vision, then the tight spiral of the tunnel walls; but he did not see them.

Andy Quam was seeing something quite different, and far worse.

The radiation from that glittering mist of nuclear fire that had flamed for ages in the spherical cave was deadly.

The flyer's instruments had measured its intensity. They were reliable. Quamodian had installed and checked them himself. If they said that the maximum safe dose was one hour, then there was no question, give or take a minute or so, allowing for possible error.

It was not Quamodian's own safety that concerned him, nor Monitor Clothilde Kwai Kwich's, nor the boy's.

How long had Molly Zaldivar been held prisoner in that cave, soaking in those deadly rays?

Quamodian's calculation could be little more than a guess. But it was eighteen hours or more since she had been stolen from the little bedroom of Rufe's house. It was not sensible to suppose that less than half of that time had been spent in the cave.

And if it was in fact true that she had been there that long, or anything close to that long, Molly Zaldivar was already as good as dead.

24

They burst out into the cold night air. And even in his fear and anguish Andy Quam stared incredulously at the sky.

Overhead lay a lacy net of blue and violet fire. Great pale slow lightnings of color writhed through the heavens, soundlessly and immense; they were so bright that trees cast shadows on the rocky hillside, blurred shadows of color that moved with the supple shifting of the aurora.

The carnivorous citizen thrust its long muzzle forward, past Quamodian's cheek. He felt its hot, faintly fishy breath on his ear as it whined softly, "This spectacle does not appear usual. Can you explain it?"

Quamodian said simply, "I think our own sun has gone rogue. I don't know why."

"But that's impossible," cried the girl. "Sol is not an intellectic body! No trace of volition has ever been detected!"

Quamodian spread his hands, indicating the violence of the aurora. "Then you explain it," he said.

The distant chorus of the grass-green spirals chimed in, "We have recorded reflected intensity of stellar emissions. They have approximately doubled. Three conjectures: One, that this star is prenova; improbable. Two, that previous soundings to determine intellect in this star have been in error; improbable. Three, that it has acquired volition."

"You mean it's gone rogue?" the girl demanded. "What probability do you give that?"

"No assessment," chanted the spirals. "No known data for comparison."

"Report to Almalik!" ordered the girl. "You, citizen! You have transcience facilities!"

But the spirals replied, "Our signals from Almalik are disordered. We cannot comprehend their meaning. Nor can we receive acknowledgment of our own reports."

Quamodian had had enough. "Forget Almalik!" he ordered. "And never mind about the sun, either; we can worry about that later. Right now I'm worried about a girl. A human girl named Molly Zaldivar. Perhaps she is somewhere nearby, with or without the rogue intellect. Can any of you detect her?"

Silence.

"Try!" roared Andy Quam. Then, sulkily, the predator citizen lifted its muzzle.

"For some time now," it bayed softly, the transcience receptor in Quamodian's ears converting it into words he could understand, "I have registered the presence of quarry on that far hill."

"Quarry?"

"An ancestral trait," the citizen explained. "It is a particular refinement of chemosampling in ambient air. What you call the sense of smell. But—is not Senior Monitor Kwai Kwich 'human girl' and are not you 'human male,' Monitor Quamodian?"

"Certainly! What about it?"

"Then this quarry cannot be what you seek. It is male. And it is severely injured."

They skimmed over the pitted road, dropped toward the hillside where the carnivore citizen had scented a man. Its sense of smell had not been in error.

The man was the Reefer, huddled against the trunk of a bent evergreen tree. He looked gray and ill in the flickering colored lights of the aurora. One arm, badly swollen, was in a sling. He gazed up at the flyer apathetically as Quamodian jumped out.

"I want a word with you," Andy Quam shouted.

The Reefer growled hoarsely, "Make it short. I'm a sick man."

"Where is the rogue? Where is Molly Zaldivar?"

The Reefer shifted his weight awkwardly, flinching from the movement of his arm. "Gone. I don't know where."

"When?"

The Reefer shook his head wearily. Pale with pain, he pulled a short black stick from his pocket, gnawed the end off it and began chewing grimly. "A root that grows on the reefs," he said, his voice almost inaudible. "Filthy to chew, I guess, but it eases pain. It has always been my personal substitute for Almalik. When did the rogue go? I don't know. It dumped me here this afternoon. Couple hours ago something went on over there—" he gestured weakly at the hill that lay over the cave, "and I saw something bright in the sky."

"The aurora?" Quamodian demanded.

"No! That's been going on since dark. This was something else. I think—" his voice trailed off; he shook himself and finished, "I think the rogue is out in space. Maybe took the girl with him."

Monitor Clothilde Kwai Kwich interrupted. "Andy! This man is dying. I suggest we get him to a hospital."

The Reefer grinned painfully, working his lips for a second, then jetted a stream of black liquid at a rock. "Good idea, miss," he said. "Only it's too late for the hospital. I'm going to the church."

"Gosh, preacher!" breathed Rufe, wide-eyed behind Andy Quam in the shifting auroral lights. "Never thought *he'd* say that!"

"Never would," rumbled the Reefer, "if I had the choice. Knew it was coming. Your robot inspector told me weeks ago, 'Malignant fusorian virus,' he said, and acted like he was enjoying it—much as a robot can enjoy anything. And he said the Visitants could clear it up, but no doctor could. Expect he's right."

"So you're joining Almalik," said Andy Quam.

The Reefer shrugged bitterly, and winced from his slung arm. "I've tamed my last sleeth. My free life's ended." A spasm of pain whitened his face beneath the scars and the dirty beard. "Don't think I like it, Quamodian! But half my body's on fire."

"Good!" cried Andy Quam. "That's fine! Now, if you want a ride to Wisdom Creek, you can start paying the fare!"

The boy gasped, and even Clothilde Kwai Kwich darted a sudden incredulous look at Quamodian. The Reefer licked his lips, staring at Quamodian. "What're you talking about? I'm too sick for jokes!"

"That's good, because I'm not joking. I'm going to leave you here to rot—unless you make it worth my while to take you in."

"How?"

"Easiest thing in the world," Quamodian said tightly. "Let's just start by telling me the truth about what you and Cliff Hawk were doing."

Under the many-hued gleam of the auroras the Reefer's eyes glowed whitely, furiously. If he had had the transcience powers of the sleeth, Andreas Quamodian would

424

have been stunned or dead in that moment; there was madness in his look, and a rage that could destroy planets.

But it passed. The Reefer looked away. His jaws worked; he gulped, spat a thin black stream of the juice of his root and said, "Why not? Makes no difference any more, does it? After all, the Visitants will soon be burrowing in my brain and exposing all my secrets for Almalik to know. Might as well tell you now as have you find out that way —but let me sit down in your flyer, Quamodian. I'm telling the truth about being sick."

Andy Quam opened the bubble for him, and painfully the huge man sank into the cushions. The autonomic circuits of the flyer compensated for his weight and he sat bobbing slightly, looking down on them.

"Truth is," he said, "Cliff Hawk was only working for me. Insolent pup! I knew he thought he was pretty high and mighty, chasing after pure knowledge and all that stuff. But all I wanted was a cure for this virus. Ever since I picked it up on the reefs, more'n twenty years ago, it's been sleeping there inside me. I didn't mean for it to kill me, Quamodian. But I didn't mean to take on the Visitants, either."

He soothed his splinted arm with rough, blunt fingers, staring up at the many-hued sky. "I did like some of the things the Visitants had to offer, of course. Physical immortality, just about. A cure for this fusorian poison. Power—the rogues were my way of getting those things, without letting those parasites into my body. Hawk was just my engineer."

"So you knew Cliff Hawk was creating a rogue?" Quamodian leaned forward to search the Reefer's lax and bloodless face.

"Two rogues, Quamodian. The first got away." He grinned with a spasm of pain. "Looks like the other one did too!"

"I see," whispered Andy Quam, staring up at the angry aurora. "The first one entered our sun. Now it's rogue too!"

The Reefer shrugged.

Clothilde Kwai Kwich cried, "Monitor Quamodian! This must be reported at once. Since our citizens are not in contact with Almalik, we must return immediately to Wisdom Creek and report via the transflex station there."

"It's been reported already," said Andy Quam.

"Impossible! How could it be? We just found out . . ."

"By Rufe's parents. They knew about it, didn't they?" The boy nodded, looking pleased and excited. "And they've gone to Nuevo York to pass the word along."

The Reefer scratched his ribs cautiously, winced and groaned. "So that's about it, right? Now how about taking me in to Wisdom Creek?"

"Not just yet," said Andy Quam, deadly quiet. "One more question. What about Molly Zaldivar?"

"That witless little thing! She ruined Cliff Hawk. In love with her, he was; she tried to stop him, and messed everything up."

He gasped and leaned forward, clutching his chest. "But I don't know where she is now, Quamodian," he moaned. "Please! Isn't that enough? Won't you take me in before this thing kills me?"

On the way to Wisdom Creek Andy Quam used the flyer's circuits to contact the control dome for priorities. "Thirty-minute delay on all messages, Monitor Quamodian," said the dome. "I will inform you when your circuits can be cleared."

Grim-lipped, Andy Quam ordered the flyer to the Starchurch. Now that he knew what was wrong with the sun his responsibility was at an end. Almalik would cope with the problem—somehow—or Almalik would fail; Quamodian didn't care. At that moment the only thing on his mind was Molly Zaldivar, stolen into space by the rogue and doomed to early death by the lethal rays of the old power source in the cavern. As for the Reefer, Quamodian didn't care in the slightest whether he lived or died.

Yet there was a sort of grandeur in what happened at the Starchurch. They were greeted by the new robot inspector, his egg-shaped black body bobbing with excitement at the presence of so many illustrious visitors. Even though this was not a Starday, a circle of the saved were kneeling on that wide floor beneath the imaged suns of Almalik, and Quamodian and Monitor Clothilde Kwai Kwich led the procession that brought the limping, sullen figure of the Reefer to the Visitants. Behind him the carnivorous citizen, the green spiral citizen and the cloud brought up the rear.

The kneeling worshippers chanted their praises of Almalik. Then Juan Zaldivar stood up to ask the Reefer the statutory question—if he understood the nature of symbiotic life; if he had chosen of his own free will to accept

426

the fusorian symbiotes in his body, blood, brain and bone; if he understood that this choice was made forever.

To each question, the Reefer croaked, "I do."

He knelt, and the inhabited saved ones knelt with him, their golden brands glowing in the gloom. They chanted again, their voices rolling solemnly against the mighty dome that held the thirteen suns of Almalik.

The Reefer gasped a sudden protesting cry.

He rose half to his feet, turned with a sudden look of wild alarm, then pitched forward on his damaged arm.

Quamodian heard a sharp, hissing crackle. Fine golden sparks were dancing up from the glowing marks on the bodies and faces of the saved ones, floating delicately toward the prone body of the Reefer. They flew together, gathering into a tiny cloud of golden fire that hovered over him.

The yellow fireball sank hissing into his skin.

An arm of it darted around his body, touched his cheek, retreated to rejoin the rest. The air was suddenly heavy with the sweet reek of the Visitants.

The Reefer's moans subsided.

Then the chanting ended. He stirred, opened his eyes, stood up easily and came to shake Andeas Quamodian's hand.

"Thanks, friend," his great voice boomed. A serene and gentle smile had fallen over his scarred ferocious face. The star of the Visitants now glowed faintly above his ragged beard. "All my pain is gone."

Juan Zaldivar came to take his hand. "You are saved now. You'll feel no pain again," he said solemnly.

The control dome had been' in touch with Almalik. But there were difficulties. Quamodian blazed, "What difficulties? I must communicate with Almalik at once—go there as soon as possible!"

"Regret," sang the control dome sweetly. "It is a matter of priorities."

"That's what I demand, emergency priority!"

"But Monitor Quamodian," sang the control dome, "when you arrived yesterday you stated the emergency was here."

"It *was* here. Now I have new facts! I expect a most serious danger to the suns of Almalik!"

Clothilde Kwai Kwich whispered, "Andy, may I speak to him? Perhaps he will listen—" But Quamodian froze her with a glare. She subsided without comment. She had become a softer, more feminine person since the visit to the cave, the discovery that Andy Quam's fears were not groundless.

"State these facts," the monitor rapped out melodiously.

"They are already available to Almalik," said Quamodian. "They exist in the mind of a man called the Reefer who has just received the Visitants. I wish to be on hand among the stars of Almalik, to assist with the interpretation and use of this new information."

He did not add his more urgent private reason; it would have been of no use, since it was not the sort of thing that would influence the control dome's transcience patterns. But he clung to a wild, despairing hope that Molly Zaldivar might appear with her captor, somewhere about the multiple suns of Almalik. If she did, Quamodian wanted to be there.

"Moment," sang the monitor dome. Andy Quam shifted uneasily in the seat of the flyer.

Clothilde Kwai Kwich frowned thoughtfully. *"We* have priorities," she stated, as if to no one.

"What about it?" Quam demanded.

"Nothing, Andy. Except that the rest of us can go to Almalik at once and plead your cause."

"Agree," chanted the chorus of the grass-green spirals. "Impatient. Urgent. Suggest no delay."

And the cloud citizen sighed, "There exist great forces deployed against Almalik. It is necessary to prepare immediately."

Quamodian said stubbornly, "Do what you like. I am going anyway."

Clothilde looked at him doubtfully, but said nothing. She was saved the need to, anyway; the control dome spoke in all their ears, through the little communicator plugs:

"Monitor Quamodian, your request is denied, Senior Monitor Kwai Kwich, your priorities, and those of your party, are withdrawn. There can be no travel to that destination now."

The news struck them all with consternation. The green spirals whirled furiously in their interlocking orbits, their collective thoughts a babel of whispered fear and excitement, just below the threshhold of comprehensibility for the others. The predator citizen whined mournfully and edged closer to the boy, Rufe, who stared wide-eyed at

428

Andy Quam. The pinkly glowing cloud citizen whispered somber predictions about the disasters that lay ahead, and Clothilde Kwai Kwich's hand crept out, unnoticed, to take the hand of Andy Quam.

"Why?" he demanded furiously. "We are monitors! We cannot be denied priority rights!"

"All priorities are withdrawn," said the control dome somberly. "Our headquarters report anomalous astronomical phenomena among the planets and multiple suns of Almalik. Robot inspector, please clarify."

Unnoticed, the black egg-shaped form of the robot had drifted across the square toward them. Its oval sensor was cool and bright and blank. Its high voice hummed: "That is correct, Monitor Quamodian. The outer planet of Almalik Thirteen has suddenly stopped in its orbit. It is moving on a collision course toward its primary at many times the normal acceleration of gravity."

Quamodian's eyes narrowed. His mind whirled with chaotic flashes of foreboding. Molly was there! He was certain of it now, and certain that he must get to her. "Not surprising!" he barked, surprising himself. "That is precisely what I hoped to prevent! I must get there at once to limit the damage, avoid it if I still can."

"Impossible, Monitor Quamodian," the robot whirred. "The collision of the anomalous planet with Almalik Thirteen is expected to occur within a few hours. All transflex facilities are in use for the evacuation of the threatened planets. Even so, they are inadequate. Only a fraction of the population can be saved. Under these circumstances, no incoming travel is permitted."

Clothilde Kwai Kwich gasped. The predator citizen lifted his snout and emitted a long, mourning howl.

Quamodian stammered, "But—but I must go there! To help! It is still possible to do something . . ."

The robot did not respond. Its bright black case hung motionless.

Rufe whispered fearfully, "Preacher, what's the matter? Is it dead?"

Quamodian shook his head, staring. The robot's plasma sensor flickered, darkened, went out. Three thick black effector whips slid out of its body shell and dangled limply below it, brushing the dusty pavement of the square.

"Robot Inspector?" Quamodian called querulously. Beside him the girl whispered, "There's something terribly wrong! It's out of communication entirely."

429

But abruptly the effectors snapped back into the case. The sensor glowed again.

"We have received a further instruction from headquarters," it hummed. "The information states that a powerful rogue invader has destroyed the native intellects in two of the suns of Almalik. The invader has established its own transcience patterns in these suns, and it is now attacking the planets of Almalik Thirteen."

Quamodian caught a sudden, rasping breath.

"Call Cygnus!" he demanded.

"Sacred Almalik, spokesman star of Cygnus, is calling here," the robot's high whine interrupted him. "Your transflex travel priority has been approved. You and your party may depart from the Wisdom Creek transflex station at once."

25

Light-millennia away, the rogue's consciousness grew and sharpened in the heat of a cosmic fury. The huge sentience of stripped electrons and plasma soliloquized to itself like a stellar Hamlet:

My seas boil dry . . . my magma bleeds from glowing wounds . . . my core itself is shattered by those savage plasma spears . . . still I hurl myself toward the great white sun ahead . . .

The inner planets of the sun spread wider in their orbits as it approached. They began flashing backward past it; it was hours only now until they, and all the space about, would be dissolved in the blazing debris of the sun the rogue was about to destroy.

And still the sun did not resist.

Swelling vast ahead of the rogue, it lay serenely white, beautiful and quiet, undisturbed by the rogue's attack.

By now the rogue was ancient and mature—in its own terms at least; it had existed and learned through billions of cycles of its picosecond reflexes. It had learned a full complement of "emotions," or at any rate of those polarizing tropisms which did for it what the glandular byproducts called emotions did for human beings. It had

430

learned anger, and the calm pride of the target sun called forth anger in the rogue:

If it would only recognize me! If it would only admit causing the sun of Earth to strike at me! If it would offer some apology for deceiving me, for its contempt of me—then perhaps I could yet stop my blow . . .

But it ignored him.

The rogue was not entirely ignored. Though the great white star blazed on passionlessly, benevolently, still the rogue found itself the target for great forces from elsewhere. Another sun of Almalik had joined the attack upon it. The blue companion of the golden giant stabbed at it with a twisting shaft of plasma, a monstrous snake of glowing ions and transcience energy, which pierced to the rogue's heart, withdrew and jabbed again.

An agony of meta-pain jolted the rogue to its innermost plasma swirl; but it was not destroyed. It gathered its forces and sought for a weapon to hurl back the thrust of the blue star.

And it found one. Passing by the great fifth planet of the unresisting white sun, the rogue reached out with its plasma arms to snatch a string of moons. It gathered them to itself, fused their shattered mass into its own body, linked their electrons into its transcience patterns. With its new mass it strengthened its defenses.

And secure in its new strength, it drew more strength from the attacking stars themselves. It sucked their transcience energies, through the blue bolts and the golden ones, tightened its transflection fields and hurled its new mass always faster toward the maddening white star that glowed on, contemptuous of all the rogue could do.

And that phase of the battle ended.

Though the rogue had never struck back at the twin attacking giants, they were beaten.

Their plasma coils had exhausted even their giant strength. The coils withdrew, collapsed, disintegrated. The blue giant shrank and dimmed; its golden companion swelled and reddened.

And then they were both dead. Their fusion fires still blazed on—but mindlessly now; the intellects that had animated them were drained empty.

Sentience had fled from them. Anger and fear and purpose had gone. The blue star swelled again, the golden companion shrank back to normal size; they had become

431

merely globes of reacting nuclear gas, normal atomic engines no longer controlled by any transcience intellect.

It was a clear victory for the rogue—but its major enemy, the bright white star in its path, was still the same.

It was not defeated. If it was even threatened, it gave no sign.

The rogue felt its vast quiet mind watching, alert but strangely unafraid. It was anomalous, the rogue considered, that the target star did not request mercy, or a discussion of terms. Anomalous—and somehow disturbing.

But the rogue would not be deterred from its purpose. It plunged on to smash the white star and its haughty pride. It sought and found new fuel for its vengeance. Passing a cloud of asteroids, it swept them up and added them to its mass. It reached ahead to gather in the barren satellite of the fourth planet, and crushed and fused the new mass into its own as it sought to crush and fuse all the suns of Almalik.

Already in anticipation, it tasted the acrid joy of victory and destruction.

Thirteen suns would die or be driven to mindless burning. A hundred planets, and a thousand inhabited worldlets would be destroyed. A million billion living things would go up in white-hot plasma as the stars died . . .

And among them, thought the rogue with a bleak stab of pain, would be the trivial living blob of organized matter called Molly Zaldivar.

I *do not wish Molly Zaldivar to die. She must die. I will not save her. But I do not wish her to die, because I love her.*

In its deadly plunge toward the white star it sent thin threads of plasma effectors ahead to seek her out. Its sensor filaments ranged the cubic miles of void, and found her at last, still on the sleeth, far ahead of the rogue and dropping toward the atmosphere of the third planet. The arm of the golden giant that had freed her from the rogue was gone now, with its master's death; but Molly Zaldivar still lived.

And felt the rogue's delicate tendril touch.

She looked up unerringly toward the point in space where his massed energies were driving the planet down to its primary. "Monster?" she whispered.

The rogue was silent. It merely watched, and listened.

"Monster," she said, more confident now, "I know you're there. I don't mind."

She was silent for a moment, leaning forward over the sleek black skin of the sleeth, staring toward the cloudy world below. "You've done so much harm, monster," she sighed, "I wish—and yet you've tried to be good to me. Monster, I'm so sorry that you must make war on Almalik!"

The rogue did not answer. But it probed her interior spectrum of thoughts and energies, registered the dark shadow of sadness and, with it, a pale golden glow of—of what? Love? Fondness at least, the rogue considered.

It contracted its tendril to the merest whisper, content only to observe her, while it considered. Its strength was so immeasurably greater than her own that it could lift her from the sleeth in an instant. The energies that had hurled planets about and slain stars could fold both her and the sleeth back into its own fused and glowing mass effortlessly, carrying them with it into the collision with the proud white star ahead.

But it did not.

It watched her carefully, but without interfering, as she darted, secure in the sleeth's shimmering transflection fields, into the ionized border layers of the third planet's atmosphere and dropped swiftly toward the cities on its surface.

The third planet was a blue-green world, and beautiful. It was a world of peaceful seas and friendly continents. Dazzling cities dwelt along its oceans and rivers, inhabited by all the many kinds of creatures that were companions of Almalik.

The rogue watched her drop into the towering spires of one of the cities. It was not yet too late; it could sweep her up even there, and bring her back in the effortless recoil of one of its plasma arms.

But it stayed its energies. It merely watched, as it drove on toward the collision, now little more than an hour off, which would sear and melt this world, and destroy the organized mass of matter that was Molly Zaldivar.

433

26

The flyer, with its organic passengers and trailed by the green spirals and the pink cloud citizen, fell endlessly through the transflection distances, and emerged into the exit port of Kaymar, crown city of the planet of Kaymar, central world of Almalik.

Clothilde Kwai Kwich's hand tightened in consternation on Andy Quam's arm. Beside him the boy gasped. "Preacher! Looks like we've come to a bad place!"

The great central dome of the city seethed with citizens of all kinds. Many were human, in this central city of the worlds of Almalik; calm Terrestrials, bronzed giants from the reefs. But there were citizens in a myriad shapes and in no shapes at all, liquid citizens and gaseous citizens, citizens that had no form of matter to clothe the bare energies that constituted their beings. The diaphragm of the transflex cube behind them was already contracting on a full load of refugees lucky enough to be on their way to some other world. The shouts, cries, hissing whistles, electronic pulses and other signals of the countless thousands who had not yet been so lucky added up to a vast chorus of pleas for help. Twenty crystal citizens hung just before them, their razor-sharp edges of bright blue transparency flashing in the suns of Almalik. Quam dropped the flyer to the ramp, opened the door and led the way, ducking under the crystal citizens.

"Got to get out of this crush," he panted. "Headquarters of the Companions of the Star is just over here— I think . . ."

Clothilde Kwai Kwich cried breathlessly, "Yes, Andy! They'll still be functioning; we'll go there, and—" but she had no breath to finish. It was all they could do to urge their way through the incredible press of citizens. There was neither violence nor outright panic; these were not the enemy. But there were so many of them, so many countless thousands more than the transflex cube could evacuate in the few score minutes left, and backed by so many thousands of thousands more that had not yet managed to make their way even into the central dome of the

434

city. They were orderly. They were brave. But each of them knew that most of them were doomed.

They fought their way to a clear space and paused for breath. The carnivore citizen was the least affected of them; he glanced at young Rufe and bayed a laughing comment which the translators in Quamodian's ear rendered as: "Let the cub ride my shoulders! We'll never make it any other way."

"Naw!" flamed Rufe. "I can keep up if you can. Come on, preacher, let's do what we came to do!"

The pinkly glowing cloud citizen was worst damaged of the party. Little cloudlets of his material had been detached; some were still floating after him, rejoining the central mass of his being; others were hopelessly lost in the crush behind them. The grass-green spirals had merely tightened their orbits, maintaining exact spacing and speeds.

"All right," said Andy Quam. "Let's go!"

But a great shout from the dome behind them made them turn.

Every citizen, warm-blooded or cold, humanoid or amorphous, was staring upward, through the crystal ceiling of the dome, with ten thousand thousand eyes, photoreceptors, radar scanners, sensors of every description.

There, streaked like a child's bright daub on the calm blue skies of Kaymar, hung the bright and glittering globe of the invading rogue star. Lightnings played about its blazing body as it shot across the sky, its motion visible even though its distance was many million of miles.

Andy Quam tore his eyes away. "Come on," he muttered. "We've got even less time than I thought."

The Grand Hall of the Companions of the Star was empty. The thirteen suns of Almalik blazed down from the ceiling on an auditorium that could seat thousands, and now held no one at all.

Senior Monitor Clothilde Kwai Kwich said dolefully, "I can't understand. I thought here at least we'd find someone who could help . . ."

The chant of the grass-green spirals sounded in Andy Quam's ears: "No indications! No operative functions being performed! This construct not inhabited!"

The boy clutched Quamodian's arm. "But, preacher," he said. "Almalik told us to come here. Didn't he?"

Quamodian said, "He gave us permission. Directly.

435

Yes." He turned, searching the vast room with his eyes. "But perhaps something has happened."

The weary sigh of the cloud citizen whispered: "There exists a large-scale entity which is observing us."

Quamodian flung himself into a chair, trying to think. Time was so short! He had counted on finding the order of Companions of the Star still functioning. Perhaps it had not been realistic, but in his mind he had expected to find the great hall thronged with worshippers, the many offices and administrative sections busy about the endless tasks of Almalik. If he had thought at all, he had thought that a robot monitor of a citizen would have greeted them at the entrance, led them directly to someone in supreme authority, received his information about the rogue—and acted. Acted in time to save this world, and all the worlds of Almalik.

He had not expected that the building would be empty.

The others were waiting quietly for him to act. He realized that, right or wrong, he would have to make the decisions for all of them. And there was less time with every passing clock-tick . . .

He stood up. "All right," he said, "we'll go back to the transflex cube. Perhaps the monitor there can help us."

"Through that mob, preacher? Impossible!" cried the boy.

"Impossible or not, that's what we'll have to do. Unless you have a better idea . . ."

But then, as they turned to leave, a Voice rumbled softly in their ears.

"Wait," it said.

They froze where they stood. The girl looked imploringly at Andy Quam. She did not speak, but her lips formed a word: "Almalik?"

He nodded, and the Voice spoke again:

"Behold," it said, and the great dome lifted on its transflection forces to reveal the splendor of the heavens of Almalik themselves. It was daytime now; the glittering stars that the dome was designed to reveal could not be seen. But the bright smear of the invader was there, blighting the beauty of the calm clouds. And near it in the sky, dropping toward them . . .

"It's Miss Zaldivar!" shouted the boy. "Look, preacher! It's her and the sleeth!"

They were in that great hall for less than a quarter of an hour, and in all that time Quamodian could not afterward remember taking a breath. He was overpowered by the immense majesty of Almalik himself, brooding over them, watching and helping. Even the nearness of the girl he had crossed half a universe to find could not break him free from the spell of that immortal and immense star.

Though what was said was surely catastrophic enough to rouse him to action; for Molly Zaldivar, she said, was dying.

"Dear Andy," she whispered across the vast gulf of the chamber, her voice warm and affectionate in his ears. "No! Don't come any closer to me. I'm charged with radiations, Andy dear—the old ones from the Plan of Man machines, new ones that our little monster-star used to try to save my life. Or to give me life again; because I was dead. Anyway, if you come near me now it will be your death . . ."

Even so, he rose to run toward her; but she stopped him with a gesture. "Please," she whispered. "Now. What was it that you came from Earth to tell?"

He stammered out the story the Reefer had told him, While Clothilde Kwai Kwich and the boy, one on each side of him, stood silent and awed. Molly Zaldivar listened gravely, her face composed though her eyes widened, then danced, as she saw how Clothilde's hand sought his.

Then she said, "Thank you, Andy. You've always been the best friend I could ever hope to have. I . . ."

Her composure almost broke for a moment, but she controlled herself, and smiled. "I don't mind leaving this world much, dear Andy. But I do mind leaving you."

And then she was gone, mounting once more toward the sky on the great, patient back of the sleeth, while the enormous dome of Almalik swung majestically back into place to blot her out.

27

The rogue sensed the fear in that distant watcher, the fear of a father for a threatened son. It thought to call for help, but the distance was a thousand times too far. Even here, its thin thread of sensor had been snapped; it had lost Molly Zaldivar and her sleeth.

It tried to find them again for many picoseconds, but in vain. Some force larger than itself had shut her off, blinded it to her activities. A sense that in a human might have been called foreboding filled the rogue; but it had no time for even meta-emotions; it was driving ever closer to its enemy sun, and it needed all its forces for the task ahead.

The third planet had fallen far behind it now. It flashed through the orbit of the second planet, now hidden from it at inferior conjunction by the expanding white sun. The great white disk grew ahead of it.

Still the star ignores my attack. It refuses to resist. It offers no apology for the attacks it has made on me through 'ts lesser stars. Still it is watching—mocking me . . .

"Monster! Stop for me."

The thin filament of the rogue's probing sensor was alive again, carrying a message for it. The rogue energized its perceptions and saw that Molly Zaldivar was pursuing, racing after it on the black and shining sleeth. There was a power flowing from her that the rogue could not quite recognize, but that made it uneasy, unsure of itself. The feeble human figure of organized matter that was the girl should not have been able to dispose such powers. Not even with the energies the rogue itself had bestowed on her; not when her life was close to an end, and all her accumulated strengths were being disposed at once.

The rogue considered for some nanoseconds the possibility that these forces came from its enemy, Almalik. But it dismissed the possibility. It simply did not matter. Contact was only minutes away. Already the thin solar atmosphere was boiling around it. It did not stop, perhaps could not stop; the gathered mass of its planetary body was plunging too fast to be diverted now.

But it sent a message through its plasma effector, shaking the thin atmosphere that the sleeth carried with it though space. "What do you want, Molly Zaldivar?" its tiny voice piped. "Do you love me now?"

Her answer sent a seismic tremor through the core of the planet it had made its body: "Love you, monster? I don't know. I cannot imagine it. And yet—yes, perhaps I do. If it matters . . ."

The rogue shook in its mad plunge. Its boiling seas loosed huge clouds of vapor as, for a moment, its grasp ⌐lackened; lightnings played through its tortured skies.

⌐t Molly was still speaking:

"But I have no life left to love anyone, monster. My

438

body is dying, and I must tell you something. Monster! Please listen. *Almalik is not your enemy.*"

A shock of doubt shattered the rogue's great joy.

"Listen monster! Almalik never hurt you. Almalik has renounced all violence. He could not harm you, nor any sentient thing. Ever!"

Rage shook the rogue now. The crustal rocks of its planetary body snapped and white-hot magma spewed forth. In the air around Molly Zaldivar its tiny voice shrieked: "Lies! Lies again! The sun of Earth that tried to kill me was Almalik's vassal. Its twin stars that tried to kill me again—they were Almalik's companions!"

But Molly Zaldivar's voice came strongly. "No, monster. I lied to you once, yes. Because I was afraid of you. But Almalik has never lied, nor has he tried to harm you. The sun of Earth that struck you—it was your own brother!"

The rogue called back the huge effector that it had lashed out to strike her. Puzzled, its shrill voice repeated, "Brother?"

"Yes, your brother! Another synthetic sentience, made before you. It occupied the sun of Earth and tried to destroy you—came here before you, and tried to destroy you again through the twin stars of Almalik. But you defeated it, monster. And now it is gone, and you must stop before you destroy great Almalik!"

The rogue paused, while its sentient plasma revolved the startling new concept. "Brother?" its tiny voice whispered again. A dreadful doubt shivered through its core.

If it were wrong, it thought—if it were wrong, then it was doing a dreadful and irrevocable deed.

For if it were wrong, then Almalik had always been its friend. And it was within minutes of destroying Almalik forever.

Methodically, patiently, the rogue rebuilt its net of sensors, threw out probes to scan the patient white star before it—so close now, and so vulnerable!—and all of space around. Its velocity, hard driven and accelerated through hundreds of millions of miles, was huge. Unstoppable. It had thrown its enegies in profligate abandon into thrusting the dead planet toward the white star. It was simply too late to stop.

With care and speed it calculated possible trajectories to divert its own plunge, not to stop it—for that was utterly

439

impossible now—but simply to deflect it enough to miss the star and plunge on into the dark space beyond . . .

Impossible. It was too late.

Well, then: to pass through the star's corona, destroying itself in the process, of course, and working great havoc with the star's internal energy balance, but leaving most of it intact . . .

Also impossible. Also too late.

In what passed in it for desperation, the rogue computed its chance of plunging through the skin of the star but on a tangent that would miss the core, leave the star wounded and erupting with enormous violence, but perhaps not entirely destroyed . . .

Also impossible, and finally impossible. Its energies were too great, its time of collision too near. It would strike the white sun almost dead on, whatever the rogue did now. And rogue and white star together would erupt in the ultimate violence of a supernova, destroying themselves and everything for a light-year or more around.

I regret, thought the rogue. *I feel pity. For Molly Zaldivar. For Almalik. For all the myriads of beings on Almalik's doomed planets. And for me.*

It sent out a message on the thin, stretched filament of energy with which it had been in contact with Molly Zaldivar, to say that there was no longer any hope.

But it could not make contact.

Once again it searched all of space nearby, seeking Molly Zaldivar and the sleeth. Uselessly. Somehow, Molly Zaldivar was gone.

The patterns of energy that made up the essential being of the rogue were shaken with grief and pain. Despairing, it thrust with all the energies it possessed at the calm white disk of its target sun, now so near and so vulnerable. Great spouts of flame boiled from the star below it; the rogue's own planetary body split and shattered in the violence of its effort to undo what it had done. But it was no use. The fragments of its planet, continental in size, massive as worldlets themselves, drove on unchecked.

Look, little one. Take that blue star. Use its energies, if you will.

The rogue darted out sensors in all directions, seeking the source of that soundless, gentle voice. The sensors found nothing. But the rogue knew where it came from:

it was Almalik, speaking to it from the enormous, swelling, flame-ringed solar disk so near below.

The blue star?

Experimentally the rogue threw out a sensor toward it. It was empty, untenanted since it had destroyed the mad sentience that had inhabited it. It was waiting for it.

Something helped the rogue, something to which it could not put a name: not merely Almalik, not just the star it was so close to destroying, but a congeries of sentiences, a pooled strength of living and stellar creatures, all urging the rogue on, supporting it, giving it help.

It drove along the lines of its sensor and entered into the waiting star.

New energies flooded its webs of sentience. The resources of a giant stellar furnace were now its own to command.

It reached out to the planet it had abandoned, hurtling down on the white star, grasped it with the mighty plasma arms of its new body. White arms from Almalik himself joined the rogue—and with them, golden arms. The rogue puzzled over that for a few electron-orbits; surely the golden star was dead, unable to take part.

Yet it was taking part. The golden arms linked with the blue and white ones, and together, smoothly, strongly, with infinite speed they pulled the planet aside.

The planet did not survive those mighty forces; it crumbled into a million billion fragments, streaming past the great white orb of Almalik and heading out into space on cometary orbits.

But it had missed. Almalik was safe.

And the rogue had time to realize what it had gained, in the might of its new stellar body—and what it had lost. It sensed the joy, the proud approval, of that far-off fatherly watcher—which was now more akin than ever, but no longer all rogue.

The great tolling chorus of the stars welcomed it into brotherhood. *Join us, brother,* said a great collective voice. *Be one with us. Be one with all things that share the bonds of mind. Be one with Almalik.*

And a part of the rogue rejoiced, and a part of it ached with an unpracticed grief for Molly Zaldivar, doomed to death in her frail human body, lost forever.

The slow, gentle voice held a hint of amusement, and

441

wry pity. *Look, brother,* it said. *You gave her your strength. We gave her our empty sun for a home.*

And the rogue struck out, unbelieving, with a bright blue plasma sensor toward the golden star; and it met the rogue's sensor with one of its own. Gold thread and blue touched and joined, while the stars watched and rejoiced.

The voice that spoke to the rogue was not a human voice, but there was something of humanity about it— something soft and merry, something very like the voice of Molly Zaldivar and dear.

"Hello, monster," it said. "Welcome. Welcome forever."